Titles by James Paddock

Novels

CJ Washburn Mysteries
Deserving of Death
Sailing into Death

Time-Travel
Before Anne After (Book 1)
Time Will Tell (Book 2)

Sabre-Toothed Cat Suspense
Smilodon (Book 1)
Sabre City (Book 2)
The Last Sabre (Book 3)

Other Suspense
Lost & Forgotten
Elkhorn Mountain Menace
(Previously titled Angels in the Mist)

Novelette
Hot Roast Beef with Mustard

Connect with James Paddock Online

Facebook: https://www.facebook.com/DesertBookshelf
Twitter: http://twitter.com/jameswriter/
Blog: http://www.desertbookshelf.com/blog/

Published by Desert Bookshelf Publishing

Acknowledgements

Where does one start with acknowledgements? How does a Novelist thank everyone who provided input into the writing of a work of fiction, especially when they had no idea they were providing such input? Every person a writer meets in some small way assists in the novel writing process. So, for that, I thank the entire world. You are my research platform, an endless source of unique plots and characters.

After the world, of course, I must thank my parents even though they left this earth long before I completed my first novel. Without them I wouldn't be here, struggling to get every word correct in this, novel number ten. They gave me life and guidance to eventually wander off on my own in pursuit of.... myself. It has been well over forty years since they tearfully saw me off on my first airplane flight and the beginning of a career in the U.S. Navy. Have I found myself? Verdict is still out.

In the process of looking, however, I did find Lynn, the mother of my three children. Thank you Lynn for twenty-five fine years and also for your support in those early, short-story writing days as I went from one bad draft to the next not quite so bad draft. Thank you for your faith.

Of course I must thank my three wonderful children, MeLynda, Carrie and Matt, for loving everything I write, or at least pretending that they do. Who would love us unconditionally if not our children?

At the top of the list I must thank Penny, my number one pal for the past sixteen years and for the remainder of this lifetime. How she puts up with me, I have no idea. How do I tell her when she thinks I am not listening to her that I'm being distracted by the voices in my head plotting out the next scene in my current work-in-progress? There is something to say for a spouse who not only puts up with her husband's inattention and his need for isolation, but also all his other idiosyncrasies. Her reward, of course, is a new novel to read once every year or two. Not only does she get to be the first to read it, but also the second and third, maybe even the fourth. As my #1 editor for content, plot and grammar, Penny pores through my finished work multiple times.

Thank you Penny for always being there.

Specifically for Sailing into Death I must thank my son, Matt, for advising me in the area of arms and explosives. When it comes to deadly force, he knows his stuff.

By the way, Matt, thank you for your service to our country. Also thanks go to my daughter-in-law, Nina (Matt's wife) and to my son-in-law, Ryan. All three proudly serve in the United States Navy.

For everything else that is not covered above, I thank the Internet. Research is always just a few keystrokes away.

Most especially...

Thank you to all my loyal readers.

SAILING
INTO
DEATH

A CJ Washburn Mystery

James R. Paddock

Chapter 1

Clinton Joshua Washburn–CJ to his friends, Clint to his fiancée, Clinton only to his mother–stared at the man standing before him. *Sales Associate* the badge read. Roger Miller it also read. CJ considered commenting on the name, whether he'd ever heard of "King of the Road" or "Dang Me" or "You Can't Roller Skate in a Buffalo Herd." He then wondered if Sales Associate Miller even knew who the King of the Road was, likely a toddler when the Nashville singer, Roger Miller, died. Of course, CJ knew better than to make fun of someone's name. It'd been nearly two decades since he'd dropped his use of Clinton in favor of CJ to keep the hecklers off his back.

"How may I help you, sir?" Miller said, smoothly turning about so as to come alongside CJ. "Looking for a gift for your wife or girlfriend? You've come to the right place. You or she, or both, must have great taste as these are the most popular lingerie ensembles in the store, the entire mall for that matter, maybe all of Tampa."

CJ turned his head away from the sales associate as though admiring a sexily clad mannequin and rolled his eyes.

"Any woman would *die* for the opportunity to slide into bed in one of these," Miller said, stroking the fabric on the mannequin, "especially if she was sliding in next to her man."

"How much?" CJ asked, if for no other reason than to deflect the man's spiel before he got more personal.

"We've got this little piece priced special for the weekend at only $219.99. Can I gift wrap that for you?"

CJ exited the mall empty-handed. When he'd picked up the rental at the airport he'd decided to make the gift selection his first project because he knew that once he started focusing on the investigation, he'd forget, or he wouldn't remember until he was in route back to Tucson, having to pick up something from the Atlanta Airport mall. No matter how nice it would be, she'd somehow know. There was no way he was going to get Stella an airport gift. No way!

He started the car and thought about what brought him to the west coast of Florida on a job that was paying nothing but expenses. Contrary to what he would have suspected, business had been good since the serial killer fiasco four weeks back. Maybe it had to do with his name and picture in the news as being the individual who was, first, the prime suspect and then who later shot and killed the cop who turned out to be the killer of eight young women. CJ didn't have much choice at the time. The cop, one Tommy Clark, confessed his crimes while squeezing the life out of Stella with a deadly chokehold, his brother pressing a gun to CJ's daughter's temple. CJ didn't flinch when the opportunity presented itself. He put a bullet through Tommy's eye. The resulting publicity had clients coming out of the woodwork to the point that CJ had to turn people away, some of whom seemed as crazy as Tommy Clark.

It was all because of a vendetta that Clark had against prostitutes, and then women in general, and then CJ. The Clark brothers were insane, no doubt about it, the result of dysfunctional and abusive childhoods, according the slew of criminal psychologists that popped up on every news network.

But that was all over, an ugly chapter closed and gone; at least it would be gone if everyone would just leave him alone about it. Stella and Trish continued to suggest that he seek counseling. The more they picked at him the more he dug in his heels. They attended counseling themselves, sometimes together. He understood that. Hell, his daughter was kidnapped twice and then watched her father kill her kidnapper. Trish was still a kid, only 21-years-old. His little girl. It probably screwed her head up good. And it was hell on Stella, too. The two of them had been through a lot and the counseling seemed to be helping them.

But he was fine. Tommy Clark deserved to die and CJ just happened to be in the position to pull the trigger. Not one person that he talked to disagreed. What should he need counseling for? He did the right thing.

As the air conditioner pulled the temperature down in the rental, CJ paged through the folder he had on Douglas Rothbower, the brother-in-law of Gianna Onassis, CJ's attorney and biggest client. CJ was her number one private eye. While in the throes of the Tommy Clark fiasco CJ had landed in jail three times. Gianna came to his aid for two of those, pro-bono, only to have Tommy target and kill her niece, Alexandria Rothbower. It was the day that they found her body that CJ put the bullet in Tommy's head. The death of many of the women Tommy killed weighed heavy on CJ, but none more so than Alexandria. Tommy went after her only because of CJ, and Gianna knew that, but she didn't blame him... much.

CJ still carried a heavy burden of guilt.

He thought about the meeting he'd had with her two days after her niece was murdered. She was dressed in black, her meeting with CJ her last stop before departing to escort her niece's body home to Indiana.

"I'm running out of time so let's talk business," she'd said. "I came to your aid pro-bono when you were in jail. Now I ask the same courtesy from you."

"Name it."

"Alexandria's father walked out of their lives five years ago, at least that's what I think. Alexandria's mother, my sister, thinks otherwise, that something happened to him."

"Why would she think that?" CJ asked.

"He gambled; got in over his head. She thinks someone killed him and buried his body somewhere."

"If he owed money, what would be the advantage in killing him?" CJ asked.

"Exactly."

"Has she ever been contacted by anyone wanting her to make payment on his debt?"

"Not that I know of. Reason her theory seems off to me." She reached across her desk and picked up a white envelope. As she handed it to him she said, "This is the information you'll need. My sister's number, friends, business associates, etcetera."

"I'll do everything I can."

"When I say pro-bono, I'm referring to your time only. If you have expenses, such as travel to Indiana, or anywhere for that matter, I expect to be billed. Is that clear?"

"Certainly."

"No stone unturned."

"You want him found no matter what."

"Exactly."

And so now here CJ was, following a lead to Florida, the only viable lead he'd come up with during his trip to Indiana the week before.

Three weeks after Alexandria's funeral, CJ had visited Gianna's sister, Kassandra, in her Indiana home, the home deserted, voluntarily or otherwise, by her husband and then hollowed out with the tragic loss of her daughter. When he called on her he found a wife alone and broken, a mother forever in mourning. CJ stood before her, wanting to be anywhere but there, looking at a woman in desperate need of help. Aged beyond her years,

Kassandra thanked CJ for coming, offered him coffee or water, obviously out of gracious habit, for she appeared to fear that he would accept. He thanked her and declined, asked questions, got no answers and a flood of tears. She said she'd wished Gianna hadn't sent him, that it was a waste of his time.

"Your sister says that you think he might have met foul play; that he might be dead."

Kassandra had sighed, wiped at her tears and then apologized. "I was angry back then, said some things I probably shouldn't have said, like I hoped he'd gotten himself killed. I may have thought or may have even wished that he did, but I really had no reason to believe it to be true."

"Then you do think he is alive," CJ had said to her.

"I assume he is."

When he left her home CJ doubted that much would come of the two names and phone numbers he was able to force out of her, but one must investigate everything, follow every lead as though it would be the case breaker. Although it didn't break the case, one name did lead CJ in the direction suspected by Gianna and sort of confirmed by Kassandra, that Douglas Rothbower simply walked away from his family and his job. Reason... unknown or unwilling to say. The source was Douglas' best friend, Paddy McLane. CJ found him at *Paddy's Irish Pub* in Indiana.

"I couldn't o' asked for a better friend," Paddy had told him in a thick Irish brogue.

"Why did he leave?" CJ asked.

Paddy shrugged. "Can't really say."

"Don't know or won't say?"

"You have any Irish blood in you, Mister Washburn?"

"Can't say that I do," CJ admitted.

"Then you shant know of the thick blood of Irish friendship, now do you? It's as thick as our brogue, you see; thick enough to stand a fork on a hot, windy day."

"That's pretty thick," said CJ.

"You got a friend like that, someone who, as you police type like to say, has your back?"

CJ thought about Detective Dan Payne, his best friend in Tucson. "Yes, I do."

"Well, with us, we have each other's back, front and sides. A man, you see Mister Washburn, with an Irish heart takes care of his friends..." he paused for a long time and then added, "and his family."

CJ just looked at him, trying to read the deeper meaning in his words. "Are you saying that Douglas Rothbower was Irish?"

"You don't know?"

CJ leaned in closer. "Know what?"

"Doug was pure Irish. Don't let the name fool you."

CJ sat back. "Rothbower?"

Paddy held up his hand. "No. That is German. Doug was born of an Irish mother in Ireland and was presented with the name Douglas O'Reilly. She supposedly died when he was three days old."

"Supposedly?"

"Aye. Can't say for sure... word of mouth you see. Anyway, the father could not be found. So the baby, in some underhanded, under-the-table deal, was adopted by a couple of wealthy Americans by the name of Rothbower and brought to Chicago. The rest, as they say here in your country, is history."

"The rest may be history, Paddy, but there are some interesting questions. Did Doug know any of this? When did he find out?"

"Can I buy you a pint o' Guinness, my friend?" Paddy said, looking down at the half consumed soda in front of CJ.

CJ's gut response was to decline, however, he had to remind himself that he was a private investigator, not an on-duty officer of the law. He also had a hunch that Paddy was not finished talking, had additional info to provide. He just needed a little more time and maybe a little more lubrication.

"Thank you, Paddy. I'd like that."

Paddy held up two fingers to the barmaid and said, "A couple o' pints of the black stuff." In just over a half minute they had two foaming mugs of dark beer.

CJ pointed to his mug. "Black stuff?"

"The finest Guinness that'll ever pass your lips." Paddy drank down a quarter of his and then said, "Have you ever been to Florida, Mister Washburn?"

"We be Guinness-drinking buddies now, Paddy. You can call me CJ."

Paddy slapped him on the shoulder. "CJ! A fine name. What does the C stand for?"

CJ looked at him for a long time and then admitted, "Clinton."

Paddy threw back his head and laughed. "No wonder you go by CJ." He took another swig of his beer. "Again I ask, have you ever been to Florida?"

"I can't say that I have," CJ said.

"Well, if you ever get down in the area of Tampa, you need to visit St. Petersburg. You'll find a couple o' Irish pubs worth looking up. One is much like this one here in which you be enjoying a fine Irish lager."

"St. Petersburg?" CJ said.

"Aye. St. Petersburg. That's all I have to say about that. Now don't let that Guinness go flat on ya, CJ."

CJ took a swig.

"By the way," Paddy said, "Doug knew all along he'd been adopted. He didn't learn of the sordid details until five or six years ago."

After checking out the other name and phone number given to him by Kassandra, which led him to poking around Douglas' old work place, to no avail, CJ returned to Tucson. With Stella's help he typed 'Irish Pubs St. Petersburg Florida' into Google. St. Petersburg had several, one of which was called *Paddy McGee's Irish Pub*. Its website banner displayed the same slogan in the same Irish-like font that CJ had seen hanging over the bar in *Paddy's Irish Pub* in Indiana.

Where your friends are ours, and our friends are yours

"...one much like this one here..." Paddy McLane had said when he recommended the Irish pub in St. Petersburg. CJ didn't believe in coincidences.

Chapter 2

CJ drove along Bay Shore Drive, finding it hard to keep his eye on traffic while stealing glances at the single and double masted sailing yachts moored on both sides of one pier after another. There must have been hundreds of them of all different sizes. He'd never seen anything like it.

He turned east onto 1st Avenue–what appeared to take him to where he could view the yachts closer–noted *St. Petersburg Sailing Center* on the right and then St. Petersburg Marina to the left. Choosing neither, he went straight into *Demens Landing Park* where he parked and got out. For the next hour he walked, gazing upon the yachts with mast after mast pointing to a cloudless sky. He watched people coming and going with coolers and packs, many dressed in sailing attire, others in well worn shorts and T-shirts, smiles on their faces, laughter in the air. He looked across the harbor where more yachts came and went, feeling like a kid in his first candy store, but with no means to try a sample. He wondered what it would take to learn to sail.

After a time he exhaled a lungful of air and turned away. He was a landlocked landlubber, always had been, always would be. He knew nothing about this life, suspected in any case that it was too rich for his blood. He started the car and looked once more out at the masts jutting into the air and thought about Stella, wondered if she'd enjoy sailing. Maybe, when they got married, they'd go sailing for their honeymoon.

After another sigh he entered the address to the Irish pub into the GPS and headed out.

Paddy McGee's Irish Pub was little more than a half dozen blocks from where CJ had been admiring the sailboats. A few cars littered the parking lot just shy of 4:00 in the afternoon. CJ stepped through the entryway and stopped. As he waited for his eyes to adjust to the dark interior, a young woman breezed by.

"*Céad míle fáilte!*" she said. "Welcome to Paddy McGee's; have a seat anywhere and I shall be right with you," she added and then was gone. CJ approached the bar and sat. He looked at the menu and drink specials until the young woman appeared in front of him. "What can we do for you today, me friend?"

"Kade meal... whatever you said. What does it mean?"

"*Céad míle fáilte.* It means, 100,000 welcomes."

"Ah." CJ pointed at a board that read *Daily Specials* and said, "What's a *Car Bomb*?"

"Tis a bit early for that, I should think."

"I don't necessarily *want* one, just curious."

"We give you a pub glass o' Guinness stout, half full, and a shot glass o' Irish Whiskey and Irish Cream. You then carefully drop the shot glass into the stout and in the blink of an leprechaun eye, drink it all down before the cream curdles."

CJ noted her grin, wondered if the brogue was real. "Sounds a bit out of my league." He pointed to the specials board again. "I'll have the $7 Angus burger and Guinness draught."

"Aye. Fine choice me friend." A minute later when she presented him with the draught, she said, "Burger in five. Obviously you're new to Paddy McGee's. What brings ya to our fine establishment?"

"For one, I'm hungry. Been a long day flying."

"Arms must be tired."

He chuckled. "You also were recommended by Paddy McLane in Fisher's, Indiana."

"*Paddy's Irish Pub.* Paddy's cousin Paddy. You a regular of Irish pubs? A reviewer of fine Irish pub grub maybe? If so I'll tell Paddy to spice your burger up a bit, throw in some chips on the house."

"Sorry. Not a food critic. Is that Paddy McGee himself doing the cooking?" CJ nodded toward a middle aged guy working over a grill down at the end of the bar.

"Aye, tis he."

"I'd appreciate a chat with him when he has an opportunity."

"And who shall I say tis beggin' for his attention?"

CJ pulled a card from his pocket and handed it to her. "CJ Washburn."

She looked at the card. "Private eye, aye, Mister Washburn? Haven't had one in here before, least not one who'd admit it. Arizona? Indiana? Now Florida? Must be important."

"Every case I pursue is important to someone."

"Aye. Very true." With that she walked back to the grill and handed the card to Paddy McGee. He glanced toward CJ, said something to the girl and pocketed the card. When she returned she said, "Why don't you make yourself comfy in one of the booths? Paddy will join you with your burger in short order. I'll make sure he throws in an order of chips even though you're not a critic."

"You just never know. I might want to moonlight as one if I can be bribed with food." CJ picked up his Guinness, thanked her with a wink and then made his way to a booth well away from other patrons.

CJ sipped at his Guinness and thought about Stella. He visualized the two of them on a yacht in white boat shoes, white shirts and shorts, hair blowing in the breeze, his hand on the helm, sails and shirt sleeves billowing as they tacked along the surface of a mildly choppy sea. He had to admit, though, that he wasn't sure what it meant to tack. He was more and more wanting to find out.

"Mister Washburn."

CJ looked up as his burger and chips were placed before him. The man stuck out his hand and CJ took it. "CJ, please."

"CJ. I'm Paddy McGee. Welcome." He slid into the booth across from CJ. "I understand my cousin sent you me way."

"In a way, yes," CJ said. "During a chat I had with him a week back he mentioned that if I ever got down this way I ought to look you up."

"Me cousin tis like that. Always trying to send business me way.

I often try to do the same by him. Only a week ago, is that so? I spoke with Paddy about a week ago as well and it seems to me he might have mentioned you."

"Then you know why I'm here."

"Aye, I do. Something about searching for Douglas Rothbower. Don't know how I can be o' much help. I don't know o' Douglas being around here. You may have wasted your time... and your money. Me cousin was just being kind to recommend me establishment. You maybe became a bit confused when he mentioned St. Petersburg in the same conversation as was mentioned Mister Rothbower."

"Tis odd," CJ said, "that you and your cousin should discuss Douglas Rothbower when, apparently, the name holds no importance to you."

"I didn't say that the name doesn't hold importance, Mister Washburn. We are a close family. Me cousin and I talk frequently. When I last spoke with him he mentioned that a PI had been to see him, looking for his best friend who went missing five years ago. I knew Douglas, met him many years back when visiting up in Fishers so it was not that unusual for Paddy to mention your visit, that after five years there was someone looking for him." He took a swig from a bottle of water he had brought over with him. "Me cousin cares about his friend and, therefore, so do I. That's the importance to me, Mister Washburn, but I know nothing of his whereabouts."

"Did your cousin by chance mention why I'm looking for him?"

"No, can't say that he did. You and Douglas were mentioned just in passing. It must be mighty important to have someone like yourself chasing about the country. Wife suddenly desperate to find her husband I gather?"

A memory of CJ's meeting with Kassandra Rothbower flashed through his mind. She'd looked broken, but how much of that was losing her daughter? Did he just assume she was still mourning her husband's disappearance?

"In addition to the wife, Douglas had a daughter, Alexandria," CJ said. "She was killed about a month ago. The family felt it important to find Douglas. He has a right to know."

Paddy sat back, the shock evident on his face. "That is awful. How did it happen?"

"She was murdered."

He shook his head. "Most dreadful. As a father myself..." he looked away for a brief few seconds, and then back at CJ, "I understand. However, I'm afraid I cannot help you. I do not know o' Doug's whereabouts."

CJ had followed Paddy's eyes to the barmaid and now sat back and considered the man, the typical image of the owner of an Irish pub; round face, red hair, rosy cheeks, a tad robust with a bit of a potbelly. Instead of a bottle of water he just needed a beer mug and a pipe to make the picture complete. The barmaid was his daughter, CJ concluded. This was a family business.

"Well," CJ said, "to avoid wasting a trip I may just indulge myself with a little tourist time. I've never been sailing. You have any recommendations along that line?"

"Sailing?"

CJ sensed that Paddy was relieved by the change in topic.

Paddy snorted. "Never been myself, never even considered it. Prefer something with a motor. I'd never trust the wind."

"But they do have motors from what I can tell, in order to get in and out of the harbor, and as backup I imagine," CJ said.

"Aye, they do, and that makes for an interesting point. Why all the trouble to install and put up and down the sails if ya have to put a motor on it anyways?"

"Save on fuel?"

"From what I can see, those who can afford to keep one of those yachts, can afford the fuel for a real boat."

CJ laughed.

"Look up *Bay Shore Charters and Sailing School*. They might be able to answer your questions about lessons and all that. Go straight east from here until you hit the water. You can't miss them."

CJ wrote it down. "Thanks."

"Well, I'll leave you to your fine Angus burger. I've got more cookin' a waitin'."

CJ pulled out a another business card and pushed it across the table. "I'll be in town until Saturday. Give me a call if you think of anything."

"Where are you staying?"

"The Hilton over on 1st."

"Hilton Bayfront. I know of it. Nice place." Paddy pushed the card back at CJ. "I have your card already." He shook CJ's hand. "Nice meeting you, CJ. The luck 'o the Irish be with you."

CJ took a bite from his burger and then turned to be able to gain a better view of the establishment. Another waitress had apparently arrived, an older woman. Paddy's wife maybe or an employee clocking in before *Happy Hour* starts up, he surmised. He watched her for a bit, noted how she seemed to be in charge of the younger girl. He considered the resemblance between the two. *Mom*, he concluded and then glanced over at Paddy. He was scraping the grill with one hand, the other pressing a phone to his ear.

Curious, CJ thought. When Paddy had referred to Douglas Rothbower as Doug, CJ wondered if it was a slip. There also seemed to be a lot more shock than CJ had expected when he mentioned that Alexandria had been murdered. Maybe Paddy knows Douglas better than he lets on.

Paddy put his phone away, glanced at CJ and then bent over his kitchen tasks.

Chapter 3

Bay Shore Charters and Sailing School was not open when CJ went by. He'd lingered too long at *Paddy McGee's Irish Pub*, hoping that the call that Paddy had made was to Douglas Rothbower, letting him know that someone was looking for him. CJ suspected that it wasn't going to be that easy. Maybe he had it all wrong, that Paddy knew nothing about Douglas' disappearance, that the call he'd made was to order more Angus burger patties. Maybe this trip to St. Petersburg was, in fact, a dead end.

He wandered south along Bay Shore Drive, stopped to read a *Manatee Basics for Boaters* sign and wondered what it'd be like to see a real manatee up close. He continued on until he could turn east onto 2nd Avenue. A minute later he was gazing upon more sailing yachts, hundreds of them for sure. He wished Stella had come along. At least then the trip wouldn't have been wasted. He walked along a pier-side parking lot until it ended and the avenue continued onto St. Petersburg Pier which appeared to extend a quarter mile out into Tampa Bay. He kept walking toward the end where stood what appeared to be a five-story inverted pyramid-shaped building. He walked around it, gazed at some of the shops, and came to a stop when he couldn't go any farther. Signage told him he was on *The Pier*, the official name of the architectural wonder. He stood gazing at the shoreline on the far side of the bay, wondering what was over there.

After a time he turned around and walked back to his car, taking another slow stroll past the yachts along the way. He reset the GPS for the address for the *Hilton St. Petersburg Bayfront Hotel*, waited for it to calculate, and then pulled into traffic.

CJ was surprised to find out that the hotel was only a few minutes away. Bay Shore Drive ran for about a mile and he'd initially parked at the north end. The hotel was near the south end, a block or so west, *Al Lang Stadium* sandwiched between it and the bay. He could have checked in first and then gone for the stroll. He thought maybe he'd do that anyway, just to get a sunset view of the harbor, maybe take some pictures to send to Stella, if he could figure out how to do that on his phone.

After checking in and hauling his baggage up to the 9th floor, CJ stood at his window and looked down at the stadium. He could see part of the field. If it had been baseball season and the schedule worked he'd have considered taking in a game. The field, however, was setup for soccer. While checking in he'd noticed that the hotel offered ticket discounts for the game on Saturday, *Tampa Bay Rowdies* versus *Atlanta Silverbacks*. He was not a soccer fan so it wasn't all that appealing. Besides, he doubted he'd be there two more days. Paddy was likely right. He'd wasted his time. He should call Stella and have her change his flight reservations.

His gaze lifted beyond the stadium, to the sailing yachts coming in from or going out to Tampa Bay. The yearning rumbled once more in his center. He was scheduled to fly back on Saturday. Maybe he'd leave that as it was and spend Friday getting a sailing lesson.

He watched the boats for a time and then turned with the intent to go out for the sunset walk he'd planned when there came a knock at his door. He paused, expecting to hear a female voice say, "Housekeeping!" but heard nothing.

The knock came again.

He stepped to the door and peered through the peephole. Two men in nearly identical suits that screamed FBI awaited. CJ hadn't much respect for the FBI until a month back when his son, Josh, who he hadn't seen nor heard from for more than a half decade, turned up as one of several FBI special agents assigned to the serial killer case where CJ had been the prime suspect. Together they unraveled the mystery, found and killed the perp, and in the process patched up some old wounds. CJ looked on the FBI with a new set of eyes.

Maybe, he thought, this wasn't going to be a wasted trip after all. Who did Paddy McGee call?

He opened the door.

Chapter 4

"Clinton Washburn?" the taller of the two men said.

"CJ Washburn," CJ replied.

They presented their IDs. "We're with the Federal Bureau of Investigation. We'd like you to come with us."

CJ waited for them to expound on why. When they didn't he said, "For what reason?"

The two looked at each other as if neither of them expected to be challenged as to their reason for fetching him.

"We'd rather not discuss that here, Mister Washburn. This won't take long. We'll deliver you back here in a couple of hours at most."

"Let me see your IDs again."

They held them out. CJ wasn't sure he could identify a fake or not, but at least he felt better going through the motion. He committed the names to memory.

"What's this about? Did I forget to return a library book?"

The short one, Special Agent Ryan Coulter according to his ID, rolled his eyes.

His partner, Special Agent Howard Blain, said, "Douglas Rothbower."

That was the reason CJ was hoping to hear. "Fine." He retrieved his keycard and then followed them to the elevator.

Nothing was said during the descent or as they walked out of the hotel toward a dark gray Dodge Charger. Coulter threw the keys to Blain.

"You can drive," Coulter said.

Blain looked surprised, but said nothing, climbing in behind the wheel. And still they remained silent for the next few minutes, until

Blain took the on-ramp onto I-175. When he had the vehicle up to speed and moving with the westbound traffic, Coulter turned toward CJ in the backseat and said, "Have you ever heard of the *Battle of the Bogside*, Mister Washburn?"

CJ shook his head. "A *World War II* battle?"

"No, but good try. It was a three day skirmish, you might say, between the Unionists and the Nationalists in an inner-city development in Derry, Northern Ireland called Bogside. Took place in August of 1969."

"I was all of a year old. Although I should recall it, my memory fails me."

"Then I'll try to fill you in without going into all of the political history of the region. Basically, the population of Derry was over 60% Catholic or you might say, Nationalist. However, for the previous half century the Unionists, or Protestants, controlled the city thanks to a bit of creative sleight-of-hand when drawing the electoral wards boundaries. At least that's the opinion of most Nationalists. Every time it looked like the Nationalists would gain a bit of control, the boundaries would get redrawn, thus allowing the Unionists to maintain a majority on the city council. It allowed them control over public housing, thus creating a housing crisis for the Catholic population. There were also accusations of employment discrimination against Catholics. It was Catholics versus Protestants, you might say, a small but important piece in the Irish versus British puzzle. In August of 1969 this all came to a head."

Blain directed the car onto I-275 northbound.

CJ said, "Was that the beginning of the Irish Republican Army?"

"Oh hell no. The IRA has been around since your grandparents were babes-in-arms, but you're close. The events of 1969 split the IRA, thus spinning off the Provisional IRA and the Irish National Liberation Army. These two factions were most of what you saw in the news for the next 28 years or so, car bombings and such, but that's another story all together."

"What does this all have to do with me and my search for Douglas

Rothbower, who, if my guess is correct, wasn't much older than me in 1969?"

"Actually, Mister Washburn, Rothbower was younger than you. He was born August 13, 1969 in Derry, smack in the middle of the *Battle of the Bogside.*"

"Okay. I'm getting the picture. In the middle of all this car bombing and rock throwing, Douglas' mother went into labor. I understand that she gave him the name, Douglas O'Reilly, then died three days later."

"The fact is it's not known when she died, or if she actually died at all."

"But there is a birth record?"

"Of sorts, yes."

"Who's the father?"

"Not named."

"But she gave the baby the name, O'Reilly."

"Had to be completely false. Would be like giving him the name, Jones, here."

"Why would she do that? Why not her own name?"

"Good question."

"What was her name?"

"Éibhleann Ó Caiside, believed to have also been false."

"Why's that?"

"Ó Caiside is a very old name, I mean centuries old. It is spelled o space c-a-i-s-i-d-e. It has been replaced by the more common version, Cassidy, spelled as you'd expect. And there was no Éibhleann to be found in that family."

"Pronounce the first name again," CJ said.

"Long a, v and then lin. So it sounds like Ave-lin. Spelled e-i-b-h-l-e-a-n-n."

"Hm," CJ said. "She must have been one mixed up little girl. Seeing as she was able to name him, she had to have made it for at least a day or so."

"Long enough to leave the baby and her homemade birth certificate on the hospital doorstep."

"Homemade birth certificate?"

"That's what I meant by 'of sorts' when you asked if there was a birth certificate. It wasn't an official hospital record, but she tried to make it look like one in her young and naive way."

"What did the note say?"

"Why do you think there was a note?"

"If I was going to leave a baby on a doorstep, I'd try to give some reason, even if was a lie, something to assuage my own guilt, a reason I could live with telling. There'd most definitely be a note."

"It said that both parents were dead, that the baby had no other family."

"There were no other records?"

He looked at his partner and then back at CJ. "His adoptive parents were told that his parents were both dead. End of story."

"But that's not the end of the story, is it?" CJ said.

"Why do you say that?"

"How many people died during the *Battle of the Bogside*?"

"Numerous injuries, as I've already said. No deaths."

"So officials had reason to suspect that the parents being dead was a lie, but for whatever reasons, they didn't care. Maybe they just wanted to hand off another ward of the state to someone else to feed. A rich American family sounded perfect at the time."

The agent turned forward with no comment.

"I was told that the adoption was illegal, *under the table* were the words. Anything having to do with the circumstances around the birth or death of the parents seem to me to be rather suspect."

"Possible."

"Was there any effort on the part of hospital officials or police to locate the parents? They... he... she... someone left a note and a handmade birth certificate."

"There was a search and police investigation, but nothing turned up. As I already said, it was believed that the last name given to the baby was false. It'd be like naming a baby here Douglas Jones before dropping him off on a doorstep. Unless one got lucky with DNA, one would be hard-pressed to trace the parents, alive or dead."

"And of course, back then, there was no DNA technology," CJ said. "So... a baby was dropped off on a doorstep with the name of Douglas O'Reilly and then illegally adopted by a rich American family, the Rothbowers. As fascinating as I find all of this, I fail to see what's so important that the FBI should be getting involved in a baby drop and then an illegal adoption that took place 43 years ago in another country. Also, what does it have to do with Rothbower abandoning his family five years ago and then disappearing?"

"We believe that Rothbower learned who his parents actually were and went off on a quest to locate them."

"Them?"

"He believes they are both still alive."

"Ah," CJ said. He'd been leaning forward, elbows on his knees. He flopped back against the seat. "And the FBI is involved because they also believe the parents are still alive and living in the United States. Fugitives from the law would be my guess? Maybe what you said a few minutes back, that is that the activities of the Provisional IRA and the other one you mentioned are not relevant, was in fact a lie."

"That's not what I said."

"'But that's another story all together,' is actually what you said. You want these people and it has *everything* to do with the violence that went on in Ireland from 1969 until sometime in the late 90s when it ended."

"It came to a stop with a ceasefire in 1997," Coulter said, turning back to face CJ, "and then a signed-by-the-powers agreement on Good Friday in '98. In summary the agreement stated that the majority of Northern Ireland people wanted to remain part of the UK, but recognized that a *substantial section* of the people wanted a united Ireland. What it came down to was that if a majority of the people, at some later date, wanted a united Ireland, the two governments, British and Irish, would be obligated to make it happen."

"So it *didn't* end," CJ said.

"The bombing, fighting and killing ended, but the mission of the IRA and all the spinoffs did not. They have been working behind the scenes, both above ground and underground, to sway opinion. Recently, in the last few years, there has been an increased groundswell of rebirth."

"And violence?"

"Some, though not enough to make headline news like that in the 80s and 90s."

"And that's the reason you're looking for the parents. They're still alive and well and in the center of the groundswell, maybe the violent part."

The agent didn't say anything.

"They're operating out of Florida somewhere and Douglas is close to finding them," CJ said. "Is that it then?"

Coulter looked at his partner and then turned forward in his seat again. They were leaving land and crossing over Old Tampa Bay, the reverse route CJ had taken when he drove into St. Petersburg from the Tampa airport.

The remainder of the trip passed in silence, CJ curious as to where they were going. After a time they left the interstate, made a few turns and wound up cruising through a commercial park, a minute later coming to a stop at a gate. With a special handshake or wink or something that CJ didn't see, the gate opened and they passed through. As they left the car and proceeded inside, he wondered how his son, Special Agent Joshua Washburn, was doing and whether his office in Denver looked anything like this. Josh had invited him to come up for a visit and tour. CJ would have to take him up on that, another step in healing old wounds.

The two agents dropped him off in an office in front of a desk which, according to the name plaque, belonged to John Taffer. The initials ASAC were below the name, in a smaller font. He was asked if he wanted coffee, water or soda. A minute later he had a bottle of *Mineral Springs* and was told that Special Agent Taffer would be with him shortly. He looked at the plaque for a time, sipping on the water, trying to recall the rank structure of the FBI. The SAC he knew was Special Agent-in-Charge, therefore, the ASAC must be the Assistant Special Agent-in-Charge.

A few seconds later, a man several inches taller than CJ's 6'2" walked in, his hand immediately extended.

"Clinton Washburn," he said, swallowing CJ's hand. "John Taffer. Sorry to keep you waiting. Got a call from the wife as you were brought in. She had to let me know we've got a new grandson."

"Congratulations."

Taffer moved around to his desk and sat down. "That's number two for us. You have any grandkids, Clinton?"

"Not yet, and please call me CJ."

"CJ. You have two kids, though. Patricia and Special Agent Joshua Washburn."

CJ wasn't surprised by the fact that Agent Taffer already knew that. He'd probably been briefed about CJ's entire life, likely knew more than CJ knew himself. He certainly knew that CJ had no grandchildren. So why the *let's bond and be friends* ruse?

"Yep," CJ said. "Just the two. Can we get to the point? I was summoned from my hotel room because I'm searching for Douglas Rothbower. Why is he so important to the FBI?"

"Okay. To the point. If you were anyone else we'd have simply told you to drop your investigation and go home. However, your file has a couple of stars on it, making you a friend of the FBI."

"I have a file?"

"Of course. You have an interesting history."

CJ wasn't sure how to respond to that, so he went with, "How is it that *my file* has stars?"

"First, you're the father of one of our special agents. Family and all of that. Second, you served as a police officer, honorably. Third, you and your son were instrumental in solving one of the worst serial killer cases seen in Arizona's modern day history and you, personally, took the guy out. You have the respect of the bureau."

"I'm honored. So what does it all mean?"

"It means that we want to be a bit more open with you, as a courtesy you might say, to help you understand why we need you to back off."

"Your two agents filled me in about the IRA. I see nothing there that warrants my walking away."

"They didn't tell you everything and probably a lot more than they should have. Again, respect and all that."

"Okay. What's the part that I don't know yet?"

Taffer formed a steeple with his fingers. "Douglas Rothbower is an informant."

"Informant?"

"Deep cover. If you by chance find him you could be risking his life, and yours for that matter, and jeopardize a very important operation."

"But he's not an agent," CJ said.

"No."

"I didn't think the FBI did deep cover with civilian informants."

"This is a special case. We are working closely with other agencies and foreign governments. Rothbower was a perfect fit and he was more than willing to do it."

"What exactly is he doing?"

"I can't really divulge anything further."

"I gather I've gotten close. Why else would you have intercepted me?"

"Close enough."

CJ considered what he had just been told and then said, "You might have a problem."

"How's that?"

"I got a little too close too easily for his being deep cover. "

"That is being taken care of."

"The cousins?"

Taffer just smiled and tilted his head.

"My client is not going to be happy," CJ said.

"I'm sure you can make her understand."

"Then you know who my client is."

"Certainly. My condolences to Ms. Onassis and her sister."

"I'll be sure to pass it along," CJ said, adding a tad of sarcasm to his voice. "Does Douglas know that his daughter is dead?"

"He's been out of the country, so I don't think so."

"Are you intending on telling him?"

"When the time is right. Things are coming to a head right now so passing that news to him could be detrimental, and it's not going to bring his daughter back."

No it won't, CJ thought, but if I were Douglas, I'd be pissed when I find out the FBI was withholding the death of my daughter.

CJ and Agent Taffer chatted for a few more minutes about CJ's son in Colorado, the FBI in general and a little about the serial killer case that made CJ so famous. And then the two agents returned him to his hotel.

"Go home," was the last thing Taffer said to him. At this point, CJ wasn't making any commitments, though he had to admit that it seemed he had hit a federal brick wall. Was it worth trying to break it down?

He'd have to do more thinking on it.

Chapter 5

Hot, wet, tangled. CJ struggled from sleep, trying to push away the dream, or nightmare, whatever it was. As the fog cleared he kicked away the covers and lay listening for Stella's breathing, but heard nothing. Seconds ticked by as he recalled that he wasn't in Arizona, that he'd flown to Florida alone, that the unfamiliar shapes in the near total darkness belonged to his hotel room in St. Petersburg.

He looked at the time. 6 a.m. In Arizona it would be daylight at 6 a.m. He got up and pulled back the drapes; not even a hint of sunrise. His internal Arizona clock knew it was actually only 3 a.m. back in the desert. He should still be asleep. He pushed the drapes all the way open to allow city lights to enter, then lay back down on top of the spread and stared up at the ceiling.

He'd talked to Stella after Agent Blain dropped him back at the hotel, but didn't tell her anything about the FBI meeting. He only told her that he'd be returning on Saturday as scheduled and that he'd fill her in on his progress after he'd kissed her a whole lot. He didn't mention wanting to take a sailing lesson. He wasn't ready to divulge his honeymoon idea until he had found out if he'd even like it himself, if he was capable of handling a sailboat.

The Rothbower thing bugged him. His initial gut reaction had been to tell Agent Taffer to stick it up his ass, but then he got his gut under control. He understood an operation of the nature the agent was talking about, had his own experience with working between multiple agencies; at the city and county level anyway. It wouldn't take a whole lot to kill an operation that had taken weeks or even months to set up. A deep cover informant, though, with multiple federal agencies over possibly several years... CJ couldn't imagine. Apparently Rothbower was key to the entire thing, whatever the entire thing was.

By the time CJ had left Taffer's office, he knew he couldn't not agree to back down. They could make things difficult for him, probably would have if he wasn't already related to the FBI by blood. They could start playing hardball and CJ didn't even have a bat.

They didn't have to be courteous.

He got up and headed for the shower.

CJ was in the hotel dining room using a piece of toast and his fork to gang up on the last bite of egg when a shadow fell over him. He looked up.

"Mister Washburn?"

CJ blinked for a few seconds, recalling the various pictures he'd seen, then released his fork and sat back. "Douglas Rothbower."

The man looked over his shoulder as though expecting someone to be listening in, and then looked back down at CJ. "Douglas O'Reilly." CJ was sitting on the booth side of a table, his back against the wall. Rothbower, or O'Reilly, pulled out the chair on the opposite side and sat. "It is said that you have been looking for me."

CJ noted a twist of Irish Brogue, nothing like the two Paddys, however.

"Yes. But I didn't really expect to find you after I spoke with the FBI last night."

"FBI?" Douglas sat back in his chair. "Had no idea." He looked around the dining room again then leaned forward, lowering his voice. "Then you must know about UIRA."

Douglas looked away for a few seconds and CJ wondered if the man had said something he shouldn't have.

"Then you know what it is I am doing," Douglas added.

CJ leaned closer and lowered his voice, though there was no one close by in the hotel diner. "I know you're deep undercover."

"And so you *do* know."

"They asked me to back off because you're involved in a sensitive operation. Didn't want to put you in danger or jeopardize the mission."

O'Reilly looked just as surprised as CJ. "Yes, I could see them telling you that. But I didn't know they talked to you; surprised they trusted you. I heard by another channel that a private eye from Arizona, Tucson they said, was looking for me and that it was important that I meet with him."

"They?"

"Well, he."

"Paddy McGee?"

O'Reilly ignored the question. "Something about family. Me sister-in-law, Gianna Onassis, lives in Tucson. What's she sticking her nose into now?"

"You didn't know that your daughter was living in Tucson?"

"Alexandria? Aye, I do. Going to school."

"But you don't know of anything going on."

"I have been in and out o' country, mostly out. Returned just three days ago after a couple o' months in Northern Ireland. When I'm there I don't talk with my handler; only just checked in yesterday. They trust me to do what I have to do."

"And what is that?" CJ asked, wanting to add, *that would have you deserting your family?* Instead he said, "Sorry. I shouldn't ask."

"No. You shouldn't. And I shant tell you. So what about me family that Gianna deems it so important to hire you to find me? I can't imagine that Alex would hire you. Has something happened to Alexandria or Kassandra? I spoke to Kassandra earlier in the summer. Everything was fine."

"You talked with your wife?"

"I check in with her every few months, was planning a call in a day or so. When you do what I do, it's a little tricky. Just coming here to meet with you wasn't easy."

"She never told me, led me to believe she didn't know where you were, hadn't heard from you in five years."

He smiled and nodded his head. "She *is* good. Together we built a cover story. I left because of gambling issues or some such thing, ran out on me family. She even has people believing I'm dead. I don't gamble and as you can see, I'm not dead."

"Really?" CJ was shocked. "Kassandra went along with this?"

Douglas dropped his head for a second and then looked back up at CJ. "I am not proud of how it all started. The story we concocted, in the beginning, was not far from the truth. I did walk out on my family and yes, Kassandra didn't know where I was for nearly four years. Although I have since regretted it, I've gotten into something that is a lot bigger than me." He straightened his back and added, "We'd just started talking about patching things up. When this is over, I'll go back."

"When might that be?"

"Soon. The summit..." He stopped as though he'd caught his tongue getting ahead of his brain again. "It's all coming to a head so it'll be soon. I don't know if she'll have me back, but I'm ready to give it a go."

CJ sat back again and considered his next words. He had to lock his jaw against things like, 'There's nothing to go back to. You've waited too long,' or 'You think you've had regrets, wait until you hear this,' or 'You're an ass, Douglas O'Reilly/Rothbower.' Until Douglas had walked in, CJ was prepared to leave Florida without further effort to find him, telling Gianna that he'd failed, or telling her the truth. He hadn't quite thought that through yet. Now the bag was open and there was no getting it closed.

He looked straight into the man's eyes. "There's no easy way to say this, Douglas, but Alexandria is dead."

Chapter 6

Delivering the news to Gianna's brother-in-law took more out of CJ than he would have ever imagined. He'd have thought that with his mission accomplished he would have felt free to spend the day playing tourist, taking a sailing lesson or at least checking out a beach and shopping for a gift for Stella. Instead, he'd sat for some time in the hotel dining room, thinking. After a bit he found himself standing just outside the hotel entrance, wondering where to go. Noting a *Starbucks* next door, he went in.

The place was busy. A college-aged blond, hair wrapped up in a bun, worked the order counter while an older woman and man filled the orders behind her.

"What's your major?" CJ asked after placing his order for a regular Grande.

She gave him a surprised look.

"Florida State nearby. I made the assumption you're a college student."

"Oh!" She presented a huge, white-teethed smile. "Environmental Science. Third year."

"Will bet there's a lot of jobs in that field in Florida."

"Hope so. I... ah..." she pointed behind him.

CJ got the hint and moved aside for the next customer in line. While he waited for his order to be filled, he watched the girl, thinking about how much she looked like his daughter, maybe the reason he'd struck up a conversation with her. Minutes later he was still in deep thought about Trish and her move back down to Arizona from Idaho where she'd been going to school, when his name was called. After adding one sugar to his coffee, he stepped back out into the sunny Florida morning.

The coffee still too hot to drink, he wandered across the stadium parking lot to the waterfront, taking little or no notice of the yachts coming and going, his thoughts, instead, not only on Trish, but also on Alexandria and the look on her father's face. He thought about Trish and how close he'd come to losing her to an insane cop turned killer; that if he had, it would have been all his fault. He thought about Josh and all the years that were lost when he took off, angry at his parents, again CJ's fault, and how close he came to losing him when he'd finally returned, saved by a bullet-proof vest. He had no doubt he'd have been at fault on that as well. CJ would never say another bad word about bullet-proof vests.

After giving Rothbower the news of his daughter's death, CJ had told him the story of Tommy Clark, or as much of the story that was important to be repeated to a devastated father. CJ then watched him walk away, regret and fault fighting an internal struggle like a couple of entwined snakes. CJ never mentioned how at fault he felt himself, how Tommy killed Alexandria because of him.

There was plenty of blame to go around.

He wondered if he should call Gianna and give her the report now, or wait to do it face-to-face. He sat down on a bench facing the harbor, set his *Starbucks* coffee next to him, pulled out his phone and pressed the speed dial icon for Stella.

CJ had forgotten about the 3-hour time difference until he heard Stella's voice and realized it wasn't even 5 a.m. for her.

"Sorry," he said. "Go back to sleep. I'll call back later."

"No," she said. "That's fine. What's wrong?"

"What do you mean, what's wrong?"

"You sound different."

CJ wondered how she could read him after he'd said only a handful of words. Now he wished he hadn't called because she'd twenty-question him until he gave it all up. Why was he holding back on her anyway? She was not only his fiancé, but his assistant in *Desert Investigative Services*. Correction; she was his partner.

"I just talked to Douglas Rothbower," he said.

"Oh! That's great!"

"Yes it is, however..."

"However what?"

"I gave him the news about his daughter."

"Oh. That had to have been hard."

"Yeah, it was. Watching his reaction got me to thinking about Tommy Clark again, and how much worse it could have all been. Trish. Josh. You. I could have lost you all."

"But you didn't. Okay? We're all still here and you're still here."

There was a long silence because CJ didn't know what else to say.

"So... how did you find him?"

"He just showed up. Walked up to me while I was eating breakfast."

"So someone you talked to got the word to him that he was being searched for. Was it the guy at the Irish pub?"

"It had to have been, though at first I thought it was the FBI."

"FBI? You talked to the bureau? When was that?"

CJ put his head in his hand. *Damn!* "Last night. They came to my hotel room and took me to the Tampa field office."

"After you and I talked? That was late, wasn't it?"

CJ let out a long breath, then took in another. "No. Before we talked. They wanted me to stop my search."

"You had already met with them when you called last night? Why didn't you tell me?"

"I don't know. I was still trying to sort it all out."

"Damn it, Clint! We've talked about this. Open communications! You're on a case and I'm your assistant slash secretary slash partner. That's what you told me anyway. I really wanted to come with you, but you talked me out of it, saying you'd keep me up to speed. Well, I'm way behind now."

"I'm sorry."

"Catch me up. They wanted you to stop searching for Rothbower? Why?"

CJ told her about the meeting at the Tampa field office and then Douglas O'Reilly showing up, that Douglas had been talking to his wife all along, that they'd been using a cover story and even after Alexandria died, she never broke his cover, even to her sister.

"You would have thought she would have said something after Gianna hired you," Stella said.

"That's my thought, too. She could have just said that she knew where he was and that it was her job to tell him. That would have been enough to stop Gianna. And Gianna thought she was doing something for her sister."

"The sisters aren't talking to each other, it seems. It's that lack of communications thing I mentioned a minute ago."

"I hear you."

"Any idea what he's into?"

CJ's butt was getting sore so he stood and stepped out onto the sidewalk that ran along the harbor. He caught a movement at the corner of his eye and suddenly realized he was stepping into someone's path, but in the process of trying to avoid the person, they collided.

"Sorry!" CJ said as he stumbled to the side.

"Sorry!" the guy said, grabbing CJ by one arm as though to steady the two of them. "My apologies." He then released his grip and continued on his way, fast-walking south.

"What was that?" Stella asked.

"Nothing. I just bumped into someone." For a few seconds CJ watched the man, who didn't seem to be bothered at all with the collision. "Walked right in front of him."

"Oh. So, any idea what Rothbower or O'Reilly is into?"

"He says he spends a lot of time in Northern Ireland. Put that with the history Agent Coulter gave me, I would say it has something to do with the resurgence of the IRA. Agent Taffer refused to elaborate."

"He was concerned that your poking around could get Douglas killed; is that right?"

"Or me, he said. And jeopardize the mission, whatever the mission is."

"You've done what Gianna wanted. I think you need to get out of there. You've got paying clients stacking up here."

"I'll be home tomorrow afternoon."

"I'll be at the airport. So what do you have planned for today?"

CJ looked out at the rows and rows of yachts. "I don't know. Explore the city a little, do a bit of window shopping, maybe find some fresh-caught fish for lunch."

"Sounds nice. Remember to get receipts. I can't bill Gianna for expenses unless you have documented receipts."

"Yes ma'am," CJ said, wondering what he did with the *Starbucks* receipt.

They talked a bit longer about Trish's new job and Stella's sister in Albuquerque, exchanged I-love-yous and then hung up. CJ was really glad he'd called, glad to get the entire Rothbower/O'Reilly thing off his chest and out in the open. Communications. Yes, he'd do better at that.

His gaze fell to the sailboats again.

Except for the sailing.

He continued walking north toward *Bay Shore Charters and Sailing School*. He really wasn't ready to share with Stella what might be nothing more than a midlife crisis urge, *his* dream, but not necessarily hers.

CJ stood with his hands in his pockets, staring at the closed sign on the front of the small building. *Bay Shore Charters and Sailing School* didn't open until 9:00. It was only 8:05. He strolled away to walk along the walkway and look at the variety of vessels tied to the piers, wondered if any of them were the ones on which the classes were held. Not all of them were sailboats. More than half were strictly power boats; big power boats; not the kind with a small outboard hanging off the back. He wanted to get closer but the fence and locked gate precluded it.

His attention was momentarily drawn up the street where a police car and then a fire apparatus screamed by, heading south on Bay Shore Drive. Less than a minute after they disappeared from view their sirens died. Another could be heard off in the distance, coming closer. CJ wondered only briefly what was going on.

He returned to Bay Shore Drive and walked South to 2nd Avenue where he stopped to look at sailboats again. He watched people come and go, several pulling wheeled carts down to their boats. They were dressed a lot different than CJ. That got him to thinking that he needed to return to his hotel room and change into shoes more appropriate for sailing. The shorts and light-cotton off-white button-down shirt he was wearing would certainly be okay, however, his dress oxfords weren't going to cut it. Why he put those on this morning, he had no idea. He had a pair of *Nikes* with him.

As he walked along between 2nd Avenue and 1st Avenue, in route back to his hotel, he spotted the commotion of emergency vehicles up ahead a quarter of a mile or so, right next to *Al Lang Field*. There were three police vehicles that he could see, an unmarked sedan, a fire truck and EMS, as well as an official-looking white van. As he got closer several men in full-body wet suits appeared from around the van, one looking to put on scuba gear, getting ready to go into the water.

A body, CJ thought.

Professional curiosity kept him from crossing the street as he normally would have to make his way to his hotel. When he got to within fifty feet of where the action was concentrated, which was not but a few yards from the bench where he'd sat and called Stella and where a diver was now doing something with a scuba tank, a police officer stopped him.

"Cross over to the other side of the street and go around," he told CJ.

CJ backed up a couple of steps and then just watched. One diver without a tank was already in the water handling what did in fact appear to be a body. The other diver went in, tank on his back, goggles on top of his head.

"Sir!" the cop said. "I need you to move along."

CJ looked over at him.

The cop pointed at CJ. "You! Move away! Cross over to the sidewalk on the other side or go back. Go about your business. There's nothing here for you to see."

A little more pushy than Tucson cops, CJ thought. Not wanting to get tied up in something that certainly wasn't his business, he crossed the street and then cut through the stadium parking lot to get over to the street on which sat his hotel. It was 8:35. If he hurried he had just enough time to change shoes and get back to *Bay Shore Charters and Sailing School* when it opened.

CJ stepped out of the hotel front entrance twelve minutes later and walked down to the sidewalk. He looked to his right at the *Starbucks* next door and wondered what he did with the coffee he'd bought earlier. He didn't get any more of it than a hot sip. He turned his face up to the sky and tried to remember where he left it.

Oh yeah! He'd set it down on the bench when he called Stella, then walked away without it. It was probably history now, dumped by the scuba divers who'd been using the same bench.

He weighed the urge for another coffee against getting to the sailing school when it opened. He figured they didn't start right at 9:00 so he turned toward the *Starbucks*. Hopefully there wouldn't still be a long line.

There was a woman and a man in line, both standing a good five feet back from a police detective at the counter. CJ could tell it was a police detective because, one, they all looked the same, and two, there was a uniformed police officer next to him, the same officer who gave CJ a hard time just fifteen minutes before. The detective was showing something to the girl behind the counter, the girl who served CJ and who reminded him of Trish.

The girl shook her head while lifting her hands and shoulders, the universal sign of *I don't know*. Then she looked past the detective's shoulder to CJ. Her eyes got big. She pointed and her mouth moved.

The detective and police officer swiveled around and CJ suddenly felt like he'd forgotten to put on his pants.

The police officer moved first, stepping toward CJ and pointing at him, his other hand sliding to his weapon. "You! Don't move!"

CJ didn't move.

"Are you Clinton Washburn?" the detective asked of CJ after the officer had taken him by the arm and guided him outside.

"Yes," CJ said.

"Private investigator from Arizona; *Desert Investigative Services*?"

"That's right. How...?"

"Let's see some ID?"

CJ reached to his back pocket, but found it empty. He checked his other pockets but found only the key to his rental, his cell phone, his hotel room keycard, and some change.

"I must have left my wallet in my hotel room. I can go up..."

"Do you know a Douglas O'Reilly?" the detective interrupted.

Surprised, CJ said, "Yes."

"How do you know him?"

"I met with him this morning, at breakfast in the hotel."

"Why?"

"He was the subject of my current investigation. I'm here in Florida on behalf of a Tucson, Arizona client."

"He *was* the subject?"

"Yes, was," CJ said, again surprised by the question. "The investigation is concluded. I've accomplished what my client asked of me."

"And what was that?"

"To find her brother-in-law."

"And then kill him?"

CJ's mouth dropped open. "Douglas is dead? Son of a..."

"Yeah. It's a bitch alright. It's a bitch that you dropped your wallet while pushing a knife into Mister O'Reilly and then throwing him off the seawall. It's also a bitch that the credit card you used to purchase the coffee you left at the scene was in your wallet along with the receipt, and that the gal in *Starbucks* remembers you."

"I need to call my client," CJ said.

"How about you call your attorney instead?" the detective said.

"My client *is* my attorney."

"You're under arrest, Mister Washburn, for the murder of Douglas O'Reilly."

With that statement the uniformed cop pulled CJ's arms behind his back and began applying handcuffs.

The detective continued. "You have the right to remain silent. Anything you say can be used against you in a court of law. You have the right to consult with a lawyer and have that lawyer present during the interrogation. If you cannot afford a lawyer, one will be appointed to represent you. You can invoke your right to be silent before or during an interrogation, and if you do so, the interrogation must stop. You can invoke your right to have a lawyer present, and until your lawyer is present, the interrogation must stop."

CJ had all kinds of things he wanted to say, but he was in another state where nobody knew him and he knew nobody.

"I invoke my right to silence and my right to an attorney," he said.

"Smart man," the detective said. "It's rare that I get to arrest a smart man. I doubt your client and attorney in Arizona is licensed to practice in Florida. I would normally allow you to contact her anyway, however, since as you say, you are here on her behalf, maybe killing her brother-in-law on her behalf, I am invoking my right to refuse. We will be happy to assist you in finding a local attorney."

They walked him back across the stadium parking lot to a patrol car and pushed him into the back. As they started to close the door CJ said, "Detective."

The detective looked in at him.

"This is extremely important. Contact John Taffer, Assistant Special Agent-in-Charge at the FBI field office in Tampa."

"And why should I do that?"

"He'll be able to tell you who Douglas O'Reilly really was and maybe shed a little light on the direction your investigation should go to find the real killer."

"Other than you?"

"I didn't kill him. I came to find him to inform him of the death of his daughter. Agent Taffer intercepted me last night, wanted me to back off my search for fear that it would get Douglas killed."

The detective only tilted his head at CJ.

"Douglas was an FBI informant. I really shouldn't say anything more, leave it to Taffer to fill you in."

The detective straightened up and appeared to pause in consideration of what CJ just told him. CJ started to open his mouth to say something else when the detective plucked his phone from his belt clip. CJ closed his mouth and watched him punch a few buttons and then hold the phone to his ear.

After a bit, the detective said, "John, good morning. Parker DuPont here."

CJ smiled at the fact that Detective DuPont was already on a first name basis with Special Agent Taffer.

"Going well. Kids are good. How is Gail doing? Still in chemo?"

"Yeah, know what you mean. Listen, I've got a body down here on Bay Shore. Not even cold and I already have a suspect in custody."

"Yeah, they should all go this easy. Here's the twist, however. The guy in custody dropped your name. I hope to hell you're not going to tell me he's out of bounds or some dumb ass thing."

"The suspect's name is Clinton Washburn. The dead guy is..." DuPont's eyebrows went up. "Yeah. That's right. Douglas O'Reilly."

DuPont moved the phone a few inches from his ear and CJ heard Agent Taffer yell, "Dumb ass!"

"Tell him O'Reilly came to *me*," CJ called out the door.

Detective DuPont pushed the door closed and walked away.

Chapter 7

"Believe it or not, Agent Taffer is vouching for you," Detective DuPont said after he'd left CJ in an interview room for way too long after a uniformed cop dropped him there. CJ knew the drill. Let the suspect stew with his own thoughts, hopefully be ready to spill his guts as soon as someone walks in. "That's not enough, though," the detective added. "How did your wallet wind up in the bay with the body?"

That wasn't a hard one to figure out for CJ. He'd had two hours to think through the entire morning, develop his own time line. He told DuPont about colliding with the man when he stood up from the bench. "Long pants, khaki. Some kind of hiking boots, brown. Black shirt. Didn't see his face; got only a profile."

"Hair color?"

CJ shook his head. "Not dark. I'd say blondish, but I'd be guessing. Other than that, sorry. I was talking on my cell phone at the time. It was obviously planned. Pick my pocket and then kill Douglas. Plant the wallet so that the blame would fall on me. These guys can think and act on the fly."

"Guys?"

"I guess it could have just been one person. He or they; take your pick."

"You think someone found out he was an informant?"

"Certainly. He had to have been following him when Douglas came to see me. They probably became suspicious after my visit to the FBI last night."

"How would they have found out about that, do you think?" DuPont said.

"That's a good question, isn't it. The only other person in Florida who knew why I was here was Paddy McGee, the owner of *Paddy McGee's Irish Pub*. The pub was the first place I went after flying in yesterday afternoon. I met with him for ten minutes or so. We talked about Douglas. He claimed to have only met him once, many years back, in Indiana, but otherwise didn't know him. When he went back to his grill he immediately made a phone call. I suspected at the time it had something to do with our conversation; too coincidental. I don't know who he called, but three things have happened since. First, the FBI picked me up to have a chat about my looking for Douglas. How would they have found out about me? Second, Douglas visited me this morning to find out why I was looking for him. He didn't already know about his daughter's death and he was surprised that I'd talked to the FBI. Where did he find out about me? Third, Douglas was killed right after he left the hotel."

"So, what are you thinking?"

"A couple of possibilities. Paddy called one person who then notified the FBI and the bad guys."

"Not highly likely," DuPont said.

"I agree. He either called the bad guys or the FBI or Douglas. If he called the FBI, his phone may be bugged. I have my doubts he called Douglas."

"Why's that?"

CJ looked at DuPont for a few seconds, trying to surmise whether the detective was humoring him or was seriously following his train of thought.

"Because when I told Douglas of his daughter's death, he looked genuinely shocked and devastated. There is no way a father could act that out. If Paddy had called him to tell him I was looking for him, he would have told him why, wouldn't you think? Douglas' daughter being murdered would certainly be worth mentioning."

"Murdered?" Dupont said.

"Yes. Murdered. A serial killer."

The detective pointed his finger at CJ. "You're not talking about the cop who went berserk in Arizona a month or two ago, are you?"

"Tommy Clark. Yes."

The detective leaned back and looked up at the ceiling. "Washburn. I knew I recognized that name from somewhere. You were the subject of a nationwide manhunt."

"Glad to hear that my notoriety precedes me. I'm also the one who put Clark down."

"That's the story that's out there. Shit just kind of follows you around, doesn't it?"

CJ ignored the last comment. "The thing is, Douglas' murder is unrelated fallout. In Tommy Clark's twisted mind he started targeting me by going after people close to me. My attorney, who was also my biggest client and a good friend, had a niece attending school in Tucson. After failing in an attempt at my daughter, Clark targeted and killed her. She happened to be Douglas' daughter. As a favor to my attorney, Gianna Onassis, I took on the task of finding Douglas and informing him. He'd disappeared some five years ago; just walked away from his family."

"Douglas Rothbower," Dupont said. "You found him. Now he's dead, too."

CJ looked at him, a bit surprised. He hadn't yet mentioned Douglas' real name.

"Agent Taffer filled me in. He's considerably pissed. A lot of bureau effort and manpower on this IRA thing has gone out the window."

"I really didn't have anything to do with it. After Taffer told me to back off, I had no intention of doing otherwise. I was looking forward to playing tourist for a day and then flying home tomorrow and briefing my client on what I'd found. I didn't do anything so there's no need to be pissed at me."

"I think he sees it a little different. If you hadn't shown up asking questions, Douglas wouldn't have broken his cover to see you. He'd still be alive and the FBI's operation would still be intact."

CJ sat back. "Yeah, well, I had no way of knowing." When DuPont didn't say anything more, CJ said, "So... what now?"

DuPont leaned over and unlocked the cuffs that had been keeping

CJ married to the table. "Get the hell out of here. Do like you said you were going to do. Play tourist and then be on the plane tomorrow back to Arizona."

"Thanks."

"Stay out of trouble."

"What about my wallet?"

"Oh yeah. Forgot about that." The detective opened the door. "Hang tight for a minute."

CJ stood and stretched in an attempt to soften some of the sore spots that resulted from sitting in a hard chair for so long.

The door opened again and DuPont came back in. He dropped a plastic bag on the table. "I left it in the evidence bag for you. It's a tad soggy."

CJ picked it up and looked at it. "Great. Just great."

Chapter 8

When the taxi driver looked at the soggy twenty dollar bill and then gave CJ a "You've got to be kidding me!" look, CJ told him to keep the change and headed into the hotel, his Tampa Bay-soaked wallet still sequestered in the evidence bag gripped tightly in his hand. He hoped that housekeeping had already taken care of his room because all he wanted to do was turn on the TV, use the blow dryer to dry what could be salvaged and then hibernate until it was time to go to the airport on Saturday. He'd had about as much of Florida as he could stand.

As he passed through the lobby he noted a family poring over a map, and a woman wearing sunglasses, sitting off to the side by herself paging through a newspaper. Dark glasses in a dark hotel interior; curious, CJ thought. She looked up and he smiled. She didn't smile back but did seem to study him longer than passing curiosity would normally entail. The thought left him as soon as he passed out of her view, down the corridor to the elevators. Entering one, after stepping aside for two people to exit, he punched the button for the 9th floor. He decided he'd put out the *do not disturb* sign whether housekeeping had been in or not. Shoes off and then getting horizontal on the bed was all he could think about.

Just as the elevator door started to close, the woman with the sunglasses slipped in.

"What floor?" CJ asked, prepared to punch another button.

"Are you Mister Washburn?" she said.

He looked down at her, a good ten inches shorter than him. "Yes."

"Then I'm going to your floor."

CJ stood back and considered the woman. She wore a black skirt, calf-length, and a black blouse buttoned high. A narrow black scarf sat atop her head, tied under her hair in the back. In her hands in front of her was a black clutch purse. Her shoes matched her ensemble. All that was missing were black gloves.

She was most certainly a woman in mourning. CJ took a wild stab. "How did you know Douglas?"

She looked at him, surprise in her eyes. "He was my husband. I am Rebecca O'Reilly."

CJ raised his eyebrows.

"I would rather not talk in here. Your hotel room, please."

CJ nodded and the elevator stopped. She followed him to his room and as he swiped his key card she opened her purse and pulled out a phone. She flipped it open and speed-dialed a number.

"He is here," she said into the phone. "Room 915.

"Yes. Of course." She closed the phone and put it away.

"Who did you just call?" CJ asked.

"My mother-in-law."

CJ raised his eyebrows again.

"We talk with you together. She won't be long."

Despite his almost overwhelming curiosity and the numerous questions forming in his mind, he agreed. He offered her the best chair and then busied himself spreading out the contents of his wallet, glad that housekeeping had been in. He retrieved a towel and started drying off credit cards and the receipts he'd been collecting. When he noticed her questioning look, he said, "My wallet found its way into the bay."

"Oh."

CJ noticed a slight up-turn at one corner of her mouth. Despite her dark mood, she found his situation amusing. He wondered what she looked like without the headdress and sunglasses. All he could really see were a pair of prominent cheek bones and a light colored mole on the left side of her jaw.

He was pushing hot air into the crevasses of his wallet when there came a knock. He shut off the hair dryer and opened the door. The woman who stood before him was maybe in her mid-sixties, though the grief she obviously carried added some years. Her ensemble was similar to the younger woman's, though, a full length dress, but without the sunglasses.

He stepped aside and let her pass into the room. Without waiting for him to do so for her, she pulled the only other chair over next to Rebecca and sat.

"What have you told him?" she asked of Rebecca.

"Only that I was Douglas' wife and that you were his mother."

"*Am* his mother. I will always be his mother, even when he is dead."

Rebecca dropped her head. Her cheekbones seemed to become even more pronounced.

The older woman looked up at CJ. "Sit down, Mister Washburn."

He sat on the bed.

She handed him a business card. "I am Eveleen Danohough, Douglas' mother. This is my daughter-in-law, Rebecca O'Reilly. We know that you are a private investigator. We want to hire you."

CJ glanced at the business card and then set it aside. "For what purpose?"

"We want you to find Douglas' killer."

"I am licensed only in Arizona, certainly not in Florida."

"I fail to see why that should be an issue. You don't have to have a license to ask questions."

"No, but the local police would frown upon my snooping around, especially when they are already investigating his murder, and especially since they've already told me to go home. I found the police here to be quite efficient. Let them find the answers you want."

"They won't find anything."

"How do you know that?

"I just know."

"I see." CJ looked up at the ceiling and then at the two women. "Are you aware that Douglas O'Reilly was a false name, that Douglas was actually someone else?"

The old woman's mouth tightened and it seemed for a few seconds that she ground her teeth. "Mister Washburn. The other name you're going to refer to is Rothbower. *It* was the false name, given to him illegally. O'Reilly was the name I gave him when he was born and the name he took back when he found out what happened. Douglas Edmond O'Reilly."

"Then you must also be aware that he had another family as Douglas Rothbower, a wife and daughter."

Rebecca looked up, surprise evident on what little of her face that was visible.

"Yes," Ms. Danohough said.

Rebecca's head swiveled to the older woman, her mouth dropping open. "How?" was all she managed to say.

Ms. Danohough closed her eyes for a few seconds as though gathering her thoughts, her patience. She turned to Rebecca and said, "Douglas wanted to tell you, but I convinced him not to. What was the point? You were married in Northern Ireland, both his and your motherland. That should hold precedence over an illegal marriage in a foreign country."

"Are you a member of the Irish Republican Army, Ms. Danohough?" CJ asked.

Her face went flat as she seemed to consider the question.

"It's not a complicated question. Either you are or are not."

"No. We are not members of the IRA."

"How about the Provisional IRA or the Irish National Liberation Army?"

"Why do you ask, Mister Washburn? I don't see the relevance."

"You want to know who killed your son. I have reason to believe it had something to do with one of these three groups I just mentioned. Which one were Douglas and yourselves associated with?"

Ms. Danohough looked at Mrs. O'Reilly, who was staring at her feet. Her mouth tightened and she turned back to CJ.

"The Provisional IRA, Mister Washburn. Have been a member since before Douglas was born."

"August 13, 1969 in Derry, Northern Ireland during the Battle of

Bogside, is that right? You were also reported to have died shortly after childbirth, thus the reason Douglas wound up in a new home."

A little more teeth-grinding. "You're well-informed."

"Except about the dying in childbirth part. Apparently I was misinformed." Not waiting for a comment back he addressed the younger woman. "How about you, Rebecca? How long have you been a member of the Provisional Army?"

She brought her chin up, said, "Just since we've been married," then lowered her head again.

"When was that?"

"They were married a year ago, last month," the elder woman said.

"You do realize that there is a Mrs. Rothbower who would argue that she is the rightful widow. Seeing as her marriage took place in this country and both she and Douglas were residents at the time, she'd have a very legal leg to stand on. America frowns on a man having more than one wife."

"As does Ireland."

"Mrs. Rothbower trumps with longevity, twenty-plus years."

"She kicked him out."

"Is that what he told you?"

"Yes. And then they got divorced, so it makes no difference anyway."

CJ opened his mouth to argue and then realized he wasn't completely sure what the cover story was that they created. Did he abandon them like he said or did she kick him out? Douglas did say that the cover story was an extension of the truth, that it was years before he made contact again. Did she kick him out but let everyone, including her sister, believe that he packed up and left without telling her anything, that he just disappeared? There was no mention of a divorce.

"Never-the-less, Mister Washburn, we want to hire you to find his killer. You seem to know a lot more about my son than I expected. You believe it has something to do with PIRA?" She pronounced the group as one word.

"What is the mission of PIRA?" CJ asked.

"I haven't read the mission statement in some time, so I couldn't tell you. Something to do with putting the Irish back into Ireland I would imagine."

"Through armed or peaceful means?"

"Peaceful, of course." She seemed to raise her chin a bit when she said it. Then CJ remembered something Douglas had let slip in the hotel diner.

"Or is it UIRA?" He pronounced it as one word as had Douglas, and then spelled it out, a total guess on his part. The look on her face told him he'd hit pay dirt. "What does the U stand for?" he added.

She glared at him.

"United?"

She relaxed the glare. "Yes."

"We're not supposed to talk about it, Eveleen," Rebecca said, a little harsher than CJ would have thought her capable of against her mother-in-law.

"It appears that Mister Washburn just figures things out on his own," the older woman said. "Maybe it is a good thing that we hire him."

"What if you don't like what I come up with?"

Her shoulders slumped and she looked down at her feet. "My son is dead. What is there to like?"

"I'm suspecting that UIRA had something to do with Doug's death."

Her head came up. "How can you think that?"

"Are you aware that Douglas was an FBI informant; had been for a year or two?"

Eveleen Danohough opened and closed her mouth a couple of times before saying, "That's impossible."

"Not only is it possible, it's true. I had a long conversation with the FBI last night and with Douglas this morning, less than an hour before he was killed."

"I don't..." She closed her mouth and looked at Rebecca. "Did you know this?"

CJ had been watching the younger woman when he disclosed Douglas' secret. Her face went through at least three emotional changes. First was surprise and then her jaw set and her lips compressed into one solid line. Just before Eveleen turned to her, her face went slack and she dropped her chin to her chest.

She shook her head. "No." A small tear rolled from under her sunglasses.

"I still don't believe it," the elder woman said. "You've got it wrong or you're making it all up."

"What would be my motivation to concoct such a thing?"

"What would be the purpose of his being an informant?"

"That, I don't know. Douglas did tell me that whatever it was, it was almost over, that he'd be returning to his family... in Indiana." CJ watched for additional reaction from Rebecca, but saw no change from her interest in her little black purse in her lap. "In his words," he added, "it'd be soon." He did notice that Rebecca's knuckles were turning white from her grip on the purse. "He never mentioned he was divorced. Neither did Mrs. Rothbower when I spoke to her last week."

Suddenly the older woman stood up. "I do not believe we require your services after all, Mister Washburn. Sorry to have troubled you."

CJ and Rebecca rose together. She made no attempt to wipe at her single tear. As she followed her mother-in-law to the door she raised her chin and turned halfway back to face CJ. She said nothing, but the look she gave him was altogether different from the three she'd previously displayed. He wished he could have seen her eyes.

And then they were gone.

CJ put his hands in his pockets and walked over to the window, thinking about the visit from the two women. After a time they appeared in the parking lot below, the wife two steps behind the mother. What exactly did he see in that final look? Was she trying to convey a message? Was it anger, concern, a warning, or was it, "Nice to have met you, Mister Washburn. Have a nice day?"

He doubted it was the later.

He also wondered how long the daughter-in-law, mother-in-law relationship would last now that it was obvious that the marriage was not legal, that there was no family relationship, that there was no reason for Rebecca to bow her head to Eveleen. Would Rebecca cower, or would she step up?

CJ had a feeling that that final look said, "I'm done with this bitch," and "I'll be back." She didn't impress him as one who would cower when set free. She'd want answers.

And then CJ thought about what else he noticed when she turned that last time to look at him, when she gave him her profile, a very interesting profile.

Yes, she'd be back, he thought. First, he needed to make a phone call.

Chapter 9

"Good morning, CJ," Gianna Onassis said after Eleanor transferred him over. "How are things in Florida this time of year?"

"Warm and a bit humid. Otherwise, not bad."

"Better or worse than warm and a bit dry?"

CJ stood at the window looking beyond the ball field, to the bay. "Verdict's still out. Do like the water, though, and the boats."

"So I gather you have something to report," Gianna said.

"I do and you're not going to like it."

"Did you find Douglas?"

"That I did. Talked with him this morning; delivered the news about Alexandria. An hour later he was dead."

"Dead!"

"Murdered."

CJ listened to the prolonged silence for a time and then said, "There's more."

"More than he was murdered?"

"A whole lot more. I was going to give you the report tomorrow afternoon when I returned, but developments require that I give it to you over the phone now. I'll need to know what to do next."

"I gather, then, that this isn't a short report."

"No."

"Give me five. I'll call you back."

CJ never moved from the spot at the window, his eyes following the yachts, his mind rehearsing his words. He decided to give it to her in the same way he'd received it himself; chronological.

When she finally called back, fifteen minutes later, she said, "You've got my full attention now. What happened?"

CJ told her about the visit to the Irish pub and then being escorted into the FBI office, followed by the visit from Douglas "O'Reilly" the next morning. He finished up this part of his report with his being arrested after Douglas' body was found in the bay with CJ's wallet floating nearby.

"Arrested? You never called me!"

"When I told them that my attorney was also my client, that you hired me to search for Douglas Rothbower, they decided you'd possibly hired me to find and kill him, that a local attorney would be advised."

"That's ludicrous!"

"It never got to that. I put the detective in touch with the FBI agent I met with. They just happened to be on a first name basis. I was shortly thereafter released and told to go home."

"Good advice, it sounds like." She let out a sigh. "I'll call my sister and tell her, or maybe I ought to fly up there and tell her face-to-face."

"I think after I tell you the rest, you'll want to do the face-to-face."

"The rest?"

"I haven't gotten to the good part yet."

"There's a good part?"

"Maybe *good* is the wrong word. If we were watching a movie, this would be the *good* part; might even require a second bag of popcorn."

"Just give it to me, CJ."

"The reason why I might need further instructions, why you may not want me to close the case just yet."

"Damn it, CJ! Stop beating around the bush. Out with it!"

"I just had a visit from Douglas' mother, Eveleen Danohough, and his *other* wife, Rebecca O'Reilly."

Gianna seemed to choke on something before she responded. "You sure it's not part of this FBI undercover profile, two people acting the part?"

"I don't think so. The mother seemed quite convincing, said that the adoption and all were illegal, that despite reports to the contrary, she did not die in childbirth."

"Why did she give him up, then?"

"She didn't say, though I've a feeling it was forced upon her, or she had no other choice. She said that once Douglas discovered who he was, he returned to the fold. He and Rebecca were married in Ireland a little more than a year ago."

"I'll be damned."

"I'm not done, yet."

"What else?"

"Rebecca is pregnant. She didn't say so but I noticed the baby bump. No more than a two or three months."

"It just keeps getting better and better."

"I'm still not done yet."

"Oh, Christ, CJ! What else can there possible be? A third wife? Another mother? What?"

"Your sister has been talking to him regularly."

"She's what?!"

"This is straight from Douglas this morning. Either he ran off or she kicked him out in the beginning. That part is a bit unclear. It was a number of years before he made contact again, by which time he'd found his biological mother and his history and wormed his way into the United Irish Republican Army and somehow or other got hooked up with the FBI. Because of his undercover mission they, Douglas and Kassandra together, concocted a cover story that he'd run off and she hadn't heard from him at all."

"She never told me," Gianna said.

"She didn't tell anyone apparently; played her part superbly."

"Alexandria didn't know?"

"I don't think so. They, Douglas and Kassandra that is, didn't talk often, July being the last time, he said. He didn't already know about Alexandria having been killed. He'd been out of country for the last few months, in Northern Ireland. Just got back. "

"Jesus Christ, CJ! How could they do that? What was so important?"

"That, I don't know. Agent Taffer wouldn't reveal the mission. Whatever it was, it was coming to an end."

"How so?"

"In Douglas' words, 'When this is over, I'll go back.' When I asked when that might be, he said, 'Soon. Very soon.' That could be a couple of days, a couple of weeks or a couple of months.'"

"With this *wife*, Rebecca, pregnant?"

"I don't think he knew about that. My hunch is that she hadn't told him yet."

"If you saw it, how could he not?"

"Maybe for some reason she was hiding it, waiting for the right time. He'd only just returned from Ireland, so..."

"What are you thinking, CJ?"

"If he was planning on returning to Kassandra, he would have had no intentions of building a family with Rebecca, maybe had made it clear from the beginning that he didn't want kids. She was being used for cover and she didn't know it, thought this was the real deal, the reason she hadn't told him about the baby yet. She wasn't sure what his reaction was going to be."

"How do you know she didn't know anything?"

"Because of her reactions when she learned of Douglas' other family, his involvement with the FBI. I don't think she is that good of an actress. Doug's mother, on-the-other-hand, knew everything except for his being FBI undercover. They came to me because they wanted to hire me to find Douglas' killer. When they left, Eveleen had rescinded that request, however I think Rebecca is now, more than ever, a pissed off widow. She wants answers and after she gets rid of her so called, mother-in-law, she's going to be back."

"So, you're wondering now if I want you to continue with this?"

"Yes. I've accomplished what I came for, to find and inform Douglas of the death of his daughter. Sometimes investigations are like this. You go to dig for a worm only to wind up in a nest of snakes."

"An accurate analogy, CJ. I'm going to try to get a flight out today to talk to Kassandra tonight. She's also going to need an attorney and since I'm not licensed to practice at all in Indiana, I cannot be her attorney of record. Besides, my specialty is criminal law. I will have to bring on a consultant. The question of illegal adoption muddies everything. Was Doug a legal U.S. resident? Does his marriage to my sister come into question? Is his name Rothbower or O'Reilly? Even if Rebecca is not his legal wife, she is carrying his child. Who becomes the rightful heir? How is Eveleen Danohough going to fit into it? There may have to be DNA testing to prove she is his biological mother if she starts making claims."

"Wow!"

"Yeah, it gets complicated."

"And right now I doubt Rebecca is thinking any of that," CJ said. "She is wanting to know who killed her husband."

"Give her more credit, CJ. I'm sure right at the top of her concern is whether or not he was in fact her husband. A woman isn't going to let that slide by for very long. She will be wanting to know who this person was, this father of her child. The rightful heir issue is just a fuzzy cloud out there, yet to be recognized for the storm it may turn into."

"I suppose that if in fact he had been communicating with Kassandra all this time," CJ said, "there could be no claim of abandonment. All of her assets are also his assets, thus subject to claims by heirs."

"Now you're getting the idea, CJ. When's your flight back?"

"Tomorrow morning."

"Hang tight, then. I'll call you tonight. Might be late. If you do any more, you'll be on the clock. No more pro-bono."

"Thank you. If Rebecca returns, it may be to ask me to get on her clock. As long as I'm working for you, I'll decline her request, however..."

"You'd like to find some answers for her. I get it. Technically, you can't work for her as you are not licensed in Florida, but you can work for me in Arizona. Florida is where your investigation has led you."

"The local police told me to go home."

"They can tell you anything they want, but unless you've broken some law, they have no enforcement power."

"True."

"I'll get back to you tonight. Become a tourist for a few hours."

"I need to buy Stella a gift."

"Perfect!"

The next call CJ made was to Stella.

Chapter 10

"I'm coming there," Stella said after CJ had recited the entire story, including his arrest and his conversation with Gianna.

"That's not necessary," he said.

"The hell it isn't. Someone has to watch your back, keep you out of jail. They're going to start charging you rent."

"Funny."

"The way I see it, whether you're working for Gianna or this so called Irish wife, you won't be coming home tomorrow. You're going to need a second pair of eyes, a partner to bounce things off of. Gianna has deep pockets and can afford the additional expenses."

"But Rebecca O'Reilly may not, and I may be working for her."

"It'll be what it'll be. We owe it to Alexandria." And then Stella's voice became sultry. "Besides, I miss you."

CJ smiled. "That's all I needed to hear. When can you be here?"

"I'm making the flight reservations right now. Hold on a second."

CJ was amazed at how fast Stella could book a flight. He listened to her breathe, say, "Hm" a couple of times and then...

"I fly out at 7:00 a.m. and will arrive in Tampa at 2:15, via Atlanta."

They talked about the weather for a few minutes and then Stella said, "Trish and I went to our joint counseling this morning."

"How are you doing with it?" CJ asked. The two of them had counseling separately once a week and then together every other week.

"I'm doing okay, I think, but Trish is still struggling. She went through a lot more of it than I did, having been kidnapped twice, hit by a car and had a gun pressed to her head. Hell, she was almost killed... twice. And then Clark killed her friend in Idaho. It may be years before she'll be able to get past it."

"If at all," CJ added. He'd pulled the chair over to the window where he could relax and look out onto Tampa Bay. "I know something that might be good for you while you're here."

"I don't hear that, *I can't wait to get you into bed voice*, so what else are you thinking might be good for me?"

"What do you think about going sailing?"

"Sailing?"

"Don't sound so excited," CJ said. The tone in her voice deflated his balloon a bit.

"Sorry. It's just that... well, I don't know."

"What don't you know?"

"For one, I don't know how to swim."

"Neither do I."

"So you think it would be a good idea for two people, neither of whom know how to swim, to go out on the ocean in a little sailboat?"

"They're not sailboats; they're sailing yachts."

"What's the difference?"

"Yachts are much bigger." Actually, CJ had no idea if there was any difference. It was the only thing he could think of. "And it's not an ocean, it's a bay."

"That's supposed to make me feel better? Would that be equivalent with handing the keys to a Mac-truck to someone who has never driven and turning him loose in a crowded parking lot?"

"Tampa bay isn't crowded. I'm looking out at it right now and there's hardly any boats."

"That's probably because the smart ones kstay on dry land."

CJ opened his mouth to say something about the fact that they'd have to take lessons, but concluded she'd just have another snappy comeback. "Maybe it's not such a good idea," he finally said.

"I didn't say that."

CJ looked up at the ceiling. "Okay. What are you saying?"

"I'm not sure what I'm saying. The idea scares me, however..."

"However what?"

"It might be romantic if we sailed with someone who knew what they were doing."

"Just go along for the ride? Sit in the back and cuddle?"

"Yeah, I guess so."

It wasn't exactly what CJ had in mind, but it could be a decent compromise. "Okay. We can check that out."

"And if you still wanted to go sailing, just the two of us, I'd have to insist on lessons first, and lifejackets always."

CJ looked up at the ceiling again. "Lessons. Yes. Definitely. I should have thought of that. And lifejackets, of course."

When CJ set the phone down ten minutes later, his stomach growled. He hadn't eaten since breakfast in the hotel diner seven hours before. He recalled the bistro at the corner of 2nd Avenue and Bay Shore Drive. He'd looked at the menu briefly, could almost taste the Atlantic Salmon or the Cajun Fried Grouper Sandwich. He wasn't sure he'd ever had grouper, but it was worth a try.

He checked that he had his key card and then went out the door.

As the door closed behind him, a young man in an official hotel uniform approached from the direction of the elevator.

"Mister Washburn?" the man said, noting the room he'd just come out of.

"Yes."

"I was told to bring this up to you." He handed over a note.

CJ ripped the tape holding the folded note closed, opened it and read it quickly. "Was it a man or woman who gave this to you?"

"I got it from the check-in associate at the front desk. I don't know who gave it to her."

"Thank you," CJ said. He fished around in his pocket until he came up with a few dollars, and then handed them over.

The young man pocketed the money, turned and walked back to the elevators.

CJ read the note again.

You are being watched and followed.
Meet me at Paddy McGee's at 3:15.
Make sure you lose them first.

R

Chapter 11

CJ stood in the hallway for some time considering the note. The "R" could only mean Rebecca. Why the need for a clandestine meeting? Was Paddy McGee's the best place for it? He looked at his watch. It was 2:32. He returned to his room.

He pulled out a T-shirt that he'd brought along, white with a picture of the Grand Canyon and the words, *Grand Canyon National Park*. He put it on. The shirt he'd been wearing he left on the bed. He sorted through his suitcase again until he came up with a burgundy shirt of the same style. With that rolled up tight and tucked under his arm, he grabbed his car key and headed for the elevators.

In the hotel gift shop he looked for ball caps. Sure enough, they had two colors, white and black. He purchased a white one that said *St. Petersburg* in gold script. He had the clerk put it in a bag to which CJ added the shirt.

When he'd gotten off the elevator a few minutes before and walked through the lobby, he'd noted a man in an Hawaiian shirt sitting in the same spot where Rebecca O'Reilly had been earlier. He was paging through a travel magazine, taking no more than a subtle notice of CJ as he passed by. When CJ came out of the gift shop, the man was on his feet in a position to be able to see the shop entrance, talking on his phone. Except for a brief glance toward CJ, he displayed no obvious interest in anything beyond his conversation. CJ headed back to the elevators.

Once inside he punched the buttons for the 2nd and 9th floors. He got off on the 2nd floor and found the stairs where he could exit out onto the parking lot. He was smart enough to know that just because he snookered the Hawaiian shirt guy, he likely wasn't going to get away scot-free. There was certainly someone with eyes on his car. As he pulled the car out onto 1st Street, he got to thinking that he should have just walked out the front door. Now they may actually suspect that he is aware of them and trying to shake them, causing them to become more vigilant.

Oh well; it is what it is, he thought. He noted all the vehicles parked nearby, one in particular being a dark green Chevy Impala with one man sitting in it. CJ couldn't help but notice the surprise on the man's face as he passed by. CJ watched his mirrors until the Impala came out of its street parking spot, stopped briefly to pick up the Hawaiian shirt guy who'd come running out of the hotel, and make a quick U-turn. Good, he thought. Now I know who's following me.

He slowed to allow the driver to get into a conservative following distance, deciding that he didn't want them to get the idea he was trying to shake them. He then casually made his way along the streets of downtown St. Petersburg.

Once CJ was within a few blocks of Paddy McGee's, he began circling. He wasn't sure he'd find what he was looking for until he spotted it. It was a parking garage at Sunshine Lane and 1st Street, a little farther from McGee's than he wanted, but still close enough. He exited the garage on foot onto the *Whitney National Bank* parking lot where the green Impala, not surprisingly, was now parked. He entered the bank from the parking lot and then went straight through and directly out onto the street side, dodged traffic to cross over and into the *White House and Black Market*, exited from there out a side door, crossed a landscaped breezeway into another shop, put on the hat and shirt without stopping, stuffed the bag into his pocket and stepped out onto 2nd Street, nearly two blocks and several buildings away from where he'd left his escorts. From there it was a four-block walk to the Irish pub. A sophisticated surveillance team would not have let him slip away so easily, would have had all exits from the bank covered immediately. CJ had glanced out from inside the bank. They hadn't even left the car. Who were these amateurs?

Just in case, though, CJ added a limp and then lifted his shoulders and bent forward as though plagued with a humped-back. He tilted the hat brim low over his face and then slowly approached the pub, looking about for any suspicious vehicles. There were none with people sitting inside. He entered the pub and looked around. While his eyes adjusted, the same young barmaid from the day before called from the bar.

"*Céad míle fáilte!* Welcome to Paddy's. Have a seat anywhere."

CJ nodded and continued to scan the darkened interior. There were no women sitting alone, none even who resembled Rebecca O'Reilly lounging anywhere. Of course, if she changed from her widow outfit and removed the sunglasses, he'd likely not recognize her at all unless he sat down in front of her and could study her cheek bones. He continued with his limp until he was seated in the same booth as the day before, facing so that he could see anyone who came through the door, whether Rebecca or one of his newly found friends. He opened a menu and pretended as though he was looking at it until the barmaid approached, less than thirty seconds later.

"What can we do for you today, me friend?" she said.

"Just a Guinness," he said.

She bent down and peered under the cap-bill. "Tis Mister Washburn," she said, her voice low. "Follow me. Mrs. O'Reilly tis awaiting you."

Surprised, CJ slid from the booth and fell in behind the young woman. He noticed that Paddy was not around, that another man at least ten years older was busy cleaning the grill. Business was apparently slow on a Friday mid-afternoon.

They passed by the bathrooms, through a door with a sign that read, EMPLOYEES ONLY, and into a wide hall lined with shelves packed with goods of all sorts. The hall opened into a storage room. She opened another door and stepped aside. CJ entered and the door closed behind him. Paddy McGee sat at a desk. In a chair off to the side sat Rebecca O'Reilly, still in black, sans the sunglasses.

"Have a seat, Mister Washburn," Paddy said.

CJ removed his hat and sat in the only other chair.

"I have to say I'm not happy about the turn o' events and then

Becca asking you to meet her back here. I hope that you made sure you weren't followed. I can't have my pub being connected with all of this."

"What exactly is *all of this*?"

"We left Ireland because we wanted to be away from the violence, the not being able to be friends with someone just because they was different, the always having to be on guard. And now here it is again, right here in America. My sister's husband is dead."

CJ looked over at Rebecca who sat stone-faced, eyes alert, focused, angry. Even with that he could see the resemblance, she at least five years younger. "Rebecca is your sister?"

"Yes."

CJ sat back and thought about it. "The two of you and your cousin in Indiana came to America together?"

"In 2000. Just me cousin and me at first," Paddy said. "Twas 2006 that Becca joined me, after our *màthair* died o' grief."

"*Màthair*?"

"Our mother. We lost our *athair*, our father, to the troubles in '98."

"Troubles?"

"The troubles what we call 'em, the violence in Derry that began in the late 60's. For nearly thirty years it tore our country apart. In 1998, after it was supposedly all ended, a marketplace was bombed in *Omagh*, less than 50 kilometers south o' Derry. Our parents had gone there to enjoy the day. Our *Màthair* had just gone in search o' a toilet when the bomb went off less than a dozen feet from where she left our *athair* standing. He died in her arms."

"I'm very sorry. I gather, then, that you are not a member of UIRA."

"Neither the UIRA, or PIRA, or IRA, or any o' the other splinter groups. I do know that Douglas was involved in some o' that, and despite my disapproval, Becca supported him."

CJ looked at Rebecca. "You haven't told him, I gather."

She shook her head. "No."

"Told me what?" He looked at his sister. "Told me what, Becca?"

"Doug was..." she said. "I didn't know."

"Doug was what?"

"Doug worked for the FBI," she said, barely above a whisper.

Paddy looked between his sister and CJ. To CJ he said, "This is true?"

"He was an FBI informant, yes."

Paddy put his elbows on the desk and his head in his hands. "Mother o' God! And you didn't know, Becca?"

"I had no idea."

"Did Eveleen know?"

"I don't think so."

"I was the one who told Eveleen," CJ said. "Either she was an exceptional actor or she was truly shocked and angry."

"I'd *say* she'd be angry. She's a major player in the UIRA, or at least used to be. I'm assuming that if he was with the FBI, he'd have been spying on her organization; hell, spying on her."

"*Her* organization?" CJ said. "Define major player?"

"She's one o' the four who founded the group, the reason I was so much against Becca marrying him."

"Ah," CJ said. "That brings us around to another small item. Your marriage, Rebecca. Did you know before today that Douglas was already married?"

"I knew that he had been married and that he was divorced," she said, then her voice took on an edge of anger. "I *did not know* that he had a daughter. He led me to believe that he had no children at all."

"You'd never heard of the name, Rothbower?"

"No."

CJ said to Paddy. "But you knew."

"I knew that he'd gone by Rothbower at one time, but I also thought he was divorced, without children. I was shocked yesterday when you told me his daughter had been killed."

CJ snorted a laugh. "It appears there are a few communication gaps in all of this. Everybody knew some piece. If you'd all gotten together and talked about it, you might have known everything."

"We all thought he was divorced and that he had no children," Paddy said.

"Why did you never tell your sister about his real name?"

"Despite how I felt about Eveleen–believe me, there's no love lost there–in my opinion he was born an O'Reilly, and that was his real name. I liked Doug; I just didn't like his association with UIRA thus my reason for not approving o' his marriage to Becca. We came to America to be free o' the troubles, not to start more."

"Starting more may be right," CJ said.

"What do you mean?"

"Douglas told me that whatever he was undercover for, it was about to be over. I got the impression there was something major brewing and the FBI was about to engage it and bring it down, at least the part on this side of the Atlantic."

Paddy nodded. "I guess I shouldn't be surprised."

"Why's that? What can a group accomplish from 4,000 miles away?"

There suddenly came a knock on the door, and it opened. They all looked up to find the barmaid with a tray and two mugs of beer.

"Just bringing Mister Washburn his Guinness," she said.

"Thank you," CJ said, taking a mug of foaming brew from her tray.

The second mug she handed to Paddy.

"Thank you, Hannah?" Paddy said.

As Hannah left, CJ noted that Rebecca already had a dark beverage in a regular glass. He recalled the profile she'd provided him as she left his hotel room and was willing to bet that the beverage was non-alcoholic. "How far along are you, Becca?"

She gave him a little bit of a surprised look and then said, "Twelve weeks."

"Congratulations," was the only thing he could think to say.

"Thank you."

"I ask again," CJ said after taking a sip of the beer, "what can UIRA accomplish from 4,000 miles away?"

"There are thousands, no probably tens of thousands o' Irish Catholics in the United States willing to provide some amount o' monetary support. With that a small group can do a lot o' damage, gain a lot o' attention."

"And it all has to do with ridding Ireland of British rule?"

Paddy held up his hands. "Let us slow down. A lot o' people don't understand what exactly has been going on. They think o' Ireland as one country when actually it is two. In 1922 Ireland split into two factions, northern and southern. Northern Ireland, consisting of the six northern-most counties, chose to remain under British rule while Southern Ireland, the remaining twenty-six counties, chose to move away, to become an Irish Free State. This was finalized in 1948 when Southern Ireland became the Republic o' Ireland and severed all ties with the British Empire."

"So the problems are in Northern Ireland?" CJ said. "The Catholics want to become part of the Republic of Ireland, too, and the, what, non-Catholics don't?"

"Protestants. Unfortunately, that is how it is perceived. Actually it is the Unionists verses the Nationalists. Since the majority o' Unionists are Protestant and vice-a-versa for the Nationalists, our wonderful press has turned it into a Protestant versus Catholic thing. Ones religion really has nothing to do with it."

"Am I to assume that you are not Catholic, however you do support the Nationalists?"

"You assume correctly. I would be in favor o' falling away from British rule, but not at the cost o' lives on any side o' the issue."

"So," CJ said, "all these organizations, IRA, PIRA and UIRA, are Nationalists."

"Those and a few other smaller ones, aye."

"The goals are to end British rule."

"Aye, some by peaceful means and others via violence."

"UIRA?" CJ said. "By what means are they using?"

"I think they walk the line." Paddy turned an expectant look onto his sister.

"I..." She wiped at her eyes with a Kleenex. "I didn't think they were violent. But you think they killed Doug?" she said to CJ.

"Yes I do. Who was following me, and why?"

"I don't know."

"You must know something. After all, you warned me. Average folk don't generally pick up on tails. They aren't that aware or that suspicious. Why were you suspicious enough to have seen them?"

"When Doug returned from Ireland this last time, he told me there had been some things going on."

"Like what?"

"I don't know. He didn't say, but every time we went somewhere together he was concerned about being followed. One time he actually pointed out two men. I didn't know what to think."

"And you apparently spotted them this afternoon."

"One of them, yes."

"In the hotel wearing an Hawaiian shirt."

"Yes."

"You didn't ask Douglas why he was being followed?"

"Of course I did. He brushed it off as having something to do with his work."

"His work. What exactly did he do?"

"He was a beer import and distribution specialist."

CJ looked between her and Paddy for a couple of seconds. "He sold beer?"

"Yes."

"He must have done fairly well at it."

"He had clients from Miami to Savannah and handled imports primarily from Ireland, though some from Scotland and Germany. It paid the bills."

"What do you do?" CJ asked her.

"What do I do?" she asked as though not understanding the question.

"Job. What kind of employment do you have?"

"Oh! I keep the books for Paddy and sometimes wait tables."

CJ turned to Paddy. "You have quite a family business going. Wife, daughter and sister?"

Paddy smiled. "I never told you that my wife and daughter work here. How did you figure that out?"

"Simple observation. The big question is, who did Doug think was following him? I doubt it had anything to do with his work. Corporate spies in the beer business would be after secret recipes, new product developments or trying to steal customers. They certainly wouldn't be following around a beer salesman, nor would they have any interest in a private eye after their charge is dead."

"You said that you thought UIRA had something to do with it," Rebecca said. "Do you think that someone found out Doug was an informant and killed him?"

"Or had him killed. It's a theory, nothing more at this point. It could also be someone from the other side, the Unionists."

Paddy shook his head. "The Unionists aren't violent. I can't see that happening."

"There must be some resistance to UIRA. If Doug was perceived to be involved in something, there certainly could be motive to eliminate him."

"I see what you're saying," Paddy said.

CJ looked up at the ceiling for a few seconds and then said, "But I doubt it."

"You just said it was a possibility."

"I did, except everything seemed to go haywire *after* Douglas met with me, which was the morning *after* I was intercepted by the FBI which was the evening *after* I met with you. Between you and the FBI, I talked to no one, thus either you called them or you called someone else who called them."

The siblings looked at each other and then Rebecca said, "He called me. I called nobody. I didn't even know about Doug's involvement with the FBI until I learned it from you a few hours ago."

"But you still told someone that I was in town looking for your husband?"

"No one."

"No one? Not even your husband or your mother-in-law?"

"Well, yeah. I told them."

"When?"

"Doug last night, but I didn't tell Eveleen until this morning, after Doug was killed. It was she who wanted to visit you in your hotel room."

"Did you tell Doug in person or on the phone?"

"In person. I told you, I did not call anyone after Paddy called me."

"Did Doug call anyone last night?"

Rebecca considered the question for a few seconds and then said, "No. We were together until we went to bed about 11:00. He never made a phone call."

"What did he say when you told him I was looking for him?"

"He didn't say much, only that it probably had something to do with his ex-wife."

"You weren't curious?"

"Of course I was curious. As a matter of fact, when he didn't tell me anything more, I got pissed off. When I get pissed off he gets quiet, which pisses me off even more. We watched TV last night in silence and then went to bed in silence. He left earlier than usual this morning, didn't even wake me up to kiss me goodbye." She bit on her lip. "Now he's dead."

CJ watched the pain in her face and then said to Paddy, "So you didn't tell your sister why I was here."

Paddy shook his head. "Their marriage is their business. All I told her was that you were a private investigator from Arizona and that you were staying at the Hilton. I knew something was about to hit the fan. I wasn't about to do any of the slinging."

"And you didn't call anyone else after you spoke to your sister?"

"No."

"Who else did you tell?"

"No one."

"Not your wife or daughter?"

"I said I told no one. I didn't talk to anyone else about you or Doug until I heard from Becca this morning that he had been killed."

CJ turned his head to Rebecca. "It seems that your phone has been bugged."

Her eyes got big. "By whom?"

"I would say, by whomever has been keeping an eye on Douglas, someone from UIRA."

"Why wouldn't the FBI have a bug on his phone?" Paddy said.

"It's reasonable that they would have, however, I don't know how they operate with a deep undercover. When you called your sister, did you call her house phone or cell phone?"

"He called my cell phone," Rebecca said. "We don't have a house phone. Doug and I each had a cell phone."

"If the FBI tapped a phone, it likely would have been Doug's, not yours, and it would have been with Doug's knowledge seeing as he was working with them. It had to have been the UIRA who was listening in on your phone, Rebecca, or on yours, Paddy. Maybe both."

"Mine!" Paddy appeared surprised, and disturbed, by that prospect. "I don't have anything to do with the UIRA, for or against. What reason would they have to be paying attention to me? I simply have a small, struggling business here. I don't play any of their political games."

"They may not see it that way, Paddy. You're part of Douglas' extended family. If they have been questioning his loyalty to the extent that they started tailing him, physically or electronically, then everyone in his family falls under the suspect list. They might start thinking that Paddy's Irish Pub is a front for anti-UIRA activity. If they'd been suspecting that Douglas was other than he said he was and could trace that back to you and then back to your cousin in Indiana and Douglas' other wife, other family, then keeping at least a tab on you would only be logical."

Paddy dropped his chin to his chest and closed his eyes.

"I'd be willing to bet that as soon as they lost me over at the parking garage, discovered that I was not actually in the bank they watched me go into, that at least one of them came here. Can you get Hannah back in here?"

"Certainly." Paddy stood and walked out.

While they waited, CJ said to Rebecca, "Douglas wasn't happy about becoming a father, was he?"

She shook her head and looked down at her hands. "I only just told him a few days ago."

"You're showing. How could he have not known?"

"He'd been gone for two months. I knew before he left, but I was scared to tell him. I wanted this child, was scared that he'd try to talk me into an abortion."

"So you knew he didn't want kids."

"Yes, I knew, but I didn't know why? Maybe I had some silly notion that once I was pregnant, he'd change his mind."

"He didn't change his mind."

"No."

"You fought about it."

"Yes."

"He'd been home for what, two days and you had two fights."

"Three days. Yes."

Paddy returned with Hannah.

"Hannah," CJ said. "After you escorted me back here, did a single man come in, look around and then immediately leave?"

Hannah's eyebrows went up. "Aye. Just a few minutes ago."

"What kind of shirt was he wearing?"

"An oversized Hawaiian shirt. Red."

"Thanks."

When CJ didn't say anything else, Hannah looked between her father and her aunt and then returned to her duties.

"So," CJ said. "When they lost me, this was the first place they thought to look. Curious, wouldn't you say?"

Paddy didn't look happy.

CJ leaned forward, elbows on his knees. "Douglas had been concerned about being watched, so this may not have been spontaneous, that is his death may have been only a matter of time. Maybe they suspected there was a plant, or a mole, but weren't sure who. Maybe they had several suspects and were watching all of them, waiting until one made a mistake. Coming to see me may have been Doug's mistake, however, I only just showed up yesterday so this person or persons were able to think on the fly, form a conclusion and then grab an opportunity when it was presented to them... in other words, me."

Rebecca was still sitting in the chair, her head leaning against a file cabinet, eyes closed. She didn't respond to CJ. Neither did Paddy. He didn't expect a response when he was thinking out loud.

"They managed to pick my pocket after I'd been seen meeting with Douglas, then kill him and drop him and my wallet into the bay together, all in bright daylight without witnesses. That takes a well organized team."

"You don't think it could have been just one man?" Paddy said.

"Possible, but doubtful. Also, I spotted two men following me."

Hannah poked her head in again. "Someone asking for you," she said to Paddy.

"If it's a vendor, get his name and I'll call him back. Now's not a good time."

"Not a vendor, Dad. He didn't show me ID or anything, but he looks like a cop."

"Looks aren't everything, darlin'. Just get his name and tell him I'll..."

"John Taffer," said the man suddenly looming up behind her.

Hannah jumped like she'd been goosed by a ghost.

Taffer stepped next to her and put his hand on her shoulder, ducking slightly under the door frame. "My apologies," he said and presented his ID. "Special Agent John Taffer, FBI." He looked down at CJ. "Mister Washburn. Interesting finding you here. Detective DuPont told me you were leaving town."

"My flight wasn't until tomorrow."

"Wasn't?" Taffer said.

"Sometimes things change," CJ said.

"It's okay, Hannah," Paddy said.

Despite being curious, she turned and rushed off.

"You must be Rebecca O'Reilly," Taffer said to Rebecca. When she nodded he added, "I'm very sorry for your loss."

"Thank you," she whispered, but kept her eyes downcast.

"What can I do for you, Agent?" Paddy said.

"I'd like to talk with you and Mrs. O'Reilly." He tilted his head toward CJ. "In private."

"Mister Washburn is working for me," Rebecca said. "He needs to be here."

"Working for you? In what capacity?"

"I've hired him to find the person who killed my husband."

Taffer looked at CJ for confirmation. CJ raised his eyebrows and tilted his head.

"I really don't think that's a good idea, Mrs. O'Reilly. You should let the local police handle it."

"If I called them up could they tell me anything I don't already know?"

Taffer shook his head. "I doubt it."

"That's probably because they don't know anything."

"I believe they know a lot more than you think, however they will not normally divulge information while in the middle of an investigation."

"What have they got so far?" CJ said. "I was seen with Douglas O'Reilly, then my wallet was found next to his body and a Starbucks coffee was discovered near the scene, which I'm sure, if they haven't run them already, will divulge my fingerprints. Do they have anything that points to anyone besides me?"

Taffer smiled. "I couldn't say."

"How did you find out that I was in St. Petersburg looking for Douglas?"

Taffer just looked at him.

"You sent two men to pick me up last night. I'd only been in town maybe five, six hours and had only talked to Paddy here and he'd only talked to his sister, Mrs. O'Reilly. By deduction we've come to one conclusion. You were listening in on Paddy's call to his sister. That's a wiretap. Don't you need a court order to do a wire tap?"

"Not if we already have permission."

"Permission!" Rebecca suddenly came alert. "Whose phone did you have permission to listen in on?"

CJ noted a brief break in Agent Taffer's façade. Just as quick, he had it back.

"Seeing as your husband owns the account under which both of your phone numbers reside, we had permission to listen in on both."

Rebecca's mouth hung open, not knowing what to say.

CJ stepped in. "Seeing as the account owner is now deceased and the responsibility for the account is naturally passed to the surviving spouse, I would advise that the surviving spouse, my client, revoke permission for said line tapping."

Rebecca glared at Taffer. "Stop it, now!"

"Very well, Mrs. O'Reilly." He turned around and closed the door. "Actually, we've already ceased monitoring your phones."

"Because Doug is dead," she said.

"Yes. However, we do have a situation going on. With great respect for you in your time of grief, we are asking that you allow us, the FBI, and the St. Petersburg Police, to pursue the investigation into your husband's murder in a manner that will not impede an ongoing operation, that is, without a third party to add a level of confusion."

"And what is this operation?" CJ asked.

"That, I am not at liberty to discuss or reveal. I will say that Douglas spent much of his time giving of himself to get to where we are today. He would not want it all to be destroyed when we are this close."

"This close to what?" Paddy said.

"Again, I cannot say."

CJ said, "Who is the man in the Hawaiian shirt?"

Taffer looked at CJ like he didn't know what he was talking about. "What man in a Hawaiian shirt?"

"Several men had been tailing Douglas since he returned from Northern Ireland three days ago. These same men have been tailing me this afternoon. We'd come to the conclusion that they were members of UIRA. Now I'm wondering if they were FBI."

Taffer shook his head again. "No. We are not tailing you. We have no interest in you whatsoever."

"Well you probably should," Paddy said. "He's the only one who appears to be coming up with answers so far. Maybe if you followed him around, you'd find your killer."

"Don't encourage him, Paddy," CJ said.

"How do you know they were tailing Douglas?" Taffer asked.

"Doug told me," Rebecca said. "He pointed out one of them for me yesterday. I saw the same man at Mister Washburn's hotel this afternoon when I went to visit him."

"She warned me and then I was able to confirm it when I left the hotel to come here. They're not very good. I shook them easily. I'm inclined to believe, however, that they may not be your killers."

"Why's that?"

"The man who bumped into me, thus who took my wallet, was not the man in the Hawaiian shirt. Although I hadn't gotten a good look at the other man following me–he has only been in the car, the driver–I did catch a brief glimpse of his profile when I drove by where he was parked. Outside of his clothing, all I got of the man who took my wallet was his facial profile. I was on the phone, a bit distracted."

"Must be why it was so easy to pick your pocket," Paddy said.

"Embarrassing, yes. The point I'm trying to make is that the two profiles don't match."

"Does Detective DuPont know about the tails?" Taffer asked.

"Haven't talked to him since he cut me loose."

"I'll let him know. He'll probably be calling you for descriptions."

CJ didn't say anything and the room suddenly went silent. After a time Agent Taffer said, "Again, I have to ask you to stay out of the investigation unless you are called upon."

"It might be easier to remain away if we had some idea what the operation was all about," CJ said.

Taffer didn't respond.

"You mentioned last night that there were other agencies involved. I'm assuming that would be Homeland Security if, as I suspect, UIRA is on the terrorist list."

Again Taffer said nothing.

"I can assume, then, that UIRA has set up shop in the United States to organize something. Either people or weapons or... explosives."

In addition to CJ, Paddy and Rebecca were staring at Agent Taffer, anticipating some kind of response. When still none came, CJ continued.

"A lengthy undercover leading up to an event as large as you're leaving us to believe would require all three, plus a target."

"Please, in the interest of national security, I ask that you stay out of it. Let us do our work." He looked at Rebecca. "I don't think your husband would want all his effort wasted."

Rebecca looked between her brother and CJ, then finally said, "Okay."

CJ said to Taffer. "How do I get rid of my tails?"

"Go home, Mister Washburn. That would certainly do it."

Chapter 12

CJ was again standing at his hotel window, looking out over the bay, his eye on one particular single-masted boat appearing to work its way to the harbor entrance, maybe coming in after a day of fun in the sun. He wasn't thinking about sailing, though, at least not consciously. When he left the pub and made his way back to the parking garage, he didn't see the car that had been following him, nor the Hawaiian shirt guy. Just in case he would need to use the disguise again, he'd stuffed the hat and shirt back into the bag. When he entered the hotel through the main entrance, he was glad he did. There was Hawaiian Shirt, in his place, holding a Gentleman's Quarterly Magazine. He certainly didn't look like a GQ kind of guy, but then CJ had no idea what a GQ kind of guy looked like. He'd never actually seen anyone reading the magazine who wasn't trying to pass time while in a waiting room or a hotel lobby.

In addition to watching the sailboat, CJ had been keeping an eye on the cars on the street below. His attention was drawn to a dark green sedan approaching from the north. It slowed and then parked. From his vantage point he couldn't be sure it was a Chevy Impala, but when no one got out, he could only assume. A minute later Hawaiian Shirt came out and got in the passenger side. The car didn't move. Both of his shadows were back in place.

So why all the manpower to keep him under surveillance? What were they afraid of?

After Taffer left the pub, CJ had stayed around to eat and watch the happy hour crowd trickle, and then flood in. When he'd become aware that he wasn't in a happy hour mood, he paid his tab and made his departure. Now he was getting bored.

He looked at his watch. It was 6:56. He tried to remember what time the sun set the night before, guessed at maybe 8:00 or so, and decided to go for another walk. He pulled his phone off charge and went out the door.

There was still police tape around the crime scene, including the bench where CJ had sat earlier. Also still in residence was one marked and one unmarked police vehicle as well as the dive van. Two men stood on the seawall looking down, one in a wet suit, while a uniformed cop watched the onlookers and rubberneckers. CJ stepped up to where a few other people were watching, some 50 yards north of the tape, and looked toward the activity in the water. There was one man with a tank on his back slowly moving back and forth. Occasionally he'd disappear.

CJ made note that Hawaiian Shirt had also joined the rubberneckers. He had a cell phone pressed to his ear. CJ turned his back to him and the scene and started walking north, along the seawall.

As per her promise to Agent Taffer, Rebecca had withdrawn her request for CJ's services, however, CJ had made no promises and he still retained a client. Until Gianna called and told him otherwise, he was still on her payroll. He had no intention of going home, rather hoped that she would give him more of a reason to stay.

He approached 1st Avenue where turning right would bring him onto *Demens Landing Park* and access to *St. Petersburg Sailing Center* or *St. Petersburg Marina.* He paused to consider if he wanted to go into the park or continue along Bay Shore Drive when Hawaiian Shirt suddenly appeared right next to him.

"Mister Washburn," he said. "I have quick access to a gun." He pointed toward the bridge that fed 1st Avenue into the park. "Please go this way."

CJ looked at the man, two inches shorter then himself, though stocky and muscled. As he considered his options the man took a step away and put his hand behind his back, under his shirt.

"I'm quicker than you are thinking, Mister Washburn," he said.

Apparently CJ's options were slim. "Seeing as you said please," he said and turned toward the bridge. Hawaiian Shirt fell in behind him. The Chevy Impala appeared beside them for a few seconds and then moved on ahead, turning left toward the marina. Following Hawaiian Shirt's instructions, they continued on foot, following the route of the Impala until they stopped at a foot-gate entrance where the driver of the Impala was waiting. He opened the gate with a key and they entered a walk area that provided access to all the covered slips.

They walked along the slips for a time, driver in front, Hawaiian Shirt behind, until they stopped at a boat with a pair of outboard motors. The outboards, each having the number 300 stenciled on the back, seemed a bit much for what appeared to be a small boat, if in fact the 300 stood for horsepower. But then, what did CJ know about boats?

Hawaiian Shirt pointed. "Get in and sit down there."

CJ stepped across and sat. "Where're we going?"

Hawaiian Shirt ignored the question. The driver fired the motors to life. CJ was expecting something a bit louder, with a deep-throated rumble. Instead, they were quiet and smooth. The driver jumped off, threw off the lines and jumped back on. Hawaiian Shirt stayed in place, keeping an eye on CJ, while the driver stowed the lines.

And then they were moving.

Hawaiian Shirt reached into a compartment and came up with a set of handcuffs. He threw them at CJ. "Put these on. Hook up to the rail." With that he pulled out a handgun, a small Colt automatic.

CJ considered the cuffs for a few seconds before attaching them between his right wrist and the four-foot section of rail.

Hawaiian Shirt put his gun away and then seemed to relax.

"Nice boat," CJ said. "I imagine it has some get-up-and-go with 600 horses on the back." He made like changing position and tested the strength of the rail. It moved back and forth about a half inch. He wondered how strong it was. "Where're we going?"

Hawaiian Shirt ignored him.

"What is that?" CJ pointed toward *The Pier* and its inverted pyramid-shaped building as they slowly motored by.

Hawaiian Shirt continued to ignore him, not even turning his head.

"Why are we going so slow?" CJ sort of knew the answer to that question as he'd read the *Manatee Basics for Boaters* sign when he was walking around the day before. It said that boat speeds in Manatee waters was either *slow* or at *idle* between November and March. This was September so CJ surmised that it was a habit for the locals to travel these waters slow all year round. Then CJ noticed another boat passing in the opposite direction, two men on board. It had the words, *Hillsborough County Sheriff,* stenciled on the side, and it looked to be just as fast if not faster than the one in which he was sitting. His captors were going slow because they didn't want to attract the attention of a few of the counties finest.

Too bad for them, CJ thought and tightened his grip on the rail.

Chapter 13

The timing wasn't perfect, CJ knew, but if these guys were motoring out to deep waters with the intent to shoot him in the head and then leave him for the sharks, there wasn't going to be a better time. With the sheriff within view, now was the best he was going to get.

CJ twisted in his seat, tensed and then delivered a kick aimed for under Hawaiian Shirt's jaw. Hawaiian Shirt, though, was definitely quicker than CJ was thinking. He dodged to the side while reaching back for his gun. CJ's kick caught him on the ear, dazed him for just enough time for CJ to regain his equilibrium. Hawaiian Shirt shook it off and rose to his feet, bringing the gun out. CJ kicked out again, this time straight at the man's chest with all the power he could muster.

At first, like a martial arts kicking bag struck by a young student, nothing appeared to happen. Time stopped. Everything became suspended; CJ's breathing, heartbeat, even his fall. It all seemed to just hang there, until he noticed the gun in Hawaiian Shirt's hand, pointing... and then it went off.

The explosion, the slam to the bench and the deck, the lightning burst of pain and the sight of the back of Hawaiian's Shirt's legs as he flipped backwards off the side of the boat, all came to CJ in the next split second. Trying hard to ignore the burning pain in his side, CJ pulled himself onto the bench and looked up at the other man who was turned and looking at him. Anticipating another physical confrontation, CJ rose to his feet. The driver punched the throttle forward, throwing CJ against the back of the boat. He'd gone completely out if not for his being attached to the rail.

He came to his feet again and looked back, expecting to see the Sheriff's boat in hot pursuit. To his disappointment, however, they were almost at a complete stop, and a lifebuoy ring went flying through the air.

CJ started attacking the rail. He jerked at it, kicked it, did everything he could think to break it from its hold on the boat, but it wouldn't budge. Then he chanced to look at the driver again. He had a gun pointed at CJ and was pulling the trigger, over and over, but nothing was happening. The man looked at the gun as though it had purposely misfired, and then released the clip. It was empty. If not for the burning in his side, CJ would have laughed. The man turned away, to get another clip, CJ assumed, and he had to make a fast decision. Either continue to attack the rail in hopes of breaking free and jumping overboard, or attack the man, though as with Hawaiian Shirt, only with his feet. He was definitely within range. As a matter-of-fact, the area was so small that the man couldn't get far enough away from CJ unless he climbed over the windshield and up onto the bow.

CJ turned, gritted his teeth against the pain, and kicked the man square in the kidney. The man jerked on the wheel as he dropped to one knee. The boat veered port and CJ was again thrown down. As he struggled up he saw that the man still had the gun in one hand and was busy bringing the boat back on a straight course. CJ set himself for another kick, but the man glanced back at him, grinned and then jerked the wheel to the right. CJ hit something and the pain he'd been feeling ignited like fire.

When he was able to clear his head and get his feet back, the man had found the second clip and this one was not empty. As he looked down to slide the clip in CJ turned to kick and then noticed a sailboat just off the starboard bow. It was crossing and by CJ's amateur assessment, they were on a collision course. A woman and a child were looking their way and a man was scrambling for the helm.

CJ pointed and yelled, "Collision!"

The man slammed in the clip, looked over his shoulder to what CJ was pointing, turned around, swung the wheel and pulled back on the throttle. The resulting forward momentum forced on CJ set him up to issue another kick. As the man turned back, CJ hit him in the side of the head.

The man fell against the throttle, the gun exploded, the engines roared, and CJ flew back, his head slamming into something hard. The man tumbled after him, tangled briefly with CJ and then disappeared. CJ saw sky and boat and snatches of water just before everything went black.

Chapter 14

CJ awoke only seconds later, his chin striking the fiberglass seat with each bounce of the boat, his arm about to be jerked from its socket. The pounding seemed to be in sync with the blood pulsing through his head and the mind-numbing throb in his ribcage. It took a full minute to pull himself up.

He was alone on the boat and it appeared to be running at full throttle.

He looked back and saw nothing but a few boats off in the distance and land way beyond that. He wondered how long the boat would run before it ran out of fuel. Then he remembered that he was in Tampa Bay and likely he'd hit land first.

He turned around, noted the low hanging sun and then..."Holy shit!"

Land was close and rapidly getting closer. A small red and white plane passed from his right to left and landed just beyond the rocks at which CJ was racing.

Albert something Airport was all he could recall as he threw a kick at the throttle in hopes of hooking it with his toe and pulling it back. All he managed to do was shove it harder against the stops. The effort flopped him onto the deck again. He gritted his teeth against the pain as he pulled and bounced back to the seat. He looked at the approaching wall of rocks, and then at the throttle and...

The wheel!

That, he could reach, though he could do little more than kick it then drop to the deck.

Without pause he struck at it. It turned a little and the boat started into a left turn, though not nearly enough. He scrambled to his feet and then hit the wheel again. When he got back to his knees, leaning heavily on the bench, only his adrenaline was cutting through the pain. The boat was running almost parallel to the rocks, but they were close enough, CJ could swear, that he could spit on them. He pushed up to his feet, took as much of a breath as he could, gritted his teeth and struck the wheel one more time. With that, he fell hard, a lightning bolt of pain radiating out from his center.

And then he blacked out.

When he awoke thirty seconds had gone by, and he was still bouncing, which meant that he hadn't hit the rocks. After a time he pulled himself up onto the bench and looked ahead. There were no rocks, nor any land or boat threat, at least not for a few minutes. He turned his attention to the rail. It was then that he spotted a crack in the fiberglass.

He kicked it and then staggered until he had to sit down. He wondered how much fuel there was, how long it would run like this, how many times he would have to try to steer it away from land before he couldn't do it anymore, how he was going to be able to see land once it turned dark. He closed his eyes and willed for the pounding in his head to stop, certain that it only made it worse. He looked where it felt like Hawaiian's Shirt's bullet slammed through his ribcage. There was no blood. He didn't understand. He'd have sworn he'd been shot.

"Cut... engines!"

CJ looked up to find the Sheriff's boat running maybe fifty feet away, lights flashing, a mike to one officer's face.

"Cut your engines!" the deputy yelled into the mike.

CJ stood. He held up his arm with the handcuffs attached and made like trying to stretch to the throttle, shaking his head. The officer turned to the deputy driving and appeared to say something. The Sheriff's boat eased closer.

"Can you reach the kill switch?" the officer said.

Kill switch? CJ looked but could not see what he was referring to. He held his hands out and gave the I don't know sign.

The officer appeared to speak to Hawaiian Shirt who was sitting off to the side, still dripping from his rescue. Hawaiian Shirt said something. The officer put the mike back to his face.

"Red lanyard left of the wheel. If you can reach it, pull it."

CJ looked and saw a red lanyard hanging down to the left of the driver's seat. He could reach it with a foot, but there was no way he was going to be able to grab it and pull... unless he could hook it with a toe.

He took off a shoe and sock, then stretched. His big toe could just touch it between bounces, but the resulting pain in his side was excruciating. And his head just kept pounding. It was the pain that kept him from reaching. If he could block the pain he could stretch farther. He needed to stop the bouncing, stop the pounding. Whatever additional pain it caused, he had to push through it so that it would all stop.

"Push!" he yelled and then reached. "More! More!" The toe hooked around the lanyard. "More! Damn it!" CJ swiveled his foot to ensure the lanyard was well-wrapped, pulled and dropped.

The boat's two 300 horsepower motors went silent. CJ lay where he landed, appearing to be dangling between the handcuffs and the lanyard, feeling the somewhat more tolerable pain and listening to the Sheriff's boat coming around and then alongside. As he enjoyed the lack of pounding and bouncing, while waiting for the deputy to board, his cell phone started playing the Gummy Bear song. Gummy Bear was Stella's ringtone. He didn't have the energy to answer it, maybe due to the crash after the adrenaline rush or the injuries he'd sustained, but that was alright. Just her song was enough connection to make him smile.

Chapter 15

CJ sat on the edge of a table in the emergency room with his arms up while a nurse wrapped a wide elastic bandage around his midsection. Special Agent Taffer had just come in and sat down, sending the deputy away. When the nurse finished and then left, saying a doctor would be in shortly, Taffer said, "I wish the hell you'd gone home."

CJ carefully shrugged. "I was planning to tomorrow, then shit happened. I didn't go looking for it. It all came looking for me."

"You're like a bad magnet. So, what the hell happened?"

CJ told him again about the two guys who had been following him and the one in the Hawaiian shirt forcing him into the boat.

"Rory Pickens," Taffer said. "Northern Ireland citizen. Has been in our country only three days. Has never been on our radar."

CJ slid from the table and picked up his shirt before going on to tell the FBI agent about the boat ride and his hunch that it was to be his last ride anywhere, that he was to be killed and dumped.

"When I kicked Pickens overboard," he said, "I thought I'd been shot. Obviously it was only a bad landing; broke a couple of ribs."

"The nurse said it was just one rib and it was only cracked," Taffer said.

"Yeah, well, it feels like a couple of compound fractures to me." With great care CJ pulled on the T-shirt while trying to avoid the bandage on his head. "Although I blacked out, they don't think there's more than a mild concussion. I'm starting to wonder about your medical system here."

"You think you should be admitted?"

"Hell no! I'm fine."

Taffer shook his head, smiling. "You *are* going to leave us tomorrow, aren't you?"

"My Arizona client will be contacting me tonight to let me know whether or not I should continue my investigation. In any case, my partner is arriving tomorrow afternoon, so I have to say, no, I'm not planning on leaving. We'll be hanging around for a bit, either working or playing."

"How about you and your," Taffer made quote marks with his fingers, "*partner*, walk the beaches, soak up some Florida sun, and then go home. I hear she's a looker and that you two are engaged. I was lead to understand that she was your secretary, not your partner."

"She's kind of both. She's a full partner but still handles most of the administrative duties. She's started working on her PI certification. We hope to hire a part-time secretary when she has her license and we have a reasonable caseload."

"Humph!" Taffer said. "Personally, I don't know if I'd like to be working in the same profession as my wife, certainly not as a partner. Hope it works out for you."

"It will."

"Famous last words."

Taffer gave CJ a ride back to the hotel after the doctor dropped in long enough to write a prescription for a pain killer and give orders to take it easy. "No strenuous exercise for at least a month," he said. "Preferably six weeks. Remove the bandage a couple of times a day and leave it off for a quarter to a half hour. Take some deep breaths during that time. Ice it periodically, at least once a day.

"Check in with your doctor when you get back to Arizona," he'd added.

"I definitely will." CJ had no intention of seeing another doctor.

At the hotel front desk he inquired as to the nearest pharmacy. They asked what had happened when they saw the bandage on his head. "Boating accident," was all he said. He knew they wanted to hear more. He wasn't talking. They directed him to a pharmacy that stayed open late–midnight they said–just a couple of blocks away. Getting in and out of a car wasn't easy–it was a struggle getting in and out of Taffer's car–so driving would certainly not be any easier. He decided that he'd walk.

He dialed Stella and set out at a pace only slightly faster than a crippled old man.

"I called earlier," she said when she answered, the obvious question in her voice.

"Yeah, I heard it, but I was tied up."

"Oh."

"Literally," he added.

"What do you mean, literally?"

She didn't buy the humor when he tried to make light of being strung between handcuffs and a kill switch, so he told her the whole story, downplaying his injuries, not mentioning the emergency room visit.

"I don't like this case, Clint," she said. "You've found Douglas. Now I think you should tell Gianna you're done and come home tomorrow."

"If she wants me to continue, it'll be on the clock, which means a paycheck."

"Not much point in it if you're dead, is there?" She didn't wait for his answer to her obviously rhetorical question. "This is international crap. The FBI doesn't want you there, Mrs., or whatever she is, O'Reilly doesn't want you there anymore, and UIRA, or whoever these guys are working for, not only doesn't want you there, but also, for some reason, want you dead."

"That's just it," CJ said. "What possible reason do they have for wanting me dead? What kind of threat am I to them?"

"I don't know and I don't care," Stella said firmly. "Take the hint and come home."

He thought about the sailboats for a few seconds, realized that in his condition, any kind of sailing would probably not be a good idea.

"Maybe you're right. I really wanted to do some vacationing with you, kind of like a pre-wedding honeymoon."

Stella laughed. "I like your idea, but how about somewhere a little less stressful, like Cancun. We could spend a week down there."

"What better way to heal than to sit around on the beach? How about next week?"

"Heal! Heal from what?"

"Ah..." *Damn*! "I got a little banged up in the scuffle on the boat."

"How much is a little?"

"A slightly cracked rib."

"You broke a rib!"

"It's not as bad as it sounds."

"A broken rib is a broken rib."

"A week in Cancun sounds really good."

"How about we talk about it when you get home."

CJ started to say, okay, when a St. Petersburg Police cruiser stopped just past him and two uniformed officers got out.

"Clinton Washburn?" one said, his hand on the butt of his weapon. The other officer came around from the driver's side.

"Yes," CJ said.

"We need you to come with us."

"What's going on?" Stella said.

"Am I being arrested?" CJ asked, the phone still to his ear.

"Not at this time. Detective DuPont would like to have a few words with you, sir."

CJ actually considered asking them to say please, then thought better of it. The cops didn't look like the humorous type. "I'm being summoned in to see Detective DuPont of the St. Petersburg Police," he said into the phone. "I'll call you back later."

CJ sat in an interview room with his head resting on his arms on the table, waiting on Detective DuPont, wishing for sleep or at least his pain meds. The police officers had refused his request to stop by the pharmacy first. He was ready to give the Hillsborough Sheriff a good review–he'd likely be dead now if not for them–but he was having second thoughts about the St. Petersburg Police Department.

When DuPont walked in, CJ was actually asleep. He awoke slowly.

"If you have a concussion," the detective said, "I'd think you shouldn't be sleeping."

"Humph!" was all CJ managed.

"We might have a little bit of a problem," DuPont said. When CJ just blinked at him, he continued. "Rory Pickens claims that he was taking you out to do a little fishing and you went nuts. He had to overpower you and handcuff you to get you under control. Was afraid for his life."

"You're kidding, right?"

"I don't kid. He says that when he spotted the Sheriff's patrol boat and started to flag them down, that you pushed him overboard."

"What did he say about the other guy?"

"He said that it was just the two of you on the boat. No one else has been found."

"The deputies in the Sheriff's boat didn't see anything?"

"They heard a gunshot. When they looked there was a man in the water and one at the helm, and the boat was racing away."

CJ thought about that for a minute. "There's a big hole in his story, you realize."

"There is, but I'll let you tell me what you think it is."

"A couple, actually. First, the deputies likely have a rough description of the man at the helm, and they probably said he was wearing a yellow shirt. If you notice, I'm wearing a white T-shirt, the same one I was wearing then."

DuPont nodded.

"Also, and this the deputies can readily confirm, I was handcuffed in such a way that I would not have been able to stand at the helm."

"How do you explain them only seeing one person on board?"

"After I kicked Pickens overboard, I fell to the deck. The deputies would not have been able to see me. By the time I came to my feet, they'd been focused on recovering the guy in the water."

DuPont sat back with his hands folded on his belly.

"One more thing," CJ said.

"Yes."

"What about the fishing poles? If we were going out fishing there would have been fishing poles. I never saw any."

"He said that you threw them overboard when you went nuts, and all the gear, too."

"And why were we going out fishing just before sunset? Also, do folks who go out fishing routinely carry handcuffs in Florida?"

"You've hit it all, Washburn, and some I didn't think about. The holes have grown so big, you could drive his boat through them."

"By-the-way," CJ said, "why are *you* questioning me? I thought this was a county sheriff case."

"As it appears to be related to the O'Reilly murder, they passed it over to me. They saw through the guy's story right away and were glad to get rid of him."

"How do you figure it's related to the murder?" CJ asked.

"Contrary to how it may look, St. Petersburg police officers direct traffic around crime scenes for more than just the thrill. They're trained to watch people, make note of who is hanging around, sometimes taking pictures or videos. Rory Pickens was seen a number of times, as were you. My sharp-eyed officer also made note that Pickens followed after you from the crime scene this afternoon, that the two of you appeared to have a *conversation* just before he lost sight of the both of you when you turned into the park together."

"He didn't happen to make note of a dark green Chevy Impala, did he?"

"Not that I know of. Why?"

"The other guy was driving that car when they were shadowing me, was right next to us when we walked into the park. It may still be parked at the marina. I can give you the plate number, if you'd like."

"I'd like."

CJ gave it to him and DuPont left, saying he'd be right back. CJ put his head back down on the table and wished for darkness.

Chapter 16

The darkness lasted about a minute before CJ's phone started playing the ringtone that was anyone else besides Stella. He pushed the fuzz from his brain and dragged the phone from his pocket. The screen indicated that it was Josh calling. He had talked to Josh only once since his son returned to his field office in Denver a couple of days after the Tommy Clark incident. He hit the answer button and put it to his ear.

"Hi, Josh."

"Dad. What the hell is going on?"

"Ah... having some fun in Florida. Who you been talking to?"

"Stella for one. Assistant Special Agent-in-Charge John Taffer for another."

"Stella called you?"

"I called her after Agent Taffer called me. I tried you first but you went to voice mail."

"Oh." CJ recalled ignoring his phone while in the police cruiser. He hadn't even looked at it. He didn't think it was a good time to be having a chat. "Then you must have most of the story. And why did Taffer call you? I didn't ask him to."

"Initially I thought it was a courtesy call, just to keep me informed. He said you got rather banged up, that you were lucky you didn't get killed."

"Yeah, well, probably a bit of an overstatement. I'm just fine. A small boat accident."

"Accident? Not the way I'm hearing it. Here's the thing, Dad. Taffer and my boss are on a secure conference call right now and I have a feeling that what I thought was a courtesy call is actually a request to loan me out to the Tampa field office."

CJ looked up at the ceiling. "You've got to be kidding! No! I don't need to be babysat by my son... again."

"I quite agree," Josh said. "However, I don't think it'd do much good for me to try to decline the assignment."

"Conflict of interest," CJ said. "Too personal. You couldn't be objective."

"My thoughts exactly, though I think if you convinced them that you're flying home tomorrow, that might do it. There'd be no point in sending me if you aren't there."

"Really!" CJ said. "Are you part of the conspiracy to get me to leave?"

There were several seconds of silence on Josh's end before he said, "What do you mean?"

"Taffer doesn't want me here, but being as it's a free country he can't really force me to go, at least not without a court order of some kind, I imagine. Stella is now worried for my safety and wants me home. I figure the two of them have asked you to intercede and you figured a little reverse psychology might work."

Detective DuPont walked back in the door.

"That's not how I work, Dad," Josh said.

"Sure. Listen, I've got to go. I'm in the interview room at St. Petersburg Police Headquarters and the detective just came in. Talk to you later."

CJ put the phone away as DuPont sat down.

"That your girlfriend?" DuPont said.

"My son."

"The FBI agent?"

"The one and only."

It looked like DuPont was going to continue his interrogation along that line and then seemed to change his mind. "The car is registered to one Samuel Blight." He showed CJ a picture. "And the car is gone."

"That's him. I gather then that Nicole Blight is his wife or sister."

"Nicole Blight?" DuPont tilted his head at CJ. "Where did you come up with that name?"

"Sheriff's deputy. I was within earshot when they determined who the registered boat owner was."

"Ah," DuPont said and nodded. "Yes, she's the wife. Boat's in her name. Car's in his."

"Wonder if she knew her boat was to be turned into a killing platform?"

"We haven't located her yet."

"I'd say Samuel Blight made it to shore, collected his car, contacted his wife and then together they have gone into hiding."

"That's a good theory, however, we have reason to believe she is currently not in the country."

"Let me guess. Northern Ireland."

"Correct."

"Are they and Pickens all members of United Irish Republican Army?"

"We believe so, yes."

"And you are buds with Agent Taffer."

DuPont tilted his head again. "We are not *buds*, that is we don't have each other's number on speed dial. We are, occasionally, on a first name basis."

"Are you a rider on his bus then, the one that included Douglas O'Reilly as an undercover informant?"

"That bus, as you refer to it, Mister Washburn, is a bit exclusive, filled with FBI and HLS. Not much room for a lowlife St. Petersburg detective."

"So, until I showed up you didn't even know there was a bus. Something is about to go down in your jurisdiction. Shouldn't the FBI be bringing you in the loop?"

"That would certainly seem logical, now wouldn't it? And you're right. I knew nothing about his little operation until you landed in my lap."

"You're welcome, then."

"Actually, I don't know whether to thank you or throw you into a cell until we can put you on a westbound plane."

CJ considered his options for a time and then said, "How about I work with you, give you all the scoop that I've dug up so far, including what I've learned from Taffer and his people."

"He's apparently told you more than he's told me. Why *is* that?"

"It's not that he's told me all that much, but that I've put together puzzle pieces from him, Rebecca O'Reilly, Eveleen Danohough and Paddy McGee. Also from Douglas just before he was killed."

DuPont leaned back and crossed his arms. "You'd have made a good detective. Why did you leave the force?"

CJ shrugged. "Tried to save a dying marriage. By the time it was obvious that it, the marriage that is, still wasn't going to work I was full speed ahead into the PI business, lease on an office, a box of letterhead with *Desert Investigative Services* at the top, enough business cards to last a lifetime, and I was kind of liking not having to answer to everyone with more rank than me."

"Let me tell you, it gets better when you shed the uniform and put on a shirt and tie," DuPont said.

"My best friend made detective about the time I left the force," CJ said. "I've watched him and am not sure it's all that much better."

"I didn't say it was a *lot* better. I just said it was better. I've played with the thought of going independent like you, though, I have to say I kind of like the steady paycheck."

"I know what you mean." CJ sat back in the chair trying to find a position where his ribs didn't hurt. "When can I get out of here? I haven't filled my prescription for painkiller yet."

"I'll give you a ride. Wife has probably given up on me and put dinner in the refrigerator."

In DuPont's car, CJ said, "Back to my offer. I don't know for sure that I'll be hanging around. If I do, I'd be glad to consult with you, feed you whatever I learn from my contacts, and that includes Taffer and his crew, though I have to say he may find a way of deporting me back to Arizona."

"Tell you what... Can I call you Clinton?"

"You do and I'll take your service weapon away from you and shoot off your kneecap. Call me CJ, please."

DuPont laughed. "CJ then. I go by Parker. As I was going to say, you keep me informed and I'll make sure the welcome wagon has your name." He pulled up in front of the drug store that CJ had originally been headed for. "This is your stop. I assume you can make it from here."

"I can use the walk." He shook DuPont's hand. "Thanks, Parker. I'll let you know if I stay or fly."

The wait for the prescription wasn't nearly as long as CJ expected. "Take with food," the pharmacist said. CJ purchased a bottle of water and a pre-packaged apple turnover and had it all consumed before he'd walked a block. He checked his watch as he dropped the discards into a trashcan. It was 11:15. He wondered what time zone Fishers, Indiana fell into and then remembered from his trip there to see Douglas' wife, Kassandra, that it was on Eastern Time.

Why hadn't he received a call from Gianna by now? She'd had plenty of time to get there, meet with her sister and then call him. He found her speed dial icon and punched it. When the connection was made he immediately wished he'd not made the call.

"...don't give damn what you think I want!" a woman yelled. "You killed my daughter and now my husband. And then you come here thinking you know what's best for me? What I want is for you to stay out of my affairs! Out of my life!"

"You're not being rational, Kassi."

"Get out!"

CJ wanted only to hang up the phone, wished he had waited for Gianna to call him. He felt bad for her, even more so for her sister, could only imagine the anguish they were both going through.

"I'll call you back, CJ," Gianna suddenly said into the phone, her voice sounding exasperated, tired.

"Was that *him*?!" Kassandra screamed just before the connection was broken.

He returned the phone to his pocket and continued walking until he came upon a bench. Just the sight of it suddenly made him feel exhausted and sore. He sat down and put his head in his hands.

Kassandra was pointing the blame at the wrong person. Tommy Clark threatened to go after people close to CJ and when he couldn't get to his family, he went after his friends, and then the family of his friends. Gianna was his attorney, his client and his friend. Gianna's niece, Kassandra's daughter, was the target Clark could get to and so he killed her. And now, in an effort to notify Kassandra's husband, at Gianna's request, CJ may have gotten him killed as well.

Gianna played no part in the blame on this. Kassandra was definitely pointing her anger at too many people. He was the only common factor.

The *Gummy Bear Song* started playing from CJ's pocket. He pulled the phone out and said, "Hi."

"You sound tired," Stella said. "I've been waiting for you to call back. Where are you? Are you in bed?"

"No. Sitting on a bench in downtown St. Petersburg, thinking."

"It's late there. What are you thinking about?"

"Tried calling Gianna to see what she wanted me to do. I interrupted a fight between her and her sister." CJ went on to tell her what he'd heard.

"Wow," Stella said.

"I think you're right. I should drop it all and just go home. When Gianna calls back I'll tell her I can't do any more."

Stella was silent for a time before she said, "What was the thing with the detective?"

"The sheriff turned things over to him when it came to light that it was related to his case, that is, Douglas' murder, and he wanted to question me directly, get my statement face-to-face. That was pretty much it."

"How are the ribs?"

"Sore. I just filled the prescription for pain meds. Hasn't had time to work yet."

She was silent for a time again, and then said, "I don't think you should come home."

CJ was surprised by that. "Why?"

"For one, when I booked my flight to Tampa, I cancelled yours. Now that flight is full. I can't get you out before Sunday."

"And two?"

"And two," she said. "I think it's important to find Douglas' killer. I don't think you can say, 'Oh well,' and walk away."

CJ nodded but wasn't sure he actually agreed.

"And I don't think you should be doing it alone. I expect to see your face when I get off that plane tomorrow."

"I'll be the guy with a bandage on his head and a big grin."

"Bandage on your head? I thought your injuries were just your ribs."

"Ah... didn't I mention that I bumped my head?"

"No. You did not. How bad?"

"It's nothing. Really. So minor I didn't even think to mention it."

"Not a concussion, is it?"

"No more than a mild one if anything at all, the doctor said." CJ felt the bandage and wondered if he could replace it with a small Band-Aid. If he combed his hair just right he could probably leave it off altogether and it wouldn't be noticeable. "Really. It's nothing. The doctor wouldn't have made so light of it if it had been a concussion."

"Humph!" was all Stella said.

By the time they'd finished up the call, CJ was walking again and feeling better. As he was entering the hotel elevator, Gianna called him back.

"Sorry you had to hear all that, CJ. Kassi is rather distraught."

CJ looked at the ceiling as the elevator climbed to the 9th floor. It stopped. "I completely understand."

"I haven't decided yet what more I want you to do. Has there been any developments there?"

CJ fetched his key card from his pocket as he walked to his room.

"As a matter of fact, I've got a lot to tell you." Without turning on the lights, he sat at his window where he could look out at the lights defining the edge of Tampa Bay. He then proceeded to tell Gianna about his 600 horsepower adventure.

Chapter 17

CJ had all he could do to struggle out of bed Saturday morning. It was the urge to pee that motivated him to find his feet and shuffle to the bathroom. There didn't seem to be a muscle, joint or square inch of skin that didn't hurt. He took his pain meds with water and then carefully removed the bandage wrap around his ribcage. The bruise looked like he'd been hit with a baseball bat. Brushing his teeth, showering and shaving, those things he'd taken for granted, took three times longer, requiring much deliberate care. By the time he stepped out of the shower, however, he had gained better control of his movements and his head felt a bit clearer. He was even able to cover the bump and scab on his forehead with his hair. Still, he put on a new bandage.

He took as deep a breath as he could and considered not putting the wrap back on, though he had to admit it did feel a bit better to have the security of it there. He just couldn't breathe the way he wanted to. He decided to go down to breakfast and then come back up and put it on afterwards.

He got dressed.

CJ sat at the same table as the morning before, empty plate before him, sipping coffee and running the events of the last two days through his mind. What he couldn't figure out was why he'd become a target. What were the motivations of Pickens and Blight, or the people they worked for, to take him out and kill him? In what way was he a threat?

Maybe they thought he knew something. Maybe they weren't intending to kill him, but were taking him somewhere to be questioned as to what he knew. Did they believe Douglas told him something or gave him something? Eveleen Danohough was a big wig in UIRA. If

UIRA was involved in all this, wouldn't she know about it, have to put her blessing on it? In CJ's opinion, she didn't look like the type who would have her son killed and then hire a private investigator to find the killer afterwards.

But... could it be that someone else in the organization is going behind her back? Paddy McGee had said that she was one of four who founded the group. Maybe one of the other three had discovered that there was a mole right under Eveleen's nose and took matters into his own hands. Kill the mole and then kill the last person he talked to.

Still, that didn't make sense. They can't just kill everyone that Douglas talked to. What was there about CJ that led them to thinking he needed to be eliminated?

Then, again, was the intent no more than transporting him to another location where the boss could question him. Elimination may not have been the reason at all. If that were the case, what did they think he knew? And why handcuff him? They could have just told him that someone wanted to talk to him, asked him nicely to come along for a boat ride. He may have cooperated.

But then, maybe he wouldn't have.

If they were killing people, who was next? Rebecca? Eveleen? The McGee family? How big was this thing?

He needed to talk to Eveleen.

CJ went next door to Starbucks to get a proper coffee. When he got up to the counter the same girl as the morning before asked for his order and then recognized him.

"Ah," was all she said, though her head kept swiveling to and fro as though looking for a cop or someone in authority.

"It was all a big misunderstanding," CJ said to her, giving her his sexiest smile. "I'm really quite harmless."

"Okay," she said, though obviously not convinced.

"I'll have a Salted Caramel Mocha, hold the cream."

She repeated it back to him then turned away, going straight to filling his order ahead of the woman who had placed her order first.

When she pushed his drink toward him less than a minute later, he handed her a ten dollar bill and said, "Keep the change," and winked.

Back in his room he fetched the business card that Eveleen had given him the day before. He sipped his mocha and considered the card. Eveleen Danohough was the owner of the *Coffee Bean Boutique*.

What is a *Coffee Bean Boutique*? he wondered. There were two phone numbers, business and cell. He dialed the cell number and was immediately directed to her voice mail.

"Ms. Danohough. CJ Washburn here. I'd like to meet with you. Please give me a call." He recited his number and then called the business.

"*Coffee Bean Boutique*," a sultry voice said. "This is Sandra. How may I help you?"

"Eveleen Danohough wouldn't happen to be in, would she?" CJ said.

"I'm afraid she is not," Sandra said, her voice losing most of its sultry edge. "We don't open for another hour. She'd normally be here on Saturday mornings, but, sadly, she's had a death in the family. I doubt we'll see her or Eddie before Monday."

"Eddie?"

"Eddie Hall, Eveleen's partner. Is there anything I may be able to do for you?"

"Afraid not. I've left a message on her cell. If she does come in ask her to call CJ Washburn. She has my number."

"I will."

"Thank you very much."

CJ put the phone down and considered what to do next. After his conversation with Gianna and Stella the night before, it was decided, seeing as Stella was going to join him anyway, that together they should go ahead and continue the investigation into who killed Douglas and why. Gianna couldn't just walk away from it and her sister. "In for a pence, in for a pound," she'd said. "But be careful," she'd added. "I don't want to lose anyone else."

That got CJ to thinking about how dangerous this whole thing was and the fact that Stella was joining him. If something were to happen to her he might as well handcuff himself back to the boat and kick the throttle wide open. There would be no way he could live with the guilt.

He carefully wrapped his ribcage with the elastic bandage and then dug out *Paddy McGee's Irish Pub*'s business card that Rebecca had handed him as he was leaving the pub. On the back she'd written her phone number. He keyed in the number and then pressed the call button.

A half hour later CJ was parked on the street directly in front of *Banyan Coffee and Tea* in Downtown St. Petersburg, about a mile and a half drive from the hotel. He waited until it was a few minutes shy of 9:30 before going in and ordering two regular coffees. Although he'd already eaten breakfast, he added a couple of Danishes. Just as he walked out an outside table with a big red umbrella became available, so he took it.

The sky was a rich blue and cloudless. The forecast called for rain later in the day, but for the moment it was a very enjoyable morning. A sudden breeze rattled the umbrella and sent an empty sugar packet sailing off the table only to be replaced by several leaves from above. He looked up at a beautiful oak tree under which he was sitting–at least he thought it was oak–considered the pleasantness of the location, birds chirping, the enjoyable Florida aroma. Most of the pains throughout his body had disappeared and his ribs weren't feeling too bad. He sipped at his coffee and watched as Rebecca pulled up and parked on the other side of Martin Luther King Jr. Street. As she crossed the roadway in what appeared to CJ to be the same mourning outfit as the day before, except for a different purse, he rose and pulled out a chair.

"I took the liberty of ordering for you," he said. "Regular coffee. I hope that's okay."

"Fine," she said as she sat. "Thank you." She tore open two sugars and dumped them in the coffee. "What's with the bandage on your head?"

"Your two friends, Hawaiian Shirt and the other guy, took me out for a boat ride. It didn't go well."

"Oh."

"Hawaiian Shirt is one Rory Pickens. He's being held in the city jail at the moment. The other is Samuel Blight. The last time I saw him he was flying off the back of the boat. He either drowned or swam to shore."

She just looked at him, her mouth hanging open.

"Do you know either of those two names?"

She shook her head. "No."

"Doug never mentioned them?"

"Other than just pointing them out to me, no. Never mentioned names."

"I know that you told Agent Taffer you'd not retain my services to find out who killed your husband."

She started to say something but CJ put his hand up.

"That's okay. However, my partner is arriving this afternoon and together we're going to look further into this. It's now personal for me seeing as the boat ride last night was forced upon me for the purpose of killing me and dumping me at sea. At least, that's my opinion. Also, my Tucson client is asking that I continue with the investigation."

CJ's cell phone suddenly played a one-second tune. He pulled it out and looked at the text message.

"My partner just boarded her flight in Tucson."

"Your partner? As in another private investigator?"

"Yes. Let me answer her real quick." With one finger he slowly keyed in "Okay," and then "Love U." He punched "SEND" and then put the phone away.

"So you're bringing in help," Rebecca said.

"Yes."

She looked down at the Danish and then back up at CJ. "If this Roy guy..."

"Rory," CJ corrected.

"Rory. If he's in jail and the other guy is possibly dead, haven't you done as much as you can do? Don't you figure they're the ones who killed my husband?"

"Currently there's no proof. There's a third guy, the one who lifted my wallet. He's likely the guy who killed Douglas. Unless Pickens and Blight are working with him, I'm thinking they're off the hook for that. Rory Pickens will likely be out this afternoon, if he isn't already. There's nothing at this point to tie him to Douglas' murder and it's his word against mine as to what happened on the boat. What witnesses there were didn't see all that much. The sheriff and Detective DuPont both believe me, and so does Special Agent Taffer, however, there's nothing on which to hold Pickens. I can file a complaint against him, but that probably wouldn't go too far."

"What are you going to do?"

"This thing is bigger than these two guys, bigger even than the one who killed Douglas. Someone had to have ordered the hit. That same person also put the order out on me. I don't take that kind of thing lightly."

They were interrupted by another cell phone, this time a full ringtone. Rebecca reached into a side pocket of her purse. She looked at the readout, pressed the phone to her ear and said in a flat tone, "Hello."

CJ turned his head and looked down the street, his way of demonstrating that he was not intentionally trying to listen in on her call.

"Who's saying that?" she said.

The sudden sharp uptake in her voice told CJ this wasn't a social call.

"Onassis? What?"

That brought CJ around to looking at her.

"Gianna Onassis! Who the hell is that?"

CJ raised his eyebrows.

"Arizona?" With that Rebecca's eyes came up to meet CJ's.

CJ pointed to her phone and said, "Who you talking to?"

"Eveleen," she said. "An attorney is trying to take claim of

Douglas' body when the police release him and have him transported to Indiana."

He indicated to Rebecca to give him the phone. She handed it over. "Ms. Danohough. This is CJ Washburn. Gianna Onassis is not only a powerful attorney, she is also Douglas' sister-in-law. She is representing her sister in Indiana."

"That marriage, Mister Washburn, was a sham," Eveleen said. "They have no right."

"Actually, they may have every right."

"She kicked him out!" Eveleen nearly screamed the words. She took a deep breath and lowered her voice. "Now that he's dead, she wants him back?"

"The fact is, she didn't kick him out. He left on his own."

"I don't..." Whatever she started to say, she changed her mind. "Whichever makes little difference. He left and changed his name. He was no longer a Rothbower."

"You and I can argue it, Ms. Danohough, but in the end, if you pursue it, it will be the U.S. courts who'll decide and I'm fairly certain which way that decision would go."

CJ would have sworn he could hear her teeth grinding.

"She wants him cremated," she said. "We don't."

"I'd be willing to bet that she's basing that on his wishes, likely a legal document filed with his will, which Gianna, I'm sure, has in her possession by now."

"Any will he had would have been null and void when he changed his name. I don't see how the courts could ignore that."

"What the courts are going to see is that Douglas' name change was necessary in order to infiltrate the UIRA organization as an informant. I'm sure the FBI will provide testimony to that affect. His marriage to Rebecca was part of his cover."

"*This* was his life!" she screamed into the phone. "This was not some *God damned cover*!"

CJ considered telling her again what Douglas had told him just before he was killed, that he'd intended on returning to Indiana, to his first and legal wife. He could already see, however, that Rebecca was turning white, her chin against her chest, her eyes closed, tears streaming down her cheeks.

"The thing is, Ms. Danohough, you may have bigger problems right now, you and Rebecca both."

"Problems? What are you talking about?"

"I have reason to believe that you may be on a to-be-killed list."

"A what!"

"I think Douglas was only the first and that you are possibly next, and maybe Rebecca as well."

With that Rebecca's chin came up. She wiped at her face with her wadded up napkin and looked at CJ.

"We need to meet someplace safe," he said into the phone, "where I can tell you what has happened since we last met and why I believe you're in danger."

The silence that followed was so long that CJ thought he'd lost connection.

"Ms. Danohough?" he said.

"I'm still here. I'm thinking. How about Paddy McGee's Irish Pub? I can give you the address or Rebecca can guide you there."

"No," CJ said. "That's not a good place."

"You sure?"

"Quite sure."

"Where are you now?" she asked.

CJ told her.

"I'll come to you, then. Give me half an hour."

While they waited, CJ got a second coffee, and a juice for Rebecca. She visited the ladies room. She then told him how she'd met Douglas. It was in her brother's pub when she was working. They'd flirted with each other, but kept it strictly as a patron to waitress relationship. Then one morning Paddy invited Douglas for breakfast at the house. They were married a few months later.

"A bit quick, don't you think?" CJ said.

"When you're in love," she said and then stopped. She looked down at her hands and then picked up her juice and took a sip. "I thought we were in love. I was. Now I'm not sure about him. Was he just acting?"

CJ didn't know how to respond.

They sat in silence for a bit, CJ sipping coffee, Rebecca sipping juice. Just when CJ considered getting a third coffee, Rebecca said, "There she is." She was indicating a southbound car.

As it passed by, CJ stood and raised his arm. Eveleen glanced his way and then continued on to a parking place a quarter-block farther down the street. She setup to parallel park but seemed to be bothered by a red truck that had pulled up close behind her. When traffic allowed, the driver of the truck swung wide and turned into a drive a hundred feet or so beyond. Eveleen began maneuvering her car into the parking spot.

Something about the truck bothered CJ. Although he often didn't pay close attention to what was going on around him, there always seemed to be a 6th sense at work with him. It was this sense that had him thinking about when he'd first noted the truck. He was fairly certain that it had arrived maybe ten minutes earlier, slipping into a street slot north of where Rebecca parked, facing south. No one had gotten out. CJ had then observed it pull out when Eveleen passed by, falling in behind her. From his angle he could see that the drive it pulled into was the far end of a parking lot, the near end having an exit back onto the same street, this side of where Eveleen was parking. The truck seemed to just drift through the lot, as though the driver was looking for something. There were plenty of parking spots open, but he wasn't parking. It was more like he was waiting... circling.

Waiting for Eveleen to get out of her car? CJ stepped away from the table and out onto the street. "Stay here," he said to Rebecca and began a slow jog in Eveleen's direction.

Eveleen's car door opened and the truck began moving faster. It turned toward the parking lot exit and CJ picked up his pace.

When Eveleen stepped out of her car, CJ was directly across

from the truck. "Eveleen!" he yelled. "Get back in your car!" He then dodged a northbound car and rushed directly at the truck. It's front wheels contacted the street, whereupon it turned and began accelerating. "Eveleen!" CJ yelled again and then flung himself at the driver's door, knowing there was nothing else he could do other than distract the driver. With a roar of the truck's engine and a screech of its tires, he bounced off the door, landing in a sprawl on the street. There came another screech of tires, a horn blast almost in CJ's ear and then a cacophony of metal against metal. Somewhere in it all, a woman screamed.

Chapter 18

CJ looked up to find a car bumper and a black wheel swimming just a few feet from his face. As the fuzz and the pain in his ribcage dissipated, the glare of the morning sun brought him to full alert. He turned his head expecting to see Eveleen in a bloody heap somewhere down the street. What he found was that her car door lay broken and mangled some fifty feet beyond her car, the truck gone. She was nowhere in sight. A man came running across the street to the gaping hole in Eveleen's car and looked in. A few seconds later Eveleen's head appeared and the man helped her out on wobbly legs.

Suddenly Rebecca and another man were kneeling next to CJ. "Are you okay?" they said, almost in unison.

CJ looked at Rebecca's frantic face and then let his head settle back onto the pavement, taking as deep a breath as he could. There were certainly going to be a few more bruises, but there didn't seem to be anything new broken.

"Yes," he said. "I'm fine. Did you get the license plate number?"

She shook her head. "No. It happened so fast."

"Neither did I," said the man. He looked around. "I hope someone did."

As he sat up, Eveleen arrived at his side.

"Are you alright?" she said. "I don't think you should be moving around until the EMS gets here."

"I'm fine."

"But you got hit by that truck."

"No. Actually, I hit the truck; bounced off. Are you okay?"

"Yes! Yes! I'm just fine. My car though..." She looked over at it. "He was trying to kill me, wasn't he?"

CJ nodded. "Yes."

"How did you know?"

Another individual joined the gathering and announced, "I called 911."

CJ stood with the assistance of Rebecca and the man, gathered his balance and then led everyone to the side. "Rebecca," he said. "Use your phone to get a picture of Eveleen's car with the door in the background, as it lies now, and then go drag it off the street. We don't need any more instances."

"You get the pictures," said the man who'd helped Eveleen out of her car. "I'll get the door for you."

"Thanks," CJ said.

CJ walked back to the table where he and Rebecca had been seated and sat down. He pulled out his phone, found a name and hit the call button. When the call was answered, he said, "Parker. CJ Washburn here. I hope you don't have plans for the day."

EMS arrived less than a minute after two St. Petersburg cruisers. By the time Detective DuPont showed on the scene, the circus was in full swing; statements, names and pictures were being collected by the officers. Once the EMS techs determined that their services were not required, they departed, taking with them the bulk of annoying strobing lights. When the officers had done as much as they could, including issuing a BOLO on the truck, they left Eveleen Danohough and CJ in the good hands of the detective. The witnesses and the curious gradually dispersed.

The four of them, Eveleen, Rebecca, CJ and Detective DuPont, sat around the table outside *Banyan Coffee and Tea*, fresh complimentary coffees from the management–tea in Eveleen's case–sitting before them. They sipped at their beverages while CJ spent some time outlining his theories.

DuPont tapped his plastic spoon on the table top for a time after CJ was finished, then said, "So you're thinking that all three of you are on this hit list?"

"Yes."

"Why?"

"That's the big money question, isn't it," CJ said, looking at Eveleen.

"How would I know?" she blurted.

"Something's been going on inside the United Irish Republican Army. You're a cofounder of the group."

She held up her hand. "Sorry that I may have given you the wrong impression, but I haven't been active for quite some time. I've been busy with my shop."

"The *Coffee Bean Boutique*?"

"Yes. If UIRA is up to something, I don't know about it."

"*Coffee Bean Boutique*?" DuPont said. "I've heard of your place. Don't you supply beans to shops up and down Florida's west coast?"

Eveleen nodded. "Starting to pick up a few out toward Orlando, too, and a couple on the Atlantic coast.

He pointed at her tea. "Didn't I hear you tell the manager at this place that you only drink tea?"

She shrugged and smiled. "What can I say? I love the smell of coffee, prefer the taste of tea. Doesn't mean I can't sell coffee. You sell what the market demands. America is not a big tea market."

DuPont saluted her with his paper cup of coffee and took a sip.

"Back to UIRA," CJ said. "So what you're saying is that you're no longer actively involved with them, that you have no idea what they've been up to?"

"That's what I'm saying. I was enjoying having my son back." She closed her eyes for a few seconds in an apparent attempt to squelch a building emotion. She swallowed and took a deep breath. "I know he had joined the group, but I'd lost interest in it a long time ago. The only reason I knew anything was going on was because of Douglas."

"You no longer agree with their mission?"

"To unite Ireland? Of course I agree. It's just that I'm getting too old for the politicking and such. It's been over sixty years, 1948 to be exact, the year I was born, since the country was split. I truly believe it will come back together, however, I doubt it will be in my lifetime. The fight will continue until I'm long gone."

"Douglas didn't talk to you about what was going on?"

"Not really. He'd meet with some people over in Apollo Beach occasionally. I didn't pay much attention, though."

"Do you know the names, Rory Pickens or Samuel Blight?"

Eveleen shook her head. "No. Who are they?"

"They're the two who picked me up, maybe tried to kill me."

"Did they kill Douglas?"

"I doubt it. That may have just been one individual. Pickens is currently in the city jail, though I doubt he's going to be there very long. Blight's whereabouts is unknown."

"Could he have been driving the truck?"

"Maybe, but probably not. I'm thinking it was the same guy who killed Douglas. I couldn't get a good look at him through the smoked windows. How many people are involved in the UIRA here in Florida?"

"I don't know?" Eveleen said.

CJ had been sitting back in his chair, talking quietly. Now he leaned forward and got directly into Eveleen's face. "This is serious, Ms. Danohough. You need to stop playing the 'I don't know anything' card because it's not going to keep you alive."

"But I *don't* know anything."

Her whine irritated CJ. "I'd be willing to put money down that you know more than you're letting on, or more than you think you do." He looked at Rebecca. "And you, too. You don't live with a man, sleep in his bed and call him your husband without noticing things about his routine or deviations from his routine. What do you know about this beach?"

"Beach?" Rebecca said. "What beach?"

CJ looked at Eveleen. "What was it you said? Pollo Beach?"

"Apollo Beach. It's a community east of here, the other side of the bay."

"How do you get there?"

"You take I-275 north or south. It's just a loop in from I-75. Either way will take you out of St. Petersburg, over one of the bridges onto, what many locals call, the Florida mainland."

CJ considered that for a few seconds, trying to match what she'd just said with the image of Tampa Bay he had in his head. "Can you get there by boat?"

"Straight across the bay? Sure."

"What are you thinking, CJ?" DuPont said.

"What if the boat ride Pickens and Blight took me on wasn't to kill me and dump me at sea? What if they were in fact taking me to this meeting location in Apollo Beach for some other reason?"

"What other reason?"

"To question me as to what I knew. Pickens and Blight aren't the brains. They're likely just gophers. Someone else is calling the shots. That someone may be who Douglas was meeting with in Apollo Beach. It still may be that my ultimate destination was the deep sea, but they first had to find out what I knew and who I told."

To Eveleen he said, "You either know something or they think you know something. Either way, you're on the hit list. For the same reason," he turned to Rebecca, "so are you."

The two women looked up and down the street. "So what should we do?" Rebecca said.

"I'll see if I can't put some officers with you for a time," DuPont said.

"That may not be necessary," CJ said.

They all just looked at him.

"My guess is that they're running out of time and at some point they may conclude that anymore of this cloak and dagger hit squad crap is useless. They'll realize that it's too little too late and they'll either abandon whatever it is they're getting ready to do, or they'll accelerate their timeline. "

"Timeline for what?" DuPont said.

"That, I don't know. I'd recommend you call your buddy, John Taffer, and ask him."

"I'll certainly do that."

CJ turned to Eveleen. "What's the history of the IRA and splinter groups as far as obtaining arms and explosives from the states?"

"You think that's what's been going on here?"

"The United Irish Republican Army is organizing something and doing it outside the Irish borders. It's much too far away to be gathering and training manpower. Planning something in secret, though, is more effective if it's accomplished well away from the battlefield where it would require only leadership and a select few lieutenants."

"You make it sound like they're intending an all out assault in Northern Ireland."

"That may be exactly what I'm saying. I'm thinking that they're gathering arms here in the United States where no one pays attention and are getting ready to load and ship them to Northern Ireland, and I've a hunch that this place in Apollo Beach may be the warehouse."

DuPont sat back. "That's an awfully big leap, CJ. Can you really believe they'd come this far from their country to organize a takeover?"

"I doubt they're considering a takeover against the British government. That's not only stupid, it's suicidal. I imagine what they're trying to do is gain attention, maybe sympathy. Isn't that what it's usually about? And I'm surprised that you're surprised, Parker," CJ said. "You of all people should know how easy it is for nefarious-minded people to organize in secret in the United States, land of unlimited freedoms. With far right-wings, left-wings, KKK, white supremacists, drug runners, border jumpers, extremist groups of all kinds, who's going to look twice at a bunch of Irish and Irish Americans getting together in Central Florida? This is the perfect place to organize."

DuPont nodded. "I see your point."

"It wouldn't be the first time," Eveleen said.

Everyone looked at her. "This has been done before?" CJ said.

"A fishing boat was seized coming into Ireland from Boston in '84. It was loaded with tons of guns and explosives. I remember it because PIRA was blamed. Turned out it originated from the Irish Mafia in Boston."

"So PIRA had nothing to do with it?" DuPont said.

Eveleen shrugged. "In '90 some IRA supporters attempted to smuggle a home-made missile system into Ireland. About the same time there were the black market Stinger Missiles in Miami. Arms purchases in Alabama; also in Colorado. All linked to the IRA."

"Really?"

"Really. After the Battle of Bogside in '69, during which I went into labor and then gave birth to Douglas, PIRA, brand new at the time, received support from Irish Americans in the United States in the form of submachine guns, handguns and ammunition; a huge shipment. I was there for that one. There have been a lot more throughout the years: Boston, Miami, New Jersey, Detroit. The list goes on. Even support from people as far out as Montana."

She took a long sip of her tea and then continued.

"After the Good Friday Accord in '98, I got angry. I and three others started the *United Irish Republican Army*. When everyone laid down their arms in 2005, the so-called disarmament, I considered giving up. As far as I was concerned, we'd lost and I was discouraged. As far back as 2002 there had been talk about relocating UIRA headquarters to the United States. The actual move took place in 2004. In November of 2005, after the arms lay down, I joined them in a rather weak last ditch effort to revitalize myself in the cause. Florida weather, age, and concern about my retirement years, easily took over and by the end of 2006 I'd become a small business owner. In everything but name, I walked away from the *United Irish Republican Army* and ensconced myself in St. Petersburg and the Florida west coast. I love Ireland, always will, but I've no desire to go back there. Not even for a visit."

"Who are the other three?" CJ said.

"Other three?"

"You said that there were four founders of the UIRA. Who are the other three?"

"One is dead. Heart attack I'd heard, in 2007, or maybe '08. He'd not actually come over; stayed in Northern Ireland with his family."

"The other two?"

"Would rather not say."

"Are they here?"

"Yes."

"Active?"

"As far as I know, yes."

"As far as you know? I think you do know and it has to be one or both of them who put the hit out on Douglas and likely out on you and Rebecca as well."

She looked away. "I don't see... I don't know." She wiped at her face with a napkin. "With much regret I gave up my son because of it all in 1969. Now, 43 years later, I've lost my son again because of it, this time for good."

"Then you need to tell us who could possibly have ordered the hit."

She sat back, folded her arms over her chest and closed her eyes. "I'm done!"

DuPont went back to tapping his spoon on the table while CJ rubbed at his shoulder. He wondered if maybe he *had* done something to it when he hit the truck.

DuPont pulled out his phone, punched at it and then put it to his ear.

"John," he said. "We've got new developments... Right. The Douglas O'Reilly case. We need to meet." He looked at Eveleen who was still turned away, her eyes closed. "No, not this afternoon. Crime doesn't take Saturday mornings off, John. Attempts are being made on people's lives in the apparent name of your little Irish operation. We need to meet now!"

He listened for a few seconds.

"I'm at what could have turned into a horrific crime scene if not for quick actions by an Arizona private eye."

He held the phone away from his ear while Agent Taffer spit out a phrase—it included a profanity and the name, Washburn—which everyone at the table could hear.

"CJ Washburn. Yes. Who else do you think I'd be talking about?"

He listened for a few seconds.

"Downtown St. Petersburg." He recited the address. "We'll be waiting."

DuPont looked around the table. "Sorry about that. He'll be here in ten minutes or so. He lives in St. Petersburg and is right now at his kid's soccer match. I'm not going to feel bad about that. I can probably count on one hand, with fingers left over, the number of my kids' events I've been able to make it to over the last ten years *and* have stayed until the end. It comes with the job."

CJ thought about that statement and his own time on the force as a police officer during the formative years for Trish and Josh. He thought about his fights with Pat, his now ex-wife, concerning that very subject, and then he thought about his too-little-too-late attempt to fix it all by leaving the force and becoming a private investigator. He recalled Trish's disappointment and Josh's anger when it still ended in divorce.

He wondered if Detective DuPont and Agent Taffer were possibly heading down that same road.

And then he thought about Stella. Would they be different? They wouldn't have kids and she worked with him. Maybe it'd work.

"What are you going to do about your car, Eveleen?" Rebecca said.

Eveleen opened her eyes and turned her head toward where the car was still parked, the driver's door poking out of the trunk. "I have *Triple A*."

"You can still drive it," CJ said.

She presented him with her saddest smile and shook her head. "No way am I driving around St. Petersburg in anything that looks like that."

"You can use Doug's car," Rebecca said.

Eveleen looked at her for a few seconds, apparently thinking about the fact that her son would never drive it again. "Thank you. I'll keep that in mind if my insurance company doesn't foot for a rental."

"And you do have Eddie," Rebecca said.

Eveleen closed her eyes again and took a deep breath. "Yes, I do have Eddie."

After a short bit of silence, CJ got up and retrieved a map from his car. He opened it on the table and said, "Any idea where in Apollo Beach this meeting place would be located? It would need to have waterfront access if the operation requires shipping arms to Northern Ireland."

DuPont pointed to the community on the map. "Pretty much everything in Apollo Beach has waterfront access, CJ."

CJ bent forward and looked closer. "Oh." He blinked a couple of times. "It looks like almost every home would have a backyard to the water, and it all feeds to the bay."

"Fifty-five miles of canals," DuPont said, "with access to Tampa Bay and, thus, the Gulf of Mexico and the Atlantic Ocean."

"These places must be expensive. There are hundreds of homes."

"Not top dollar, but close, CJ. And there are thousands of homes."

CJ sat back. "Somebody in this organization has deep pockets. Is there much commercial waterfront property or businesses?"

"I don't think so, at least not along the line that you're thinking. No warehouses with loading docks where one, unobserved, could load up a big ship worthy to sail or steam for 5,000 miles."

CJ considered that for a moment and then said, "But it is possible, I'd assume, to park a ship out in the bay somewhere and then shuttle a smaller boat to it from a house in Apollo Beach?"

"That would be *anchor* a ship out in the bay, CJ. Certainly it's possible. Realistically? I'm not seeing it."

"Why would it be so hard? You get a big house on the water. You truck in guns, ammo and such into your attached garage from where you can haul everything into your living room, or large bedroom. Nothing larger than could fit into a van or SUV. Hell, you could use the entire house if its only purpose is as a warehouse with a kitchen. That can be done in daylight hours, everyday for as long as it takes; in other words, weeks or months."

"It'd be a lot of activity in a residential neighborhood."

"Who's going to pay attention to a private vehicle coming and going from a garage once or twice a day? That's all that would be needed if these people are smart. Once you have everything staged, which can take as long as required, you bring in the sea-going vessel, park, er... ah, anchor it out a ways and then start shuttling until it's loaded. The shuttling can take place at night. Again, a little at a time."

"Great theory, my friend, but nothing but a theory. There's no meat there. It's just a supposition. Can't get a warrant on a supposition."

All the time he and the detective where discussing Apollo Beach, CJ was noticing Eveleen's seemingly uninterested attitude. When he first brought out the map, she'd given it a bare glance and then turned away as though activity elsewhere was of much greater importance.

"What was the true reason you gave up, Ms. Danohough?" CJ said.

"What do you mean," her voice said, but her face told him she knew exactly what he was asking.

"You said that after the arms were laid down in 2005, you gave up."

"It wasn't so much a lay down as a destruction. Everything was made unusable."

"And that made you angry."

"Yes."

"I thought you wanted only a peaceful solution, at least that's what you attempted to lead us to believe."

"The United States wants a peaceful solution to unrest around the world. I don't see *them* laying down and destroying their tanks, ships and planes. That would be stupid."

CJ responded only with a nod.

"When we laid down our arms and walked away it was the same as saying to the British government, 'You won. We'll do whatever you say.'"

"That's why you left Northern Ireland. You couldn't stand being under British rule. Why didn't you just move south, to Independent Ireland?"

"I considered it, actually, seeing as that was where I was born and raised, lived until the mid '80s. I didn't really want to go back there.

My parents were gone. I had no other family. Also, I'd be doing exactly what the British wanted. 'If you don't like it, there's the border.' I'd heard that from the Protestants too many times."

"Why didn't you just stay?"

She didn't answer.

"Because this is where UIRA headquarters went." CJ pointed in a direction he thought was east. "Right over there, in Apollo Beach. It's hard to hide in Ireland or even Europe. You, or your cofounders, brought UIRA to North America. You know exactly where the warehouse-headquarters are located, don't you? You could tell us the square footage, maybe even a close estimate of the tonnage of military armament staged there right now."

She tightened her lips and looked away again. "I know nothing about military armament. There's no..."

"What's the address, Ms. Danohough?" Detective DuPont said.

But Eveleen Danohough's attention was no longer on the conversation. She'd become tense, her gaze suddenly focused on something down the street.

DuPont leaned toward her. "Ms. Danohough!"

In a sudden rush to get to her feet, Eveleen shoved her chair over backwards. It hit the cement sidewalk with a clank! CJ followed to where she was looking and then jumped to his feet as well, disturbing the table and sloshing drinks all around. The truck that had tried to run her down little more than an hour before was back, and coming toward them. The passenger window started coming down and the speed picked up.

"Everyone on the ground!" CJ yelled and grabbed for Rebecca. DuPont looked, saw what CJ and Eveleen were seeing and lunged at the older woman. Chairs scattered, Rebecca screamed and the four of them landed face-down, the two men partially covering the women in a gallant attempt to protect them. *Gun* was the only thing CJ could think of as the front grill of the truck came into view between his rental and the car parked in front of it. They were about to be exposed. In a split second reflex, he reached out and grabbed a table leg. As he flipped the table, with umbrella, on its side he saw an arm and then a hand in the window and then something, an object the size of a giant coffee mug, flying out. Only it wasn't a mug. It was a...

"Bomb!" CJ yelled as he tucked his head between his arms and into the space between Rebecca's shoulder blades. The last two things he thought about before the explosion was the pain in his side and the fact that Stella would have no one to meet her at the airport.

Chapter 19

There were hands on CJ, muffled voices, shoes shuffling, someone kneeling. "...you...k," a man said. CJ rolled off of Rebecca onto his back and looked past a face and then another face, past the branches of a tree and up at the sky. "Are...," one face said but CJ couldn't make out anything else. It was like the explosion was still roaring in his head.

He looked over and saw the other three stirring at about the same speed as him. DuPont sat up, said something, then put his hands up to his ears. CJ pointed to the detective's arm and said, "You're bleeding," but it sounded like he was talking from inside a barrel.

Both women were struggling to their hands and knees and CJ heard someone say, "Stay down! Don't..." After that the words trailed off into the barrel.

CJ looked past DuPont to his rental car. The hood was up and buckled, the front end mangled, collapsed to the ground, the front tire that he could see shredded, the rear tire flat. The rear end of the car parked in front of it was also badly damaged, tires flat. The table and umbrella, except for a corner of the umbrella that was shredded, seemed to be completely intact. There was no fire, no smoke. He looked at the rental again, at the tremendous damage and remembered the object flying toward them. How was it possible that they'd sustained no injuries beyond the detective's bleeding arm and their temporary, he hoped, loss of hearing? The roaring in his head was now a high-pitched ringing.

"It's best... don't move."

CJ looked up at the person speaking and recognized the manager from the coffee shop, the one who'd provided complimentary coffee and tea after the earlier event when the same truck had come after

Eveleen. He understood why the man was recommending that he not move, however after assessing his body parts, testing his limbs and feeling the bandage on his head, CJ decided that sitting up would not be an issue. He rolled to his hands and knees and then sat back on his heels. His ribs were throbbing.

He noticed that one of the windows to the coffee shop was gone, the other intact. "Anyone hurt?" he asked of the manager, pointing at the window.

The manager shook his head. "Lucky," was all CJ heard.

CJ turned his head and found that Rebecca was already propped in a chair, looking around, in a daze. Eveleen was sitting on the ground, her head between her raised knees, while Detective DuPont was on his feet, looking up and down the street, still apparently unaware that there was blood running down his arm, dripping from his fingertips.

"Parker," CJ said, noticing that the barrel effect seemed to be fading a bit. He wished the ringing would stop. When there came no response from the detective, CJ raised his voice. "Parker!"

DuPont turned to look at CJ.

CJ pointed to the detective's hand. "You're bleeding."

The detective looked down and started to pull his hand up to his face. That was as far as he got before he fell to his knees and then plopped over sideways against the table legs. CJ shoved the table aside and dropped down next to the detective, immediately checking for his pulse. Not only did he find a pulse, and a strong one at that, but he also discovered a nail sticking out of the side of the detective's head.

And then there came the sirens.

Chapter 20

CJ stood with his hands in his pockets watching expectant faces of people milling around inside Tampa International Airport, wanting to sit down because his cracked rib was giving him issues, not able to sit because, one, he was too nervous, too keyed up, and two, there were no seats except one near a woman with four kids. He sort of felt like they looked, wiggly and whiney. He certainly didn't need to join their fray.

"Are you always like this, Mr. Washburn?" said the FBI agent standing next to him.

Between the occasional ringing in one ear and the on and off pressure, CJ still had to focus when someone was talking to him. He wondered how long it would take for his hearing to return to normal. "Like this what?"

"It's as though you have an itch that you need to scratch but don't know how to put your hand down your pants without anyone noticing."

CJ turned his head to look at Special Agent Coulter. "When did the FBI start checking for the bullet point, *well dressed comedian*, on prospective agents' resumes?"

Coulter didn't smile or even move.

"How long does it take the academy to teach you the stance: Feet twelve to eighteen inches apart, jaw set, eyes and head swiveling like an owl scanning for field mice, hands protecting your manhood?"

The corners of Coulter's mouth lifted just a little.

"You grin too much like that they'll have to send you back for a refresher."

The agent smiled a little more. "I heard the manhood comment from a thirteen-year-old... girl, only she preferred the word, dick."

CJ shook his head. "What's the world coming to?"

"She was the daughter of a senator. I swear they're the worst."

They went silent and CJ continued shuffling his feet as though trying to pace in place, noticing a shuttle arrive from the gates, the third one so far. There was no vantage point from which one could see inside the shuttle, had to wait for people to come out into the waiting area. He shuffled some more until, finally, a few people started wandering out, dragging their most precious possessions behind them, backpacks or purses slung off their shoulders. And then Stella appeared, a huge smile on her face.

CJ met her halfway and gave her a big hug, wanting more than ever to never let her go. When she started becoming uncomfortable, he pulled back and walked her toward the agent. "Stella, this is Special Agent Ryan Coulter. He'll be spending time with us today."

She shook his hand and said, "Why?"

"They have some crazy notion that there may be more attempts on my life."

"More?"

"Someone threw a bomb at him this morning, Ms. Summers," Coulter said.

"A bomb!"

CJ held up his hand, wishing Coulter hadn't jumped to it so quickly. "Not so loud. You'll have the airport being evacuated."

Stella took a deep breath and looked directly at CJ, pulling her eyebrows together. "What does he mean, bomb?" she whispered.

"It wasn't necessarily thrown at *me*. I was sitting at an outdoor table with Rebecca O'Reilly, Eveleen Danohough and Detective DuPont. I think the actual targets were the women."

Stella looked CJ up and down as though checking for missing body parts. "And?"

"And what?"

"What the hell happened? This baa... *thing* was thrown at you and you're standing here. Fortunately, it must not have gone off."

"It went off, alright. DuPont is in the hospital with a nail in his head, or, ah, it's not in his head anymore. They took it out. He also caught a staple in his arm, one of those huge ones, like a ten-penny nail bent twice."

"I know what a huge staple looks like, Clint. Was this a small bomb? Why didn't anyone else get hurt?"

"It did a lot of damage, could have easily killed any one of us except that..." CJ suddenly noticed a familiar figure separating from the stream of people coming off of the next shuttle, a bureau image wearing a Washburn face.

Stella looked over her shoulder. "Oh yeah. Forget to tell you. Ran into Josh in Atlanta. We had the same connecting flight. You didn't tell me for sure that he was coming."

"I didn't think he was. Apparently he didn't see fit to call and tell me."

"Call and tell you what, Dad?" Josh said as he hugged his father.

"I never heard from you after the conference call between your boss and Agent Taffer. You suspected you'd be loaned but you never called to confirm, so I just figured it wasn't going to happen."

"Sorry. It was so last minute. I don't always have my bags packed and affairs in order in preparation for a field assignment. Had a lot to do."

Coulter stepped forward and extended his hand. "Special Agent Brian Coulter. I, also, wasn't briefed as to your pending arrival, Agent Washburn."

As the two agents shook hands, Josh said, "Just got off the phone with Special Agent Taffer. I expect you'll receive a call shortly." Josh turned to his dad. "Taffer filled me on the IED. How is Detective DuPont doing?"

"The last I heard, he was out of surgery. The nail didn't penetrate far. The staple, however, nicked the humerus, tore up some muscle on the way in."

"It was an IED?" Stella whispered at Josh. "I thought those were roadside bombs, or devices buried in the ground waiting for someone to step on them."

"IED stands for Improvised Explosive Device," Coulter said, "and it can be anything someone could build in their garage or kitchen and it can be buried, hidden under or inside something, or thrown. Improvised is the key word here. There are no rules."

"Oh. Not exactly comforting."

"The scene is being scoured for bomb fragments right now to see if we can figure out how it was built. It appears to have been a chunk of explosive material inside a sealed container around which was taped nails, staples and sharp pieces of metal."

"Over-sized coffee mug," CJ said.

"Could be," Coulter said.

"No. I mean that's what came to mind when I saw it coming at us. It could have been something else, I guess. I recall camouflage, like green camouflage duct tape with something else taped to the outside of it. Maybe a timing device, like a cell phone."

"There *have* been shreds of duct tape found," Josh said. "It's often used to adhere a layer of enhancements to the outside of a container loaded with explosives."

"Enhancements?" Stella said.

"In this case the enhancements were nails, staples and other pieces of shrapnel. Taffer said something about pieces of a phone also being discovered. They may have used that as the timer. As a drive-by, the individual could start the timer, let's say five seconds, just before tossing it. Plenty of time to get far enough away so as to not be affected by the blast, but not enough time for someone on foot to react and run away or find cover."

"I still don't get it," Stella said. "You saw it coming at you and then it exploded, but here you are, standing right before me. What happened?"

By this time they'd all moved toward the baggage claim area, remaining a distance back so they could talk without being overheard. Agent Coulter's phone rang and he moved away to answer it.

"The only thing we could figure out," CJ said, "was that the device hit a tree. There was a good sized tree right next to where we were sitting. Or maybe it hit the table or umbrella. Whatever the case, it bounced back into the street and rolled up against the inside of the car wheel. The wheel and the car absorbed the bulk of the blast. Only a couple of pieces of shrapnel managed to find Detective DuPont, who was the closest to it and who basically shielded the rest of us."

"Agent Taffer said that there was hearing damage," Josh said. "It appears your hearing has recovered."

"About 80 percent in my right ear," CJ said. "Rebecca seemed to be recovering okay, too. I do worry about Ms. Danohough and Detective DuPont. They were the closest. Eveleen was having a hard time; constant ringing, near totally deaf in her right ear. I heard the emergency medical tech say something about bleeding from hers and the detective's ears. I don't think that's good."

"No it's not," Josh said, and then he and Stella stepped away to fetch their bags from the carousel.

When they returned, Stella said, "Is it a long walk to your rental, Clint?"

"Ah... That's right; I haven't told you that part yet," CJ said. "The car under which the IED got lodged was mine. I don't think it's going anywhere under its own power ever again."

"Oh."

"The rental company is already involved. They weren't happy, but it wasn't my fault after all."

"Did they give you another car?"

"Yes, but I haven't picked it up yet. My hearing and balance are still having issues, so I thought I'd wait."

"I guess you all are rolling with *me*, then," Josh said.

Agent Coulter stepped back into the circle, stuffing his phone back into his pocket. "That should work out fairly well since I'm officially turning the responsibility of these two people over to you, Agent Washburn. I've been directed back to the crime scene."

As Coulter walked toward the elevators that would take him back to the parking garage, appearing to be pleased with his change in assignment, Josh stared after him.

"Is there a problem, Josh?" CJ said.

"I told you on the phone yesterday, and you agreed, that I didn't think it was a good idea to send me out here just to babysit you again. I didn't really mean it literally. I thought I would be more instrumental in the investigation and the operation."

"Sorry to disappoint you. You know that Taffer is going to have his own people in the center of it."

"Yeah, but this is one step above fetching coffee. It's not what I'm trained to do."

"Nice to know we're above coffee," Stella said.

"You *are* still a rookie," CJ said, "despite what happened in Arizona."

"I realize that, still...."

"You might say the Tommy Clark case accelerated you through preschool and kindergarten. You're in first grade now."

"Thanks for that image, Dad."

CJ put his arm around his son, even though it hurt his ribcage and his shoulder to do so, suddenly realizing Josh was as tall, if not an inch or two taller, than his father. "Baby steps, Josh. Baby steps. Be sure to find out how Taffer likes his coffee."

Chapter 21

CJ directed Josh out of Tampa, across the bridge into St. Petersburg and toward the area of town where the bomb blast took place. They took the exit off of I-375 and turned left onto Martin Luther King, Jr. Street. Josh found it necessary to navigate around two news media satellite trucks and people standing in the street gawking. At the police roadblock he presented his credentials and they passed him and his two passengers through with barely more than a word. Josh parked the car and they headed out on foot for the last block.

"The cop at the roadblock must have radioed ahead," CJ said, nodding toward the FBI agent coming toward them. Before CJ could make introductions, Taffer extended his hand to Josh.

"Special Agent Washburn, I presume," he said. "I'm John Taffer, Assistant Special Agent In-Charge. You'll be answering to me while you're here."

"Good to meet you, sir," Josh said.

Taffer pointed. "Check in with Agent Coulter, who you already know. He'll bring you up to speed. I need to have a few words with these two."

Josh nodded and eagerly headed toward Agent Coulter.

Taffer turned to CJ. "Quite a mess we have here, Mister Washburn."

"It's not my mess, John. I'm just one of the victims."

"Sure. Wrong place, wrong time. The consensus among law enforcement here is that you should have stayed in Arizona."

"Or Douglas Rothbower, aka, Douglas O'Reilly, should have kept his adopted name and stayed with his wife and daughter in Indiana. He's the only reason I came here."

"He's dead. Why are you still here?"

"One of his widows wants me to stay."

Taffer snorted. "I thought we sorted that out yesterday afternoon."

"She's having second thoughts."

Taffer made a face.

"I'm Stella Summers, by-the-way," Stella said, stepping forward and extending her hand. "Clint's partner."

Taffer accepted her hand. "My apologies, Ms. Summers. Nice to meet you. Can I expect that you'll keep this guy out of trouble?"

"Either that or we'll find more trouble to get into together." She gave him her matter-of-fact grin. "My understanding is that we still have a case to work. There has been an attempt upon our client's life as well as several upon my partner's. It seems to me, Assistant Special Agent In-Charge, John Taffer, that your operation is unraveling. I hope you can get a handle on it before it leaves the confines of the US borders."

CJ couldn't help but smile.

Taffer's face seemed to be teetering between laughing or throwing them outside the police barriers. He looked between CJ and Stella and said, "How much do you two actually know?"

"Not really sure," CJ said, "We don't know what we don't know and no one will tell us, thus a lot of what we think we know is speculation. You wouldn't want us running around speculating incorrectly, now would you?"

"I don't want you running around at all. So speculate for me right here, right now. Tell me what you think is going on."

"Big picture?"

"Yeah. Big picture. A few details wouldn't hurt."

"Is this your way of finding out if we know something that you don't know so that you might be able to, as Stella said, stop your operation from unraveling?"

"Just spill it, Washburn."

"Fine." CJ twisted his torso a bit in an attempt to relax the pain spikes suddenly surging around his ribcage. When it seemed to settle a bit and he was able to get a reasonable breath, he said, "The *United*

Irish Republican Army is stockpiling arms and explosives in Apollo Beach in preparation to shuttle it all to a waiting cargo ship before it steams off to Northern Ireland."

Taffer lifted his eyebrows about two inches. "That's it?"

"What do you mean, that's it?"

"That's all you have? That's your big picture?"

"Pretty much, yes," CJ said. "Isn't that enough? I can give you some details, local players and such, but I think that's the gist of it. I have no idea what they're planning in Northern Ireland, though my guess would be something specific as timing appears to be a growing issue."

"Why do you think that?"

"Something Douglas said just before he was killed."

"Like what?"

"It's not so much *what* he said, but what he almost said. He mentioned that he was intending on returning to his Indiana wife when it was all over, and that that'd be soon. Something about a summit."

"A summit?"

"He wasn't specific. He used the word, summit, and then it was like he caught himself. Maybe it was nothing."

"Maybe." Taffer's attention seemed to shift down the street, or off into another world inside his head for a few seconds. "So," he finally said, "who do you think some of the players are?"

"There's, of course, the guy who killed Douglas. and then the two who tried to kill me, Rory Pickens and Samuel Blight."

"You don't think Pickens or Blight killed Douglas?"

"Neither of them was the one who lifted my wallet, so no. They may have been involved. No way of telling there. Initially I thought that Blight was the truck driver but I really don't have any basis for that. That may have been a fourth person. The one who threw the device from the passenger seat of the truck could be a fifth. All I saw was his hand. Male, I'm fairly certain, but that's it. Altogether there are as many as five men. Then there's Eveleen Danohough, who is more involved than she's admitting. I don't think Rebecca O'Reilly knew much of anything until the last few days. The McGee family, I'm fairly sure, is out of it, though Paddy McGee did know something about what Douglas was doing, maybe in a way, supported him. That's all the players I know about."

"Humph!"

"Oh, there's the boat you or the sheriff impounded, the one on which I nearly performed a suicide mission. Maybe that was to be the shuttle."

Taffer shook his head. "For what you're thinking, too small."

CJ crossed his arms and grinned. "Then I'm damned close, aren't I? That was just their run-a-round vessel, wasn't it? Or maybe that boat had little to do with it at all, a convenient vehicle at the time to transport me from one point to another, or from the St. Petersburg Marina to a deep, open-water body dump site. Samuel Blight's wife, Nicole, may have had no idea her boat was being used for murder or she may be a player."

Taffer removed his sunglasses and ran his hand over his face as though he was trying to wipe away an annoying spider web. He put the sunglasses back on. "Here's the thing, Mister Clinton Joshua Washburn. This entire operation has gone to crap because they haven't actually started the stockpiling yet, if that's what they're doing. If they'd had weapons and explosives gathered at the Apollo Beach location like we thought they were preparing to do, and had started their shuttling, we'd have them and their ship now, but you arrived just in time to give Douglas the opportunity to break cover and tip his hand before he could get fully debriefed by us. Now they're playing this game of eliminating anybody and everybody associated with him while in the meantime, we suspect, they are writing up an entirely new game plan.

"The shuttling was to begin tomorrow, we think. Where it was coming from, Douglas wasn't able to find out. What vessel it would all be shuttled to, Douglas wasn't able to find out. The location of the other two pickup points along the US coastline, Douglas was not able to discover. He wasn't able to find out much of anything as far as the US side of the operation goes because he'd been in Ireland for the last few months, or maybe he did know a lot more but he didn't have time to pass it along to us. I say that because he had requested a meeting which was to take place tonight. That request came through only an hour before he met with you. What we did learn from him, though, is that whatever they are planning to do is to happen very soon, within the next week. And, since we'd not gotten confirmation on weapons shipment, we're not even sure that's what it is. It could be something else altogether. As a matter-of-fact, we are beginning to believe that some of what we thought we knew was as a result of false information being purposely leaked to us.

"By who?"

"That's not important right now because, Mister Washburn, all our efforts have gone south since you showed up. Why is it I should feel sorry for you in any way, or entertain the thought of involving you at all in this operation?"

"Because I'm already involved whether I want to be or not."

"If you went home you could become uninvolved."

Stella, who'd been watching the exchange from off to the side, stepped up close beside CJ. "My partner is one hell of an investigator. You should be excited to have him on your team." She pointed toward where Josh was talking with several agents. "You already have one Washburn. Now you have the opportunity to have three."

Agent Taffer's eyebrows went up. "Three?"

"As Clint's fiancée, I'm as good as a Washburn."

Taffer shook his head. "I don't believe it."

"I'm suddenly not feeling guilty anymore," CJ said.

Both Taffer and Stella looked at him.

"I thought that Douglas was killed because he came to see me, *tipped his hand* was the way you put it, Agent Taffer. Actually, it appears to me that making contact with you is what did the final hand-tipping. They were already suspecting him of something, having two people shadowing him. Then he was witnessed contacting you. That's what did it. My only involvement was that I was someone they saw him talking to after talking to you and before they had a chance to kill him."

Taffer's jaw tightened as he glared at CJ.

"I'm just a victim here, Agent Taffer. You all are the ones who got him killed."

Taffer pointed back the way they'd come, south toward the police barricades. "Out! Get out of my crime scene. Go do something tourist-like until you can get a flight back to Arizona. If you can't get one by tomorrow morning I'll get a court order and have you escorted."

"I'm a victim and a witness in this explosion," CJ said, "as well as a onetime suspect and witness in Douglas Rothbower's death. I don't think I should be leaving town."

"If I want you for anything I'll call the Tucson field office and have you interviewed via video conference."

CJ looked at Stella. She shrugged. He glanced over at Josh who appeared to be waist-deep in evidence gathering. And then he remembered the glimpses of news he'd spotted while waiting for Stella at the airport. The mysterious explosion in downtown St. Petersburg had the police baffled. There was some speculation that it was a terrorist group, seeing as the FBI and HLS had both shown their presence at the scene, but that was quickly overridden by the local news station reporting that there was rumor of gang retaliation for something or another, and a Federal spokesperson made a point of not denying the rumor. CJ recalled someone at the airport, who was also watching the news, saying to the person he was standing next to, "Gang violence in Tampa? You don't see that very often."

CJ wondered if the FBI started the rumor. No one was talking about anything having to do with the *Irish Republican Army*.

"Okay," CJ said. "You're the boss." He took Stella's arm. "Did you happen to notice what networks those satellite trucks were from, partner?"

She looked back toward where the trucks waited, just beyond the barricades, and then smiled. "CBS was one of them," she said. "Didn't notice the other."

He pointed. "Oh, look. There's a third one. Wonder if we can find CNN's number?" With that he started walking the two of them up the street.

"Hey!" Special Agent Taffer yelled at them.

CJ looked over his shoulder. "What?"

Taffer pointed toward a dirty gray Dodge Charger with government plates, the one Agent Coulter drove. "Make yourself comfortable over there. Don't talk to anyone and stay out of the way."

CJ looked at the Charger. "And do what? Stand around bored with our hands in our pockets? I'd rather go catch a cab, retrieve my replacement rental and make some phone calls." He swiveled his head to look up the street again. "It was easy to get by those cameras on the way in. Not so sure it's going to be that easy on the way out. Think they'll pay for a scoop? Lord knows this is turning into a rather expensive assignment. Hope my insurance covered the car."

"You didn't get the extra insurance?" Stella said.

"No. I figured my regular insurance would be sufficient."

"Is the regular insurance going to pay for your rental car being blown up?" Stella asked.

"If I explain to them that it was an Irish terrorist group, they should be okay with it, don't you think?"

"You know you can't be spreading that information around," Taffer said. "You'll have rioting in the streets, anti-Irish slogans written on walls, Irish families bullied. What do you want?"

"I want to be able to continue my investigation into Douglas' death as requested by my clients," CJ said. "That's clients, plural, both of whom want the same thing. You can go off and find your arms shipment or whatever the hell it is."

"The two are interlinked; you do know that don't you?"

"Of course. And if I discover something that'll help you, I would be quite happy..."

"Obligated," Taffer said.

"I'll be happy and *obligated* to inform you. On the flip side, I'd appreciate anything you find out about Douglas' death."

"If I do, it'd just be a courtesy. No obligation does the FBI have. If it was the organization that killed him, you will likely never know who it was. Hit men disappear into the rank and structure?"

"And then it may be simpler than that. Both of my clients want to know why. My Arizona client wants to know a bit more about Douglas' illegal second marriage, his birth name, his adopted name, his mother's name, his father's name and if said father is still alive. There are unanswered questions all over the place. His last will & testament comes into play to benefit who? What about the yet to be born child that Rebecca O'Reilly is carrying. There also appears to be an issue over where he is going to be buried, memorial services, cremation or not. Many fingers in the morbid pie. Much to do, Agent Taffer. Much to do."

Taffer's phone rang. He looked at it, pointed at the Dodge Charger again and said, "Wait there," and then walked away with the phone pressed to his ear.

CJ said to Stella, "Do you have your *iPad* thingy with you?"

She rolled her eyes. "My *iPad* thingy is in my purse."

"Good." He lead her over to the Charger. "Pull it out and Google something about a summit in Ireland."

"You know about Google, Clint? You becoming a techie on me?"

"Everybody knows about Google." He put his arm around her. "Not everyone knows how to Google like my girl, though."

"Your girl?"

"My partner."

"Better." Stella laughed and extracted the rectangular device from her purse.

"Is that new?" CJ asked, pointing at her purse.

Stella looked down. "What? My *iPad*?"

"No. The purse. Never saw it before."

"Very good, Clint. Nice of you to notice. Yes, it is new. Needed something that would hold my *iPad*, among other things."

"What other things?"

"I'm a woman. I have other things. Want to poke your hand in and find out."

CJ took a step back. "No. Just noticing is all. Bigger than what you usually carry."

"Yes it is. I have more things, like this *iPad*." With that she turned it on.

CJ leaned against the car, his arms crossed over his chest, and watched Stella's fingers dance across the face of the *iPad*. He hated having to type on the little smart phone screens, but he had to admit that the screens of these larger devices were intriguing. Maybe he'd have Stella show him how to use an *iPad*.

"The only thing I find is the 38th G8 summit, which was already held this year at Camp David."

"Is it held once a year?"

"I think so." She poked around for a time and then said, "Yes. It's once a year, in the summer, normally June or July."

"That doesn't sound like it's worth pursuing. What other kind of summit would Douglas have been referring to?"

"Hold on," Stella said, bit on her lip and swiped her finger up and down a couple of times. "The next summit location hasn't been announced yet, but the county of Fermanagh in Northern Ireland is on the list of prospects."

"That's rather interesting. When would that be?"

"June of next year."

"That's still nine months away. I don't see how it'd be relevant."

"Me neither."

"And what would they hope to accomplish with guns and explosives? I could see a demonstration to gain world attention, maybe world favor if it was done peacefully. Violence wouldn't be productive. I think that's been proven over the last half century."

"It's been proven over and over again, throughout the millennia," Stella said, "but it's still going on all over the world. There is always going to be some idiot who's able to talk a whole group of like-minded idiots into believing that killing someone or blowing someone up is going to progress their cause."

"True."

Stella put the *iPad* away and joined CJ, arms crossed, staring off into the distance.

"You didn't see anything about any other summit?"

"Nothing."

After a period of ensuing silence they noticed Josh and Agent Coulter break away from the activity in front of the coffee shop and rush their way. The two agents climbed into the Dodge Charger against which CJ and Stella were still leaning. CJ pushed off the vehicle and caught the passenger door before his son got it closed.

"Sorry, Dad," Josh said. "Can't talk right now."

"Where you going? What's happening?"

Josh looked over at Coulter who was pulling on his seatbelt. He shrugged and put the key in the ignition.

"They may have found the truck."

"Then I'm going with you."

"I don't think so."

"I'm the only one you have right now who really saw the truck so therefore can tell you for sure that it's the right one."

"We can't have civilians compromising a crime scene."

"Give me a break, Josh. We're in the business. We know what to do at a crime scene and you know that."

Josh looked over at Coulter again.

"Get in," Coulter said.

CJ and Stella were still buckling in the backseat when they cleared through the police barrier. "Wonder what Taffer will say when he finds out we've gone along on this?" he whispered to Stella.

"He said to stay near this car, didn't he?" she said.

CJ chuckled. "I love the way you think."

Chapter 22

"It was discovered in a parking lot on the northeast corner of Mirror Lake," Agent Coulter said as he turned the Charger east onto 4th Avenue, hardly slowing down. "No more than a mile away."

"That would make sense," Josh said. "After failing to run over Ms. Danohough, he probably called his buddy who met him in that parking lot with the IED. Afterwards, they dropped the truck back there and took off."

"Truck has to be stolen," CJ said. "They wouldn't be stupid enough to use their own."

"That's our assumption, yes. I suspect that the locals will know more about that by the time we get there."

There were two St. Petersburg Police cruisers blocking the truck and tying up a nearly full parking lot when they arrived. Coulter stopped the Charger behind one and they all piled out. While the agent presented his identification to one uniformed officer, CJ, Josh and Stella walked over to the truck. A second officer stepped out in front of them.

"FBI?" he said.

Josh pulled out his ID and the officer nodded and stepped aside.

"Yep. This is the one." CJ pointed to a dent in the driver's door. "That's where I slammed into it." They walked around to the front. "Broken headlight, and there's a chunk of glass missing. Will bet if the area around where Ms. Danohough's door was taken off is scoured closer, the missing glass will be found."

"It's been scoured," Josh said. "Likely already have it in evidence."

They continued around to the passenger side, the door of which was hanging open. The uniformed officer followed along. They all peered in. CJ pointed to a crucifix hanging from the rearview mirror. "Just before he threw the device, I saw that crucifix. Didn't even think about it until now."

"A bit ironic," Stella said.

"No doubt," Josh said. "Owner is not going to be happy once he learns that his truck was used in an attempted murder."

"She," CJ said.

"He or she," Josh corrected.

"I'll put money on she," CJ said. "The cleanliness of the truck and the crucifix tell me that the owner is female."

"He's right," the officer said. "The registration has already been pulled from the glove box. The owner is female."

CJ smiled at Josh.

"You're the guy who was there with Detective DuPont?" the officer said to CJ.

"Yes," CJ said.

"Washburn?"

CJ nodded. "Have you gotten any new word on Detective DuPont?"

"Just that he's recovering nicely at *St. Pete General*. Probably a day or two before they release him though."

Agent Coulter stepped up next to them. "The owner of the truck is a Pamela Moore. She lives alone in an apartment in Seminole, about ten miles west of here. Two officers are already with her. She claims that she didn't even know that the truck was gone."

"She's probably telling the truth," CJ said. "An apartment complex early on a Saturday morning is a great place and time to steal a vehicle. People are less likely to take notice compared to a weekday when they're all streaming out to go to work."

"Our forensics team is on the way," the officer said.

CJ considered what he'd noted over at the coffee shop. "I figured they'd be busy with the bombing site."

"You'd think." The officer glanced toward the agents and added so that only CJ could hear, "The FBI put a squash on it, wanted to use their own people."

CJ nodded his understanding. "Doubt they'll find anything except maybe fingerprints. The hand I saw was not gloved, so you may get lucky there." He looked over toward the lake and up and down the street. He noted a sign in front of the nearest building.

Mirror Lake, World's Largest SHUFFLEBOARD CLUB

"Shuffleboard?" he said.

"You've never heard of shuffleboard, Mister Washburn," Coulter said.

"Of course I've heard of shuffleboard. I just didn't know anyone actually played it."

"This is Florida, the favorite destination of mature adults. Shuffleboard, bingo, bocce ball, lawn bowling and pickleball are the sports to keep an eye on."

CJ turned his head to look directly at Agent Coulter. "Pickleball?"

"They play that down in Green Valley, Dad," Josh said.

CJ just looked at his son.

"Green Valley is south of Tucson."

"I know where Green Valley is, Josh. It's where the *really old people* live. I recall those words coming out of your mouth when you were maybe fourteen. How do you know so much about the r*eally old people*?"

"Dated a girl in high school whose grandparents lived there. We went to visit once."

"Did you play pickleball?"

"No, but we did play bingo."

Stella laughed and CJ smiled.

"If you all are through reminiscing," Agent Coulter said.

CJ took on his serious face. "Sorry."

"You're right. I doubt we're going to get much here. Still have to go through the motions, however."

CJ nodded and leaned back against the neighboring car with Stella and Josh. Looking at the truck, it was quite obvious there was nothing there. Pamela Moore was a tidy person, almost to the point of fastidious. The inside of the truck virtually sparkled. If the perps had left even a slice of fingernail, it would stick right out. He wondered if she'd been told about it being used to take off Ms. Danohough's door.

Except for people trying to negotiate their vehicles in and out of the parking lot, there were few gawkers. Passersby were pretty much ignoring the police cars with lights strobing. After a bit, one man in blue shorts and a shirt sporting scattered and angled images of palm trees and the word, Florida, walked up to the uniformed officer.

"Is it possible to get my car out?" he said.

"Which one is yours?" the officer asked.

The man pointed to the sky-blue Toyota Prius against which CJ was leaning.

Before the officer could respond, CJ, Stella and the two FBI agents surrounded the man.

Agent Coulter presented his ID. "FBI Special Agent Brian Coulter. Your name is?"

"I'm Willis Horton, Willis Patrick Horton the Second."

"Okay, Willis. We'd like to ask you a few questions."

"I just parked here," Willis said. "I don't know anything about anything."

"Chances are you didn't see anything, but we still need to ask. Was this truck here when you arrived?"

The man looked at the truck. "I don't think so."

"Are you sure?"

Willis looked at the truck again. "I'm sure. I believe there was a Jeep Wagoneer parked here. Can't say I really paid that much attention. I just parked and went straight in."

"Do you remember what time you arrived?" CJ asked.

"Of course I remember. I may be eighty-four but I've the mind of a forty-year-old. I parked at exactly 11:43 because I had a meeting at 12:00 with the shuffleboard activities committee. I like to be early."

Josh said to his father, "What was the exact time the bomb was thrown?"

"Between the manager of the coffee shop and a woman from across the street, it was either 11:47 or 11:48."

Josh turned back to the old man. "Were there many others arriving for this committee meeting?"

"Four others."

"Did any of them arrive after you?"

"I was the first so, yes, they all arrived after me."

"Are any still in the building?"

Willis thought for a minute and then said, "Ruth Bebee was getting ready to leave right behind me. She'd withdrawn to the ladies room. All the others left some time ago. She and I are kind of hitting it off, if you know what I mean. We hung around for a long time after the meeting and chatted. She has two Great Danes and I have a Tibetan Mastiff."

"Thank you, Mister Horton. Could you take us in and show us to Ms. Bebee?"

"Certainly. She's much younger than I, only about sixty-five. My son thinks she's too young for me. If I didn't know better I'd be thinking he wants her for himself. He's sixty-six and got divorced a few years back."

They were following along with Mister Horton as he led them into the building.

"But he has a fight on his hands if he thinks he's going to barge in on his old man's territory."

CJ looked at Stella and stifled a snicker. She poked him in the ribs. "Ouch!" he said.

When she realized he wasn't faking it, she said, "Sorry. I forgot."

They all stopped ten feet shy of the ladies' room, except for Stella. As she started to reach for the door to go in, a woman came out.

"Are you Ruth Bebee?" Stella said.

Appearing perplexed, the woman looked between Stella and the group of men sequestered behind her. "Yes."

"Ruth," Willis Horton said. "These folks are from the FBI."

"FBI?"

Again, Coulter produced his ID. "I'm Special Agent Ryan Coulter, Ms. Bebee. Please don't be alarmed. We're just trying to find witnesses to an event that occurred about the time you arrived here for your meeting."

"Oh."

"Could you follow us outside, please?"

She looked over at Willis.

"It's okay, Ruth," Willis said.

She nodded to the agent. "Sure. I guess so."

CJ held the door and they all filed outside, Stella last. She took CJ's hand and said, "How bad are your ribs?"

"Still sore. Throwing myself at the truck and then almost getting blown up haven't helped much in the healing process."

"How about your head?"

"An ignorable low-grade headache." They walked along hand-in-hand, well behind the group until Josh looked over his shoulder at them. They dropped hands. "I have to say, though, it all feels much better now that you're here."

"You're glad I came, then?"

"Most definitely, yes."

At the truck, Agent Coulter said, "Ms. Bebee, do you recall noticing this truck when you parked?"

"Yes, as a matter-of-fact, I do. And I'm still a bit irritated about it now that I'm reminded of it."

"Why's that? Tell us about it."

She pointed east. "I was coming from that direction on Mirror Lake Drive when I saw Willis' car parked right here. There was another car, like a jeep or something, starting to back out of the spot next to his car and I thought, 'Well, that's nice. I can park right next to Willis' pretty little Prius.' I really like his Prius. It's so quiet and he keeps it really clean."

"That's nice, Ms. Bebee."

"I'm hoping he'll take me for a ride in it one day."

"You do?" Willis said, appearing rather surprised.

"Yes, I do."

"I'm sure you and Mr. Horton can work that out," Coulter said. "We're just interested in the truck."

"Yes. Of course. Anyway, just as I got to the turn into the parking lot, this truck came barreling around me like it was a race or something and then cut me off. By the time I got to here," she pointed down to the ground upon which she was standing, "the truck was in my spot. I was considering stopping and giving the driver a piece of my mind when two men flew out of the truck, ran across the parking lot to another car and then sped away."

"Where, exactly, was *that* car parked?"

She turned and pointed to the next row over. "That's my Taurus over there. The yellow car. That's where they were parked. I took their spot as they pulled out. They almost backed into me as I came around."

"Can you remember anything about the men?" Josh said. "Description, what they were wearing?"

She shook her head. "No. Not really. The driver was taller than the other guy. The other guy was wearing a black T-shirt I think, and blue jeans. The driver, I don't know. Black shirt also, khaki-like pants maybe, not shorts. They both had dark hair, medium length. The other guy drove the car. That's about all I remember. It all happened so fast."

"How about the car? What do you recall about it?"

"Blue. I know it was blue, like a sedan. Not blue like Willis' car. Much darker."

"That's it? Anything else?"

She shook her head. "Don't know much about cars. It was a dark blue sedan."

"Any dents, scratches, license plate number? Was it licensed in Florida or another state?"

"I think I'd have noticed if it wasn't Florida, but I can't say I even looked."

"Okay. Thank you very much, Ms. Bebee." Agent Coulter presented her with a clipboard and pen. "Write down your contact information in case we have further questions." He added his card to the clipboard. "Please give me a call if you should think of anything else."

CJ and Stella leaned against one of the patrol cars. "So. What next?" Stella said.

"I don't know. I'd kind of like to get something to eat and then sit in a quiet place and think about it all for a bit."

"You've got my vote. All I've had today is a breakfast muffin and a cup of coffee. Airplane snacks don't count for much."

CJ had just straightened up to look up and down the street for a place to get some food when Ruth Bebee handed the clipboard back to Agent Coulter and said, "The driver of the car might be Irish."

"Irish?" Coulter said.

Everyone's attention was suddenly back on the woman

"Why do you say that, Ms. Bebee?" CJ said.

"Because of the flag decal."

"Where?"

"On the back window. It was green, white and orange; the national flag of the Republic of Ireland. Not to be confused with the Italian flag, green, white and red. It's the only European flag that has orange unless you consider the Royal Standard of the Netherlands, the official flag of the Dutch monarch, which really doesn't count as a flag of countries."

"You're certain it was a Republic of Ireland flag?" Coulter said.

"I know my flags, or at least a lot of them."

"And I can vouch for the fact that she knows all the European flags for sure," piped up Willis Horton.

Ruth Bebee nodded her head. "And I know what I saw."

While they were talking with Willis Horton and Ruth Bebee, dark clouds had started rolling in from the west and a breeze began picking up. As they moved vehicles to allow Willis Horton to get his car out, the rain began.

"I think we're done here," Agent Coulter said. "We'll let the locals do the forensics."

With that they returned to the bombing crime scene where evidence gathering had halted while everyone stood or sat undercover from the pouring rain. CJ, Stella and Josh jumped from Coulter's car to dash into Josh's rental in which they headed off to fetch CJ's new rental. An hour later and after only a minor amount of hassle and additional paperwork, CJ and Stella had their own wheels, and they were ready to take a break from it all.

"There's nothing more Stella and I can do at the crime scene," CJ said to Josh. "Why don't you head back over there. We're going to go find something to eat."

"You sure?"

CJ could tell that that was exactly what Josh wanted to do. He was an FBI agent and he wanted to be in on the middle of the investigation. "I'm sure. Go."

As Josh drove away, Stella said, "Give me the key."

"Why?"

"You've a head injury and a cracked rib so I'm driving. You're also not hearing so well."

"What?"

"I said...." She saw the grin on his face and took the key he was presenting.

"I've a chauffeur now," CJ said. "Nice."

"Where to?"

"The food is good at *Paddy McGee's Irish Pub*."

Chapter 23

Contrary to what CJ experienced the previous two days, *Paddy McGee's* appeared busy when they pulled the rental car into the parking lot. "It just occurred to me that it's Saturday night," CJ said. "Don't know if I want to fight a crowd."

"Normally, I'm good for a crowd," Stella said, "especially after a stressful day. But considering what's going on, having dinner at an Irish pub, I'm not so sure."

"You think the bombers are looking for us, and they're hanging out here hoping we'll show up? Maybe we should have kept Josh as a body guard."

She looked at him for a few seconds and then said, "Seriously?"

He made a face to indicate he wasn't serious.

Stella pushed her head back against the headrest. "I don't know what I'm worried about. I do have to say, though, that this whole Irish army thing does have me a bit spooked. Throwing bombs isn't supposed to happen in this country. And if it does, it should be coming from Middle East terrorists, not from Irish Nationalists."

"First of all," CJ said, "to put your mind at ease, the only reason they were doing this was to shut people up. By now they should be figuring out that it's too late, that whoever they're trying to silence is now talking to the FBI, that all their efforts have failed and that they'd be smart to cut their losses and run.

"Second of all, if they *are* after anybody, they're after Eveleen Danohough and Rebecca, and the two of them are likely someplace together, safe."

"Do you know where that is?"

He shook his head. "No. To be truthful with you, I kind of lost track of them when I begged Agent Taffer to provide someone to run me to the airport to meet you. Rebecca's car was across the street from the blast. The fact that her tires were flattened and the car was inside the cordoned off blast zone means she wasn't going anywhere with it. Ms Danohough's car was already out of commission and she was adamant about the fact that she wasn't going to drive around without a door. Being hit by the same truck from which the bomb was thrown makes it crime evidence anyway. If the two women went anywhere, they had to have been picked up."

"Maybe they're under FBI protection somewhere."

"Good point. I'll ask Josh next time I talk to him." He looked out through the steady drizzle, to the simple painted sign that read, *Paddy McGee's Irish Pub*. "In any case, maybe a happy-go-lucky crowd would be good for us right now."

Stella hit the button on her seatbelt, pulled out the key and put her hand on the door handle. "Okay, then. Let's do it. I hope the food is as good as you say because I'm hungry."

CJ opened the door to the pub for Stella and then followed her in. They stopped side-by-side, brushing water from their heads and shoulders and looking about. The crowd, though not as heavy as expected, was anything but happy-go-lucky. It was like any normal American restaurant, couples and groups sitting at tables, eating, drinking, conversing, music playing in be background, in this case, Irish folk music; a bit more subdued than they would have guessed. Two men sat at the bar watching a silent soccer game on one of three widescreen TVs in the room. Paddy's wife was behind the bar doing what bar-keeps do. The man CJ noted the day before was again on the grill and Hannah was picking up empty mugs from a table. As she crossed the room she glanced toward CJ and Stella and then stopped, her face lighting up in a smile. She shifted the mugs to one hand, held up a finger and then turned and ran past the bar, toward the back where CJ knew was Paddy's office. Seconds later she was back, Paddy right behind her. She stopped to get rid of the mugs as Paddy continued on, straight at CJ, a big grin on his face.

"*Céad Míle Fáilte* Mister Washburn!" he declared in a baritone loud enough to be heard in the parking lot, and wrapped his arms around CJ. "How the hell are you my friend?"

"I'm just fine, Paddy." CJ managed to break out of the hug and then noticed Rebecca O'Reilly had followed him out. He wondered if Ms. Danohough was here as well.

"You saved me sister's life. For that you will forever be an honored guest in me pub." Paddy turned to Stella and took her hand in both of his. "I am Paddy McGee."

"Stella Summers," Stella said, "CJ's partner."

"*Céad Míle Fáilte* my friend! You, as well, are my honored guest." He touched her burgundy hair. "You are maybe Irish?"

"No. Actually I'm half Scottish."

"Scottish!" He laughed. "We'll try not to hold that against you." He threw an arm around her. "Come with me. I'll give you the best table in the house. Did you know that Scotland was built by the Irish?"

"No, I didn't."

"It is true. There is Irish in all Scots."

"All Scots?"

"Well... there are some who say Scotland was settled by the Germans or the Greeks or the Egyptians or the Australians. However, when you start mixing them all together with strong Irish blood and heritage, all the way back to the *Dal Riata* in the 6th century, guess who rises to the top."

Stella grinned. "The Irish?"

Paddy removed his arm and pulled out a chair. "CJ, you have an intelligent and beautiful woman here. If I weren't already married to an intelligent and beautiful woman, I'd be having to ask you to leave."

"Fortunate for me then," CJ said.

They sat and then Paddy sat with them, his face and his tone becoming serious. "I must apologize for my countrymen. They mean well but go about it in a bad way."

"Bad isn't even the word for it, Paddy. They're trying to kill people to protect their mission which is to do what? Kill more people to make a point? And in the name of what? Your parents died because of this and if not for a little luck, and I do mean luck, so would have your sister. I wouldn't be calling them my countrymen if I were you."

"You are right, CJ, and it is *that* that keeps me awake at night."

Hannah dropped two menus on the table. "*Céad Míle Fáilte.* A couple of Guinness draughts, Mister Washburn?"

"That would be perfect," CJ said. "Hannah, this is my partner, Stella. Stella, this is Paddy's daughter, Hannah."

Hannah shook Stella's hand. "*Fáilte.* Nice to meet you."

"You, too," Stella said.

With that, Hannah departed and Paddy stood. "I'll check back after a time and see how you're doing. I'm truly glad you came."

As he walked away, Rebecca took his place and turned her eyes on Stella. "I'm Rebecca O'Reilly. Mister Washburn said you were here to assist in the investigation."

"That's right," Stella said.

"This has all turned so crazy. I just want it all to go away so I can just bury my husband. And apparently I can't even do that because your attorney says he doesn't belong to me, that he never was my husband."

Stella reached out and covered Rebecca's hand. "I'm so sorry."

Rebecca didn't pull away. "Everything Doug told me was a lie. I gave my life to him and he lied to me and then left me alone. Not only did he leave me once when he got himself killed, but now he's leaving me again to be returned to his *real* wife." She'd extracted her hand to make quote marks in the air with the word, *real*. "Every time I turn around there are more lies. What am I supposed to do now?"

"Your brother and his family," Stella said. "It looks like you have good people around you. All you can do right now is lean on them."

"That's all I've done since our parents died... until Doug came along. Now I'm back and I have a baby growing inside of me. Douglas' baby. The baby *he* didn't want." Rebecca stared at her hands for a time, eyes closed, weeping. "My brother has his own family to take care of. He doesn't need the burden of a second."

Hannah arrived with the two mugs of Guinness plus water for Rebecca as well as napkins and silverware.

"Thank you, *Awnya*," Rebecca said.

"Will be right back for your orders," Hannah said, putting her hand on her aunt's shoulder and then rushing away.

Stella pulled out one of the napkins and handed it to Rebecca. Rebecca stared at the napkin as though not knowing what to do with it and then dabbed at her eyes. She sniffled.

"What did you call her?" CJ asked of Rebecca.

"*Awnya*." She sniffled again and smiled. "It's pronounced like on and ya. On-ya, spelled A-W-N-Y-A. That's the Irish pronunciation for her name, H-A-N-N-A-H of which Americans say, *Han-a*. My brother has shifted to what her American friends call her, maybe his way of trying to maintain a father-daughter relationship with her. My sister-in-law, Maire, and I prefer the Irish form."

"*Awnya*," CJ said. "I like it."

The mood of the pub seemed livelier, people talking with more animation, often throwing glances toward CJ and Stella, ordering more drinks. The silence at the table, however, hung on for a time before CJ thought to ask about Ms. Danohough. "Where is Eveleen?"

Rebecca shrugged her shoulders. "Home, I guess. She was here for a while and then Eddie picked her up."

"Eddie?"

"Ed Hall. Her friend."

CJ recalled talking on the phone with Sandra at the *Coffee Bean Boutique*. "Her business partner?"

"Yes. I think he's her boyfriend, too, though I don't really know that for sure. I'm not really into my mother-in-law."

CJ glanced up at a nearby TV monitor and noticed it playing a news report about the bombing. There was no sound, but the dialogue between a pair of talking heads was being run across the bottom in rolling text. Stella followed his gaze.

"It was discovered earlier this afternoon that one of the individuals who may have been targeted by this bomber was Clinton Washburn, a private investigator from Arizona, the same Clinton Washburn who shot and killed serial killer Tommy Clark just one month ago, almost to the day."

The video had changed from a wide angle of the street in front of the coffee shop to a close-up of CJ talking with a uniformed police officer. The narration continued.

"Is there a connection between the two, that is the killing rampage in Arizona and the bombing here in Florida?"

"That's highly unlikely, though I don't think it's being overruled that this could be some kind of retaliation against him for killing Tommy Clark. The FBI is not being forthcoming in the motive behind the bombing, or who or what was the actual target. Was it Clinton Washburn or one of the people he was having coffee with, one of which, by-the-way, was St. Petersburg police detective, Parker DuPont. He was the only person seriously injured in the blast."

"There was something about a murder yesterday morning in which Mr. Washburn was a suspect. Tell us about that."

"That has turned out to be interesting. The body of one Douglas O'Reilly was discovered floating in the bay by passersby Friday morning. Within an hour Clinton Washburn was taken into custody by, believe-it-or-not, Detective DuPont."

"The same person who was injured in the blast this morning?"

"That's correct. But that's not all. Washburn was released only a few hours later. Then, yesterday afternoon, it was reported that the Hillsborough County Sheriff had to chase down and disable a run-a-way boat on Tampa Bay with Clinton Washburn on board. Details there are a bit sketchy, but that case was turned over to Detective DuPont after it was discovered that it was related to the morning murder.

"And here is another twist. Sitting at that table this morning with Mr. Washburn and Detective DuPont, when the bomb exploded, was the wife of the murdered man from yesterday morning, Rebecca O'Reilly, and his mother, Eveleen Danohough."

"I'd say coincidences are out the window here."

"We have now learned that the FBI agent who was called in to assist in the serial killing in Arizona a month ago has also been called in again to assist in this horrific event in Florida. He is Clinton Washburn's son, Special Agent Joshua Washburn."

The video changed once again to CJ, Josh and Stella getting out of Josh's rental, Agent Taffer walking toward them.

"The woman with them is Clinton's assistant, Stella Summers. It seems that she and Special Agent Washburn arrived in St. Petersburg this afternoon, together."

"This is getting more and more curious. Has there been anything at all as to the motive behind this bombing?"

"Next to nothing so far, but like I said, the FBI is being tight-lipped. Of course the first thing that came to mind was middle-east extremists and our own white supremacists, but no one has come forward to claim

responsibility. One rumor that popped up, but was immediately rejected, was the IRA."

"The Irish Republican Army?"

"Right. Like I said, it was rejected, even by the news media."

"Great!" CJ said and turned his attention back to the table. Rebecca was gone

"They could at least get it right," Stella said to CJ. "I'm your partner, not your assistant." After a few seconds of contemplative silence, Stella opened the menu and said, "So, what's on the agenda for tomorrow?"

"To be honest with you, I don't know if there's anything we can do. As far as the bombing and Douglas' murder, the FBI and the locals have control of that. Searching down the legality of the will and all is a bit out of our league. I'd say let's just hang around and play tourist."

"I feel bad for Rebecca. Is there anything we can do for her?"

"The only help we can give her is help she probably doesn't want, and that would be assistance in getting Douglas' affairs in order and shipping him to Indiana."

"I think she's angry enough at him that she may be more than happy to get rid of him," Stella said. "A woman scorned and all that."

"Maybe, but Eveleen Danohough may want to step into the fight. She'll have to prove that she's his mother first, which may be a challenge in US courts. Even with that, I don't know if she'd have power over Kassandra Rothbower, the legal wife in Indiana."

"Eveleen gave him up as a baby, abandoned him on the hospital doorstep. Doesn't she lose her right to him?"

"Abandoning him to an alleged illegal adoption. I don't know what kind of twist that'll put on it. In the end, though, I believe it'll all be for not. It all took place forty-three years ago in another country. There may involve a statute of limitations that will allow the courts to turn a blind eye and say that Douglas Rothbower is his legal name and his marriage of twenty-some years to Kassandra takes precedence over everything.

"I also believe Gianna Onassis will do whatever it takes to win this for her sister."

"What's Shepherd's Pie?" Stella asked of Hannah a minute later.

"You've never enjoyed Shepherd's Pie?" Hannah said. "That's like saying you've never had ice cream. You must not be Irish."

"I'm Scottish, actually."

"Oh! That's that cute little country to the north, just beyond the Irish Sea. They's fine people, they is, but they know little o' Shepherd's Pie. Will give you a break on that."

Stella just looked at her, apparently not sure what to say.

Hannah put a hand on her shoulder and grinned. "Don't take anything we say here in Paddy's seriously. Tis all in fun, except the Shepherd's pie. It be serious for your supper. Tis ground top sirloin o' beef sautéed with onions, peas, and carrots, all baked in a casserole. It be topped with mashed potatoes."

CJ tilted his head at Stella. She shrugged.

"Let's have two of those, *Awnya*."

Hannah grinned at the use of her Irish pronunciation. "Perfect. Refill on your Guinness?"

"Sure. Why not."

"So," Stella said after Hannah rushed away with their empty mugs in hand, "we're just going to hang around and play tourist?"

"I think we can do that and keep our ears and eyes open at the same time. Let's go sailing tomorrow."

"With your broken rib?"

"First of all, it's just cracked."

"What's the difference?"

"Second of all," added CJ, ignoring her question, "we let someone else do all the hosting, jibbing and tacking. We'll just sit, snuggle, and enjoy the day on the bay."

Stella considered it for a time. "I don't know. I'm not a water person."

"Neither am I. We won't be in the water. We'll be on the boat, wearing life vests and hats, smelling of sunscreen, enjoying the exhilaration of skimming across the surface under the power of a warm ocean breeze. What could possibly go wrong?"

Chapter 24

After arguing with Stella over who was going to carry her luggage into the hotel and then trying to hide the pain while hauling only her computer bag, all CJ wanted to do was remove the wrap and drown himself in a hot shower.

Stella helped him with the wrap, making a face at the huge bruise occupying his entire left side, pushed him into the shower and then joined him.

"I don't think I'm in shape enough for sexual calisthenics," he said.

"No sex," she said. "We're going to wash up and then I've got something special planned for you."

"No sex, huh? I can't wait." He pulled her chin up so that he could kiss her. "I might have to give you a raise."

She reached down and touched him. "It seems to me the raise is all yours, Mister No Calisthenics Guy. What I have in mind will most definitely take care of that."

CJ smiled, thinking that a little horizontal smooching might not be all that bad, but ten minutes later he lay on his side while Stella applied a bag of ice to his ribs, the smile, and any thought of sex, gone.

"The doctor should have mentioned this," Stella said. "Maybe you forgot."

"That's cold!" CJ complained. "I'm sure that if the doctor did mention ice, he didn't refer to it as, 'something special.' This is worse than when I got thrown around the boat. Can we go down and sit in the whirlpool after this?"

"No. No heat for at least three or four days. Rest and relaxation only."

"Tell that to the guy who threw a bomb at me."

"I also don't think sailing would be a good idea," Stella added.

"I'd think that'd be resting and relaxing while someone else did all the work."

She made a pouting face at him.

"You're a poop head."

She put her hands on her hips. "I'm a what?"

"No sex. No sailing. No whirlpool. What next?"

"No Superman stuff. No jumping tall buildings and rescuing maidens in distress."

"That proves it. You're a poop head."

"Say that one more time and I'll..."

"You'll what? Poop head! Poop head! Poop head!"

She hit him in the head with the bag of ice.

"Owww!"

Sunday morning dawned with Stella fetching CJ's pain medication and more ice. After the round of ice torture, he lay on his back until the meds took effect, watching Tampa's Bay News 9's morning special report on the bombing before switching over to CNN. No one had come forth to claim responsibility. Somehow or other the UIRA angle had not been picked up by any of the news agencies. CJ could see the FBI keeping tight lipped about it all, but he was surprised with the locals. He had to give a nod of respect to the St. Petersburg Police Force. Still...

"Something's not right about all this," CJ said to Stella.

"Someone threw a bomb in downtown St. Petersburg," she said. "What could possibly be right?"

"In Tucson, even with the FBI in the middle of it, there would have been detectives swarming the scene with their forensic teams, and a hell of a lot more uniforms. Other than Parker DuPont, who *I* called, I've seen no other detectives. The few uniforms that were present were nothing more than traffic guards, statement takers and lackeys for the Feds. The forensic team that was there was strictly FBI."

"Okay," Stella nodded. "I see what you mean, but..."

"But what?"

"I don't know. Just *but*. Where're you going with this?"

CJ pointed at the TV. "That's why no one is picking up on the Northern Ireland connection. The Feds have a lid on it, and I mean a tight lid. It's also why when we threatened to talk to the press yesterday, Taffer caved so quickly. It was either that or lock us up somewhere and I don't think he's ready to go that route just yet."

He looked up at the ceiling for a few seconds. "And there's something else, and this didn't click with me until just now."

"What's that?"

"I heard a couple of agents talking about the fact that the HDRU was placed on standby. It should have been one of those 'Oh my God!' moments right then, that is if my head hadn't still been ringing bells."

"What's the HDRU?"

"The Hazardous Device Response Unit."

"A bomb is a hazardous device. Why should that be unusual?"

"The original mission of the HDRU, when it was established seven or eight years ago, was to locate and diffuse WMDs, not small home-made IEDs."

"W... M... D?" Stella said. "Weapons of Mass..."

"Destruction. That's right."

"Oh... my... God," Stella said in a whisper.

"Exactly. Chemical or Nuclear yield," he continued, "and there are only two people who can order the deployment of the HDRU; the Director of the FBI and the Executive Assistant Director for Counterterrorism and Counterintelligence. At least, that's the way it used to be. Maybe their scope has been expanded to include smaller high explosive devices."

"If it hasn't, that's scary."

"Scary indeed."

"How do you know this stuff?"

"I knew someone in border patrol when I was still in uniform. They ran a drill with the HDRU to which I was *unofficially* invited."

After a few minutes of contemplative silence while staring at the TV, Stella said, "Before you started talking about this stuff, I was hungry. Now I've lost my appetite."

"Let's go down to breakfast anyway. I'm sure your appetite will return. I'll call Josh and see if he's ready to join us."

Stella's appetite did indeed return. CJ watched her eat like it was her last meal. Halfway through the breakfast, Josh arrived.

After he placed his order, they discussed weather and life in Denver, a city neither CJ or Stella had ever visited. When Josh's eggs arrived, CJ said, "Any new news on the bombing event?"

"Nothing I can really talk about."

CJ considered giving him a hard time about not trusting his old man, then, instead, went straight for the heart of his thoughts.

"Why was the HDRU deployed?"

Josh's mouth dropped open for just a second and then closed. He squinted at his dad. "To my knowledge the HDRU has not been deployed, and I think I'd know. Where're you getting your information?"

"Then let me rephrase my question. Why has the HDRU been placed in standby?"

"Then let me restate *my* question. Where are you getting your information?"

"This is bigger than just a few guns and IEDs, isn't it, Josh?"

"Dad, who the hell have you been talking to?"

"Hey, guys," Stella said. "Stop asking each other questions and start giving some answers. Josh, I think we deserve to know the seriousness of this whole mess."

"I need to know where the leak is," Josh said. "The lid on this is tight as hell."

"The lid is a tad loose, Josh," CJ said. "It's not as though someone is purposefully whispering secrets to whoever will listen. I've got ears and enough knowledge to make conclusions out of snippets of what I hear. Your agents need to be more aware of who's hanging near them when they start discussing what they're doing, what's going on. If I can put two and two together, so can the people manning the satellite trucks and some of them have long range microphones. The lid isn't tight enough."

Josh took a deep breath and blew it out.

CJ leaned forward, pushing his plate out of the way and dropping his voice. "I've heard enough to know that a WMD of some sort may be involved. I've also heard enough to speculate that it's somewhere in this area right now or onboard a cargo ship due to drop anchor just offshore sometime today, if it's not there already. Is it chemical or nuclear?"

"Damn it, Dad! You know I can't say anything."

Stella leaned forward. "Here's a question I think you *could* answer, Josh. If you were living here, in Florida, with a wife and a baby, would you, right now, be thinking that it'd be a good time for them to visit her parents in Colorado?"

Josh considered the question for a time and then leaned back and smiled. "No," he said.

Stella looked at CJ, who had raised his eyebrows at her. "Nice approach," he said. "It's big enough to bring in the HDRU, but not big enough to worry about evacuating loved ones. Therefore, it's chemical and it's small." He turned to Josh. "Is your Intel good enough that you know exactly what it is, how big it is and what it's intended target is?"

"No."

"No to what part?"

"Target."

CJ leaned back in his chair in contemplation. After a time he said, "I think Douglas knew. I believe he'd just found out but was killed before he could impart his knowledge to his handler."

"Why do you say that?"

"It's more of a hunch than anything. One word he let slip to me was *summit*. I had Stella do a little *Goggling* to see if she could find anything having to do with summit and Ireland. She came up with the G8 summit in June of next year in Fermanagh."

Josh raised his eyebrows.

"That's in Northern Ireland," CJ added.

"I know where Fermanagh is, Dad. It's interesting, but nine months out? It's a long reach."

"Agreed. What other summit is in the works, likely before the end of the year?"

"Certainly none that I know of," Josh said. "Are you sure he used the word, *summit*?"

"Yes."

"I'll have to mention it to Agent Taffer."

"I already did, yesterday. He certainly found it interesting as well, and, like you, appeared to immediately dismiss it."

"I'm sure he didn't dismiss it, Dad. We can't dismiss anything. He probably passed it on to Washington for others to consider in the longer time-line. Right here, on the ground, we're thinking a much shorter time-line."

"Hm," CJ nodded.

"How short?" Stella asked.

"A few days; a few weeks."

"Are you thinking within our borders versus Northern Ireland?" CJ asked.

"That's exactly what I'm thinking, though it hasn't been voiced as yet from the bosses. It may be brought up at this morning's briefing, which I have to be at in," he looked at his watch, "fifty-two minutes."

Josh finished off his meal, pushed back and gulped down the remainder of his coffee. "I'll catch up with you guys later. What are you planning for the day?"

CJ shrugged. "Haven't put a lot of thought into it as yet. Might go sailing."

"Sailing?" Josh looked at Stella. "He's kidding, right?"

"He shouldn't be going out on a boat with those ribs, so yes, I hope he's kidding."

After Josh walked away, Stella said, "You are kidding, aren't you?"

"If you insist."

"I insist. So, what now?"

"Let's see if we can find Ms. Eveleen Danohough."

"Why?"

"Because I think it might be important to find out who Douglas' father is, which is an item on my checklist of things to accomplish for Gianna."

"You think he's still alive?"

"I think the chances are high. I also think that she's much more involved with all of this than she's letting on, and that if that's the case we may not be able to find her."

"Why's that?"

"Because she has either gone deep into hiding from UIRA or she's dead. She wasn't at Paddy McGee's last night so I think she's hiding somewhere."

"If she's a co-founder, why would she have to hide from them and why would they want to kill her?"

"Her son was an FBI informant. Anyone he might have talked to is a loose end UIRA can't have hanging around. They're cutting all loose ends to try and salvage their mission."

Stella sat back and stared at CJ, her mouth twisted into a thoughtful pose. "Rebecca is a loose end as well," she said after a time.

"As may be Paddy McGee and his family."

Chapter 25

Not surprisingly, Eveleen's cell phone went to voice mail, as did her business phone at *Coffee Bean Boutique*. CJ then called Rebecca.

"Good morning, Rebecca," CJ said when she answered. "How are you feeling this morning?"

"Physically, I'm fine. Mentally, I'm a wreck still happening."

"I'm very sorry. Anything I can do to help?"

"I don't know," she said. After a few seconds she added, "I don't think so."

"What I called about is Eveleen. She's not picking up on the numbers I have for her. Do you have any idea where she is?"

"No, I don't."

"You mentioned last night that her friend, Eddie Hall, picked her up. Do you know how we could get in touch with him? Maybe she spent the night at his place."

"Yes. Just a second." There was silence until she returned. "I have no idea where he lives so I don't have an address, but I do have a phone number." She recited it to him. "His cell, I think."

"Thank you. Did you go home last night?"

"I stayed at my brother's."

"Good," CJ said.

After disconnecting with Rebecca, CJ dialed Eddie's number, and then for the third time, left a voice mail.

"Now what?" Stella said. "Think you should check in with Gianna?"

He nodded and hit Gianna's speed dial number.

"CJ!" Gianna said. "I was about to call you. Was wrapped up with Kassandra all day yesterday; didn't see the news about the bombing until late last night, your name and photo in the middle of it. How are you doing?"

"Not too bad this morning, Gianna. A little banged up but my favorite nurse is here with me now."

"Nurse?"

"Stella."

"Of course. Good."

"Stella thought it'd be a good idea I call and give you a report, see if there's anything I can be doing for you on this end as far shipping Douglas back to Indiana."

"I've got it pretty well covered, although the St. Petersburg police haven't released the body yet. If you've developed any pull on that side, it'd be appreciated."

"I'll see what I can do. My best contact, however, is in the hospital."

"Detective DuPont?"

"Right. I'll go by and see him this morning."

"The other thing," Gianna said, "is that I'm hitting a brick wall with Eveleen Danohough, the woman claiming to be Douglas' natural mother. Is there any doubt in your mind that she is legitimate?"

"None at all. She's the real deal."

"Then I feel sorry for her, but I'll still have to break the wall down."

"Is it going to be a problem?"

"No."

"What about Rebecca O'Reilly?" CJ asked.

"She has no leg to stand on. The marriage will be recognized neither here in the United States, nor in Ireland."

"She's going to be left high and dry then."

"Afraid so. What do you know about her?"

"She doesn't deserve it," CJ said. "That I do know."

"Will she land on her feet?"

"She has support from her brother and his family and a part-time job in her brother's Irish pub, which will likely turn into full time for a while. In six months, though, she's going to become a single mom. Life is about to get rough."

"I've got the picture." She was silent for a time. "Tell me about the bombing. How is it that this is all tying together with Douglas' name on the bow?"

CJ considered the question for a few seconds and then said, "That part I'd rather pass to you in a means that is more secure than a couple of cell phones. I don't believe, though, that it's of immediate importance to what you have to deal with concerning wills, marriages, burial rights and the like."

"I'll take your word on that, CJ, and look forward to the entire report at a later time. What more do you think you have to do, or is it time to go home?"

CJ looked over at Stella. "Stella and I are thinking about playing tourist for a little while. I also would like to meet with Eveleen Danohough at least once more. For what reason, I'm not even sure. I do want to ask her about Doug's real father. Would that be important to know for what you have to do?"

"At one time I thought it'd be important. Now, even if he should still be alive, I have my doubts. I don't really know how productive having that knowledge would even be. Is that a worm can worth opening?"

"Or is it just an old, empty can turning rusty?"

"Another of your interesting analogies, CJ?"

"My apologies. I have to say, though, it is an itch that has been growing slowly..."

"And until you scratch it..."

"You know me too well, Gianna."

Gianna laughed. "Do what you feel you have to do, CJ. When you two are ready, go back to Tucson. If I need you for anything else, I'll let you know."

CJ put his phone down and said to Stella, "Let's go visit Detective DuPont. Look up the address of the hospital on your *iPad* thingy."

"What hospital? I'm sure there's more than one."

"The cop yesterday said, *St. Pete General*. See if you can find that."

When Stella did, they finished off their coffee and vacated the hotel restaurant.

It was only about eight miles, or twenty minutes, to the hospital according to the GPS, but with taking precautions–studying people in the lobby and anyone hanging around outside, looking for suspicious characters sitting in a car by themselves, checking to be sure no cars moved shortly after they pulled onto the street, changing routes four times in an effort to reveal if anyone was following them–they arrived in the hospital parking lot thirty-three minutes later.

"You're starting to freak me out a little here, Clint," Stella said.

"Sometimes I feel like I'm freaking myself out, but after yesterday morning I just can't help it. Common sense tells me they're done, but I can't get that to override my paranoia."

They sat in silence for another five minutes looking about, checking faces, watching for eyes having more than a glancing interest with two people sitting in a car.

"Okay?" CJ said.

"Okay," Stella said.

They got out and entered through the main doors of the hospital.

Parker DuPont was sitting in a chair, a bandage engulfing his head, his arm in a cast, nestled inside a sling, talking to a boy of about nine. Another boy and a girl, each in their teens, stood to the side, next to a woman. The older boy impressed CJ as being a younger version of Parker.

"CJ Washburn!" Parker said when he spotted the two of them at the door. "Come in. Come in. I was hoping you'd drop by."

They entered and Parker went on with introductions.

"This is my family. The tallest, but not for too much longer it appears, is my wife, Gracie. Challenging her in height is Blake, fifteen, then Tracy, thirteen and Scott here at nine." Talking to his family, he said, "Guys, this is CJ Washburn, the private eye I told you about from Arizona. And this, I assume, is Stella...?"

"Summers," Stella finished for him.

"Stella Summers, CJ's partner."

There were handshakes and good-to-meet-yous all around followed by concerns from Mrs. DuPont on how CJ and the two women faired in the explosion.

After that report, CJ said, "How are you doing, Parker? Doesn't appear the damage was major."

"Not bad at all. The nail actually fell out in the ambulance. I can already hear my new title floating around the precinct. A confidential source is telling me that there is talk of putting it on a welcome back banner when I return." He drew his free hand across the space in front of his face. "Hardhead DuPont!"

"You're never going to shake the name if they do," CJ said.

Parker snorted.

"Can we call you, Hardhead Dad?" Scott chimed in.

Parker hugged his son with his good arm. "As long as you say it with a smile on your face." To his wife, Parker said, "Can I have a few moments with these guys?"

"Of course," she said.

With no prodding, Blake grabbed Scott by his shirt sleeve and said, "Come on, Scott. Dad's having a meeting."

"We'll come back in about fifteen minutes," Gracie said. She bent over to give him a kiss on the cheek. "See you later, Hardhead."

He reached out to slap her on the butt and she playfully scooted out of his reach.

"Nice to meet you all," she said as they filed out the door.

"Nice family," CJ said after Parker's wife and kids had left and he'd propped himself upon the edge of the bed. "When are you getting out of here?"

"Believe it or not, about noon today I've been told. I haven't gotten any information about the bombing other than what I've been able to see on the news. My police force buddies keep saying they don't know anything and John Taffer won't tell me anything. What the hell is going on?"

"You know about the *United Irish Republican Army*," CJ said, more as a statement than a question.

"Yeah. I was there, remember, when you were drilling Danohough, just before all hell broke loose?"

"Well, here's what we've come up with." CJ went on to tell him about overhearing agents talking about the FBI placing the HDRU on standby.

Parker's mouth fell open and then he came upright in his chair, his eyes shifting to the doorway. Stella followed his gaze, saw no one there, and said, "I know what you're thinking, but we don't believe it's as bad as it sounds."

"HDRU means nuclear, doesn't it?" Parker looked between CJ and Stella.

"Nuclear or chemical," CJ said. "However, in this case the Feds believe it's chemical and small. Not a threat to the public as a whole, that is not to the extent that an evacuation would be a consideration."

"You're sure?"

CJ blew out a lungful of air. "No. Not one hundred percent. The agent I talked with I'm certain was being straight forward with what he knew, though I'm not convinced he knows everything. You've been watching the news. As you've seen there's been no mention of such a device. I'm sure the Feds are sharing information strictly on a need-to-know basis."

"That's standard ops with them," Parker said. "They never divulge anything unless there's a reason. You sure you're not being fed just enough to keep you off their backs? You heard something and now they're covering it over and downplaying it, at the same time making like their being nicey nice with you?"

"If it had come from Taffer, or any of his agents for that matter, I'd say you'd probably be right."

"Ah." Parker sat back again, adjusted his casted arm a bit and said, nodding his head slowly, "Your source is your son, then. He's here I assume?"

"Yes."

"You don't think he'd try to steer you wrong?"

"He may try to avoid telling me, which, of course, he did, but once he realized I was already putting two and two together, he divulged what he knew. I just don't know that he's been told everything. He's an import from Denver and a new agent. How much of the big picture is Taffer really going to give him?"

"My next question exactly," Parker said. "And here is another question. Have you seen any of my people around the crime scene; forensics, detectives, uniforms... somebody?"

CJ shook his head. "Other than first responders and traffic control, *nada*."

"That's been my understanding. Taffer has shut us out except for Doug O'Reilly's murder and your little boat incident. Seeing as I'm out for a time, Donald Gorky has taken over my cases, which means, by-the-way, you'll be hearing from him probably tomorrow, so don't leave town."

"Why should he want to talk to me?"

"Standard procedure when taking over another detective's case. Helps get familiar. You weren't planning on leaving, where you?"

CJ looked at Stella. She shrugged her shoulders.

"No, can't say we were, wanting to keep our options open, taking one thing at a time. We're trying to stay focused on what we came here for to begin with, which was Douglas Rothbower. With his death, his alias and another wife, things have become a bit more complicated."

"Add in his relationship with UIRA and the FBI," Stella said, "and the fact that his mother, his second wife, and Clint have all been placed on someone's hit list, I don't see how we *could* leave."

"So," CJ said. "there you have it."

"Good." Parker said. He cleared his throat, looked toward the door and then back at CJ. "The thing is, I have an ulterior motive for wanting you to stay."

CJ waited a few seconds. When nothing more came from Parker, he said, "And that is?"

Parker cleared his throat again. "I'd like to ride with you guys... ah... guy and lady."

Stella raised her eyebrows at him.

"You want to ride with us?" CJ said. "Why? And what would your captain say?"

"I'm now on leave and when I do return, with my right wing hobbled, I'll be stuck on a desk until I can prove my worth on the firing range. I've a hunch that's going to be a while. What I do in my off time is of no concern to the captain."

"I'd be willing to bet the captain has a different take on that."

"Maybe, but I don't care."

"So you want to ride with us because you don't want to ride a desk," CJ said.

"There's more to it than that. First of all, I know the area. I'd do a better job than your GPS. Second, I not only know the case, er... ah, cases involved here, I am a victim. Third, I want to learn how to do what you do."

"What we do?"

"Private Investigations. How did you become a PI? What did it take? How hard was it to find clients? What would you have done different if you had to start over?"

"You're thinking of quitting the force and becoming a PI?"

"Been playing with the thought for almost a year now. You showing up pulled it off the backburner, so to speak."

CJ started to ask what the real motivation was, if it by chance happened to be the same reason CJ had when he turned in his badge and hung his shingle, that is to save his marriage. Before he could open his mouth, Stella responded.

"Having someone along who knows the streets might not be a bad idea." She looked up at CJ. "We'll likely be around only another day or two. What do you think?"

CJ was surprised. "Sure." Questioning Parker's real motivation when his family was about to return to the room might not be a good idea. There'd be plenty of time to talk to him out in the field. "Why not?"

Chapter 26

After selecting a quiet outdoor table, CJ and Stella examined *Fresco's Waterfront Bistro*'s lunch menu. From where they sat at the foot of *The Pier* they could view Tampa Bay in the background, spires of sailboats in the foreground. CJ had given Stella a tour of the various piers from where they could look down at the activity around the boats on this early Sunday afternoon. He was hoping that she'd catch the sailing bug that had taken seed in him. So far, he couldn't tell. She hadn't said much.

"So what do you think?" CJ said.

"I think I'll have the Chicken Quesadilla."

CJ started to say that he meant, "What do you think about sailing?" After a few seconds of deliberation, he decided to let it slide for a bit longer.

"Chicken?" he said. "We're on the Florida coast. You can't get fish any fresher than right here."

"I'm not a fish person."

CJ knew this about Stella, however... "Fish in Arizona is not the same as Florida." He pointed down at his menu. "I'm having the Cajun Fried Grouper Sandwich."

"First of all, I don't like fish no matter what state I'm in. Second, if I did decide to try something that might hint of fish, I certainly wouldn't get excited about grouper. Just the name sounds about as appealing as pickled pig lips."

CJ laughed so hard he had to hug his cracked rib. "Oh, that hurt."

"Sorry."

"Grouper," he said once he had settled, "is just another big fish. Variety's can vary from ten or twenty pounds to hundreds."

"I don't care how big it is. It's still fish and I still don't want to eat it."

"Suit yourself," CJ said. "I don't see pickled pig lips on the menu, though."

She stuck her tongue out at him and then looked across at a couple coming toward them, one of whom had a cast on his right arm. "Here's Parker and Gracie."

CJ and Detective DuPont had agreed that when he was released from the hospital, Parker would call and they'd meet up. When the call came the two of them decided upon *Fresco's Waterfront Bistro* near *The Pier* for lunch, DuPont stating that he was anxious for some real food.

"I agreed to drop him off somewhere to meet up with you guys, against my better judgment by-the-way," Gracie said. "However, when I heard him say to you on the phone that he'd meet you here for lunch, I decided I was going to get something out of this for myself. Before I could say it to him, he asked me to go with him. Can you believe that? My husband asked me out on a date without my hinting first."

Parker started to open his mouth but Gracie put a finger up to his lips. "Don't you even say something that'll destroy my illusion.

"So," she continued, "I dropped the kids home and here we are. We haven't been out to eat together without them since I don't know when."

"December," Parker said as he pulled out a chair for his wife so she could sit across from Stella.

"Sounds about right," Gracie said, "And when we're in the middle of a nice evening together, he inevitably gets a call. He's forced to be off duty now and can't be called in, so I'm taking advantage. If I'd known it was this easy to get his attention, I'd have driven a nail into his head a long time ago."

CJ laughed again and then groaned.

In the hour or so that they'd hung around the hospital, Stella and Gracie had become good friends, hitting it off like they'd known each other for years.

Parker picked up a menu. "Have you ordered yet?"

"No," CJ said. "Just got here."

The table went silent while everyone looked over their menu. After they placed their orders, Gracie said to her husband, "Are you sure you're going to be okay running around? I think you should be resting. The doctor said to take it easy."

"First of all, the nurses watched me all night," Parker said, "and the nail in the head did no damage. Barely broke the skin. Any insanity you see has always been there."

"True," Gracie said.

He made a face at her. "You don't have to agree with me."

"Tis my job, Sweetie."

"With my right arm in a cast I can't carry a weapon or sign credit card slips. I'm not even supposed to drive. How much damage can I do?"

"To you or someone else?"

"My wife is a comedian," Parker said. "I keep saying she should take it on the road."

Gracie made the same face at him that he'd made at her.

"How long have you been married?" Stella asked.

"On a good day it seems like yesterday," Gracie said. "On a bad day it's more like forever."

"My comedian point again," Parker said. "We will have been married nineteen years this coming spring, and it has all been blissful."

Gracie snorted and then reached over and squeezed Parker's hand.

"So, when are *you two* getting married?" Gracie said.

CJ and Stella looked at each other.

"When he first asked me," Stella said, "he wanted to run off to Las Vegas right then."

"We were kind of in the middle of a case," CJ said, "so I guess the timing could have been a bit better."

"*Kind of* in the middle of a case?" Stella said. "We were being pursued by the police and the FBI." She looked across at Gracie. "His proposal was that if we got married right away we'd not be forced to testify against each other when we got caught."

Gracie's open mouth and wide eyes told Stella that Parker's wife didn't know anything about CJ's history. She said to Parker, "Clint led me to believe that he'd told you about the Tommy Clark case."

"He did, but I don't share a whole lot of my work with my wife. He certainly didn't tell me about wanting to run to Las Vegas to get married, though."

"This sounds like a very interesting story," Gracie said. "Start telling."

And so, Stella and CJ did, finishing up about the time coffee was ordered and empty plates were taken.

"So your reason for coming here was because Tommy Clark killed your lawyer's niece?" Gracie said.

"Exactly," Stella said. "And it seems this nightmare is never going to end."

"That's the thing about nightmares." Gracie took a sip of her coffee and pushed her chair back. "Seeing as you still have things to do to close down *this* nightmare and you're dragging my husband into it, I guess I'll take my leave."

"I'm glad you came for lunch," Stella said.

"Me too. Please bring him back in one piece. No more trips to the emergency room, thank you very much. Have had enough of that with the kids and he's not nearly as resilient as they are."

"We'll guard him with our lives," CJ said.

Parker just rolled his eyes.

"When you drop him off, why don't you stay for dinner?" Gracie said. "Meals out are going to get old after awhile."

Stella looked at CJ, who tilted his head in agreement. "Thank you. We'd like that."

After Gracie left, Stella said to Parker, "I like your wife."

"Yeah. Me too," Parker said. "So what's on your agenda for the afternoon? How can I be of help?"

"I want to find out who Douglas' real father was," CJ said. "For that we need to find Ms. Danohough. Rebecca said she was picked up by Eddie Hall. We can try her residence, though I doubt she'll be there. Since he may be her boyfriend and business partner, I'd say if we find him we'll find her."

"Business partner?" Parker said. "The *Coffee Bean Boutique*?"

"Yes."

Parker pulled out his phone. "That'll be easy."

It wasn't as easy as Parker thought it was going to be. After more than thirty minutes of Sunday afternoon runaround and mumbled unfavorable sentiments for a few of his fellow human beings, he said, "Got it! And you're not going to believe it."

CJ sat back in his chair. "Don't tell me. Apollo Beach."

"You're good. The seven thousand block of Fox Hill Drive."

"Did you come up with a phone number other than his cell phone?" CJ asked.

Parker shook his head. "No. I say let's head over there. You have a GPS in your car, I assume. If not we can use the app off my phone."

"We have the GPS. Wouldn't you want to go in with official backup?" Stella said. "This may be the nest or whatever."

"Or it could be just a coincidence," the detective said. "You believe in coincidences, don't you?"

CJ snorted. "I say let's go eye-ball it, see what vehicles might be parked on the driveway. Maybe you can get a plate number or two. I figure we'll either find Ms. Danohough and her boyfriend or, as Stella suggested, a nest of critters."

"If we do see anything that looks suspicious," Parker said, "we can't do anything but call it in. With me officially off duty, we are all just civilians."

Stella put her hand on CJ's arm. "That's just fine with us. I think CJ has had enough excitement for a weekend anyway."

Two minutes later, lunch tab paid, they sat in the car waiting for the air conditioner to cool it down while Stella punched the address into the GPS. When nothing came up she pulled out her iPad, brought up MapQuest and, again, put in the address. Just as with the GPS, no such address was found. She searched for just the street. When that produced nothing she said, "There's no Fox Hill Drive in Apollo Beach. This is bogus."

They all sat back in silence.

"Well I guess," CJ said after a time, "we ought to do what we should have done in the first place."

"What's that?" Stella asked.

"Go to Ms. Danohough's address. We've been assuming she's not there because we figured she'd gone off with Ed Hall so as to stay out of sight of whoever is trying to kill her. Could it be that she's simply keeping him with her as her bodyguard, so to speak?"

"Good point," Parker said. "Why the bogus address though? Where does he really live?"

"That's a very good question."

CJ dug out Danohough's address he'd received from Rebecca. Stella loaded it into the GPS and a minute later, they were on their way. Stella drove because the pain killer was making CJ feel a little woozy, almost nauseous. As she pulled out onto the street, CJ leaned his seat back and closed his eyes.

By the time they got to Danohough's apartment building, Stella looked like she was ready to shoot either the GPS or Detective DuPont sitting in the backseat overriding the GPS's irritating voice with his own version of how to get there. That was one thing CJ knew about Stella; she didn't like backseat drivers, especially when she was following a GPS.

"It's a bottom floor apartment," DuPont said and opened the car door. "I'm just along for the ride, so you guys can do the talking."

They all got out and gathered at the front of the car. "You're our consultant," Stella said.

"Seems ass backwards," CJ said. "It's your city."

"Officially, I'm not even here," Parker said. "I'm like the fly on the wall. Are either of you two packin'?"

"I told you the other day," CJ said. "Didn't want to go through the paperwork on the flight, so no."

Parker looked at Stella.

"Well..." she said, looking between the two men. "I might be."

CJ's mouth dropped open. "You're carrying? Why didn't I know?"

"You never asked."

"You took it on the plane?"

"I learned what to do. Got a hard-sided lockable case. Declared it at check in. Did the paperwork. Wasn't that hard."

Parker laughed, shaking his head. "A tad ironic, I'd say. We have a police detective, a licensed private investigator who's an ex-cop, and a yet to be licensed PI in training who's never been a cop. Guess who's packin'."

CJ snorted.

"I should have guessed by the purse she's carrying," Parker added.

"Is that what you meant by 'among other things' yesterday when I first noticed the new purse?" CJ asked.

"Yes."

"I do have to say, though," Parker said, "I don't know about the reciprocity between Arizona and Florida for carrying a concealed weapon. I'd have to look it up."

"Florida recognizes my Arizona license," Stella said.

"You're sure?"

Stella started to pull out her iPad. "I can bring up the reciprocal agreements on the Arizona Department of Public Safety website if you'd like."

Parker held up his hand. "I believe you." He turned to CJ. "Is she any good with it?"

"I can't say I even know. How embarrassing is that?"

"Before I'd marry her, I'd want to find out. You may have to brush up on your own skills. Have you seen it?"

"Of course I've seen it. It's a pink SIG Sauer MOS-22. She's had it for a few years."

"Pink?"

"I'm a girl," Stella said. "Deal with it."

"Not much punch in a little pink twenty-two," Parker said.

"It's enough if you hit what you're aiming at," Stella said. "Guys have to carry big guns in case they miss."

"Ha ha. You and my wife ought to go on the standup comedian circuit together."

"We could be the Hot Packin' Dick Wives."

Parker laughed, but CJ winced and rubbed his stomach.

"You okay, Clint?" Stella said.

"Stomach's a little uneasy. It'll pass."

"Probably the grouper."

CJ snorted.

They entered the building and navigated their way to Apartment 107. Approximately eight inches below the numbers on the door was a peep hole. CJ watched it closely after Stella pushed the doorbell, a habit that he picked up from years on the police force. Seconds passed but there came no response. She rang it again. This time a shadow passed across the peep hole as though someone stepped up close to look.

"Did you see that?" CJ said.

"Yeah," Parker said. "There's definitely someone in there and they're not answering the door."

CJ knocked on the door. "Ms. Danohough! It's CJ Washburn."

A few seconds of silence passed and then came a thump and a crash. CJ looked at Parker.

"Try the door," Parker said.

CJ turned the knob and the door inched open. He started to say, "I'll go in first," but Stella was ahead of him. She hit the door with her shoulder, rushed in and to the side taking a shooter's stance, her SIG Sauer out in front of her. CJ and Parker moved in around her, and the three gawked at the scene before them.

Stella raised her SIG Sauer to point at the ceiling. Parker took her arm and directed the weapon toward the floor. "There are apartments above, no one below. Point it down."

She nodded.

A man lay on his side next to an overturned straight-backed chair, partially unbuttoned shirt, eyes wide, blood and sweat dripping from his face. Beyond him, scattered about a small dining area, were dozens of seashells and shards of glass. A small, round table lay on its side, the window under which it appeared to have resided, stood partially open, curtains blowing about. Parker rushed to the window and looked out.

"Gone," he said, shaking his head and pulling his phone from his pocket.

"Is there anyone else in the apartment?" CJ asked of the man.

The man closed his eyes and slowly shook his head. "Just Eveleen."

"Are you Ed Hall?"

The man looked at CJ for a few seconds as though confused by the question and then nodded. "Yes."

"Where's Eveleen?"

Just before Hall bowed his head CJ noticed that what he at first took as sweat and blood, was a mixture of sweat, blood and something else. Maybe tears?

"In the bedroom," Hall said without lifting his head again.

CJ glanced into a narrow but very neat kitchen, water trickling from the faucet, a small kitchen towel lying on the floor against the far cabinet. He turned away from the kitchen into a hall where he expected to find the bedroom Ed Hall had mentioned. He stopped at the first open door to find a bathroom, then across from it to an empty bedroom. He continued on to what had to be the master bedroom. Stella was suddenly by his side, her SIG Sauer still grasped in both hands, pointed at the floor, determination etched in her face.

The bedroom door was open. CJ stepped in, took one look and then rushed back to the bathroom where he proceeded to empty his stomach of everything he had eaten at the bistro.

Chapter 27

"Put your SIG Sauer in the trunk of your car before the police arrive," DuPont said to Stella. "It'll avoid any undue questions and concerns. All you'd need to do is drop your purse and have the SIG fall out."

She gave him a questioning, "You're crazy," kind of look.

"Stranger things have happened," he said.

When Stella left, CJ helped Ed Hall into a chair while DuPont documented the scene with his camera phone. After that he sent everyone out of the apartment so as to not contaminate the crime scene any further. The last CJ saw of Hall and the Detective, they were outside the apartment door, Hall sitting on the floor with his back against the wall, DuPont taking more pictures of the contusion on Ed Hall's forehead. Blood seemed to continue to seep from under the hairline.

While waiting for the first responders to arrive, CJ and Stella sat on the front stoop of the building, he with his head in his hands, elbows propped on his knees.

"How're you feeling?" she asked him.

"Better. For a while it was like someone was twisting a knife in there. Embarrassing."

"Why?"

"I took one look at a Eveleen Danohough, blood and brains all over, and proceeded to get sick. Never done that before."

"I almost got sick, too."

"I'm supposed to be a trained professional. Been there; done it. In the words of my old captain, 'Check it at the door so you don't chuck it in the door.'"

"Obviously there was something else going on; most likely something you ate didn't agree with you. Maybe the grouper."

CJ shook his head. "No. It's not the grouper. The pain killer felt wrong before I ate. Maybe a bad combination."

One of the sirens they'd been hearing for the last thirty seconds burst into the apartment complex parking lot. A St. Petersburg police cruiser skidded to a stop right in front of them and a police officer who CJ recognized got out.

"Officer Pratt," CJ said. "Nice to see you."

"Clinton Washburn. Am I here to haul you in again?"

"I sure hope not." CJ pointed his thumb over his shoulder. "Detective DuPont is inside with two victims, one deceased, one not."

Stella stood. "Perp appeared to depart out the window. Apartment 107." She then proceeded to lead Officer Pratt and his partner into the building.

Detective Gorky arrived on the heels of the medical examiner, spoke to Parker for a minute or so and then went in. CJ had long since moved away from the stoop. He had been alternating between sitting in the rental and leaning against the trunk, depending on how he was feeling at the time. The nausea came and went, though had gradually gotten better. He was now leaning against the car.

"How much longer do you think we'll be here?" Stella said.

"The detective will want to get our statements." He looked over to where Parker and an EMS tech were standing with Ed Hall. The tech was intent upon Ed Hall's injury. Several more units had arrived and officers were canvassing around looking for anyone who had seen the perp come or go. "I'd sure like to be able to listen in on what Ed Hall has to say."

"I can't imagine they'd let you do that."

Just then Ed Hall and CJ met eyes for a few seconds, until Hall looked away. "No, no way," CJ said, "but he appears to be telling Parker something, so I'm anxious to hear Parker's report."

A dark gray Dodge Charger rolled in, blue light strobing from the dash. It stopped in such a way as to tie up the parking lot even further.

"Oh, oh," CJ said.

"What?" Stella turned her head in the direction CJ was looking. "Oh," she added as Agents Coulter and Washburn climbed out.

"The Detectives are not going to be happy," CJ said.

The two agents started toward the entry to the apartment building when Josh spotted CJ and Stella. The surprise, though quickly covered up, was quite evident. Coulter continued toward the crime scene while Josh turned toward them.

"What are you doing here, Dad?"

"It was we, us, the two of us here, who discovered the body."

Josh looked up at the sky, pulling his hand through his hair. "Great. I think I'm going to be on the carpet for this."

"Why?"

"I was supposed to be keeping an eye on you. In the heat of the investigation at the bombing scene, I became lax, let you all go off by yourself." He looked over at the apartment building. "The victim is Eveleen Danohough?"

"You already know it is. Why else would you be here?"

Josh looked toward the building and then back at his dad. "Why were you...? Never mind. You two stay right here and don't talk to anyone, including the police. We're taking over this crime scene."

CJ shrugged his shoulders. "Okay."

Josh turned to walk away, than stopped for one more question. "Anyone besides you two?"

"Detective DuPont."

Josh followed his dad's nod to where Parker was still watching the tech work on Ed Hall. "That's just great. I thought he was in the hospital."

"He *was* until a few hours ago."

"Who's the civilian with him?"

"Eddie Hall. Eveleen's boyfriend, we think, and business partner. He is also a victim. It appears the perp bashed him in the head before escaping out a window. Other than the head injury and witnessing Ms. Danohough's murder, he wasn't harmed."

"So he's our best witness," Josh said.

"Might be your only witness."

"You didn't see anything?"

"No."

"Why were you here?"

"Wanted to ask Ms. Danohough some questions concerning Douglas Rothbower, who was supposedly her son."

"Why?"

"Because it's what I was hired to do. I'm trying to get all the facts concerning his birth and life so as to help in the legalities involved with the will and next of kin."

Josh just glared at him.

CJ held up his right hand. "Honest. There was no intention of getting in the middle of whatever it is you and your FBI pals have going with the WMD threat. You can tell Taffer or whoever carpet you wind up on that I was told by you and your superiors to stay away from it, and that I went off with those intentions, wanting only to try and find out who Douglas Rothbower's birth father really was."

"And did you?"

"Did I what?"

"Find out who his father was."

"No. Never got to talk to Ms. Danohough. It appears that she is now a dead end; no pun intended."

Josh snorted. "Like I said, don't go anywhere."

"Yes, Sir, Special Agent Joshua James Washburn, *Sir*!" CJ snapped a salute and displayed a huge grin.

Josh shook his head and followed after Agent Coulter.

Noticing the arrival of the FBI agents, Detective DuPont left Ed Hall with the tech and walked over to CJ and Stella.

"Is that your son, the FBI agent?"

"That's him."

"I could see the resemblance. Are they doing what I think they're doing?" he said.

"Taking over," CJ said.

"Don Gorky is going to be pissed. Glad it's not my case anymore." He adjusted the sling holding up his casted arm and added, "I'm starting to hate this thing."

"I'll trade you that for my broken rib."

"Will you take the hole in my head, too?"

"Already have one, so no thanks," CJ said. "So what's Hall's story?"

"Some guy who he didn't know knocked on the door and then forced himself in. He wanted to know what Eveleen Danohough knew, what she'd told the FBI and police. When she wouldn't say anything he shot her in the head and then started in on Hall. He's convinced that if we hadn't shown up he'd be dead as well."

CJ looked to the far end of the parking lot where a cop was talking with a resident. "Has the canvassing turned up anything yet?"

Parker shook his head. "Not that I've heard. On a hot Sunday afternoon, I doubt they're going to find much. People are either inside their air-conditioned apartment or they're at the beach or in a mall. There's probably a one in a thousand chance that anyone will have noticed anything. Doubt anyone will have even seen *us* arrive."

"Where did Ed Hall go?" Stella said suddenly.

CJ and Parker's heads swung around to the EMS van. The two techs were busy putting things away, restoring the van for their next dispatch.

"He shouldn't have gone anywhere," Parker said and rushed away.

As Parker dashed off, CJ said to Stella, "Something's fishy here."

"When you say that, I'm learning to not reply with, 'Other than the murder?' or some such thing," Stella said. "*Now* what are you thinking that is fishy?"

"I think Ed has something to hide and he waited for the first opportunity to slip away."

"What do you think he knows?"

"Maybe he knows the killer." CJ stepped around the car to retrieve his bottle of water and then returned to lean next to Stella again. He took a swig of the bottle. "Starting to feel a bit better."

"I think we should get you out of the sun," she said.

"Yeah, maybe."

They watched DuPont leave the EMS techs to talk to a uniformed officer and then go into the building. After a short time he came out, Josh on his heel, both heading toward CJ and Stella. Detective Gorky came out right behind them, cell phone pressed to his ear, heading for the uniformed cop DuPont had talked to minutes before.

"It appears the brown stuff is hitting the fan," CJ said.

"Yes it does," Stella said.

When Josh and DuPont stopped before them, CJ said to his son, "You take over the scene and then immediately lose the only witness."

"Knock it off, Dad. It's nothing new for a witness to wander off, head injury and all of that. The locals will find him quick enough, I'm sure."

"Not if he doesn't want to be found."

"What're you saying?" DuPont said.

"I've had a lot of time to stand here and think through what took place when we arrived and everything we saw. When we first entered the apartment, what did you see?"

DuPont considered the question for a few seconds and then said, "Man on the floor, bloody head and face, conscious, table on its side, broken glass and sea shells scattered about the dining area, window open, dead woman in bedroom with what appeared to be a gunshot to the head."

"No gun?"

"Perp obviously took it with him."

"Why would you think he'd leave the gun behind?" Josh said to his dad. "Looks rather straight forward, if you ask me."

"That's what's bugging me. It's too straight forward, too obvious. I think you're seeing what the perp wants you to see."

"But you're seeing something else?" DuPont said.

"Maybe. Let's take a look at those pictures you took," CJ said.

Seconds later Stella was holding DuPont's phone so that he could scroll through the pictures with his free hand. "What are we looking for?" DuPont said.

CJ pointed to one of the kitchen. "I'm sure if this is blown up you'll see that water is running in the kitchen sink."

"Yeah. I eventually turned it off."

"Do you recall seeing water on the floor, like someone got their hands wet and then dripped? Don't know if the photo will show that, but I did see it."

"That I don't remember." DuPont said

"And then there's the towel on the floor."

"What about it?"

"I'm sure it's important, but don't know how just yet. Still trying to think this through. Show me the rest of the pictures."

One by one DuPont scrolled through them, slowing at those of the table on its side, the shells and broken glass, and the open window. He kept scrolling.

"Stop there," CJ said when DuPont got to a photo of the entertainment center in the living room. "Why did you take that one?"

"You have to shoot everything because you don't often know until later what's important."

CJ analyzed it for several seconds and then said, "This just might be one of those that becomes important. See the decorative vases displayed along the top. First, you can't see the bottom two or three inches of the vases, meaning the there's a depression that they set down into. Second, note how one of them seems out of place, like it's been moved three or four inches. From what I saw of the rest of the apartment's décor, Eveleen wouldn't have tolerated something out of place. She liked balance and symmetry." He tapped the face of DuPont's phone with a finger nail. "I think that's where you're going to find the gun and most likely an under-the-arm holster."

"I don't..." DuPont said.

"I do," Josh said. "If you're right, Dad, great catch."

"And if I'm right there is likely no prints on it because the perp used a kitchen towel to wipe it down and then threw the towel toward the kitchen, not having the time to stow it away properly with us about to come through the door."

"But why would he escape out the window and leave his weapon behind?" DuPont said.

"Because he couldn't take a chance getting caught with it," Josh said. "Chances are the police wouldn't think there'd be a reason to do that kind of search and he'd be able to return for it at some later time, like in the middle of the night, tonight. If the police are smart enough to discover it, he's wiped it clean and all he loses is his gun."

"You might be right, Josh, but I don't think so," CJ said. "The running faucet and the water on the floor have to be significant. Parker, show me the picture you took of Ed Hall before he got up from the floor."

DuPont exchanged looks with Josh and then scrolled back to the beginning, to the very first picture. "Okay. What?"

"Two things here. Can you blow up closer to his face? You can do that on this thing, can't you?"

DuPont did so. "That better?"

"Perfect. First make note of the fact that he's quite alert. This is also how he looked when we first rushed in. He eyes were open and it'd been less than thirty seconds since we heard the crash, maybe only fifteen seconds."

"So he should have seen the perp throw the gun on top of the entertainment center before he went out the window. He didn't say anything to me about that."

"See how wet his face is? At first I thought it was sweat, and then I thought it was sweat and tears, but now I'm not so sure. I think that's what he wanted us to believe, that he was sweaty from being worked over by the perp and crying over the death of his girlfriend. I believe it was a big performance."

"You're thinking Ed Hall did this and then set it up to look like someone else?"

"You're getting closer, Parker." CJ nodded his head, getting excited. "Zoom out."

When DuPont had it so that everyone could see the entire picture, CJ pointed to Ed Hall's shirt. "Note the buttons. Only the top two are buttoned. The bottom two-thirds of the shirt is hanging open."

"And this means?"

"He took off the shirt in order to remove the holster he had hidden underneath. He then threw the gun and holster on top of the entertainment center after wiping off his prints; again, the towel in the kitchen. Somewhere in it all he stopped to throw water on his face, not getting the faucet totally shut off. Probably knowing that the door was unlocked, he understood that we would bust in it at anytime. He had three things left to do and that was, button up his shirt, setup the window for his faked escape and then bash his own head in so that he'd look like another victim."

"That doesn't make any sense," Josh said. "Why didn't he just open the window quietly, step out and walk away while you guys stood outside the door suspecting no one was home?"

"That's a very good question, Agent Washburn," CJ said, looking up at the sky, thinking. "Yes, a very good question. Why didn't he just run. Right from the beginning I felt something was off with the whole picture, but with my stomach boiling at the time, I couldn't put my finger on it. Until now anyway, when he just slipped away. That's what got me to looking at him a little closer."

He turned his eyes back at Josh.

"Maybe that *was* his intent, to exit out the window and then quietly close it behind him." CJ held up a finger. "Ah," he said.

"What?" Josh said.

"How far open was the window?"

"Maybe a third, if that much," Parker said.

"I don't think he could have gotten out that window with it open only that much, or it would have been a struggle. Is it by chance stuck?"

"Good question."

"If it is, that's why he couldn't run, and in his haste at trying to force it he knocked against the table. The fishbowl full of shells hit the floor. He became desperate and had to change his plan on the fly. He had already hidden the gun with intentions of coming back for it later, so he ran into the kitchen, threw water on his face and then ran headfirst at the edge of the kitchen counter. By the time we entered, he was on the floor moaning and bleeding. We did exactly what he wanted. We formed initial conclusions and I, like an idiot, instead of asking who he was, asked him if he was Ed Hall."

"A basic rule of interrogation," Josh said. "Never suggest an answer within the framework of your question."

"Exactly! And I should have known better."

"He grabbed a hold of that answer like a drowning man to a life ring," Dupont said. "That was *not* Ed Hall."

"I'll be willing to put twenty bucks on it," CJ said. Suddenly it was like a light went on. He rolled his head back to look up at the sky and added, "I'll be damned!"

"What?" Josh said.

"I should have knew the instant we entered the apartment that that wasn't Eddie Hall. Where the hell was my head?"

"Why?"

"Hall was Ms. Danohough's boyfriend, or that's what we've been led to believe. The guy we just allowed to walk away was in his mid-thirties."

"Unless Danohough liked them young," DuPont said.

"I doubt it," CJ said. "God, I was an idiot! I'm sure forensics will find skin, hair and/or blood on the edge of a counter. With that you'll have DNA."

"He may have wiped down the weapon and holster," DuPont said, "but he touched a lot more than that. Somewhere in that apartment we also have his fingerprints."

With that DuPont took off toward Detective Gorky while Josh headed back into the crime scene.

"You're welcome!" CJ called after them.

He and Stella remained leaning against the car. "I'm mightily impressed, Clint," Stella said. "There is no way I would have seen all of that and then put it all together."

"Sometimes I even surprise myself. I'm still irked I didn't pick up on the age difference right off."

"And this is the guy who less than eight weeks ago, after I left a voicemail, an email, and a note in his refrigerator, couldn't figure out that I went to Albuquerque to visit my sister. He thought I was murdered and dumped in a dumpster."

CJ emptied the last remaining ounce from his water bottle. "No comment."

Chapter 28

The entire McGee family was on duty at the pub when CJ, Stella and Parker walked in. Hannah came right over to them.

"Is Rebecca here?" CJ said.

"Aye, she is. Refuses to be alone so came in with us. In the office. You can go on back. You know your way."

As they filed past the grill, Paddy intercepted them.

"Good to see you again, Mister Washburn. Have there been more developments?"

"Yes, and I need to tell you and your sister together."

Paddy looked between the three of them.

"This is Detective DuPont," CJ added.

Paddy nodded his understanding and then turned to lead the way.

When they entered the office, Rebecca was sitting behind her brother's desk, feet tucked underneath her, eyes closed, a magazine flopped open in her lap. As Paddy pulled a chair forward for Stella, Rebecca jerked awake. She blinked her eyes a couple of times, seeming to be a bit irritated at her privacy being invaded.

"Mister Washburn has something to tell us, Becca," Paddy said.

With Paddy's announcement, she swung her feet to the floor and sat up as though preparing for more bad news, showing a bit of surprise at seeing Detective DuPont. She set the magazine on the desk, directed her attention at CJ, and waited.

Seeing the sorrow reflecting heavily in Rebecca's eyes, CJ turned to Stella as though searching for words he couldn't come up with. Stella grimaced then leaned forward and took Rebecca's hand. "Becca. We have more terrible news."

Rebecca dropped her eyes from CJ to Stella.

"Eveleen is dead."

As though someone let the air out of her, Rebecca seemed to deflate in the chair. Stella jumped forward to prop her up, afraid she was going to fall to the floor.

"Holy Mother of God!" Paddy said. "How? Why?" He stepped up behind the chair and attempted to put his arms around his sister. "They got to her, didn't they?"

"Yes," Parker said. "We're very sorry. I need to ask you...." He held out his cell phone with one of the pictures he had taken. "Is this Ed Hall?"

Rebecca looked and shook her head.

"No," Paddy said. "That's not Eddie."

"Do either of you know who this is?"

They shook their heads.

"Never seen him before," Paddy said.

"I don't recognize him," Rebecca said, her words barely above a whisper.

"Is that who killed her?" Paddy asked.

"He is certainly a suspect. He played a rather good con when we showed up, pretending to be Eddie Hall and a victim in the crime that was committed against Ms. Danohough."

"Then where is Eddie?" Rebecca said. "He wasn't with her?"

"The police are looking for him," CJ said.

"We found an address for him in Apollo Beach," Parker said, "however, it was bogus, non-existent. Do you know where he lives?"

Rebecca shook her head. "I don't know, but..."

"But what?"

"I thought he lived in Clearwater."

"On Fox Hill Dr. by chance?"

"I don't know."

Parker looked at Paddy.

"I've no idea," Paddy said. "Only met the chap formally once, though he's been in the pub a number of times."

Parker pulled out his phone and made a call. "Don, Parker here. I might have some more info on Eddie Hall."

Silence prevailed while the detective listened.

"Oh! Good. You're ahead of me then. What was the address?" Everyone looked at him. "Figures. Keep me up to speed if you would. Thanks."

Parker put his phone away. "He was located at his home in Clearwater about twenty minutes ago. Clearwater police are sitting on him until the Feds arrive."

"How long would it take to get there?" CJ asked.

"Detective Gorky said it was north Clearwater. Probably about forty-five minutes if traffic is decent."

"He give you the address?"

"He did. It just happens that we had the address correct but in the wrong city."

"Fox Hill Drive in Clearwater, not Apollo Beach," Stella said. "How bizarre."

"We can't go near it, though," Parker said. "It belongs to the Feds now. I'm starting to get a bit tired of being pushed off the bus."

"But you're with me," CJ said, "and I have my own bus plus a relationship with someone on the Fed bus. Ed Hall was close to Ms. Danohough, thus she may have divulged some of her history to him. My interviewing him is within the realm of my investigation, wouldn't you think?"

"As a detective in the heat of my own investigation, I'd tell you to stay away. As your consultant and off duty detective in a case I'm now only on the fringe of, I'd say, *hell* yes, it's well within your scope."

They answered a few questions concerning how Ms. Danohough was killed, again expressed their condolences even though Rebecca was not all that close to her mother-in-law, and took their leave.

They sat in silence in the car waiting for the air conditioner to pull the temperature down while Stella loaded the GPS with the correct address. When finally she pulled out onto the street, CJ said over his shoulder to Parker, "How do you feel about this coincidence between Apollo Beach and Clearwater?"

"Coincidence?"

"The address listed for Ed Hall."

"Hadn't thought too hard about it yet, though I'm sure there's something there."

"Where did you wind up getting the Apollo Beach address?" CJ said.

"From the business license records. Since Danohough and Hall were partners, they both had addresses on file."

"That's what I figured. Here's what I'm thinking. Originally, when the two of them opened *Coffee Bean Boutique*, Eddie lived in Apollo Beach. Sometime between then and now he moved to Clearwater."

Parker considered that for a moment. "Why was the address listed on the business license still Apollo Beach?"

"My guess is that he made the address change to the county but somewhere along the way, whether his error or the county's, the street address was updated, but the city wasn't. It's not all that unusual."

"Of course."

"I assume you see the big picture significance of that."

"Big picture?" Parker said. "What do you mean?"

"I see it," Stella said.

CJ grinned at her. "Share, if you would."

"It means that Ed Hall had a home in Apollo Beach, likely a waterfront home."

"Right!" Parker said from the backseat. "Right! He may actually still own that home, or sold it to someone in UIRA."

"Which means that that may be the location Douglas had yet to pass to Agent Taffer, where weapons are being warehoused."

"It also means that Eddie Hall may be a player in the big picture."

Parked behind a Clearwater police cruiser was the dark gray Dodge Charger that Stella and CJ had seen plenty of in the last twenty-four-plus hours. She stopped the car behind it.

"Feds beat us here," CJ said.

"You think they've put it together?"

"I'm assuming that the two Feds inside are Agent Coulter and my son," CJ said. "I have no reason to doubt Coulter's deductive skills. My son may be green, but he has good instincts. I'd give them fifty-fifty at this point. They might need a little push."

They climbed out of the car and CJ added, "On further thought, just the fact that they're here tells me they've figured something out or they're at least suspecting something."

As they approached the door, a Clearwater uniformed cop stepped out. "What's your business here?"

Parker presented his badge. "From St. Pete. This is related to one of our cases."

The cop looked at Parker's slung and casted arm and shook his head. "Sorry detective. FBI has this locked down. Can't allow you to go in."

CJ stepped forward. "Could you get word to one of the agents, Special Agent Coulter, or Special Agent Washburn, that we're here. I'm sure they'll make an exception. Washburn may actually be expecting us."

The cop gave them all a long look and then went in.

"You're making a big assumption, CJ," Parker said. "They could just throw you out on your ear."

"But not until Josh gives me a face-to-face reprimand. You're taking a bit of a chance yourself, making like you're on duty and actually on this case. I thought for a minute that the cop made you."

"Yeah, well, I've been on the captain's shit-list for some time. What's he going to do, put me on his shittier than shit list?"

"You sound like you have a bit of an attitude, Detective. Something you want to talk about, something you'd like to share?"

"If I did I'd have to use language not appropriate around a lady. Another time."

"Oh my stars," Stella said in a sweet, southern accent. She fluttered her eyelashes and breathed, "Please don't damage my virgin ears."

Parker laughed. "How's your stomach and your ribs, CJ?"

"Not bad right now. How's your arm?"

"Feels like I've been shot. Other than that, I should be playing golf by tomorrow."

"You play golf?"

"No. But once my badge is removed I might as well take it up."

"That or pickle ball."

Parker snorted.

The door opened and Josh stepped out. "How the hell did you get onto this so fast and what the hell are you doing here?"

"I'm glad you beat us here. Means there's some hope for you."

Josh just stared at him.

"Eddie Hall is important to my investigation, Josh. You know that. We just need a few minutes with him. Agent Taffer did tell you that he okayed our continuing with our investigation, didn't he?"

"He did."

"Did he also tell you that I made a promise that anything I discovered that might be relevant to the UIRA thing would be shared with our good friends on the bureau."

"*That*, he didn't tell me, but I would assume you'd do the right thing, Dad."

"I've got information to share."

Josh's expression didn't change as he continued to stare at his father.

"Do you want to hear it?"

"I'm waiting."

"Can we come in?"

"You can tell me right here."

"I need to be able to speak with Ed Hall first. My questions to him may help you."

"In what way?"

"You know how it goes, Josh. One question can lead to other questions depending on the answers. One doesn't know all the questions until he starts hearing the answers. It's a process."

Josh blew out a lungful of air. "Wait." He went back inside.

The cop stepped back out and crossed his arms. At 6'2" CJ usually towered over people. With this cop, though, he felt small.

"What do you bench-press?" CJ asked him.

"About three-twenty," the cop said.

"When I was wearing blue I was doing maybe two-seventy."

"Not bad for your size." The cop looked at Parker.

"I'm not even going there," Parker said.

They all looked at Stella.

"I maybe can do that in ounces," she said.

The cop grinned. "Where were you a cop?" he said to CJ.

"Tucson, Arizona."

"Hot there."

"Hot here."

"You've that dry heat, though."

"And somehow or other people seem to think that's better. I've never gotten that."

"It gets hot, you sweat," the cop said. "Drink lots of fluid and wear a hat. Enjoy air-conditioning when you can."

"Exactly," CJ said. "Tucson and Tampa. Like twins."

The cop snorted.

The door opened and Josh poked his head out. "Get your asses in here."

"Your son always talk to you like that?" Parker said.

"I think he got it from his mother."

Agent Coulter sat in a straight-backed chair facing a man sitting in the middle of an overstuffed sofa, elbows on knees, head in hands, nearly bald head glowing under the overhead lights and rotating fan.

"Mister Hall," Josh said.

The man looked up.

"This is Clinton Washburn. He'd like to ask you a few questions."

CJ grimaced at the use of his full name. While Stella and Parker held back, he moved to take the chair next to Coulter.

"First of all, Eddie, I want to say how sorry I am for your loss. I don't know if the agents have told you who I am. I'm the one who discovered Eveleen earlier this afternoon."

"I know who you are," Hall said. "Eveleen..." He cleared his throat and started again. "Eveleen told me about you... you came to Florida searching for Douglas." He blinked and swallowed. "When he died she was going to hire you to find out who killed him."

"That's right."

"Did the same person kill Eveleen?"

CJ looked toward Agent Coulter and then back at Ed Hall. "I think that's in the hands of the FBI now. I'm pursuing other matters that may or may not be related."

Hall continued to look at CJ, not saying anything.

"We had assumed that you and Eveleen were together."

"We were. She spent the night here. This morning she wanted to go to church." He looked up at the ceiling and took a deep breath. "I don't do... not into church and all that. Had a fight about it. We don't normally fight, but... things been tense... Doug murdered." He looked at the floor and shook his head. "I dropped her off at church. She said she'd get a ride home. I should have stayed with her. We parted... both of us in anger."

"I get the picture. Again, I'm very sorry. The two of you owned *Coffee Bean Boutique* together, is that right?"

"Actually, it was Eveleen's business, her investment. I had citizenship so we became partners. Partners... name only."

"But you were also partners in life. You were a couple."

His shoulders seemed to slump even more. "On and off."

"No intentions of ever getting married?"

Hall shook his head. "No. Had talked about it. Just the other day, in fact."

"Other day. When?"

"The day...." Hall looked to the side, in thought, then back down at the floor. "Ah, Tuesday I think. She asked me."

"She asked *you*? To marry her?"

"Yes."

"What did you say?"

"I had to think about it."

"Why's that?"

He shrugged. "It was complicated."

CJ studied Ed Hall for a few seconds. "So, she wanted to marry, but you didn't. How well did you know Eveleen?"

Hall looked at CJ. "What do you mean, how well did I know her?"

"Simple question, I'd think. You had a relationship, a romantic relationship I assume. What did you know about her past? How long did you know her?"

"Ah... she moved here in 2005." His gaze returned to the floor. He pushed his fingers through what little hair he had and continued. "We got to know each other and started the business in 2006. I guess you could say that's when our relationship started. It really wasn't all that romantic."

"Did she ever talk about her life back in, say, the late sixties, when she lived in Northern Ireland?"

He sat back and looked at some point behind CJ. "A little, though she lived in Ireland, not Northern Ireland. Why?"

"Before Douglas showed up did she ever mention that she had a son?"

Hall blinked rapidly for a few seconds before responding. "No. I can't say she ever did."

CJ looked over his shoulder at Stella, considering where he was going to go next.

"Until...." Hall said.

CJ swung back to him. "Until?"

"Until Douglas was killed. That's when she told me he was her son."

"You didn't know?"

"No."

"Did she happen to mention who the father was?"

Rapid blinking again. "No."

"Were you curious?"

Hall's gaze fell back to the floor. "It was her business."

CJ turned his head toward Josh this time, who was standing behind Coulter. He winked and came back to Ed Hall.

"When did you sell your house in Apollo Beach?"

Hall's head came up like he'd been poked with a needle, the forest of red hair on his arms seeming to come to attention. A few seconds passed and CJ thought he was going to deny ever owning such a house. Then Hall said, "Three years ago."

"Why?"

"Why did I sell it?"

CJ nodded.

"It was too expensive. I needed something a bit smaller."

"Did it have a boat dock?"

"Yes, it did. It was a waste of money. I didn't have a boat nor any desire for one."

"Why did you buy it to begin with?"

"Seemed like a good idea at the time." Hall straightened up and looked at Agent Coulter. "I don't see what this has to do with Eveleen."

"Please just answer the questions, Mister Hall," Coulter said.

CJ leaned forward, resting his elbows on his knees, clasping his hands in front of him. "Are you sure Eveleen didn't happen to mention who Douglas' father was? Weren't you even a bit curious?"

Hall's mouth flopped for a few seconds. "Yes... I... she didn't say... I assumed she was married once. None of my business."

"Douglas was forty-three years old, which means he was born in 1969."

Ed Hall's eyes seemed to go out of focus for a few seconds as though he was mentally confirming CJ's calculation. When it appeared that he wasn't going to return to the interview anytime soon, CJ shifted the subject again.

"You bought the Apollo Beach house in 2004 and sold it in, what, 2009?"

Hall slowly came back to CJ, considered the question and said, "Something like that."

"I imagine you took quite a loss. Wasn't the market still in free-fall about that time? Nobody was selling or buying homes in 2009 unless it was a foreclosure or rock-bottom for some other reason."

"Investors were buying things up. I got lucky. And I got a steal on this place."

"An investor bought your Apollo Beach home?"

"I think it was an investor."

"What was his name?"

"I don't remember."

"What was the address?"

Eddie Hall seemed to sit up a little straighter, his voice becoming clearer. "I don't remember."

"You don't remember the address of a home that you lived in only three years ago?"

Hall shrugged. "It'll probably come to me in a bit, but right now, I don't remember."

CJ sat back and then stood. "Thank you for your time, Mister Hall."

The trio and the two agents stepped outside, while the Clearwater cop went in.

"You have something to run with, now," CJ said to Josh and Coulter.

Coulter was already punching buttons on his phone. As he stepped out of earshot he was heard saying, "We need to dig into real estate data for Apollo Beach."

"He could at least say thanks."

"Thanks, Dad," Josh said. "Did you learn anything as far as what you're looking for?"

CJ shrugged. "Maybe. I've a bit of suspicion that I'm not ready to voice just yet."

"Like what?"

"That's why I said, not ready to voice."

"Okay. So, what now?"

"I don't know." CJ looked at his watch and then at Parker and Stella. "We've got a dinner invite tonight from Detective DuPont's wife, and it's been a very long day."

"Great. Why don't I meet up with you all later tonight at the hotel or, if not, at breakfast in the morning?"

They hugged. "Stop finding dead bodies, please, Dad," Josh said.

"I'll try my best."

In the car, Stella started the engine, set the AC for full blast and said, "Where to now?"

"My place for dinner, as CJ told his son," DuPont said. "Let's talk along the way. Hand me the GPS and I'll input the address."

"So, what are your thoughts on Ed Hall?" CJ said to the detective after Stella had replaced the GPS and started maneuvering the car out of the neighborhood.

"He's hiding something."

"No doubt. But what?"

"Did you see how he blinked his eyes every time you mentioned Douglas?" Stella said. "I think he knows a lot more about that then he's letting on."

"The question is," DuPont said, "if he *is* avoiding saying something about who Douglas' father was, why? Douglas is dead. Eveleen is dead. What's the big deal?"

"Maybe *he's* Douglas' father?" Stella said.

CJ looked out his window trying to suppress a smile.

"What are the odds?" DuPont said.

Stella looked over at CJ, back at the road and then at CJ again. "You're smiling because you think I'm right. That's what you were not yet ready to voice, isn't it?" She came to a stop sign, glanced at the GPS and flipped on her turn signal. "You're thinking that Eddie Hall is Douglas' father."

"Okay, you've got me," CJ said. "The thing is, I've met Douglas. Other than not carrying the weight that Hall carries, their features are similar enough. Although Hall is near bald, with the bushy, red eyebrows and hairy arms, you can tell he had red hair. Douglas had a serious receding hair line and it was red. Had the same eyebrows to match."

"They're both Irish," DuPont said. "Red hair is almost a given. Doesn't make them father and son."

"Jaws are nearly the same, square and determined. And then there are the eyes. I think I could see Douglas in those eyes. Add in the way he blinked every time he answered a question about Douglas, and I've got a pretty good suspect."

"Why wouldn't he admit it?"

"That's a great question, isn't it. The next thing to do is to point blank ask him if he's Douglas' father. If he denies it, there isn't much more I can do. It's not like he's breaking the law. It really is his business."

They road along in silence for a time and then CJ said, "Maybe what he's denying is that he knew Eveleen 43 years ago. He'd certainly have to know her to have fathered a child with her back in 1969."

"Do you think he was telling the truth when he said he didn't know Eveleen had a son until she told him?" Stella said.

"You mean she became pregnant and then she gave birth without him even knowing about it?" CJ said.

"It could be that he knew about it, but when she gave it up for adoption she may have told him that the baby died in childbirth. Thirty-five years later they run into each other again here in Florida and their love affair reignites. He puts old troubles behind them, doesn't even think enough about it to bring it up. Different lifetime."

"Still, why deny to us that he knew her back then?"

Stella seemed to consider CJ's question for a time, then said, "Maybe what he's hiding has nothing to do with Eveleen."

"What do you mean?" DuPont said.

"It could have something to do with the UIRA, or something only slightly related, but a secret is a secret."

Further talk about Ed Hall stalled and then DuPont said, "Don't turn there. The GPS will screw you up. Go to the next light and turn."

Stella exchanged a look with CJ. He grinned. She rolled her eyes, flipped off her turn signal and continued straight, as DuPont had suggested.

CJ wanted to say something more about what Ed Hall's secret might be, but other than possibly being Douglas' father, he wasn't sure where else to go with it. Instead, he decided that the best thing to do was to put it on the backburner where it could continue to simmer. Maybe the next time he pulled it out he'd see something. To break the silence, CJ said, "You've got some great kids there, Parker."

"Yeah. They do have their moments," DuPont said and then went on to brag about their school activities and sports involvement–CJ inserted several stories about Josh and Trish when they were of the same ages–until they turned into a circular driveway in west-central St. Petersburg.

The younger of the two boys, Scott, stepped out onto the porch as they all got out of the car. "Mom said you're cookin'," he announced to his dad.

"Then that must be the case. What is it I'm cookin'?"

"Cheeseburgers."

"Is the grill hot?"

"No. I don't think so."

"I think, then, someone has to make it hot."

"You want me to do that?"

"You know what to do?"

"Turn the gas on. Hold the button for three seconds and listen for the ignition. If it doesn't ignite turn the gas off and wait two minutes before trying again."

"What did you do, memorize it?"

"No." Scott grinned.

"Go do it!"

The screen door slammed behind Scott, almost in Stella's face. Parker shook his head. "He's got lighting the grill down. We're still working on manners." He reached with his good arm and pulled the door open. "After you."

Chapter 29

The four adults sat watching the setting sun light up a trio of palm trees on the other side of a small lake behind DuPont's house, reusable plastic plates and utensils stacked to the side, the grill cooling, kids off doing whatever it is kids do.

"I love the palm trees," Stella said. "It's a refreshing change from giant cactus. Your view here is wonderful."

"Our little piece of heaven," Gracie said.

"You should see Gracie's painting of this very scene," Parker said.

"You paint?" Stella said.

Gracie shrugged her shoulders and tilted her head. "A little here and there."

"The one I'm talking about," Parker said, "you might have noticed when you came in the door... in the entryway."

"Foyer," Gracie said.

"*Par-done* me," Parker said. "In the *fa-yay*."

Stella turned her head as though she could see the artwork in question. "Oh! I remember." She looked across the lake once more. "I need to go look at it again."

With that the two women went into the house.

"You definitely have a nice home here," CJ said.

"We're financially comfortable with it only because Gracie's mother passed away early last year. She had a place down in Sarasota that turned a little bit of equity into cash, enough for us to put a sizeable down payment on this."

"Must have been tough on Gracie to lose her mom," CJ said.

"She had Gracie late in life. She was seventy-eight when she died.

Had a lot of issues that finally took her down. In a way, it was a relief for both Gracie and her mother."

CJ nodded. After taking a slug on his beer, he said, "So, how serious are you about the PI business?"

Parker considered the question for a time. "You know how some people come up with a life-changing idea and then don't do anything about it, or they put it aside until suddenly there comes a sign that tells them to get off their asses and make it happen?"

CJ just tilted his head as though saying he understood, though maybe he didn't.

"Until recently, I was that first person, the one who has had an idea for some time but who had done absolutely nothing about it. Then you fell into my lap and I was elevated to the second person. You, CJ Washburn, are my sign."

"Your sign?"

"I've apparently been waiting for a sign, and here you are." He raised his injured arm. "And then this happened. I was forced to look at my own case from a totally different viewpoint, a PI viewpoint, and I like it."

"I think that nail in your head did more damage than anyone is thinking. You do realize that you'd likely lose whatever pension that you've invested years into."

"I've thought quite a bit about that and have decided it's not worth it if I'm unhappy with what I'm doing. Tell me this. Why did you quit being a detective?"

"I was never a detective, though the roads were leading in that direction. I stepped out of the uniform, completely away from the department, because I thought it was causing too much stress on my family. My marriage was failing and I'd hoped that going private would be the answer. It wasn't."

Parker sat back. "Humph!" He thought for a few seconds. "Can't say that the family is an issue *here*, or at least not so much that I fear that Gracie and I are having marital problems. More time with the family would certainly be a plus, though." He looked toward the house as though expecting his wife to step out anytime. "Frankly, I need a change of scenery." When CJ gave him a questioning look he continued. "I don't mean that literally." He raised his good arm to indicate something off in the distance. "Out there. I need a professional change of scenery with a big slice of independence."

"How independent you'd be would be up for debate. You'd go from working for one boss to working for dozens of bosses. Every client becomes someone to whom you'd be having to answer."

"I understand."

"And they don't always like your report. A wife hires you to find out what her husband is doing at night. Sometimes what she wants to hear is that he actually *is* working on a special project for the company, not poking the assistant."

"How much of that type of work do you get?"

"Not much, actually. Sometimes a divorce involving lots of money may inspire a request for my services to investigate a spouse, hoping that I'll uncover an affair. I do a lot of subpoena serving for the county and background checking. I've gotten established with several insurance companies doing fraud investigation. I've three different attorney's who call on me to assist in discovery of evidence before a trial. I've also assisted numerous companies in investigating internal theft problems. Occasionally I wind up in the middle of a case that the Tucson Police Department has allowed to go cold. Victims want answers and those who can afford it will gladly pay for it."

"And then there was the serial killer," Parker added.

"Oh yes. There was that. Not exactly a case I was getting paid for; however, requests for my services has more than doubled in the month since. Had to turn work away in order to come here, and I'm doing this pro-bono."

Parker looked surprised for a few seconds and then said, "Oh, yes. Douglas was the father of the niece of your attorney client. A little quid-pro-quo I believe you said."

"Exactly. She helped me when I was in jail, twice. Now I'm helping her." CJ didn't see need to mention that the pro-bono was over, that he was now billing for his services. He emptied his beer and pointed the bottle at the cooler. "Is there another in there?"

"Help yourself."

CJ stood just as the sliding glass door opened and Stella poked her head out.

"Clint! Get in here. You've got to see this."

"The painting?"

"No. The news about a summit. Here, in the United States."

They all stood in Parker's living room staring at the wall-mounted television screen. Parker was punching the back button on his DVR remote in an attempt to replay the entire news segment. He overshot the beginning so they had to wait through fifteen seconds of ads before it started up.

> *"And finally this from our European correspondent, Crystal Zalinees, reporting from Brussels."*

> *"Thank you, Mark. We've just gotten word from a reliable source that the G8 is holding a mini-summit in the next few days somewhere in the United States, believed to be in Atlanta or somewhere in the southeast. It's all kind of hush-hush so attempts to gain further information as to the exact location or as to the agenda have been stonewalled by those officials who I've approached."*

> *"The G8, Crystal, is made up of what countries?"*

> *"That would be the United States, the United Kingdom, France, Germany, Italy, Japan, Canada, and Russia. This is a big surprise, Mark, because the regular summits are in June, the last one being the 38th G8 summit earlier this summer at Camp David. The 39th isn't to take place until next summer. Speculation is that*

it'll be in Fermanagh in Northern Ireland. What this mini-summit in the U.S. is all about is anyone's guess at this point."

"Would that be like the 38th and a half G8 summit?"

The correspondent grinned.

"I don't know, Mark. This is the type of thing that I probably wouldn't have spent all that much time investigating except that one person I talked to used the word, secret."

"Secret?"

"That's correct, Mark. Either the word was said in jest or this is a secret summit."

"Thank you, Crystal."

The news anchorman lifted his eyes from his monitor to the camera.

"That was Crystal Zalinees, reporting from Brussels on a possible, secret, G8 mini-summit somewhere in the southeast United States. After the break, more fires in the northwest and what you can do to lower your risk of colon cancer. Another diet breakthrough?"

Parker paused the playback. "Okay. Fill me in. What's so important about a G8 mini-summit?"

"You remember the day you arrested me for Doug's murder?"

"How can I forget? That was only two days ago."

"I met with Doug that morning, that is he just showed up at my hotel."

"Yeah. You told me that."

"He was an undercover snitch for the FBI, apparently trying to infiltrate this UIRA that had setup headquarters in Florida."

"That's what you claimed and which has since been confirmed."

"In his short conversation with me he said something about a summit. Until now I had no idea what it meant. I did discover, as Crystal said, that the next one could be in Northern Ireland, but that's at least nine months out. This news, that being a leak about a pending mini-summit in the southeast, sort of puts things in prospective. Initially it was believed that UIRA was preparing to ship a stock of weapons and explosives to the homeland for some particular event there. What if the event is a G8 mini-summit right here in Florida?"

"Stretching it, wouldn't you say, CJ?" Parker said. "Exactly who would be attending such a summit?"

"A regular summit is attended by the world leaders, that is presidents, prime ministers, chancellors, what have you. A mini-summit might not be so high level. Just a guess, really. I may be wrong about the entire thing; however, based on what we've learned from Josh, they've a WMD and they're getting ready to use it, somewhere."

"WMD?"

Stella, CJ and Parker all turned to look at Gracie, who'd been observing from the side. Her face had turned white."

"What do you mean, WMD?"

"Mom?"

With that all four of them swung their attention to young Scott, standing in the foyer, between the bottom of the stairs and the front door.

"What?" Gracie said, her voice sharp, impatient.

"Can I go over to Jeremy's house?"

"No!"

The shock on Scott's face made it evident to CJ that such a forceful denial from his mother was uncommon. Even Parker looked surprised.

Gracie looked between the three of them and then seemed to realize what she'd just said.

"I'm sorry, Scott. Of course you can go over to Jeremy's. Be back in an hour."

Scott continued to just look at her, his jaw still hanging open.

"What are you waiting for?" his mother said. She made the shoo motion with her hand and forced a softness into her voice. "Go! Go! One hour."

As though expecting that she might change her mind, Scott rushed out the door.

Gracie turned to face her husband and her guests. "Sorry. I don't know what came over me. I really don't normally talk to my children like that."

"It's okay," Stella said. "I'm not a mother but I am an aunt and I've watched my sister react in much the same way when there was a perceived threat to her family. You know exactly what a WMD is, don't you?"

Gracie looked at the television, a dog frozen in motion in the middle of the screen, an advertisement for dog food. "Please turn that off, Parker and let's sit down."

He did and when they were all seated she said, "I have what I've tried to convince myself is an irrational fear, a fear that terrorists or some foreign power will attempt to destroy our country with any means possible, including nuclear bombs."

"A lot of people are afraid since 9/11," CJ said.

Gracie nodded. "Yes, since that day it's been much worse with me. Tracy was two and Blake was four. Parker can tell you. I had all I could do to not pack my bags, take my babies and run for the hills."

"It was a rough couple of years after that, and then Scott was born," Parker said.

"Anyway," Gracie said, "I've had a low level of this fear all my life, given to me by my father and grandfather. When I said run for the hills, I meant the Tennessee hills. That's where I was raised, near the border of Tennessee and West Virginia. My daddy and his daddy were both hillbillies. They trusted no one and protected their families and property the only way they knew, with guns. When I turned eighteen I walked, or more like it, ran away from it all, but the fears they'd ingrained in me remained as my baggage. That was 1994. Seven years later, after I'd met and married this wonderful man and had two beautiful children, and thought that I'd found a great life, terrorist bastards flew planes into the towers. The fear still lives in me eleven years later because there is always something, some threat out there that's going to destroy my family.

"Yes. I know what a weapon of mass destruction is. My father called it the weapon of final Armageddon. He could quote bible scripture to support its coming faster than anyone I knew, except maybe *his* father." She looked directly at CJ. "I don't even want to hear that they were right."

CJ looked between Stella and Parker and then said, "You aren't going to hear those words from my mouth. I really do think your father was wrong. As far as a nuclear bomb is concerned, not to worry. The FBI believes that they're dealing with something chemical and not actually of mass destruction design. Something small and of low dispersal, such as into a room of selected people."

"Like those attending the summit we just saw?"

"Yes."

Gracie considered that for a few moments. "What happens, though, if you kill off a bunch of presidents and prime ministers?"

CJ took a deep breath. "That's a big question for sure." He stood. "If you don't mind, I need to make a phone call. After that we can talk some more about it."

CJ sat on the patio watching dusk fall over the lake, his cell phone pressed to his ear. Gracie's last question was still replaying in his head. What *would* happen if you killed all the leaders of the G8? What kind of turmoil would the world fall into? Could that trigger the Armageddon as Gracie's father believed?

"Dad," Josh said into CJ's ear. "Where are you?"

"Why don't you just come out and say it?" CJ said.

"Say what?"

"What kind of trouble are you in now, Dad?"

"Okay. What kind of trouble are you in now?"

"I'm not in any trouble. Thanks for your concern, though. Stella and I just had a nice dinner with Detective DuPont and his family. Now we're hanging out at their house. You have any new developments?"

"No."

"Is that no new developments or no new developments that you're willing to share?"

"Does it make any difference?"

"Certainly. If I share with you will you share with me?"

"Depends on what you're sharing."

"You and Agent Taffer would make a good team."

Josh didn't say anything.

"Did you come up with the address of the place in Apollo Beach?"

"Yes."

"What did you find?"

"Nothing."

"Nothing?"

"That's what I said."

"No guns? No explosives?"

"Not a thing, Dad."

"What *did* you find? You sound rather frustrated."

"We went in ready for an all out assault. Ended up scaring the hell out of the neighborhood, including the old couple who lived in the house. They're leasing from some guy living in New Jersey, through a property management agent."

"Looked legit?"

"Yes, it did. I just got back from there."

"I was so sure."

"So were we."

"Thanks for letting me know. Have you seen the news about the summit?"

"Summit, Dad? I thought we already talked about that."

"That was more general. This is the G8 mini-summit about to be held here in the United States."

"Mini-summit?"

"That's what I said."

"When?"

"Don't know."

"Where?"

"Don't know, but it could be in Florida."

All CJ could hear was some heavy breathing.

"I figured that this was something the FBI should be on top of. You should be telling me, not me telling you."

"Where are you getting your information?"

"On the evening news. No idea what network. Considering that it is G8 and thus world leaders, I'd recommend you make a call to the secret service, homeland security, maybe the CIA, NSA, and BSA."

"BSA?"

"That's Boy Scouts of America. They may be running with it already."

"You're a riot, Dad."

"Anyway, that's all I was calling about. Just saw it on the news; thought I'd give you a heads up seeing as Douglas mentioned a summit just before he was killed."

"Doubt it means anything, but I'll bring it up to Taffer... again."

As CJ put away his phone he thought about how he wished he'd gotten at least a thank you from Josh and wondered how long it would be before that canyon between them would shrink away. He knew he was probably expecting too much after all the years of estrangement, but still, with what they'd been through together with Tommy Clark, CJ had thought that it'd all been put aside, or at least most of it. It was as though every time they talked or got together CJ was still having to pickaxe through the cold exterior. It did seem though that the ice *was* getting a little thinner. Josh volunteered information about the raid on the Apollo Beach house.

And then he remembered the advice he'd given Josh just the day before concerning rising from rookie FBI agent to a seasoned professional. "Baby steps," he'd told him. Maybe that's how it would be to get his son back, a series of baby steps. A little over a month ago he had no idea where Josh was, didn't even know if he was alive. Now they were talking.

"I assume you called your son," Parker said when CJ came back in. "Did they know about it?"

"I don't think Josh did. But then he *is* a rookie."

"And rookies don't know anything. I should call John Taffer."

CJ held up his hand. "Do me a favor and don't. If Taffer doesn't already know about it, it'll be a feather in Josh's cap to be the one to tell him."

"Do you think Josh will be smart enough to not mention where he got his information, to come up with a plausible explanation?"

"Oh yeah. I think he can get creative."

"Did they check out the house that Eddie Hall sold?" Stella asked.

"They did, but that didn't go anywhere. There appears to be an older couple living there, leasing the place through a property management service. Owner lives up north."

"So, what now?"

"No idea. Let the FBI run with the summit angle while we stay out of the way?"

"Fine by me," Stella said.

"Me too," Gracie said, looking at her husband. "What I could use right now is a glass of wine." She looked at CJ and Stella. "How you about you guys?"

"What do you have?" CJ said.

"Don't know much about wines. It's red and cheap."

CJ laughed. "My kind of wine."

Scott returned just as CJ and Stella were standing up to leave. He eyed the nearly empty bottle of wine, with distaste as far as CJ could tell, and headed up the stairs.

"He have something against cheap wine?" CJ asked.

Gracie waited until her son was out of earshot and then said, "Our youngest thought it would be cool to try a taste when the remainder of the family was otherwise occupied."

"By the time he was discovered," Parker said, "he'd wiped out half a bottle, and it wasn't the cheap stuff either. The following twelve to fifteen hours weren't pretty."

"I have to smile at his reaction whenever he sees a bottle of wine now," Gracie said.

"How old was he?" Stella asked.

"It was just last month."

"He reminds me a lot of my nephew," Stella said. "Boys can certainly be a challenge."

"Boys of all ages can be a challenge," Gracie said, grinning at Parker.

"Ain't that the truth," Stella said.

"Glad we aren't boys anymore," Parker said.

Gracie and Stella snorted and laughed.

CJ took Stella's hand. "Time to go."

Parker walked them to the door. "Call me in the morning if you guys still need a backseat driver for something... anything."

"You can count on it," CJ said.

Back at the hotel, CJ and Stella sat in the dark, holding hands and looking out at the lights of St. Petersburg.

"I like it here," Stella said.

"You do?" CJ was surprised.

"Except for the bombs and dead bodies, it's nice. Lots of green and water."

CJ nodded his understanding. "Nice people, too. I could see Parker and Gracie becoming very good friends."

"I think they already are."

Minutes ticked by while they watched a slow moving light in the area where they knew there was only water.

"How about tomorrow we walk down to a place I know of where one can hire sailboat time?" CJ said.

She squeezed his hand. "Sure. No driving. Just sitting and cuddling."

"Hard to cuddle with life jackets on," CJ said.

"Hard to cuddle when we're drowning, too."

"I don't know. I could drag you ashore and give you mouth-to-mouth."

"Not if you don't know how to swim. How about you try practicing a little mouth-to-mouth now?"

CJ grinned and did.

Chapter 30

Incessant ringing started to pull CJ from a place where giant trees kept falling across the road in front of him. He'd turn the wheel and the road would change, creating a detour around one tree only to be blocked by another.

"Clint!"

Stella's voice blew away the visions, replacing them with darkness and the continued ringing.

"Hey!" she said.

CJ felt her hand on his shoulder.

"Clint!" She was yelling at him now.

"Yeah." He tried to force his voice to sound like he was fully awake, knowing that with his face in the pillow it probably came out as anything but.

"Hey!" she said, pushing at him harder. "Wake up! Phone's ringing. It's on your side."

"I'm awake." He didn't move.

"Sure you are." She pushed at him again.

"Okay!" he said a little too harshly and fumbled for the phone, banging the receiver across the table before he finally got control of it.

"Yeah," he said into it.

"Clinton Washburn?" a male voice said.

"Yeah. Who's calling?"

He raised his head, blinked at the filtered lights of the night peeking through the drapes and attempted to find his limbs so he could roll onto his back without igniting the pain in his ribs and shoulder.

"Hello?"

He looked over at Stella, sitting on the edge of the bed, beautiful in the dim light.

"Hello?" he said a second time, louder, irritated. After a few seconds he returned the handset to the phone cradle. "He hung up."

CJ looked at the 3:23 displayed on the clock next to the phone.

"Who was it?" Stella asked.

"Don't know. Asked for Clinton Washburn. Sounded FBIish, or at least very official."

"Police maybe?"

"Maybe."

She settled back down next to him.

"If the FBI wanted to talk to me, they'd have Josh call, and he'd call the cell phone," CJ said. "Police would use my full name, but why call and then hang up?" He raised his head and looked over at the desk where he thought he had left his phone. He couldn't see it. He started to get up only to excite a groan.

"What do you need?" Stella said. "I'll get it."

"Cell phone. I'm calling Josh."

She turned on a light and fetched the phone. After punching the appropriate buttons CJ held it to his ear and waited.

"Yeah, Dad," Josh said after only one ring, wide awake, no irritation that CJ could tell.

"You awake?"

"I come alert very fast. It's three-thirty in the morning. What's up, Dad?"

"We just got a strange call on the hotel phone. Asked for Clinton Washburn, and then hung up after my acknowledgement. I'm checking with you to see if anything is happening on the FBI side."

"No idea who it was?"

"No."

"I'll be right there. Don't open for anyone else but me."

Stella stared at CJ as he punched the end call button and put the phone down. When he didn't say anything, she said, "Well? What did he say?"

"Get dressed. He's on his way."

Stella went into the bathroom during which time CJ just sat on the edge of the bed in his boxers, waiting for various pains to settle. When she came out he rose to his feet, gave her a hug and then shuffled into the bathroom, conscious that she was way ahead of him in the getting-dressed department. After doing his business with the toilet he carefully leaned over the sink and flooded his face and head with cold water.

Is this what it feels like to be old?

Just as he reached for a towel there came a knock at the hotel room door. Josh, he thought, and then remembered Josh's warning not to open the door for anyone except for him. Now that his head was awake and clear, he understood why and expected that Stella would look through the peephole first in any case. He waited what he would later regret was a heartbeat too long before calling out, "Look before you open..."

Stella screamed and then came a crash. CJ reached for the bathroom door just as it burst open and he found himself looking at a gun, on the end of which was a silencer sporting a hole the size of a canon. This time CJ didn't wait for another heartbeat. He dodged left while whipping the towel up and into the gun, pushing it right. The gun went off and CJ charged into the man, pushing him across the small entryway into the refrigerator, slamming his head against the microwave. The man's momentary stun allowed CJ time to grab the gun.

"Eeee!" CJ screamed, the silencer burning his hand. The gun went off again just as CJ jerked it away, the report much louder. He tossed it across the room as he stumbled back, getting a momentary vision of Stella on her knees, bending over something, blood running down her side, dripping onto the floor. Fear and a sudden rage burst inside of him. He turned to rush at the man only to receive a kick to the gut. CJ slammed against the wall and dropped to the floor, red-hot blinding pain slicing through his ribcage. He tried to shake it off, tried to cut through it, knowing that he was dead if he didn't react quickly, but he could barely move. He got one foot underneath him, formulated a plan that involved charging and head bashing, fists driven into the solarplexus, and raised his eyes. The guy was standing, staring at something behind CJ, not seeming to be preparing to strike out again. CJ took the opportunity to get another couple of breaths, as shallow and painful as they where, and took the few seconds to reconsider his plan.

Ignore the pain and hit him low and hard, CJ thought.

Just as he took one last breath and tensed for the charge, the man turned and ran out.

What the hell? CJ looked over his shoulder to find Stella, in a shooter's stance, SIG Sauer in her hand, pointing at the closing door. And blood. A lot more blood.

Stella let her arms fall and then tried to sit back, only to wind up flopping onto the floor, back against the bed. Unable to do anything but get to his hands and knees, CJ crawled over to her. The blood was coming from somewhere around her left breast.

"Stella!"

"I'm okay."

"No you're not. You're bleeding. He shot you?"

"A little bit, yeah. Just a scratch."

He tore open her blouse to find a hole or tear or bullet crease in the area of her armpit. It was hard to tell with all the blood, but what he could see was that the injury was not life threatening as long as he could get her to the hospital. He saw his phone where he'd dropped it. He picked it up and hit redial, pushed the hair back on Stella's face while he waited.

When he heard Josh's voice, he broke in. "Where the hell are you? We were attacked. One gunman. Gone. Stella's shot. Call 911. Get your ass up here." Without waiting for a response, he dropped the phone, pushed to his feet and went to the door to prop it open then grabbed a towel and returned to Stella. He was applying pressure to her wound when Josh rushed in.

"They made an attempt on my dad and Stella's life," Josh was saying into his phone. "Stella was shot. EMS is on the way." He dropped to one knee in front of Stella. "How're you doing?"

She smiled at him. "Not as bad as it looks... really. Hurts like hell, though."

"It appears that it was a graze," CJ said. "More blood than anything."

Into the phone, Josh said, "Looks like she'll be okay. Not a vital hit." To CJ he said, "Did you get a look at the gunman, recognize him?"

"Got a good look, but no, didn't recognize him."

"Could it be the guy who was driving the truck or the one who threw the device?"

"Could have been either or someone else altogether."

"No sir," Josh said into the phone. "We don't have an ID."

CJ closed his eyes and thought about the bomb being thrown, the hand pushing out through the open truck window. There was a ring, a gold ring with a dark-colored stone. The hand that held the weapon with the silencer also had a ring.

"Yes," CJ said and Josh turned from his phone. "It could have been the man who threw the bomb; could have been the same ring."

Chapter 31

Stella sat on the same emergency room table as had CJ three days before, analyzing the buttons, or lack thereof, on her blouse. By the time EMS had arrived in the hotel room, CJ had managed to recover himself enough that he was able to easily refuse their help. He wanted all their attention on Stella. Besides, he didn't really think any more damage was done to his ribs even though it might have felt like it at the time.

"The buttons are all gone, Clint," she said. "What the hell did you do?"

"I thought you were bleeding to death, that you'd been shot in the chest."

"Yeah, well, they cut my bra off of me, too... didn't have to do that. Now all I've got to cover myself with is a bloody blouse with no buttons."

CJ stood and started to pull off his shirt.

"No," Stella said. "I can live with this."

"Nonsense. You need to be covered. I've got this stylish body wrap. No one will even pay attention, and if they do, it's their problem."

Stella gave him an eye-roll and then accepted the shirt. He helped her with the left sleeve and then buttoned it for her.

"This is a nice look," he said when he was done, giving her a feel through the thin fabric.

She snorted. "Don't get used to it. And I'm in no mood for any hanky-panky."

He kissed her on the forehead. "Actually, neither am I. I was just checking to see if we were both really alive."

She snorted again.

He sat back down just as the doctor returned.

"Here's a prescription. Take as needed for pain, but no more than four times a day." He looked at his watch. "It'll be a few hours before you can fill it so until then here are some samples." He handed her two small pill bottles. "Take with eight ounces of water. Change the dressing a couple of times a day."

The doctor looked at CJ with his bandaged ribs. "Aren't you the guy who was in here a few days back?"

"Afraid so."

"Did I read that you were also involved in that explosion?"

CJ grinned and shrugged. "Not been a good visit to Florida."

"I guess not." He put his hand on Stella's shoulder. "Take care of that wound and it should heal up well. The nurse will be right in."

When he departed, leaving the door open, Josh stepped in. "Is he about done?"

"Believe so," CJ said. "Waiting on the nurse to escort us out, I guess. Have you found out anything about the perp?"

"Three-thirty in the morning, nobody sees anything."

"How about the summit?"

"What about it?"

"What do you mean, what about it? Didn't you bring it up to Taffer?"

"Yes."

CJ waited a few seconds and then said, "Well? What did you find out?"

"I told him and that's it. Sometimes information flows in one direction."

CJ started to say something about that and then changed his mind. It was probably nothing anyway. "You got the guy's gun; find anything on that?"

"Still too early for a report on the fingerprints. Don't expect to get any hits if he's a foreign national, but you never know."

"What about bullets? The gun was discharged at least three times," CJ said, "and I'm sure those hotel walls aren't that thick."

"Yes, it was fired three time, but, as I'm sure you know, Dad, ballistics when we actually have the gun, is a non-event. As for where the bullets went, fortunately, the room next to yours was unoccupied. One bullet was lodged in that room's shower wall, another in the television. The one that caught you, Stella, was found in your mattress. He must have been shooting down, otherwise it would have gone through the window."

Stella nodded. "When he broke past the door, he shoved me back. I stumbled and fell. I didn't even know I'd been shot, didn't hear it. When he went for Clint in the bathroom I knew I had to get to my gun. I had a hard time getting it out of my purse and then getting my shooter's stance, couldn't make my left arm cooperate, thought I'd injured it in my fall, though I didn't feel any pain."

"The pain was probably masked by the adrenaline rush," Josh said.

CJ bobbed his head up and down. "When he ran out I looked up and there she was, mad woman with a pink SIG Sauer; enough to send any man running for the hills, even if she *was* only holding it with one shaky hand."

"You making fun of my pink gun again, Clint?"

"No. Not at all. I'm very respectful of your pink gun. It saved our lives. I kind of wish you'd shot the guy, though. A nice punch to the shoulder would have put him down enough that we could've beat a confession out him, maybe found out about the reason for all of this."

"I'll keep that in mind next time. To be truthful with you, I couldn't even see the guy. Yes, he was standing right there, not ten feet from me, but all I could see was a big blur. My eyes were watering and I had all I could do to point the gun in the right direction."

"You were crying."

"No! I wasn't crying. My eyes were watering, maybe from being shot. I don't know. But I didn't cry, Clint."

"Sure. You can just drop us at the hotel, Josh," CJ said, "so you can get back to your duties of sorting out the puzzle."

"First of all, Dad, it's six o'clock in the morning. Second of all, I'm not leaving your sides."

"Orders from Taffer?" CJ said.

"Orders from me," Josh said. "They're after you for some reason."

"I don't need a bodyguard, Josh."

"Bullshit, Dad. There've been three attempts on your life and now Stella is getting a share. You're burning through your nine lives awfully fast. The two of you are stuck with me until I get your butts on a flight back to Arizona."

CJ opened his mouth to argue and then looked at Stella. He'd almost lost her. The gunman was obviously intent on a chest shot and it was only by the grace of Stella's stumble that he'd missed. And then CJ remembered how she and his daughter were at death's door in the hands of Tommy Clark, just before CJ killed Clark, and how Clark's brother almost killed Josh hours before that. All of it was because of CJ. He came so close to losing everyone he loved because of his profession.

He dropped his eyes to the floor.

"You're right, Josh," was all he could say.

"What's that, Dad? Did I hear you correctly? Did you say that I'm right?"

"Don't push it, Josh. Just get us back to the hotel. Stella will make the arrangements and we'll get out of here."

"Tomorrow," Stella said.

Both of the men looked at her.

"I'd like to get some rest and then do a little sightseeing this afternoon, maybe go to a beach somewhere." She looked at CJ. "No sailing."

"As much as I hate to admit it," CJ said, "Josh is right. Three attempts on my life and now you're included. It's not worth it, sticking around just for the sightseeing."

"It's not up for discussion."

CJ smiled and looked up at Josh. "You bring any beach clothes?"

Chapter 32

Hotel management seemed to be tossed between providing a new room and telling CJ and Stella to take their business elsewhere. Seeing as there didn't seem to be any media attention concerning the early morning shooting, they opted to provide the room next to Josh since it had a connecting door, which only moderately satisfied Josh. What both he and CJ really wanted was a suite with two bedrooms, but there wasn't one available.

CJ stood at the window watching the sunrise–the 5th floor view was not quite as good as on the 9th floor–while Stella focused on rearranging her suitcase and personal items. Since the old room was still a crime scene, Josh had taken care of getting them moved, dumping everything into bags, not taking the time to determine what belonged to who.

"Why don't we call Gracie and Parker?" Stella said. "See if they'd like to join us on the beach. Kids are in school and Gracie said she'd taken a few days off from her work because of Parker's injuries. They also probably know a good place to go."

"Thought you wanted to get some rest. We've been up since 3:30."

"Logically, yes. Realistically, I'm too keyed up. I'd just stare at the ceiling. If I'm going to lie on my back staring at something, I'd rather it be a blue sky on the beach."

"How about lying on your back staring at my face?" CJ said.

"Men really do have a one-track mind," Stella said. "Maybe tonight. Let's see how we are both feeling."

"Okay. It's the beach, then. Can't get your dressing wet, though."

"Don't want to swim, just wade a bit. It'll be fun."

"I don't have sandals with me."

"You did bring something other than long pants, didn't you?"

"Yes."

"Wear that and then take off your shoes when we get there. You'll be just fine."

They met-up at Parker's house where he and Gracie were loading stuff into their van.

"When you called about going to the beach," Gracie said, "my first thought, with a frown on my face, was how could I go to the beach without the kids? And then as I processed the meaning of that, the corners of my mouth turned up and I called out to Parker, 'Let's go to the beach without the kids!' Do you have any idea how long it has been since we've done that?"

"Forever," Parker said.

"Sometime last century, if I'm not mistaken," Gracie said, "before we had kids."

Parker stepped up next to CJ and nodded his head toward Josh who was down at the curb at the end of the circular driveway, looking up and down the street. "What's up with your son?"

"He's playing bodyguard and taking it rather seriously."

"Did something else happen?"

CJ and Stella hadn't told the DuPonts about the attempt on their lives just five hours before. He looked over at Stella who was carrying a beach chair from the garage with her good arm. He started to jump to her assistance and then didn't, knowing she'd fuss at him about being too protective. "I'm your partner and I can pull my own weight," she'd said many times.

"We got a call middle of the night, a hang-up. Five minutes later Stella opened the door to a knock and a gunman pushed his way in."

Parker just stared at him, his mouth hanging open.

"What happened?" Gracie said, partially overhearing the conversation.

"We got lucky, real lucky," CJ said and then went on to detail the entire event. When he was done, and after Stella had put in her clarifying comments, Gracie looked as white as the day before when she first learned of a WMD.

"I just hate this!" Gracie said and wrapped her arms around Stella. "Are you okay?"

"Yes. A bit sore." Stella was wearing a light, cotton top, the dressing completely covered.

"And here you are hauling chairs." She gave CJ a critical look and took the chair away from Stella. "Can I get you something? Have you had breakfast?"

"Yes. We ate."

"How about brandy and chocolate?"

Stella laughed. "*That* just might hit the spot, but how about we wait until after we get back from the beach?"

"How about chocolate on the way there; brandy when we return?"

"It's a deal."

The beach was exactly what CJ and Stella expected: A warm breeze, a gentle surf, sea gulls vying for scraps, a scattering of people sitting and walking, some with pre-school aged children. Two blankets, five chairs and one huge beach umbrella found the five of them sitting back, iced tea or water in their hands, gazing out at the horizon.

"Is that a pelican?" Stella said, pointing to a huge bird with a long beak as it glided by and then dove head first into the water.

"Brown pelican, yes," Gracie said. She pointed to two others farther down the beach, gliding their way in their direction. "They're fishing."

Stella watched the two as they got closer. "One has a brown head, the other is white. Is that the difference between male and female?"

"No," Gracie said. "The brown head means it is a juvenile. The white head is an adult. As far a male or female, I'm not sure. Do you know, Parker?"

"I think the male is bigger and has a longer beak. Tracy could tell you."

"Your daughter?" Stella said.

Parker nodded. "She did a report in school last spring. Knows all about the birds of Florida's gulf beaches."

Josh stood and walked down toward the surf, looking out at a jet-skier seeming to come too close to the shore. The skier did a fancy whip turn, throwing up sea spray and then headed back in the direction he'd come. Josh looked up and down the beach and then back toward the parking lot before returning to his chair.

"You need to relax," Parker said. "With that silly Hawaiian shirt I gave you, you look like the body guard for a don. Do they issue those shades at basic?"

Josh ignored Parker's question. "I'll relax when Dad and Stella's flight back to Arizona lifts off the runway."

Parker looked over at CJ. "When we were sitting in front of the coffee shop Saturday morning, just before all hell broke loose, you said you thought the threats were over, that they'd come to the realization that, and I quote, 'anymore of this cloak and dagger hit squad crap is useless.' Yet Ms. Danohough is dead and here you are still being pursued as though you are carrying the secret that would unravel their entire operation, an FBI agent as your bodyguard. Have you had any thoughts as to why they're still after you?"

CJ sat in his chair looking north along the beach and toward the parking lot while Josh did the opposite, his view being toward the south and out into the water. When they set out the chairs, the arrangement, though unspoken between the two of them, had been conscious. Unlike Josh, though, CJ didn't jump at any guy who came within fifty feet, or who came barreling in on a watercraft, but he was well aware of every male individual approaching the beach from the parking area. So far, there had been none who weren't obviously accompanied by a female and who weren't wearing beach clothes. As far as Parker's question, CJ hadn't thought about much else all morning, finding that relaxing on the beach was about as successful as trying to light a barbeque in a high wind. If you weren't careful, it'd blow up in your face.

"I have to say, Parker, I'm clueless."

"Maybe Douglas told you something else that you're not

remembering and somehow they know you don't remember it, want to eliminate you before you do."

"Or maybe they just think he told me, but he didn't."

Parker nodded. "That, too."

"Either way, I'm still a target they're after."

"Do they think Stella knows something, too?" Gracie said.

"I doubt it. Killing her would just be collateral damage in going after me. As a matter-of-fact, being near me, you all could turn into collateral damage yourselves."

Gracie looked up and down the beach. "That's not very comforting."

"Sorry, Gracie. Every time I think they're through with me, that I have some idea what they're up to, I get blindsided. Now I've got everybody running down the summit angle and am no longer sure the summit has anything to do with it. I usually don't believe in coincidences, but now and then they do happen."

"More often not, though," Parker said. "I think it has to do with the summit and you know something you have yet to realize you know."

"Thanks for the confidence, but it's no help."

"I have a question," Stella said.

"What's that?" CJ said.

"When you talked to Douglas, he said he'd been back in the states for three days. Is that right?"

"That's what he said."

"And he let slip something about a summit."

"That's what I remember."

"But, apparently, the FBI didn't know anything about the summit and as far as I can tell don't seem to find it important." She turned her head to Josh. "No offense meant, Josh."

"None taken."

"If it was so important," Stella continued, "why hadn't Douglas turned it over to the FBI right after he returned?"

There was silence for a time and then Josh said, "Maybe he didn't obtain the information in Ireland."

"You mean he'd discovered it after returning and had yet to contact his handler about it?" Parker said.

"When you're undercover like he was, it's not always easy to get information out," Josh said. "You have to be careful: Initiate a time and place, plan how to get there while making it look like something very normal, be aware of everyone around you, pass the info without being observed or recorded in any way. It can be a bit complex. I have to say, though, three days does seem like a long time to let something like this slide. He should have found a way to get to his handler. In any case, his handler should have made contact with him to get a debriefing within twenty-four to forty-eight hours after his return."

"Douglas *did* check in with his handler." Realizing what he'd said, CJ jerked forward in his chair. "Holy crap!" He half exclaimed and half groaned. His rib cage didn't appreciate the sudden movement.

"What?" Parker said.

"You okay, Clint?" Stella said.

CJ took a long, slow breath, willing the pain to relax. "I'm fine. Just moved too fast." He looked over at Josh. "I can't believe I missed it."

"Missed what, Dad?" Josh considered his dad's words for a few seconds. "Are you saying that he *did* meet with his handler? Did he tell you that?"

"Yes, he did. Until just now I didn't recall it. Probably didn't recognize the significance of the statement." He thought for a few seconds and then added, "He said something about having returned three days before from Northern Ireland and that while there he didn't talk to his handler, that they trusted him to do what he had to do. And then he said, 'I only just checked in yesterday.' Those were his exact words. I'm sure of it. That was Friday morning when I talked to him which means he checked in with his handler sometime on Thursday. I can't believe I didn't put those two things together until now."

"You've got to be mistaken," Josh said. "There's no way."

"There's always a way, Josh. You put enough money or incentive on the table, there becomes a way."

"Agent Taffer said that Douglas had requested a meeting for Friday night."

"Whoever gave him that information, lied to him."

"Lied? What?" Gracie said. "I'm lost here."

Josh and CJ just looked at each other. Stella didn't say anything. Parker put his hand on Gracie's arm. "What they're saying, dear, is that Douglas checked in with his handler, but the handler didn't pass the report on to his cohorts."

"Which means?"

"The handler purposely withheld vital information to the FBI that would help thwart whatever it is that needs to be thwarted."

"Oh," Gracie said, almost under her breath.

"Who was the handler?" CJ said.

Josh had his cell phone in his hand. "I don't know, but I'm going to find out." He punched at the phone and then stepped away.

Silence ensued thereafter, anticipation evident on all faces. CJ watched a man approach the beach through the dunes, some hundred yards north; loose fitting plain blue shirt, long pants, ball cap, sunglasses. He stopped and looked both ways, seeming to pause his gaze on CJ's group, but only briefly. Another man appeared but he didn't continue onto the beach, only his head visible over the dunes. After a bit the first man turned around joined the other man and then they both disappeared. It wasn't the same approach that CJ's group had used, that being less than twenty yards away, the closest approach from the small parking lot. CJ watched the area while waiting on the results of Josh's phone call.

Chapter 33

"Blain," Josh said when he returned. "Special Agent Howard Blain."

"Coulter's partner?" CJ said.

"Yep, though I've never met him."

"It was the two of them who picked me up at the hotel Thursday night," CJ said. "Haven't seen anything of him since."

"He had a family emergency come up on Friday and took off for Wisconsin. Something about his mother."

"Convenient." Parker said.

"Taffer isn't inclined to believe that he has an agent on the take," Josh said, "but he's checking it out anyway. Needless to say, he's a bit pissed."

"No doubt," CJ said.

"I think he's reserving at whom he'll be pissed until he gets more information. You being the source of the bad news may make you the recipient. Are you one-hundred percent certain of what Douglas said?"

CJ closed his eyes for a few seconds, forcing up a recall of the conversation. "I've no doubt. He said that when he was there, in Ireland that is, he didn't talk with his handler, that he'd just checked in the day before. His words, and this is as exact as I can recall them, ' I just checked in yesterday.' That would be Thursday."

"That still leaves a 24-hour hole for doubt," Josh said. "He could have learned of the summit between the time he checked in and the time he talked to you."

"What about Coulter?" Parker said. "They're partners, aren't they?"

"Only one of them would be designated the handler, but you're thinking is right. Partners know everything about each other, have each other's back. So from Douglas' point of view, they'd both be handlers."

"Could there be two agents on the take?" Stella said.

"Taffer's pulling Coulter out of the field right now."

"I'd give a hundred bucks to be the fly on that wall," Parker said."

After a bit of silence, Gracie said, "You up for a walk in the waves, Stella?"

"It's the only reason we haven't left for home, yet," Stella said. "If I don't get my feet wet soon, I'll go crazy."

The women got up, Stella kicking off her sandals.

Josh seemed to shift uneasily in his chair, appearing tossed between staying with his father and playing bodyguard to Stella. When he looked over at his dad, CJ gave a slight nod toward the women. Josh rose to his feet.

CJ smiled. He really didn't think there was a threat on a St. Petersburg beach, but it wasn't worth the chance. He'd feel so much better knowing that there was someone watching her back. He was also glad to see her pick up her purse, her pink Sig Sauer nestled inside. And then he silently cursed at himself, again, for not taking the time to check his own weapon through airline security.

Without a word, Parker got up and moved over to where Josh had been sitting. CJ knew it wasn't so that he could watch the women's posteriors as they strolled away. He was taking over Josh's place, watching for threats. What the two of them would do if such a threat presented itself, CJ had no idea. Hobbled with injuries and no weapons, they were both about as useful as couple of children with water balloons.

CJ suddenly felt very naked.

"I hope to hell you're wrong on this one, CJ," Parker said.

"I hope I'm wrong, too."

As they talked, CJ continued to watch the beach accesses. The two guys still nagged at him. Another man stepped onto the beach, this time directly from the parking lot. He was alone, however his dress was not similar to that of the first man. He was wearing stylish shorts and a T-shirt, too tight and tucked in, wrap-around sunglasses, and a ball cap; a phone was clipped to his belt. There was no place for a concealed weapon.

"I don't like the idea of a federal officer on the take, or cop of any kind," Parker said.

"I know what you mean," CJ said.

Maybe it was the shoes. CJ couldn't tell for sure, but they didn't appear to be something one would wear onto the beach.

"When I was in uniform, we had a cop in Tampa taking bribes from a drug dealer. Turned real messy. Put a black smudge on all of us."

Whatever it was, the guy seemed out of place.

"Had the same thing happen in Phoenix," CJ said.

"Makes it real hard to do our jobs," Parker said.

The guy was looking toward the area of the beach behind CJ, to the south. CJ started to twist about to see the girls but found, with his rib injury, that he had to stand and turn. They were some seventy or eighty yards away, Stella knee-deep in the surf, Josh close by, phone pressed to his ear. It appeared to CJ that that was where the guy was looking.

"I've been watching them," Parker said. "They're fine."

CJ sat back down and found that the guy was walking back to the parking area.

"I thought there was someone watching them," CJ said.

Parker twisted around. "Who?"

"He's gone. It was nothing."

"You're getting paranoid, CJ."

"Yeah. Tell me about it."

By the time the women had turned around to come back, the guy from the parking lot had returned, only this time he was carrying an umbrella and pushing a baby carriage; big wheels, huge canopy, an over-endowed woman in an under-endowed bikini following with a diaper bag and cooler. They set up about twenty yards behind CJ.

Parker watched them for a while and then said to CJ, barely above a whisper, "A couple of square inches of material should be illegal."

"Maybe she grabbed Barbie's bikini by mistake instead of her own."

Parker snorted.

"He's the guy I was worried about a few minutes ago," CJ said.

"Really! Looks to me like he has other things on his mind."

"Like you said, I'm getting paranoid."

When Stella and Gracie flopped back into their chairs, they didn't seem to give the neighbor woman–on her stomach, top unhooked, bottom covering next to nothing–more than a glance. Parker returned to his chair so Josh could sit back down.

"Now that I'm back you suddenly feel guilty," Gracie said, "so you had to move to give up your view."

Parker gave his wife a serious look. "I figured that Josh, being single, would have a deeper appreciation for such things. I've got everything I need right at home."

Gracie put her hand on his. "You'd better believe it, sweetie." To Stella she said, "He always knows the right thing to say."

Josh just sat, unmoving in his wraparound *Ray-Bans*. After a time he said, "Talked with Agent Taffer again. He got a hold of Agent Blain. Blain said that Douglas *had* checked in Thursday afternoon, but didn't have anything significant to report. Blain didn't have a chance to file the report before he got the call about his mother and had to fly home to Madison, Wisconsin. She was in an auto accident. Nearly died."

"So sorry to hear that."

"It's still touch and go. Blain is pretty stressed out, according to Taffer. Anyway, he claims that Douglas said nothing about a summit."

"Does Taffer believe him?" CJ asked.

"I think so," Josh said. "There have only been a handful of

cases where an agent has gone on the take. The risk is so high, I can't imagine."

CJ continued to watch the beach accesses, wondering about the guy in the blue shirt. When they finally packed up and carried everything to Parker's van, he eye-balled any car he could see, but found no one suspicious, and as they headed out there was no one following. He still couldn't rid himself of the feeling that they were being watched.

Chapter 34

They stopped at a *Subway* on the way home. CJ bought. When he started to get an argument from Parker he said, "It goes on my expense tab. Don't worry about it."

Stella poked him in the ribs and snorted.

CJ groaned.

They ate their sandwiches on the deck, under a huge umbrella, overlooking the lake behind the DuPont home.

"I should have picked up something for the kids," Gracie said. "We're going to be in the doghouse when they see the *Subway* trash."

Parker glanced at his watch. "We've got time to finish up and dispose of the trash."

"If *they* did that and we caught them, we'd give them hell."

"The difference is, we're adults," Parker said.

"That means it's okay?" Gracie said.

"That means that by this time, we should have learned enough lessons to be smart enough *not* to get caught."

"That's the lesson we're teaching our children?" Gracie looked over at Stella and CJ, a sardonic smile on her face. "Meet my husband, the cop. This is the guy sworn to serve and protect, the one who lectures his children about being honest, law-abiding citizens."

"So you'd just let them find out and face their wrath?" Parker said.

"Oh, hell no. I'd either go out and get something for them or I'd dispose of the trash deep in the can and then brush my teeth to make sure I don't have sandwich breath."

CJ laughed.

"What are you laughing at, Clint?" Stella said.

"I was just thinking that we need to be writing all this stuff down. It'll come in handy when we start growing our own family."

Stella raised both of her eyebrows and tilted her head at him. "You're forty-four and I'm... well, even though there is not yet a four in my age, I do have a nine, so I'm not far behind you. My maternal clock is winding down... that is, the urge to have a child has just about run its course. You've come along just a little bit too late, Clint."

"Oh." CJ made a face of disappointment.

"You've got two adult children. You should be looking forward to grandchildren." Stella gave Josh a look.

"Sorry," Josh said. "Not even on the horizon."

"Good! Because I'm not old enough yet to be a step-grandmother, or any kind of grandmother."

"You're at that awkward age," CJ said.

"Awkward... age?"

"I mean..."

"Sure."

CJ smiled over at Parker. "Is that offer of brandy still on the table?"

Two of three children were home from school when Stella, CJ and Josh took their leave. The women as well as Parker and CJ promised to stay in touch.

"I'll be calling you," Parker said to CJ.

"About what?" Gracie said.

"Official business," Parker said. "I'm a detective. CJ's a private detective."

"Consulting stuff," said CJ.

Gracie looked at Stella and shrugged her shoulders. "Whatever." She gave Stella a hug. "I want an invitation to your wedding."

"For sure," Stella said. "And you'd better show up."

Josh pulled up in front of the hotel lobby to let the two of them out, saying that he'd be up as soon as he parked the car. Stella mentioned that her wound was hurting and that she was anxious to take a pain killer and then lay down for a nap. CJ expressed like sentiments.

"I'm trusting that you won't get in trouble in the next five minutes," Josh said.

"I think we're too tired and sore to get into trouble," CJ said. "By the time you get up to the rooms we'll probably be in slumber land."

"We should take the time to ice you again," Stella said as they struggled out of the car.

"How about later? You need to get some rest first."

"I can rest later."

A woman and two men joined them in the elevator. The woman pushed three; one of the men pushed seven. Stella pushed five. The doors closed.

"What time does the flight leave in the morning?" CJ said.

"Little after seven." Stella leaned her head against CJ's shoulder. "How long do you think Josh will be here?"

"Probably not long after we leave."

The doors opened. The woman got off.

"But then," CJ continued, "with Blain out and Coulter maybe on the sideline, Taffer may hold onto him."

"True," Stella said.

They stood in silence as the doors closed and the elevator restarted its assent, CJ looking down at the floor and the sand caked in the crevasses of his shoes. He thought about the fact that he'd walked through the hotel lobby without checking anyone out, and he was sure that there had been people. It had to be the exhaustion from a very long day. He glanced at his watch. It wasn't even five o'clock.

And then he noticed that the two men who were sharing the elevator had the same kind of footwear issues, though not nearly as bad. One pair was pointed toward him, the other away, toward the doors. They also must have been at the beach. *That's odd*, CJ thought and lifted his eyes to take a look at the them. The one facing away was wearing a loose-fitting blue shirt. CJ could sense a warning bell just beginning to go off in his head but with the brandy still burning through his system, he was slow at making sense of its meaning.

The elevator stopped at the fifth floor and the men stepped in front of the door, both turning to fully face CJ and Stella. "You're not getting off here," said Blue Shirt, producing a short-barreled gun.

CJ heard Stella's sudden intake of breath. The man standing before them, in the blue shirt, was the man who killed Eveleen and claimed that his name was Eddie Hall. The ball cap covered the contusion on his head, sunglasses covered his eyes. The other man was the one who attacked them in the hotel room.

The doors opened to an empty corridor, paused for what seemed an excessively long time and then closed.

Blue Shirt continued. "The next time the elevator doors open we will not get off. We will select the lobby. When we get there my friend here will go out first, followed by you, Mister Washburn and then your lady. I will bring up the rear, my gun concealed but ready. I will be watching both of you. You will make no facial or hand gesture. You will say nothing. If you do and I suspect that a message has been transmitted, I'll be forced to kill the other person and then the lady here."

"Why don't I just go quietly with you," CJ said, barely able to keep his voice calm. "Let her remain in the elevator. Punch a number and let the doors close. By the time she'd be able to get off and tell someone, we, you two and I, would be long gone."

"You are quite a gentleman, Mister Washburn. No. We're doing what I say, so please, don't start a bloodbath."

CJ opened his mouth again.

"You argue with me and I'll leave her in the elevator as you requested, only with a bullet in her head. Do I make myself clear?"

CJ thought about the SIG Sauer nestled in its holster in Stella's purse–about as useful now as a squirt gun–and about his injuries, thus his limitations. He'd likely not have a chance in the confines of the elevator. However, while walking through the hotel lobby, would these guys really risk shooting people in front of any number of witnesses, maybe even video cameras? Of course with ball caps they could easily keep their faces hidden.

And then he thought about Stella and what she was thinking. He turned his head and looked at her. She appeared angry and scared, pensive, her purse hanging off her right shoulder, not her left because that's where her injury was. She would have to retrieve the SIG Sauer with her left hand and then get it into her right. He could almost read her thoughts. What if he stepped in front of her to give her cover so she could make the draw? She was also shaking. If she tried and fumbled, or hesitated, or just wasn't fast enough... he didn't even want to think about it. You couldn't outdraw a man with a gun already aimed at you, no matter how experienced you were, and Stella wasn't experienced at all.

CJ took a deep breath, felt the pain around his ribcage, looked back at Blue Shirt, and nodded his acquiescence.

"Very good. I have it on good authority that you are not armed, Mister Washburn, but you," he looked at Stella, "I know better."

"She's just my secretary," CJ said. "Doesn't even carry Mace."

"Really? Well, that's not very smart. There're a lot of people in this world intent on causing pretty young women harm. You really should consider it. In any case, you don't have a very good memory, Mister Washburn. We both know firsthand about the SIG she carries." He turned his gun toward Stella. "You're going to release your purse and let it drop to the floor. You will leave it behind when we walk out."

CJ turned his head toward Stella again and saw the look on her face. He nodded and it seemed like her resolve deflated. She let the purse drop.

"Excellent," Blue Shirt said. "You shouldn't have to worry about it. I'm sure a Good-Samaritan will turn it into the desk. As long as you are cooperative, you will live to retrieve it at a later time."

During the exchange, the elevator had made its stop on the seventh floor and then as directed by Blue Shirt's partner, descended to the ground floor. The doors opened, the gun went into hiding and the partner stepped out. Blue Shirt eased to the side to allow CJ passage.

Two people, a young couple, waited to get on, each with a small backpack hanging off a shoulder. CJ made sure to avoid their eyes. He was certain, from the tone of Blue Shirt's voice, that the man knew what he was doing, that he was possibly a gun for hire, that he wouldn't refrain from following through on the bloodbath that he referred to. He'd killed Eveleen Danohough and most likely Douglas. A few more certainly wouldn't bother him."

They made their way along the passage, some fifteen or twenty yards to where they'd turn right and head for the main doors, CJ conscious of Stella close behind him, Blue Shirt following, watching every move.

Just as they approached the corner, a man started yelling.

"Miss! Ma'am!"

"Keep going," Blue Shirt said when CJ paused.

"Ma'am!" The man was right behind them, his footsteps pounding on the passageway floor. "Ma'am! Is this yours?"

The partner looked over his shoulder causing CJ to do the same. It was the young man who'd just gotten on the elevator. He ran right up to Stella, holding her purse out to her. "Is this yours? You must have dropped it in the elevator."

Stella appeared to panic and then said, "Oh my God! Yes! Thank you very much. I..."

"I can't believe you did that, Sweetheart," Blue Shirt said. "Thank you, fine sir."

"No problem," the young man said. "Have a great day." With that he jogged back to the elevator where his wife, partner, whatever was waiting, holding the door, pride for the gallantry of her young man beaming across her face.

"Where are the Good Samaritans when you actually want one?" Blue Shirt said. "Let's continue. No more holdups. No surprises. Keep your hand out of your purse."

There were no more surprises as they filed out of the hotel and across its load/offload area to the sidewalk where a two-tone blue Ford Explorer waited.

"You get in the passenger seat, Mister Washburn and I'll keep your lady... what is your name?"

Stella glared at him for a few seconds and then said, "Mariana."

CJ suppressed a smile at her defiance, providing only her middle name instead of her first name.

"Very good, Mariana. I will keep you company. If Mister Washburn does anything stupid, it'll be you who gets shot."

Stella and then Blue Shirt climbed in the back, he instructing her to drop her purse onto the floor, while the partner went around and got in the driver's side. They left CJ standing by the passenger door. Under any other circumstance, it'd be the best opportunity to make a break for it, but then Blue Shirt and partner knew that CJ didn't have any choice but to comply. He glanced toward the hotel parking lot but didn't see Josh. By now he would have parked the car and entered through the closest entrance completely out of view of the front. What will Josh do when he discovers they aren't there? How long will it take him to determine that they'd been taken, or would he not even knock on their door, figuring they didn't want to be disturbed for a while?

CJ opened the door and got in. He looked up toward the hotel entrance. There were a few people, but no one was looking their way, no one paying them a bit of attention.

"Buckle up please," Blue Shirt said. "Don't want to damage our cargo should my friend get in an accident."

There came the sounds of seat belt clips snapping and then they were off.

Chapter 35

CJ tried to memorize the route, but there were so many turns that he started to get confused. Was that their plan, and if so, why? Blindfolds would have done the trick. And there's that; why weren't they blindfolded? You don't have to blindfold your captors if you plan on killing them. Stella still had her purse. Maybe there was a chance... maybe.

They wound up on 70th Avenue, the south side of the street having homes with backyards up against the bay; at least he thought it was the south side and he thought it was the bay. Between one pair of houses he got a brief glimpse of a long bridge structure off in the distance, two towers holding up the freeway. He considered the map he'd been looking at on Saturday before the bomb was thrown, and his earlier exploration of downtown St Petersburg. The bay was to the east, but the map showed that it also wrapped around to the south where it merged with the Gulf of Mexico and he remembered an interstate highway crossing over somewhere to the south; I-275 if he wasn't mistaken. Therefore, with recollection of the map and with where the sun was hanging and the fact that, from his experiences so far, avenues ran east-west in St. Petersburg, the back of these houses had to be south.

They pulled into the circular driveway of a split-level home with a double car attached garage on one side. The garage was set back so that the entry driveway did not impede with the circular drive, allowing plenty of parking. A pair of dark green paneled vans were parked side-by-side in front of the garage. On the driveway sat a deep-red Fiat Barchetta, spoiler on the back, top down; not a car CJ would associate with an IRA or UIRA thug.

As the partner stopped the Explorer behind the Fiat, a man came out of the house. During the entire trip the partner had not said a word. As a matter-of-fact he'd not opened his mouth from the time Blue Shirt pulled out the gun and started spouting instructions. On his right hand was a gold ring with a purple stone, telling CJ that Blue Shirt's partner was the bomb thrower. He bumbled that and the kidnapping in the hotel room. Is that why Blue Shirt had delegated him to driving?

"You will get out, Mister Washburn and accompany this gentleman up to the house," Blue Shirt said. "Mariana and I will be along in a jiff."

CJ looked over his shoulder at Stella. She was tight-jawed.

"It'll be okay," he said.

She allowed a very slight, but sad smile.

"He is correct," Blue Shirt said. "It will be okay as long as both of you do exactly what you're told."

CJ had questions but he didn't want to ask them in front of Stella. He'd just told her it'd be okay and he was a afraid that the answers to his questions, if Blue Shirt provided honest answers that is, would indicate otherwise.

He opened the door and the man from the house grabbed his arm.

"Shouldn't he be handcuffed?" the man said.

"He'll be fine," Blue Shirt said. "I'm going to stay here with his girl, my gun in her ribs. When he is secured inside, I'll bring her in."

The man pulled on CJ's arm. CJ pushed back his urge to resist and allowed himself to be guided into the house.

The front door opened into an entryway which led into a large living area; a great room to be exact, living room first and then the dining room. The kitchen wrapped around out of sight, CJ assumed. Decoration was minimal. Two sofas and a pair of chairs faced a television screen of at least eighty inches tuned to a news broadcast, middle east looking people talking to men in full body armor, serious weapons slung off shoulders. Volume was low and there was no one watching it. To the back, beyond a paper littered dining table, were a pair of huge windows looking across a grassed in backyard and a paved path leading down to a dock where a fair sized boat was moored.

Beyond that stood the bay and the bridge network CJ had spotted a few minutes before.

The view drew CJ, but he was stopped midstride by a female voice, shrill and angry. "Don't bring him in here, Gabe!" A woman near sixty appeared out of nowhere. "Why the hell isn't he shackled?"

"Alan has the girl and he said..."

"I don't give a flying fart what Alan said. You take him to the FROG and you shackle him! Got that?"

"Yes."

Gabe pulled on CJ. CJ resisted for a few seconds, trying to get a look at a map spread across the table, until he noticed a gun in Gabe's other hand.

"That way," Gabe said, indicting back toward the entryway with a twist and nod of his head. "And then up the stairs to the FROG."

CJ gave him a look. "FROG?"

"Finished Room Over the Garage. Move!"

"Oh." CJ gave in and turned around. As they passed through the foyer, the woman rushed by them, heading out the door toward where the Ford Explorer sat and where Stella and Blue Shirt, now known as Alan, still resided. As CJ ascended the stairs he could hear the woman's voice but not make out her words. She wasn't very happy. He couldn't really blame her with all the bumbling that had gone on with her operation in the last few days; however, from CJ's point of view Alan had handled the abduction quite well. Except for the guy returning Stella's purse from the elevator, he'd attracted no attention and had CJ completely under his control.

Someone *had* made one mistake, though. Stella's purse, and thus her SIG Sauer, were still in her possession. CJ wasn't sure, however, if that was going to turn into good mistake or a bad mistake for the two of them.

Chapter 36

CJ and Stella sat on opposite sides of the room, shackled with handcuffs, each to their own chain which led to half inch steel rings affixed to the walls. If they stood and went to the end of their chains, they could hold hands. They did so until Stella said that between her exhaustion and bullet wound, she had to sit down. CJ certainly couldn't argue with that.

The only furniture in the room was a table and chair against the wall opposite the entry door and two overstuffed chairs in which he and Stella sat. A second door, on Stella's side, led to a bathroom. There was one window, over the table, covered with a cheap blind, too far away for them to see out. In the corner, just inside the door, lay Stella's purse, out of reach for both of them. After the woman had brought her in, handcuffed her and left, Gabe had returned with the purse, throwing it into the corner.

Stella took some time to find a reasonable position in the chair, fooling about with the chain and handcuffs. More resigned than comfortable, she settled and said, "What do you think they're planning to do with us?"

"It's all I've been thinking about since the elevator," CJ said, "and I've not come up with a thing. After I got out of the car, what did Alan say to you?"

"Alan?"

"That's what the woman called him."

"Nothing. We just sat there until the woman came out and wanted to know what he was doing, why we weren't shackled."

"What did he say?"

"He said, 'Shackling in public view draws attention. You don't want attention. As soon as I know that Washburn has been secured, I'll bring in the lady.' She said that she still didn't like it and he said, 'You hired me to succeed where your previous idiots failed. I don't fail.'"

CJ thought about that for a few seconds and then said, "So they... she... tried using her own people but when that didn't work, she hired a pro."

"That's what it sounds like. He also said something about how if she'd hired him in the beginning, the Feds wouldn't be all over it, that her mission wouldn't be on the edge of complete failure."

"That's funny considering that it was his partner who bumbled the bomb Saturday and our kidnapping this morning."

"Surprised she didn't mention it. She did spit back at him that the mission was none of his concern, that the Fed involvement was calculated, that everything was right on track."

"Calculated. Interesting. I wonder if he's still on the clock."

"What do you mean?"

"Has he fulfilled the remainder of his contract after killing Douglas and Eveleen, that is to bring us in, get *us* off the street so to speak, or is he also playing the role as our guard?"

"What difference would it make?" Stella said.

"It would be good to know who it is we're up against; him and his bumbling partner or her bumbling idiots."

"Oh." She shifted again and took a deep breath. "He left in that red car."

"The Fiat Barchetta."

"Whatever. He took me out of the Explorer and then she took over, brought me inside and up here."

"Did he leave by himself?"

"In the Fiat? Yes. His partner never got out of the explorer."

"Did Alan or his partner tell the woman or Gabe about the SIG in your purse?"

"I don't know."

"If I were them I'd have searched it and removed it. If they didn't they really are bumbling idiots."

"So you think Alan also killed Douglas?"

"Yes, I do."

She closed her eyes for a time. "Speaking of bumbling idiots, they tried killing you three times. I really hate to ask this question, but why not this time now that they've got you? It would be so easy."

"I've thought about that, too. Here's the thing. The first time was the boat ride. That may not have started as an attempt on my life, but a kidnapping that got away from them. The second time was the bomb. I'm certain now that that was Alan and his partner. I was likely not the actual target. It was Ms Danohough or her and Rebecca. DuPont and I were to become nothing more than collateral damage. As a matter-of-fact it was probably only me they intended for collateral. I'm sure they didn't know that a police detective had arrived. If they had known maybe they'd aborted. Killing a police officer can bring out all kinds of attention. They've got an agenda and I'm sure they don't need that kind of heat right now. The third time, our little event this morning, may have again been a kidnapping attempt that went out of control. I saw the gun and never gave the guy a chance to explain himself. My sudden reaction caught him off guard."

"Why do they want you alive, then? They've gone to a lot of trouble."

"Exactly. Have I come up with so many answers that they think that they just need to get me out of the way until their mission is complete?"

"They're not afraid to kill people. Two are dead already."

"True," CJ said. "If they wanted us dead they've had ample opportunity since the elevator. This is something else. I just don't know what it is."

"Then why did they try to kill us in the hotel..." Stella paused for a few seconds, "...this morning? I cannot believe that was barely over twelve hours ago. Seems like a week."

"Know what you mean. Like I said, I think I was supposed to be taken alive. Doubt that they cared about you. You were..."

"I know," Stella said with a sigh. "Collateral damage."

"The guy was surprised when you answered the door. It may be that he didn't expect me to have a guest. Maybe he thought you were a nobody, a one night stand, a call girl, dispensable. Shooting you was as a result of the surprise, a reflex. Now they know you are of value to me, thus a bargaining chip to get me to do what they want."

"I still don't see how they would know that. Who would tell them? It does seem like Agent Blain is the mole, but he disappeared Saturday morning, well before I arrived. And besides, it seems that Taffer cleared him. After I arrived, the only people who knew about me were the FBI and the police."

"Don't forget the McGee family."

Stella thought about that for a moment.

"No," she said. "I can't see any of them being on the wrong side of this."

"I agree."

"So they, whoever *they* are, have been watching us."

"No doubt about it. I first spotted the guy with the blue shirt, Alan, while we were at the beach today."

Stella looked shocked. "You didn't say anything?"

"He was just a guy who walked onto the beach and then walked off. At the time, I dismissed him. I recognized him in the elevator just seconds before he pulled out the gun."

"Oh."

"I should have noticed him when he first got onto the elevator."

"You were tired and, like me, hurting."

"I was standing there with my head down, staring at the floor instead of looking at people. I should have seen both of them when we entered the hotel. Feeling bad is no excuse. The question is, how have they been tracking us? None of us, Josh, Parker or I, ever spotted a tail when we left Parker's house. Believe me, we were looking."

"A tracking bug?"

"How would they've known we'd be traveling in Parker's vehicle?"

"Cell phone locator?"

CJ shook his head. "That's not as easy as the movies make it out to be. A bit more sophisticated than the average Joe."

"Agent Blain is not your average Joe," Stella said. "Could he still have access to the technology?"

CJ considered that for a few seconds. "Yes... Maybe... No. Not now anyway, but this morning before we notified Taffer of our suspicions, he certainly could have. His mother in a car accident kind of takes him out of the picture. I doubt he's playing the wrong side."

Stella pulled her legs up under her and worked at trying to find a more comfortable position. "I guess that makes sense. I still think..."

"Think what?"

"I don't know." She fooled with her position a little more. "I'm going to try and get a little nap. Lack of sleep last night and then my adrenaline rush are catching up with me. And then I'm going to be hungry." She closed her eyes. "I hope they bring us a last meal."

CJ didn't say anything more, didn't want to comment on her last meal statement. Watching her, he continued to think.

Stella's next comment was a light snore.

Initially CJ thought that the UIRA operation had to do with smuggling weapons and explosives into Northern Ireland. He recalled his conversation with Agent Taffer Saturday afternoon during which time Taffer actually confirmed most of CJ's suspicion. Did the FBI have it completely wrong, even with Douglas as an informant? The woman had said that the Fed involvement was calculated, that everything was right on track. Could it be that the UIRA knew about Douglas' secret all along and had been feeding him false information so as to send officials off in a direction other than the actual mission? Is that what she meant by the Fed involvement being calculated? Could Douglas have all of a sudden found out the truth and thus had to be eliminated before he could pass it along? Douglas passed it to his handler, Agent Blain, and then where?

A mole inside the FBI... Maybe.

Douglas told Blain.

Blain told somebody. Who would he tell? Taffer? His partner?

CJ very much doubted that the mole would be Taffer. Moles are generally nearer the bottom of the pecking order. That would leave Agent Coulter.

What CJ would very much like to know right now is, what is Taffer doing to figure that out? Was it false information being fed to Douglas or was it a mole inside the FBI? That and why were he and Stella handcuffed to a wall in a FROG? Another thing, secure rings and chains weren't something one did on the fly. They'd set this up a long time ago for someone else. Douglas and Eveleen? Douglas and Rebecca? Eveleen and Rebecca? Whoever it was, they were part of the plan and he and Stella were last minute substitutes.

Also, what was Josh and the FBI doing to find them? Did Josh even know that they were gone?"

Chapter 37

"Clint!"

CJ awoke groggily, aware that Stella was trying to wake him.

"Clint!"

She was calling in a stage whisper, and there were other voices off in the distance.

"What?" CJ said.

"Wake up and be quiet."

With a start CJ remembered where he was and recognized also that it was still daylight. He looked at his watch. 6:25. He hadn't been asleep very long. "What's going on?" he asked in an equivalent whisper.

"It sounds like they're having a meeting. Listen."

CJ looked over at the door which had previously been closed. It was ajar a few inches as though someone had looked in on them and not closed it all the way. The voices were leaking in from down below. The woman who earlier seemed to be in charge was the most prominent, though CJ could only make out a word or two. There were at least two other voices, male, of which he could catch nothing but murmurs. He shifted his position to get circulation back to one leg that had fallen asleep. The chain rattled.

"Hush!" Stella hissed through her teeth.

He froze. The voices didn't stop. He moved more carefully to keep from making any further noise.

"Understand," said a new male voice. "Blah...blah... world center... blah...blah...blah..."

"Blah...Tampa...blah...blah..." said the woman. She continued on during which time CJ could pick up only the words, "fifteen" and "breakfast."

More murmurings came from the other male voices, though not a single word could be made out. The woman said, "Okay," and then went on with more instruction. That's what it felt like to CJ anyway. She was giving instructions, or going over a plan, or as far as CJ knew it was a meeting of a book club and she was reading passages from *The Grapes of Wrath* or *Gone with the Wind*.

Or maybe it's a new title: *Attack on the Summit*.

That was the word that CJ was listening for but had not heard. *Summit*.

Another murmur came from a male voice and the woman said, "Listen and listen carefully. The...blah...blah...will...blah...blah...not...blah...blah." There came another question or statement, then, "I...blah...blah...a rat's ass. You...blah...blah...eating."

The conversation went a bit quieter for a time. The only other words he picked up were "vans" and "loaded."

Then all went quiet except for what he guessed was a microwave dinging and a door opening and closing a couple of times. After a few minutes, when it appeared nobody was coming up to check on them, he whispered to Stella, "What all did you get?"

She got up and pushed her chair over as close as she could get it to him and sat back down. He took the hint and did the same.

"I heard 'center' and 'Tampa'," she said, "plus 'breakfast' then nothing for a time until she seemed to get angry and said something about meeting."

"Meeting? I didn't get that."

"It was after 'rat's ass', 'you' something 'meeting'."

"I thought it was 'eating'."

"I'm sure it was 'meeting'."

"Okay. You heard 'center' and I heard 'world center'. We both heard 'Tampa'. Is there a World Center in Tampa where there is a breakfast meeting? Maybe that's where the summit is. They're getting ready to load vans to go there."

"Or the vans are already loaded."

"If they *are* loaded, that would mean that the summit or meeting or whatever it is they're targeting, is tonight or tomorrow."

"It's a breakfast summit," Stella said. "and it's tomorrow morning. I'd put money on it."

"But where?"

"You think it's a World Center in Tampa. Even if you're right, there's not a thing we can do about it."

CJ had no response to that.

The chairs were situated so that they faced the door, sitting side-by-side just over a foot apart. CJ placed his hand on top of Stella's, on her armrest.

"I'm looking forward to us getting married," he said and then for a time they talked about life back in Tucson, what they'd do once they got married, where they'd live. Then they talked about CJ's children, Josh and Trish, and about Stella's sister and brother-in-law, Sara and Bill, and their son Lucas, the three of whom lived near Albuquerque. Stella mentioned that her sister invited them for Thanksgiving and that they should bring Trish.

"Trish would like that," CJ said, "though her mother might have other plans."

"I hope we're still around to find out," Stella said.

"We will be."

"I'm really scared."

CJ squeezed her hand.

"Don't lie to me again and say that it's going to be okay," Stella said.

"If you don't want me to, I won't. But when I say it'll be okay, I think it's not so much to convince you that everything will be okay. It's to convince myself."

"Positive thoughts make for positive results. Is that it?"

"Yeah. Something like that."

They suddenly realized that the woman was standing in the doorway.

"That's a lot of bullshit if you ask me," she said. "Positive thoughts do nothing but give one a false sense of security. Action is what gets results and nothing else."

"I have to pee," Stella said.

"You're a woman. I'd be shocked if you didn't have to pee by now." She looked directly at CJ for at least ten seconds and then said, "I'm going to demonstrate the difference between positive thoughts and action. You, sir, likely have to pee as well, however, you figure that by sending out positive thoughts I'll let you tag behind Stella here so you can also empty your bladder. Your loss, I'm afraid. Stella, you see, took action and voiced her need, therefore she'll get to go. As you said nothing, I can only assume you have no such need."

With that she turned and walked out.

"What was that all about?" Stella said.

"I have no idea."

"She knew my name, didn't use Mariana like I'd told Alan."

"Interesting. Alan knew my name but didn't know yours, yet I didn't get the feeling you were a surprise to him."

"So...?"

"So, I don't think Alan is part of the organization. As I said before, I believe he's a pro hired to kill Douglas and Eveleen and then kidnap us. It does appear that she has an accurate source of information but isn't sharing it except on a need to know. I've a feeling Alan knew nothing about the overall plan, i.e., taking out a few leaders of countries. He is probably completely out of the picture now, paid and sent on his way."

Five minutes later two men came in, one of them Samuel Blight. The other guy CJ didn't recognized. He displayed a gun while Blight removed Stella's handcuffs.

"Make it quick," Blight said.

Stella did. When she came out he told her to put the handcuffs back on.

"They hurt my wrist," she said.

"Tough."

She put them back on.

"I have to go, too, Sam," CJ said.

Blight shrugged and grinned. As he and his comrade started to walk out Stella said, "I'm hungry. Will we get anything to eat?"

"I'll pass your request along to the chef," he said and closed the door.

CJ stared at the door for a time and then said, "She's demonstrating that she's in control and can be compassionate."

"I'm not impressed."

"At least you got to pee."

"There *is* that," she said. "At least I can relax a little now. You called him Sam. Do you know him?"

"Samuel Blight. He's the guy who was driving the boat and with whom I got into a scuffle before he tumbled off the back. I think it gave him a thrill to ignore my pee request."

"Oh."

"It was his wife's boat, or at least it was in her name, and chances are it is still in impound. He likely holds a bit of a grudge."

"Did you recognize the other guy?"

"No."

An hour later Sam and his gun handler returned and removed CJ's handcuffs.

"I'd let you sit in your own piss except the boss says you both need to be relaxed and focused." He pointed to the bathroom. "In and out. No dilly daddling."

CJ stood and headed toward the bathroom.

"The gun is on her," Sam added.

"I got it," CJ said. "No daddling." When he finished his business and came out, CJ said, "So what is that we need to be focused for?"

"You'll find out soon enough. Hook back up."

CJ did so.

"Food will be up in a few minutes."

Chapter 38

Dinner wound up being pizza and water, delivered by Sam.

"How about a couple of beers to go with this," CJ said. "Did you get any with jalapeños? How about pineapple?"

Sam turned and walked out without a word.

They ate the pepperoni and sausage pizza in silence. An observer would report that Stella ate hers with slow deliberation, CJ as though he hadn't eaten in days, putting away three pieces to her one. In actuality, neither of them even tasted it, their minds fully engaged with their situation.

CJ pushed the box and what was left, aside and guzzled half the bottle of water. Stella broke the silence.

"Why do they want us relaxed and focused?"

"I don't know, but the fact that they're concerned with our biological needs tells me that they're not planning on killing us."

"I hope you're right."

That's what CJ was thinking out loud. Internally, however, he was worried that they were keeping them satisfied until they did whatever it was that they needed to be focused for, and then, when they didn't need them anymore, they'd kill them both. Why would they keep them alive if they and this house could be identified? Was Stella along as a hostage? With a gun to her head he'd do whatever they wanted.

The way CJ saw it, if they didn't do what they wanted, he and Stella would be dead. If they did what they wanted, their deaths would only be delayed.

More silence ensued, CJ turning his water bottle around and around in his hand as though the answers were somewhere in the fine print.

"What are you thinking, Clint?" Stella said.

"I'm figuring that there must be a way to turn this bottle into a weapon."

"Oh."

"If I cut off the top, there would remain jagged edges that could be jammed into one's face."

"And while you're lying on the floor bleeding to death from a gunshot wound, I could be jamming the shooter in the face with my water bottle. Sounds like a great plan."

The door opened and CJ forgot about the bottle.

Sam and the gun holder came in followed by two other men, one of whom was Rory Pickens, the other being Gabe. They split, two to each side of the door. A few seconds later, the woman entered.

She didn't waste any time. "In seven hours you'll be departing with these gentlemen, in two vehicles." She pointed to CJ. "You in one." Pointing to Stella she added, "You in the other."

"Where are we going?" CJ said.

She ignored the question. "While you are in the company of these men you will do exactly as you're told; nothing more; nothing less. Stella will be with Sam and Miles. You, Clinton, will be with Rory and Gabe. If either of you fail to do your assigned task, the other will be killed... immediately. They will always be in communications with each other."

"What is our assigned task?" CJ asked.

"You will be given that information on the way to your destination."

"Why us?"

She smiled. "Wrong place, wrong time. You became convenient for our plans."

"And your plans are...?"

"You will be briefed in the vans. Get some sleep." With that she turned and walked out. The men followed, turning off the light and closing the door.

"Seven hours," CJ said to Stella, "Puts it at about three-thirty in the morning. A bit early if we're only going to Tampa, wouldn't you say?"

Stella didn't say anything for a long time. And then, "I think they're wanting us to kill someone."

"Yeah. That's what I'm thinking, too."

Ten minutes went by without either of them saying a word.

Stella said, "Let's go to Hawaii for our honeymoon."

"Sure."

"I'm serious, Clint."

"Okay. You're serious. We'll go to Hawaii."

"Or Alaska. How about we fly to Australia or New Zealand."

"We could do it all. Hawaii, Alaska, Australia and New Zealand."

"I've always wanted to see the blue penguins of New Zealand."

"Blue penguins?" CJ said.

"Yeah. They're just little guys, only a little bigger than this." She held up her water bottle even though CJ could barely see it in the dark. "They're also called fairy penguins. New Zealand is beautiful and I've always wanted to go there. You can ask Sara. We both dreamed of going to New Zealand when we were teenagers. Promise me we'll go to New Zealand for our honeymoon, to Stewart Island."

CJ didn't even want to think about anything but the predicament they were in and what was to take place in the morning. He sort of understood, though, what she was doing. She was trying to shift her mind onto something pleasant, away from what was scaring the hell out of her. It was scaring the hell out of him, too. "Where's Stewart Island?"

"It's off the southern most point of the main island. Promise me we'll go."

"Yes," CJ said, reaching his hand out to her. "We'll go to Stewart Island of New Zealand and walk among the blue penguins."

She took his hand. "Don't even say that to humor me."

"Wouldn't think of it. When we get home let's get it all planned, the wedding and the trip to the bottom of the world."

"Thank you." She went silent for a time and then said, "And before we leave Florida, let's go sailing."

CJ looked in her direction, surprised. "Really?"

"Yes, really. I want to go sailing with you."

He squeezed her hand. "Okay, then. It's a date."

Chapter 39

CJ felt the minutes tick by, all 420 of them he was sure. If anyone ever asked, if he survived that is, he was certain he would be able to honestly tell them that he counted each and every minute. The thought of sleep at no time ever crossed his mind. Occasionally he'd hear a noise and hope that it was Josh and a massive FBI team storming the house. He'd play out the entire scenario in his head and then sigh and listen to the silence.

Stella did sleep, or at least had a dozen or so short naps, snorting herself awake from what appeared to be bad dreams. He wanted so much to hold and comfort her. The way she curled up he often times couldn't even reach her; in the dark he could barely see her.

But who was he trying to kid? He needed *her* to comfort him.

At 3:10 the lights came on. Sam stood in the doorway.

"Time for potty runs and then we're heading out."

Again the gun holder, Miles, stood at the ready while Sam unlocked Stella from the chain. When she returned from the bathroom he grabbed the handcuff still dangling from her wrist and started to lead her out. She resisted. He turned and looked at her. "Don't even try to get feisty with me, woman. You're outnumbered."

"I don't want to leave my purse."

"It's quite safe here." He gave her a yank.

She allowed two steps and then dug in again. "I have to have it," she whined. "It has..."

"It has what?"

She dropped her head as though embarrassed. CJ had no idea

where she was going with her demand, praying she wasn't going to inadvertently reveal that her purse contained a gun.

"I'm... it feels like I'm... starting my period. My... tampons are in there."

"Jesus Christ!" Sam shook his head.

"You don't even want to know what it's like if..."

"Fine," Sam said, holding up his hand. "Miles, grab the purse."

Miles looked down at it as though a tampon was going to suddenly jump out and grab him by the throat.

"It's just a damned purse. Grab it and let's go. And it wouldn't be a bad idea if you took a look in it first."

Miles picked up the purse by the strap and carried it over to the chair where Stella had been sitting. He put his gun away and with thumb and forefinger proceeded to open the flap. CJ held his breath. Stella had demonstrated the purse while they'd stood outside Danohough's apartment the day Eveleen was killed. The gun and holster resided in a secret compartment, accessible only from the side, not the top. It allowed a woman to slip her hand in and slide the SIG Sauer from its holster. He hoped that Miles wasn't smart enough to look anywhere but in the top.

The flap fell back and the iPad appeared. Miles moved it back and forth, revealing her credit cards and driver's license, a change pouch and bill pouch as well as a bunch of receipts. Behind that section was another zippered area where lived her cosmetics and various personal affects. Miles carefully unzipped it, reached in and pulled out a Ziploc bag.

"What's this?" Miles said, holding it up to CJ.

"I believe that's her tampons."

Miles dropped them back in and wiped his hand on his pants.

"She carries only as much as she thinks she might need, thus the Ziploc."

"Glad I'm not a woman." Mile closed the purse and followed after Sam and Stella.

CJ grinned after them until he got to thinking about where they were heading and the fact that he was left wallowing in his darkest fears.

CJ's wallowing was cut short only a few minutes later when Rory and Gabe came in. The procedure was the same as with Stella, except he was allowed to proceed out and down the stairs without being led by the handcuffs. The fact that Stella's purse was accompanying her gave him little comfort. As he got to thinking about it, he was afraid she'd try to make use of it and get herself killed, or Gabe had already discovered the gun and removed it.

He was led out the front door and down the walk to one of the paneled vans. The other van was already gone. Rory pushed him in and hooked the handcuff to the suicide handle. Interior lights were extinguished, as well as the house exterior lights, so CJ was not able to see what was in the cargo area, if anything at all. Rory climbed into the passenger's seat while Gabe took the wheel.

Gabe guided them out of the residential area to Pinellas Point Drive which took them west and then onto I-275 northbound. After a time CJ recognized the bridge over Old Tampa Bay, the same route on which the FBI agents took him the first night he was here. As they passed back onto dry land, CJ looked off to the left toward the area where he knew Tampa's FBI headquarters resided. He called in his mind. "Hey. Look here. We're heading somewhere to do some dastardly deed. Are you paying attention?"

With each approaching exit CJ anticipated that Gabe would slow and then direct the van into the city of Tampa and toward wherever the World Center lived. But he never slowed. The only exit he took was a merge onto eastbound I-4, toward Orlando, Tampa city lights receding behind them. At no time did he use excessive speed, often five to ten miles-per-hour below the posted speed limit.

"Where are we going?" CJ asked.

They didn't respond.

"The boss *did* say I'd be briefed while in route."

Still nothing.

"For some reason I thought that the G8 summit was in Tampa?" CJ watched as the two men turned their heads toward each other. Are they surprised that he knows about the G8 summit? "It's in Orlando then, I assume, or somewhere in that direction."

"We'll be stopping for food soon," Rory said. "You will be told then what you're to do. Don't want you to have to perform on an empty stomach."

"That's very thoughtful. You do know that security at something like this will be extremely high. With presidents and prime ministers attending it'll be crawling with Secret Service and every law enforcement agency within a hundred miles. The chances of getting anywhere close to any of the people attending will be nil to none."

"That's where you're wrong, Mister Washburn," Rory said. "Presidents are not attending this one because it is not a regular summit. Each country is sending an unimportant representative to discuss midyear issues."

"What are they discussing?" CJ asked. "What's on their agenda?"

"Other than next summer's regular summit, their agenda holds no importance."

"Next summer the G8 is meeting in Fermanagh, Northern Ireland. Why not wait until then to do whatever it is you're planning?"

"You're better informed than we thought. Yes, the G8 will be in Fermanagh next year and because it will be attended by heads-of-state, security will indeed be too high. Also, discussions about the future of Northern Ireland may be on the agenda next summer. Now is the time to get our voice heard."

"Do you think anyone will be sympathetic to your cause if you keep killing people?"

"Killing people?" Rory actually sounded shocked. "What gives you the idea that we're going to kill anyone?"

"You're going to a G8 summit with weapons and possibly a chemical agent of some kind. You've already killed two people to protect your mission."

"In a sense, Mister Washburn, this is a war and in war there are going to be casualties. Those two deaths were unfortunate, but necessary."

"I can understand Douglas," CJ said, "but Eveleen Danohough? She's a founder of the United Irish Republican Army."

"Humph! In a weak sense of the word she might have been a founder. She didn't stick around very long, went off on her little coffee business. She talked a big game but to be truthful with you she's always preferred being on the outskirts of things. That would have still been well, but then Douglas O'Reilly showed up, an FBI plant claiming to be her son, and she started going squirrely in the head. Women are just too damned unpredictable."

CJ sat back for a bit thinking about that statement. "So is Eddie Hall Douglas' father?"

"I don't know about that," Rory said. "Don't even know for sure that Douglas was actually Danohough's son. He was undercover. Could have all been lies."

"But Eddie is also a founder of UIRA, isn't he?"

Rory turned forward. "Ten minutes we'll be stopping for food. You'll be briefed then."

So Eddie Hall buffaloed them all, or almost did, CJ thought. He and Stella saw the look on Eddie's face when they talked about Douglas... that of a confused or distraught father, it seemed at the time, or is that what they wanted to see. Could it really be Eddie didn't know that he'd become a father back in 1969 until just recently, maybe only within the last few days? Or maybe he never knew, his distress being over Eveleen's death. Was their relationship not at all new, but rekindled after forty-three years? She had recently asked Eddie to marry her. She'd just gotten her son back and she wanted to reunite the entire family, even if she never told Eddie the truth as to why.

But what if Rory was right? What if Douglas *had* created the entire "I'm your long lost son" scenario to get on the inside, even going as far as marrying Rebecca to seal the ruse? CJ considered his conversations with Gianna and her sister and decided that most likely, that part of the story was true, the adoption and name change and all.

Still, what if Douglas was chosen by the FBI only because he could fit the part?

And then CJ thought about Stella. Where was she and what was she thinking? If he went crazy right now he could probably cause the van to wreck. If they all died in the wreck there'd be no reason for the others to believe anything more than that Gabe had an accident and they'd have to release Stella and walk away, the mission to kill anyone at the G8 summit terminated. He looked up at the suicide handle, took a grip and calculated how he'd reach Gabe and the steering wheel with his feet in order to send the van into a tumble at seventy miles per hour. But what if instead of letting Stella go before walking away, they kill her first? He was considering the pros and cons when he noticed the van slowing and taking an exit, and then it was too late.

As they swung around an all night *McDonald's* drive-thru, CJ spotted the other van parked off in a nearby plaza parking lot.

"You say a word you get a bullet," Rory said. "Understood?"

"Yeah," CJ said, relieved to know that Stella was nearby. He sat quietly while Gabe ordered what CJ was sure was his last meal. He wasn't even given a choice.

CJ and Stella sat within view of each other, eating Sausage McMuffins and drinking coffee. They were still inside their respective vans which were parked side by side facing in opposite directions, the side doors open, handcuffs removed. CJ could also see her purse on the floor, sandwiched tight between her foot and the wall of the van.

Their captors were able to easily step across the gap between the vans, doing what they needed to do without being viewed by the outside world. CJ sipped his coffee and wondered who would be paying attention to a couple of vans in a parking lot near an all-night McDonalds well before sunrise.

Nobody.

"We're rigging up now," Rory said after hitting speed dial on his cell phone. "Right," he added and then ended the call.

Stella finished her sandwich and picked up her coffee. CJ mouthed

"I love you." She mouthed the same back and then turned her head to where Miles had gone toward the back of her van, out of CJ's view. Suddenly her eyes got big, followed by a look that CJ had never seen on her before, that of pure terror. She nearly dropped the coffee before she got it put into a cup holder. She looked across at CJ, horror still in her eyes.

"What?" he mouthed.

And then Miles appeared with a vest in his hands. CJ didn't know too much about such things, having attended only a basic introduction class while a police officer, but from his point of view it appeared to be outfitted with C4 explosives and wires.

A suicide vest!

Chapter 40

"Here's what we're going to do," Rory said after a second identical vest was pulled out and placed on the floor in front of CJ. "You're going to put these on and do exactly what we tell you."

"Or what?" CJ said.

"Or your fiancée will get a bullet to the head. Having two wearing vests is ideal for the mission, but it can be done with just one."

"After I refuse and you shoot her, I'll still refuse."

"That just means that after this is all over, a couple of us will be taking a vacation out west to Arizona and New Mexico. I'd love to meet your daughter and extend my sympathies as to your untimely death." Rory looked across at Stella. "Same with your sister and her family just outside Albuquerque. Lucas, your nephew, is a cute kid."

For a second CJ thought that Stella was leaning over to reach her purse and envisioned a shootout between her and four well armed men. And then he realized that she was only putting her head between her knees to keep from getting sick. She lifted her head for a second and looked across to CJ, her face white.

Rory turned back to CJ, who was now glaring at him. "As I was saying, the two of you will put on these vests and do what we tell you. To keep either of you from forming thoughts about doing something crazy, I'll give you one assurance."

"What's that?"

"If everything goes off as planned, there will be no reason to detonate these devices; nor will there be a reason to visit your families."

"Why should we believe you?"

"We're only making a statement today. We have no desire to kill representatives from the seven countries that have nothing to do with the United Kingdom's dirty laundry."

"What's the statement?"

"Not your concern. Put on the vest, Mister Washburn. After yours is on, secured and armed, Ms. Summers will do the same."

CJ carefully slipped on his and then watched as Stella struggled with hers.

"All of this just to make a statement?" he said.

"Sometimes before one makes a statement, one has to make sure he has everyone's attention."

"You don't want your statement swept under the rug."

"Now you're getting the idea, Mister Washburn."

Rory extracted a device from his pocket. It was smaller than a cell phone and had a pull-out antenna. Miles made a final connection on both vests, pushing together a pair of what appeared to be simple audio cables. Then Rory held up his device.

"I need you both to pay attention now," Rory said. "It's hard to see your own, but if you look across at your partner, you'll see a small bulb just under the left breast, like those small Christmas tree bulbs. It's red." He held the device out between them. "When I push this button like this..." he did so, "the bulb lights up." He made a point of looking closely at both vests. "Very good. Your vests are now armed. If I were to push this other button," he showed it to them, "the vests would detonate at the same time. It's good from a thousand yards." The device went into his pocket. "As long as everything goes as it should, this will not come out of my pocket. Just in case, though, should some smart ass get lucky and shoot me in the head, my compatriot, Sam, has an identical device. Either one can do the job."

Sam displayed his.

"Also, that last cable that Miles connected made it possible to arm the vests. Now that they are armed, trying to disconnect those cables will trigger the detonation." He'd then looked between them. "Any questions?"

"Are you truly ready to give your life for the cause?" CJ had asked him.

"None of us would be here if we weren't."

The van doors closed before CJ had a last chance to mouth good-bye to Stella.

They left the parking lot, returning to I-4, eastbound toward Orlando, Stella's van in the lead. Traffic had begun to pick up, though the sun had yet to rise. Once again CJ started thinking about trying to wreck the van, wondering if the C4 would detonate. As he got to thinking more about it, remembering the class he'd attended, C4 was extremely stable, or *insensitive* as the presenters had termed it. A bullet fired into a block of C4 would not cause it to detonate. It required a separate blasting cap inserted into it or a detonator cord wrapped around it. He looked down and could see cords coming out of the tops of each of the six blocks. They came together in a bundle and then disappeared into an inner pocket.

He looked at the arming cables, considered unplugging them and blowing this three-man team to smithereens, but that'd only take care of one van. Stella would still be able to carry out the mission and then she'd definitely be killed and maybe even Trish and Stella's family if they followed through on their threats. If he and Stella did exactly what they were told, no one would have to die.

CJ had no choice but to trust Rory's word. There was no upside to any other option.

He took a deep breath, feeling the tightness wrapped around his chest, the inability to fully inflate his lungs. Was that because of the heavy vest strapped to his body or the stress of whatever was coming, the not knowing what was going to happen, the having no power to influence the outcome? He took another forced breath, smelled his fear oozing from his pores... and something else.

He blew out the breath, held for a few seconds and then slowly inhaled, focusing on the odor, separating it from his own. It had been there ever since they strapped the vest to him, slight but definite nonetheless. Until now he hadn't given it much thought, had passed it off as a characteristic of the explosive. He thought back to the class he'd attended, put on in Phoenix by Homeland Security to familiarize local law enforcement with various military level explosives: RDX, PETN, HMX, Semtex and C4. They were able to examine samples of each, including color and smell. None of them, except the C4, looked anything like what he was wearing. The sample he'd seen in the class was packaged in a military green wrapper, gold lettering identifying it as a C4 demolition charge, along with its weight. Something better than a pound he recalled. He looked down at the six packages spread across his chest and noted that the color was more blue than green. He also noticed that none of them had words stenciled on the outside.

He set that bullet point aside and again focused on the smell.

The presenter in the class had cut open a block and encouraged the attendees to touch and smell it. Oily, a whiff of petroleum, CJ recalled; the color of straw in his mind, light brown as described by the presenter.

He looked at the end of one block, pulled the cut wrapper aside where the blasting cap had been inserted, wished he could turn on a light to see better. He sniffed again. Oily was not what came to mind. This was something else, something familiar but on which he was not able to put his finger. Whatever it was, it was important. In what way, he didn't know, but he was certain that if he kept working at it, it'd come to him.

"I wouldn't be fooling with that if I were you."

CJ lifted his head, pulling his focus away from the C4 blocks to find Rory looking back at him. He dropped his hands away from the packages.

"If you're thinking about doing something stupid, that'd be exactly what it'd be. Stupid. You'd be sacrificing your life for no reason, as well as the lives of your lady friend and, of course, your daughter. The mission would still go off as planned.

"How much longer?" CJ asked.

"We'll get there when we get there. Sit back and enjoy the ride."

CJ sat back and closed his eyes. There was no enjoyment to be had.

Chapter 41

Just as the sun started lighting the sky they took Exit 67 off the interstate, a long exit that kept bearing right until it merged onto Route 536, running due east. The Marriott World Center dominating the northern skyline. A half mile later they turned north onto World Center Drive and navigated around the huge complex.

Again they parked side-by-side, the numerous high-rises of the Marriott loaming over them. At any other time CJ would have been awed by the magnificence of it, but right now his thoughts were most certainly elsewhere, taking little more than a glance.

They sat doing absolutely nothing for a long time, side doors closed. At 8:20, by the readout on the van's dash, Rory climbed to the back and opened the door. A few seconds later the other door opened to reveal Sam. Stella was seated as before, still looking pale, and just as scared.

Sam disappeared to the back for a few seconds, returning with a handful of dark blue windbreakers. He threw one in Stella's lap. Rory appeared next to CJ with an identical handful of windbreakers. He handed one to CJ.

"Put these on and zip them up," he said loud enough for both CJ and Stella to hear. "They're large enough to cover your vests while we walk into the building."

CJ could see part of a stencil on the back of his. He held it out and looked at the gold SECURITY in big, bold letters. He had been wondering how they were going to get into the building without being noticed.

"Put it on," Sam said.

CJ did, saw that Stella was trying to zip hers up, her hands shaking. He did the same, noted that his hands were trembling a bit as well.

"You've already said it," CJ said. "You don't need both of us. Let her go. I'll do exactly what you say."

"Gabe," Rory said, an implied order to the tone.

Gabe came out of the driver's seat, climbed to the cargo area, crossed over to Stella's side and produced a handgun. He chambered a round and put the gun to her head.

"NO!" CJ yelled.

"No?" Rory said. "Then you be a smart bloke and keep your mouth shut. Do not open it unless you are told to open it. You don't ask questions, you don't make suggestions, you don't clear your throat unless you are invited to do so. You say nothing unless you are prompted by one of us. Is that understood?"

CJ looked over at Stella. She was holding her breath, eyes closed, jaws clenched, shaking so badly he thought she was going to have a heart attack.

"Yes," CJ said, nodding.

"Very good. Gabe, stand down."

Gabe did and Stella nearly collapsed from her seat to the floor.

"Now, the both of you, listen up," Rory continued. "We are going to exit the vehicles in a short time and walk as a group into the building in single file. I and Sam will be in the front, next Mister Washburn, then Ms. Summers followed by Miles and Gabe. We will all be wearing these stylish jackets and ball caps."

With that Sam produced six ball caps, same color as the windbreakers, SECURITY emblazoned across the fronts.

"Make any necessary fitting adjustments right now and put them on."

CJ's fit just fine. He watched as Stella fought with hers, shaking so bad she couldn't figure out the adjustment. Finally Rory stepped over, took the hat from her, made the adjustment and gently placed it on her head.

"Does that feel better?" he said as though they were getting ready for a picnic.

Stella took some deep breaths and nodded.

He placed his hand on her arm. "Relax. Everything will be fine and you'll have some interesting stories to tell your nephew."

Her shaking turned to a glare.

"Okay now," he said, returning to CJ's van. "We will enter the building single file. It'll be a bit of a ways but with these jackets we will not be stopped or challenged. We are heading for the Tampa Meeting Room."

Now CJ understood the confusion on his and Stella's part. They'd heard World Center and Tampa and had assumed from that that the summit was in Tampa. It was actually in the Tampa Meeting Room of the Marriott World Center in Orlando.

"The attendees will have just assembled following their breakfast elsewhere. The eight delegates will be seated at a round table set up in the middle while their staffs will be arranged in seating around them. When we enter I will go left and Sam will go right. Mister Washburn will follow me, Ms. Summers will follow Sam.

"Do you understand? This is where you say only yes or no."

"Yes," CJ said.

"Yes," Stella said, her voice barely above a squeak.

"Good. This next piece is your most important part in this dramatic play. When we stop and turn to face the attendees I will give the order for you to open your jackets fully and display your fine wares. At the same time the four of us will be displaying automatic weapons and I will begin explaining why we are interrupting their meeting. From then on you two will only have one thing to do and that is stand right where you are until you are told otherwise, keeping your vests displayed."

He looked between the two of them. "Do you both have the picture?"

"Yes," Stella said.

CJ opened his mouth, but was afraid to say anything except, yes.

"You have a question, Mister Washburn?"

"Yes."

"Ask away. The floor is open for you until I tell you it is not."

"You make your statement and then walk away. Is that right?"

"Pretty much, yes. Not something you have to worry about."

"You can be identified. You'll be tracked down."

"Not as easy as it may seem. And as long as no one dies, the charges, should we be caught, thus jail time, would be minimal in any case."

"Two people are dead already."

"We didn't kill them."

Rory's cell phone rang.

"Shut up now," he said to CJ, touched something on the screen and put the phone to his ear. "We are ready. Is it time?" He listened and then said, "We will leave in ten minutes."

He put the phone away and looked at his watch. "They are assembling in the Tampa Room right now. Prepare gentlemen."

CJ had noticed several shoulder packs, long enough to contain the automatic weapons Rory alluded to. They didn't open them, had set them aside while they adjusted sidearms that were concealed under oversized shirts. Except to a trained or knowledgeable observer, no one would take notice. As he got to thinking about it, considering the shape of the packs, they could contain Uzi-like automatic or semi-automatic weapons with attached magazines. CJ hoped he was being over paranoid about it, but what else could they be? With vests packed with C4, anything was possible, most likely probable.

Finished with sidearm preparation, they put on their jackets, donned the hats and wrap-around sunglasses and then waited.

CJ could feel his bowels loosening just a tad. He was fairly certain that now wasn't a good time to raise his hand and ask for a bathroom break. He looked over at Stella, wished she'd open her eyes so he could see how she was coping. Her head resting against the window, she was occasionally taking a deep breath. And then CJ noticed that her purse was no longer on the floor.

Where did it go and what the hell was she thinking?

They just sat, and the minutes ticked by slower than the long hours the night before.

Chapter 42

Miles moved the other van so that there was about ten feet between them and then they all climbed out and gathered in that space.

CJ figured out that Stella's purse had to be underneath the jacket, hanging from her shoulder. He tried to communicate with her with his eyes, shifting his gaze from her face to where he thought the purse resided, back and forth a couple of time. She shook her head and looked away, jaw tight. What did that mean? There wasn't much chance that she'd try anything heroic now, he was certain, with the jackets zipped up. And in the Tampa Room when they opened the jackets it'd be well too late to do something really stupid.

Of course, he wasn't without trying to come up with something really stupid to do himself. Jump one, pull his sidearm, shoot them all in the head before they could react. Certainly more downside than upside to that idea.

"Mouths shut," Rory reminded CJ and Stella and they headed out, single file just as he had instructed.

There were people all about, coming and going between the Marriott and the parking lot, but not a crowd. Those who noticed them gave no more than a curious glance.

A bunch of security people... police... look the other way, were the likely thoughts.

They'd all make terrible witnesses. No matter, though. The hotel had security cameras for certain and everything, once they entered the building, maybe even in the parking lot, would be captured for micro analysis. CJ had the four men by about two inches. The analysts would be able to pick out him and Stella easily, but that'd be about it. With ball caps and sun glasses and with each man about the same size and same complexion, CJ doubted the FBI would be able to get reasonable identification. But he and Stella could ID them. Hell, he knew the full names of two of them, one of whom had been in police custody for a time. If, as Rory had said, they were to leave CJ and Stella alive, he and Sam would be on the run forever, would likely return to Northern Ireland and disappear. Is that what they wanted? Why would they say they were going to leave the two of them alive?

Another thing CJ was curious about was, who was Rory talking to on his phone? Was it the boss lady or some other plant on the inside of the Marriot Hotel? And what was to be their exit strategy?

They entered through a side entrance, each in turn catching the door and holding it for the person after them. CJ analyzed the pack slung off Sam's shoulder, and determined that it, in fact, contained an automatic weapon. All he could picture was an *Uzi*, deadly in a small room full of people; and there were four such weapons.

It was a good minute of steady walking before they came to a stop at a door with a plaque to the side announcing the Tampa Room. The door was closed. Without a word spoken the four men released their packs and began opening them. They paused for a few seconds, looking both ways up and down the hall, ensuring that there were no observers, and then pulled out their weapons.

Bushmaster was the word that came to CJ's mind. The *Bushmaster* was the famous weapon that killed ten and wounded three others in the 2002 Washington Beltway sniper attacks. Over the years it had been referred to as a *weapon of mass destruction*. But upon closer inspection, CJ realized that this wasn't a *Bushmaster*.

What it was, he had no idea. A knock off design? Something new that was just being introduced into the U.S.? At this point knowing what it was made little difference. They were either going to kill with them or they weren't.

Rory opened the door and they all filed in like they were getting ready to do a presentation before the G8 delegates.

Rory went left and Sam right. CJ stayed on Rory's heel, as he was instructed, glancing over his shoulder to see Gabe behind him and

Stella following Sam, followed by Miles. A woman was standing in front of her seat at a network of tables forming a square–maybe G8's version of the *Round Table*– her mouth frozen in midsentence. All heads had swiveled toward the group of intruders, questioning looks turning to horror and fright when the weapons were spotted.

"Attention! Attention! Attention!" Rory called, holding his weapon over his head. "I want silence!"

Someone whispered.

"Silence now!" Rory demanded again, pointing his weapon at the individual, a young man. The man locked his jaws and bowed his head.

"Cell phones on the floor, now! If anyone manages to make a call, that person and the person closest to them will be shot immediately."

CJ watched everyone, praying that no one tried to be heroic and do something stupid.

"You!" Rory stepped toward a dark-skinned man. "Hand me your phone, now."

CJ had noticed that the man, not one of the delegates, hadn't set his phone down, though it did not appear he'd been trying to dial. He just stood there, jaw hanging, phone in his hand as though he had been talking to someone.

Rory pointed and motioned to give it up. The man looked down as though he hadn't been aware that he was holding it and then presented it to Rory, horror and confusion etched over his face. Rory looked at it, seemed satisfied and then threw it aside.

"Now listen to me carefully." He pointed to the eight delegates. "You eight... stand up and move to that wall... now!"

In some semblance of confusion, they did what they were told, lining up along the wall indicated. At the same time Miles and Gabe had moved to the two doors and blocked them closed from anyone entering.

"Everyone else, sit on the floor in front of them."

They did as they were told, some much quicker than others. All told, by CJ's calculation, two minutes had elapsed since they had entered. Roughly thirty people stood or sat along one wall, a two-to-one mixture of men and women.

"Thank you for making that easy. Ms. Summers and Mister Washburn, open your jackets now. Show everyone what you are wearing."

The gasps and utterances of horror where audible and visible as CJ and Stella unzipped their jackets and revealed the blocks of C4 and wires.

"Silence!" Rory yelled. The room went instantly quiet except for a woman sobbing. "If you don't want these bombs to go off, you will keep your mouths shut, listen carefully and do exactly what you are told. There is no need for anyone to die today."

A few heads swiveled back and forth between Stella, CJ and Rory. Others just stared down at the floor, appearing to mouth silent prayers.

"Mister Washburn and Ms. Summers," Rory said. He pointed. "You will now move all the tables out of the way, along that wall and that wall."

Stella and CJ began moving tables. When they were done there was a big open space in the middle. Except for a scattering of briefcases and purses, there was a clear line between the G8 crowd and the doors where Miles and Gabe stood, Rory and Sam in the middle.

Rory looked over at Sam and nodded his head.

From his pack Sam produced two black cloth bags with drawstrings. He approached first CJ and then Stella, handing them the bags.

Rory pointed to the two walls full of tables. "You two go sit on a table, one at each end. Put those hoods over your heads. Pull the drawstrings tight. Don't worry about not being able to breathe. You will breathe just fine."

Once they were seated on their tables CJ looked across at Stella. *I'm sorry, I love you* he wanted to call out to her. At no time in his life had he ever felt so helpless.

"Put the hoods on now," Rory said.

They did.

"I don't care what you hear, you leave the hoods on. Do not remove them for any reason. Is that understood?"

CJ took a deep breath and tried to relax.

"I want to hear a yes," Rory added.

"Yes," Stella declared, a little too loud.

"Yes," CJ echoed.

"Very good."

And then there was silence except for an occasional sniffle from the G8 crowd. CJ filled his lungs and then slowly exhaled. He closed his eyes as though such would increase the scope of his hearing. He needed to know what they were doing that required that only he and Stella be sightless. The only thing he could tell was that they were moving around, but he couldn't venture even the slightest guess as to what they were doing. Looking in briefcases and purses maybe? Doubtful. Someone came near him and then walked away. More moving around, maybe thirty seconds worth and then Rory said one word.

"Now!"

There came a rapid series of pops, fifteen... twenty of them on top of each other, like muffled automatic gun fire. In the middle of it came screams and cries.

CJ jumped off of the table.

"Sit back down, Mister Washburn," Rory said, no more than four feet from CJ.

CJ didn't move, just listened to the cries and sobs. The popping sound had stopped.

"Sit down or I'll shoot your lady in the head."

CJ felt back for the table and then pulled himself upon it.

"Very good."

None of the weapons CJ had seen had sound suppressors, so what was that? And then he considered the weapons, the design that resembled the *Bushmaster*. The magazine was not curved like the *Bushmaster*, the barrel shorter, the sights of a different configuration. And the stock... something about the stock was very different, a shape unlike any he'd ever seen. It was more like a... a what? Round. Why was it round?

It was round because it was a tank! A small compressed gas tank. These were not totally new terrorist weapons like he'd at first assumed. These were...

...paintball guns!

CJ would have jumped off the table again, ripped off his hood and attacked them physically if he hadn't remembered they were also carrying what certainly were deadly sidearms. Besides that, he was wearing a bomb and they had the triggering device.

So he sat and listened to the sobbing, trying to make sense of what had just taken place.

Rory had said that no one was going to die, that all they were doing was delivering a statement, a message, that they first had to get everyone's attention. This would certainly get everyone's attention. The media would be on this with everything they had... *UIRA terrorists play joke on the G8, shoot them with paintball guns. Not at all the bad guys like everyone would at first think... really didn't want to hurt anyone. They just wanted to make their statement, get their message out. They were very considerate.*

The media would be painting them as the "Paintball Army" who were only trying to get Great Britain to pay attention to their demands, maybe gain a bit of support from some of the other G8 countries, gratitude that it was only paint.

A big practical joke at which the world would laugh while listening to their statement.

CJ continued to listen to the noises in the room, sniffling and shuffling. There came what sounded like a door closing and then a few voices, accents, another language. A few of the G8 people were talking.

CJ cautiously slid off the table. The voices stopped. He waited for Rory's warning but nothing came. He turned his head back and forth, listening for something, anything that would give him a clue as to what was going on.

A woman whispered.

Someone shushed her.

Neither Rory, nor any of the other three, admonished them. It only meant that they were no longer in the room, that they were gone, leaving behind two and half dozen scared men and women in a room with two individuals wearing explosives on their bodies and hoods over their heads.

CJ reached up and grabbed the ties around his neck, loosened them and then paused for a few seconds. When no warning came his way he lifted the hood.

Nearly every head was turned toward him, eyes big, questioning, almost all frightened. The G8 delegates were splattered with red paint, as well as the wall behind them. The staff on the floor at their feet received only splashes from the pellets that hit their bosses. It appeared that only the eight delegates were targeted.

CJ looked closer. No, he was wrong. Only one was targeted, the British delegate of course. Those close to him received some of the splash-over.

He looked across at Stella, sitting perfectly still on her table, hood over her head.

"They're gone," he called to her as he ran across the room. In an instant he had her hood off, had pulled her from the table and into his arms, or as close as he could get her to him with a pair of vests full of C4 between them.

"What? What?" Stella struggled out of his grasp to see past him, to see what had happened.

"Paintball guns!" he screamed.

She looked at the crowd, who were starting to stir a bit more, and back to CJ. "Paintball? They shot them with paintballs?" She stumbled back against the table.

CJ nodded his head up and down. "Yes! It was all fake." He pulled off the security jacket and then bent his head down so that his nose was close to the top of the C4 packet he had earlier started to pick at. He sniffed and closed his eyes. It wasn't oily like he would expect C4 be.

"Smell this," he said to Stella.

She gave him a quizzical look and then bent forward and inhaled.

"What does that smell like?" he said. It had already come to him but he wanted to get her confirmation. He certainly couldn't afford to be wrong.

"I..."

"First thing that comes to mind," he said. "What is it?"

"Playdough?"

"Exactly! And look at the color. C4 is generally between a white and light brown. This is a medium brown, way too dark."

He put his hands on the wire that Rory said had armed the vest, that by disconnecting them would detonate the explosives.

"Stop!" Stella yelled. "What if you're wrong?"

CJ looked down again, touched the material, squeezed off a piece and put it to his nose.

"This entire operation was fake. They used fake guns to gain attention. I'm not wrong. We're wearing fake explosives." With that he disconnected the wires. Nothing happened. In seconds he had the vest off and was helping Stella out of hers. He spotted her purse.

"Give me your SIG," he said.

"Why?"

"Just give it to me." When she did, he said, "Find a phone and call 911." He stepped away and started for the door.

"Where you going?" she called after him.

"I'm going to try and catch up to them." With that he was into the hall and running. He missed a turn, doubled back and eventually found the exit door, bursting out into the bright sun. He blinked a couple of times, looking off into the parking lot where they had left the vans. Of course the vans were already gone. He looked about, as far as he was able to see in all directions. There was no sign of either of the dark-green paneled vans.

He turned around to go back in and found himself facing two men with guns pointed at him, wearing official looking uniforms with badges.

"Put your gun on the ground," one of them said with much authority.

Damn! CJ thought and carefully bent forward, placing Stella's SIG Sauer in front of his feet. This was not the time to try and reason with cops, or in this case, Marriott Hotel security. He straightened up and, without being told, put his hands behind his head and backed up two steps.

Chapter 43

It was better than an hour before CJ was reunited with Stella, in another conference room at the opposite end of the complex. The Tampa Room, as well as most of that side of the hotel, had been evacuated until it could be determined for certain that the suicide vests were in fact fakes and after they were taken away by heavily suited men in a heavily armored vehicle.

The two of them sat together at a table, sipping coffee under the watchful eye of a pair of local police officers when Agents Taffer and Washburn came in. Taffer flashed his badge at the officers.

"We've got this now."

One of the officers picked up an evidence bag and handed it to Taffer. "Detective Reason said that you'd probably want this."

Taffer looked at the gun inside the bag. "What is it?"

"A SIG Sauer MOS-22. It's registered to the woman, a Ms. Stella Summers. When her companion here, Mister Clinton Washburn, was apprehended by hotel security, he had it in his possession, brandishing it about."

"I wasn't brandishing it about."

The officer looked over at CJ. Taffer held up his hand without looking his way, the obvious sign of, "Shut up!"

CJ sat back and crossed his arms over his chest.

"That's the report from hotel security," the officer continued. "Mister Washburn claimed he was trying to chase down the perps who'd terrorized hotel guests with paintball guns and fake explosives."

"What else has he told you?"

"Other than names and descriptions of the perps and the vehicles, including plate numbers, not much. Said he wouldn't talk to anyone else except you guys. I'm assuming you know who these people are, maybe even what exactly took place here."

"We do and yes, we do," Taffer said. "We very much appreciate the time and effort you've put into this mess, keeping it low key and all. The wrong kind of press on this and we'd have a panic on our hands."

"I can't disagree," the officer said. "A bomb scare that ended up being false. A panic is what we don't need. It is worrisome, though."

"How's that?"

"It appears that they pulled this off without a hitch. What if it had been real bullets and real explosives?"

The officers departed and the agents sat down with CJ and Stella.

"I nearly turned the hotel upside down searching for you last night," Josh said. "Had to flash my badge to get them to let me look at their videos, reminding them of what happened to you two the other morning. Spotted you on camera going out with two men." He looked at Stella. "And then someone came running out of the elevator with your purse."

Stella shook her head back and forth. "Talk about scary. They made me drop it in the elevator. I about had a heart attack when the guy came out with it; thought he, or one of us, was going to get shot. That's what they told us; we'd get shot if we talked to anyone. I was shocked when I was allowed to hold on to it."

"How did you manage to keep it after that, with the SIG Sauer in it?"

"I think they forgot about it until we were getting ready to leave the house this morning. I told them I was on my period and that my tampons were in it."

Josh sat back. "Oh."

"The guy they called Miles actually searched it," CJ said, "not finding the SIG in its secret compartment. He pulled out her package of tampons and then reacted like it was a poisonous snake. It'd have been funny if the situation hadn't been so serious."

To cover his embarrassment, Josh said, "So how are you guys doing?"

"Okay now," CJ said. "It looked pretty bad there for a while."

"We thought we were wearing the real thing," Stella said. "I wasn't functioning very well." She pointed to the gun. "Nearly the entire time I had this within my reach but I could never get the guts to pull it out."

"I'm glad you didn't," CJ said. "The automatic weapons may have been paintball guns, but the pistols they were also carrying were the real thing. They'd have killed you in a second, of that I'm sure."

"Wish I'd been there to see security take you down holding a pink SIG Sauer," Taffer said to CJ. "Surprised they didn't think it was a toy."

CJ snorted a laugh. "I can't fault them. In their eyes, if it looks like a gun, it's a gun. They made the right call. Any idea where the terrorists went?"

"Best guess is back toward Tampa or St. Petersburg. We've got the house under surveillance, but we don't expect them to show up there. We had eyes on the place within minutes after the local police passed the address you gave them. The boat you talked about was gone as well."

"Think that might have been their get-a-way transport?" CJ said.

"Maybe, but if that's the case, they haven't had enough time to rendezvous with it yet. From here they'd have to drive some distance to meet it and we have a state-wide BOLO out on both vans."

"I don't see what the point of the boat would be," Stella said. "It certainly wouldn't make for a fast get-a-way."

Taffer's phone rang. He turned away to answered it.

"You were both chained up in the house?" Josh said.

"Basically, yes," CJ said. He went on to give a short summary of all that happened from their abduction to when they left for the summit.

Josh pushed the chair back and leaned forward, elbows on knees. "So they took you just to have someone to wear the vests?"

"That and to get us off the street."

"You were figuring things out too fast?"

"That's kind of what I'm thinking, yes. The fact that we were also handy to wear the vests was a bonus; maybe a solution to a problem."

"A problem?"

"They'd installed the chain, anchored to the wall, in preparation for this. It's not something one just has hanging around in case a visitor needs to be held against their will. They had someone else lined up for the job, but it fell through. Like Ms. Danohough maybe, and Douglas. They obviously knew about Douglas. Had been using him for some time, I'd bet. They'd feed him information, false information about the mission, so that it'd get reported to his handler and thus on to you guys. While you were off chasing invisible boats full of arms and explosives and bringing in the HDRU, they were busy getting ready for the G8 mini-summit."

"Then why kill him?"

"I think sometime Thursday night he got wind of the real mission and then I showed up. Not only did they have to silence him but they also had to get rid of anyone who he talked to. That was his wife, his mother and me."

"What was that?" Taffer said, pocketing his phone as he returned to the table.

"Dad thinks that Douglas and Danohough were killed because Douglas discovered the real mission, to paintball the G8 delegates, and was about to report it to us. He also thinks that they were initially lined up to wear the vests."

"And you two were recruited to take their place?" Taffer said.

CJ nodded.

"The call I just received was our liaison with the local police. One of the vans was spotted in a Wal-Mart parking lot in Kissimmee, twenty minutes or so southeast of here."

"Not west?" CJ said. "They weren't going back toward Tampa?"

"From Kissimmee they could still go anywhere; east, west, north or south. It may be that they split, each dumping their van in exchange for other, less visible transportation."

"Probably staged there yesterday," CJ said.

"Or early this morning. By-the-way, the license plate numbers you two provided were found to belong to two other vehicles, not dark green vans. Owners of said vehicles–they both live down in Naples– are being tracked down as we speak. I'd be willing to guess that they don't even know that their plates are gone.

"Also, the locals have already run the VIN on the van they found. It and another just like it were stolen from a lot in Atlanta about a week ago."

"If I were a betting man," CJ said, "I'd put money down that the second van will be found parked in another parking lot within the same distance as the first, probably in the opposite direction."

"It does appear that this was very well planned out."

"Right to the minute," CJ added. "It was as though everything was orchestrated. They had somebody inside the Marriott who reported exactly when the G8 people were finished with their breakfast and assembling in the Tampa Room."

"That could be anyone from guests to staff," Taffer said.

"Or someone hanging around acting like a guest," CJ said. "Rory Pickens, the leader of the team that raided the meeting this morning, knew exactly where he was going when we entered the building."

"Didn't the cops say there's a witness who said they saw six people with security blazers and ball caps departing the hotel this morning?" Josh said.

"That's right," Taffer said. "So there were two inside the hotel watching the movements of the summit people and they left with them."

"And I'm sure it was all rehearsed," Josh said.

"Likely a couple of times," CJ said. "You're going to have a lot of video to go through."

"If they keep the tapes that long," Taffer said.

"If this summit was supposed to be a secret," CJ said, "how did they find out about it?"

"It's not all that easy for eight countries to send delegates and their staffs to the United States without someone figuring it out and blabbing. The investigation is going to be tedious, no doubt about it."

"So, what was the statement?" CJ asked.

"Statement?" Taffer asked. "What statement?"

"Pickens said that they were presenting a statement, that they had to get everyone's attention first."

"Haven't seen anything."

"Maybe they're releasing it directly to the press," Stella said.

Taffer pulled out his phone and walked away again.

"Did you notice that only the British delegate got hit with the paintballs?" Stella said. "I couldn't tell with his people all around him, but it looked like he took one in the face. EMS transported him away."

"Paintballs aren't that much fun," Josh said. "The report is that he caught one in the eye; may have some permanent damage."

The door opened and a suit and tie walked in. CJ wondered if it was Detective Reason, who the police officer had referred to. He stopped in front of Agent Taffer.

"I'm on hold," Taffer said. "What you got, Detective?"

The detective presented him with a folded sheet of paper. Taffer glanced at it.

Taffer's surprise was evident. "Is this the statement?"

"It is. The British Delegate was presented with one, in a business-size envelope, just before he was shot with paintballs. They left several more scattered about."

"Do you know if they also released this to the press?"

"Haven't heard at this point."

Taffer's attention returned to his phone. "John Taffer here. Keep an eye on all the news outlets. Let me know what pops up in the reporting of this. There might be a statement being released by UIRA. It seems that that might have been their purpose, simply to gain attention and then release a statement of who they are and what their goals are, their mission statement, you might say." There was a pause and then he said, "How do I know they might release a statement? I'm holding one in my hand. I just want to know if it has been released to the media... Right."

Taffer put the phone away and then took a few minutes to read through the statement. When done he handed it over to Josh.

CJ and Stella looked over his shoulder.

UIRA
United Irish Republican Army
Sinn Féin of the Saorstát Éireann
We Ourselves of the Irish Free State

Dedicated toward the Sovereignty, Independence and full Irish freedom of the 32 for the reestablishment of the united and free people of Éire, the Sinn Féin of the Irish Republic.

We, the united and free people of Éire, demand to be recognised as the representatives of the United Ireland, as Sinn Féin of the Irish Republic, Sinn Féin of the Saorstát Éireann, We Ourselves of the Irish Free State.

We, the united and free people of Éire, in the spirit of the Proclamation of 1916, its ideals and principles, and the Ireland Act of 1949, declare the full and forever tireless struggle toward Saorstát Éireann, the Irish Free State.

We, the united and free people of Éire, declare the right of Irish people as a whole to flourish in national self-determination, with complete and total independence from all control–politically, militarily and financially–from Britain and the United Kingdom, bordered entirely and inclusively by the Irish Sea, the North Channel, St. George's Channel, the Celtic Sea and the Atlantic Ocean.

We, the united and free people of Éire, declare our sovereignty, and shall stand against any and all denial of our national and democratic rights.

We, the united and free people of Éire, shall not rest before the full realisation of an Irish Democratic Socialist Republic.

We, the united and free people of Éire, declare the presence of basic human rights, that is to say that in the spirit of the United Nations' Universal Declaration of Human Rights, we...

- *are all born free*
- *have the right to a fair and free world*
- *have the right to live our lives, freely and safely*

- *shall not be made slaves nor take anyone else as slaves*
- *shall not torture nor be tortured*
- *have a right to our nationality*
- *have the right to public assembly*
- *have the right to democracy, to take part in our government, to choose our leaders*
- *are all equal before the law*
- *cannot be denied our rights as they are protected by the law*

We, the united and free people of Éire, declare the presence of basic civil rights to include civil liberties, due process, equal protection of the laws and freedom from discrimination.

We, the united and free people of Éire, shall recognise the equality of linguistic diversity as well as the dominance of Irish of which shall be taught in all schools.

We, the united and free people of Éire, shall maintain the right to exercise prudent force as necessary to compel the British to withdrawal from Northern Ireland; in two words... BRITS OUT!

We, the united and free people of Éire, are the United Irish Republican Army and shall be dedicated toward the realisation of all rights and declarations as stated here within.

Signed, the UIRA council.

"This isn't much different from other statements released by the various factions of the *Irish Republican Army* over the years," CJ said. "What's the point and why go to so much trouble, take such risks? They could have easily released it without the fanfare."

"Who would have read it?" Taffer said.

"Who's going to read it now," Josh said, "and will it change anyone's mind at the levels that will make a difference?"

Taffer considered that for a moment. "That's a good question. I don't know. It does seem like there's another shoe waiting to drop here somewhere, doesn't it."

"It does," CJ said.

Taffer's phone rang again. "Yeah," he said into it. After a few seconds he said, "What network?" and then, "All of them!?"

He put his phone away and said to Josh, "Pull up CNN on your tablet. They've got the statement with pictures. YouTube has video and it is in the process of going viral."

"Video?" CJ exclaimed. "Of what?"

"The British delegate getting shot with paintballs while you two lounged around in your suicide vests."

"Lounged around?"

"It includes a voiceover of someone reading the statement."

Josh propped up the tablet so they all could watch the YouTube video, the views of which were already in the tens-of-thousands and rapidly climbing.

"Holy..." Stella said.

"Exactly," Josh said.

"So you think this is the second shoe?" CJ said.

"Actually, I hope so. I was afraid that the second shoe was going to be another attack with real bullets and/or real explosives, so if this is all it is, we can weather the storm."

"I'm glad our faces were covered," Stella said and then turned to Taffer. "Our names aren't going to be released, are they?"

"We won't give your names out, however, I can only speak for the FBI. Who knows what the locals will do."

"Can you put some pressure on them?" she asked.

"I can only try."

After a minute of contemplation by everyone, Stella said, "When can we leave, go back to our hotel?"

"Anytime," Taffer said. "As a matter-of-fact, go! Get out of here! Please check for flights back to Arizona along the way. You're starting to fall into the category of houseguests and leftovers."

"We're not leftovers *or* houseguests," CJ said.

"Yeah, but the effects are the same."

CJ and Stella looked at each other, CJ sticking out his bottom lip. "Are you ready to go home?" he said.

Stella looked between CJ and Taffer, then at Josh. CJ could almost read her mind; he'd been getting better at predicting her moods lately so he had a good idea what she was thinking, and she didn't disappoint.

"I don't think our work here is done," she said. "Besides, you promised to take me sailing."

CJ grinned. "That I did. We have a date." He turned to Taffer. "Could we get a lift back to St. Petersburg?"

Chapter 44

Following a long hot shower, another icing for him, a change of dressing for her, and a nap, Stella and CJ dressed for dinner and prepared to go out by themselves. Josh had decided that the two of them no longer needed a bodyguard, so he was off doing FBI stuff with Taffer, or doing the bidding of Taffer seeing as he was down two agents at the moment. Blain was still with his family. His mother had made a turn for the worse and then died. There remained a sliver of doubt about Coulter, despite the theory that CJ presented about Douglas being compromised and then used to feed false information to his handlers.

Agents Taffer and Washburn were back in Tampa, the Orlando field office handling the investigation of the World Center paintball attack. Josh was to remain onboard until Coulter was fully reinstated and Blain had returned, at least a week. There was still a lot of work to do trying to follow the trail of all the players, which they figured numbered somewhere between ten and fifteen.

Stella had gone online to find a restaurant, expecting that they'd drive somewhere, only to discover something to their liking within walking distance. She made reservations for thirty minutes and then they set out on foot for the less than half-mile walk.

When they stepped through the door of *z grille*, Stella said, "I don't know why I made reservations middle of the afternoon. They aren't at all busy and certainly not as fancy as I thought considering they offered an on-line reservations service."

"Would you rather we go somewhere else?" CJ said.

"No. Actually, this looks perfect, don't you think?"

CJ shrugged and looked around. "Sure."

As the name, *z grille*, implied, it was a walk-off-the-street grille;

big windows along two sides, counter seating at the grill area with a widescreen television displaying a sports commentator talking about football, indoor and outdoor seating elsewhere. The upscale twist involved a huge wall display of a variety of fine wines.

They placed their orders, choosing a wine to start, and seated themselves out on the sidewalk under a huge red umbrella and a tall palm tree. Stella sighed. "Now I feel like we are on vacation."

"After what we've been through the last few days, going back to Tucson would be a vacation," CJ said.

"No kidding." She watched him for a few minutes. "What's the matter?"

CJ had felt uncomfortable even before they opened the door. Now he was looking up and down the street, as though expecting someone. "I..." He looked over at Stella, surprised that she had noticed. "The place felt odd from the moment we walked up. Now I know why. This brings back memories of the front of the coffee shop a three days ago. The four of us were sitting under an umbrella just like this when a bomb came flying at us and all hell broke loose."

"I doubt very much that's going to happen again, but I understand your fidgetiness." She looked up and down the street as well. "We can go inside if you want."

"No. I'll get over it. It'll be fine."

"How're your ribs doing?"

"Sore. I have to say, as much as I hate to admit it, the icing does help."

"I won't say I told you so."

"Good."

"You don't have to be such a baby about it, though."

"I wasn't being a baby. It just... surprised me is all."

"Sure." She took his hand. "So, sailing tomorrow?"

"I can't wait."

After a time a waitress delivered their meals. They ate and drank wine, talked of everything expect the events of the morning, wanting to put the fake suicide vests and paintball bullets behind them, never to speak of them again. Even though it was all a sham, the fear that it raised in them was as real as it gets.

After the meal, which CJ found to be much more satisfying than he thought it would be, they ordered strawberry shortcake and double chocolate cream pie, his and hers respectively. Nothing to do to occupy his mind while waiting for the desert, CJ started looking up and down the street again. He couldn't get the bomb throwing vision out of his head.

"Why don't we go inside for dessert," Stella said. "You're starting to make *me* nervous."

The desserts arrived as they reseated themselves at an inside table. The waitress didn't question their move at all.

Except for murmurs of delight from Stella, and a somewhat more masculine agreement from CJ, they said little until their plates were clean, sharing bites back and forth. Then Stella went online and left a glowing review for the *z grille*.

"This is a different world, isn't it?" CJ said. "We eat an excellent meal and you're able to tell the world about it before we even pay for it."

"If you like something, tell someone. That's what my mom used to say."

"I think I would like her. Is she still in Cleveland with her online boyfriend?"

Stella sighed. "Yes. They seem to be doing alright, but he does have some debt he didn't disclose to her before she moved out there. She mentioned that she wanted to sell the house, but Sara and I said no."

"What is it, four years since your dad died?"

"Yes, and we think she's jumping into this thing way too fast. If she decides to sell the house, there really isn't much we can do to stop her. At least for the time being, she's listening to us. I'm just afraid that he's going to steal her heart and then steal her money. Sara and I are talking about flying up there and just dropping in on her unannounced. Sara has been there but I haven't."

"That probably wouldn't be a bad idea." CJ sat back and took a sip of the wine. "Before we go home I'd like another shot at Eddie Hall."

"You still think he's Douglas' father?"

"Yes and no. I just don't know, but I'd like to close that page one way or the other." He stared off into the distance for a time and then said, "I'm not sure that going at him directly will accomplish anything. He has already put on the mask of denial, that is that he knew nothing of Eveleen's history. I don't think he's going to back down from that. Besides, I don't think it'll be very easy to find him if he's one of the top dogs in this morning's event."

"What do you have in mind, then?"

"If he is who I think he is, Eveleen Danohough will have proof. A woman doesn't discard her history. Am I right there?"

Stella nodded. "She'll hide it, but she won't necessarily throw it away. Her apartment is probably still a crime scene. How do you propose we get in?"

"Don't we have a detective friend who's biting at the bullet to do some private investigative work?"

"He should be staying home resting."

CJ took a sip of his water. "So should we, probably."

"True."

"I'm sure he's driving Gracie crazy. She'd probably pay to get him out of the house for an hour or two."

"She might be back to work."

"Didn't she say she was extending her vacation to a week?"

Stella thought about that for a few seconds. "Maybe she did." She pulled her phone out of her purse.

A phone call and a little over an hour later, the two of them were again sitting on DuPont's back deck, admiring the view across the lake while they imparted the events of the last twenty-four hours to Parker and Gracie.

"It was all a fake?!" Up until her exclamation, Gracie had just sat there with her mouth hanging open. Now she jumped to her feet and pulled Stella into a hug. "Oh, God! That must have been awful seeing as you thought it was real."

"It was," Stella said, "and I still get the shakes thinking about it."

"When I saw it on the news this morning," Parker said, "I wondered about you guys, but thought that you'd gone back to Arizona today. Seeing as it took place in Orlando, I didn't even think to check in with my cohorts here in St. Petersburg."

Thirteen year-old Tracy came out of the house to declare that she was home from school, the last of the three to arrive, said hi to Stella and CJ and announced she'd be in her room doing homework.

Once the four of them were alone again, Stella and CJ went on to describe the looks of shock and then relief mixed with doubt on the faces of the G8 people when CJ figured out that the explosives were fakes and pulled off his vest. CJ then described his brush with hotel security, eliciting a chuckle from Parker.

"So, now the reason we're here," CJ said. He saw the concern on their faces, so he added, "It has nothing to do with that."

"Okay," Parker said.

"I'd like to be able to go through Ms. Danohough's apartment. If she was in fact Douglas' mother, she most likely has something that will prove it and maybe even spell out who his father was."

"I thought you figured it out that it was Eddie Hall," Parker said.

"There's too much doubt there, still. I'm not even sure she was his mother, though I have to say she was rather convincing. I need to find out for sure, though I don't know what difference it would make in the big picture, now that she's dead."

"You think there might be a birth certificate?"

CJ shook his head. "My understanding is that the only birth certificate was homemade and with the baby when he was left on the doorstep of the hospital and that it was believed that the mother's name that was on it was false. The father wasn't named. That would be too easy."

"Didn't she say something about giving birth in the middle of some battle in Northern Ireland?" Parker said.

"Battle of Bogside, yes. It was a riot that took place in Derry, Northern Ireland from 12 August through 14 August of 1969. Douglas was born on the 13th."

"Could it be that the mother and/or father were killed, that a friend left the baby because there was no next of kin?"

"I was told that injuries well exceeded 1,000, but that there were no deaths. Besides, Danohough told me herself that she was the one who left Douglas."

"If she was in the middle of it," Parker said, "then we can only assume that he, the father, whether he be Eddie Hall or not, was likely in the middle of it as well."

"It's a reasonable assumption."

They all sipped at their iced tea for a time, each in their own thoughts. Finally, Parker set his tea aside and stood. "Let me make a call. I could get us in there, but if the captain found out... well, I'd just rather go through proper channels, at least get Don Gorky's go ahead. As far as I know the crime scene tape has already been pulled. I would still need him to gain official access to the key."

With that, Parker walked into the house.

An hour later the three of them—Gracie saw no purpose in going along—and the building manager stepped through the door and into the apartment where Eveleen Danohough had been murdered. Although the tape had in fact been removed, nothing else had changed.

"Any idea when someone will come in to clean this place up and move her stuff out?" the building manager said. "It would be nice to have this rented out by the first of October."

"Nothing I can tell you," Parker said.

"Who did she have listed as her next-of-kin?" CJ asked.

"No one."

"No one?"

"That's right. No one. No contacts of any kind under next-of-kin. Believe me, if there had been someone I'd have called them already."

"When is the lease up?" Parker asked.

"End of the year."

"Then you've got better than three months to figure something out, is the way I see it," CJ said. "Technically, this is hers until then."

"There is still the monthly rent."

"And when is that due?"

"First of the month."

"Then this is Ms. Danohough residence for the next three weeks. Thank you for letting us in," Parker said. "We'll return the key when we're finished."

With a huff, the manager turned and walked off.

"So," Stella said. "What are we looking for?"

CJ looked over at the corner of the living room where a small desk stood with a closed laptop computer and a printer. A wooden, two-drawer file cabinet sat to the right. He pointed. "I'll start there. Why don't you go through her bedroom, look for a journal or scrapbook. It might be something she'd secure in a more personal space, such as an underwear drawer. Look in any boxes in her closet."

"I get the picture."

She headed off and CJ opened one of the file drawers.

"Clint," Stella called.

He walked down the hall to where she stood in the bedroom doorway.

"I don't know if I can do this," she said.

He looked past her to the splatter of blood and brain matter on the bed and wall. "Why don't I do this part?" he said. "You go do the desk."

She turned around and put her hand on his chest. "Thank you." She took a couple of steps toward the living room and then stopped and turned to CJ. "One thing, Clint. You'd be looking for a diary, not a journal."

"What's the difference?"

"A diary is more personal. Thrust me. If there's a journal, it would likely be out here and have to do with her business. The diary would be in her bedroom and would contain her love life and secret ambitions."

"Would a woman her age keep a diary?"

"Maybe. Maybe not. In any case she likely had one when she was a teen or young woman. There's no way she'd discard it, even after this many years and I can guarantee that his name and the birth of her baby would be in it."

With that she headed on to the living room where CJ knew Parker was already opening doors on the entertainment center. He was going to search that and then the kitchen.

Ignoring the blood and gore, keeping his head down and his eyes focused, CJ started with the bedside table, finding only tissues and pharmaceutical items in the top drawer, books and magazines in the bottom. Nothing that looked like a diary. The closet contained the expected clothing plus two file boxes and four plastic hat boxes. He opened them all and found tax and financial records and a variety of women's hats.

He closed the closet door and stood in the middle of the room, feeling the ache in his ribs and shoulder from the exertion. He kept his back to the gore around the bed. He didn't want to look at it any more than Stella did, recalled dumping his stomach the day they found Danohough's body. His stomach rolled a bit at the memory.

He looked at the dresser and then got down on his hands and knees and peeked under the bed. There were a couple of plastic storage boxes, the slide-under-the-bed kind. He pulled them out and discovered only winter clothes; wondered how often they got used in Florida. About as often as in Southern Arizona, he figured. He pushed them back, stood and approached the dresser.

And then he hit pay dirt. In the back of the underwear drawer, the third drawer he'd opened, he discovered three bundles of letters and a used-to-be-white diary with a broken lock. He pulled the things out and went through the rest of the dresser, finding nothing more. He then carried them into the living room and dropped them onto the kitchen table.

"I think I've found it," he said. In seconds they were all sitting at the table.

"I've found nothing," Stella said.

"My neither," Parker said.

"What should we start with?" CJ asked.

"Let's look at the postmark dates on the letters," Stella said.

Each of them took a stack, removing rubber bands and looking at postmarks.

"The oldest I have is March of 1972," Parker said.

"I have..." Stella flipped through a couple, squinting at smeared ink. "I think this is October of 1969."

"CJ looked at his. I've got 1978. I think you've got the prize, Stella."

CJ and Parker bent toward Stella to get a look at the 1969 envelope.

"I can't read it," Parker said.

"I think it's addressed to Éibhleann O'Donoghue."

CJ took the envelope from her and looked at it closer. "You pronounced it wrong," he said. "The e-i-b-h is pronounced ave, not eeb. The last part is lin, not le-ann. Together it would be Ave-lin."

"And you know this... how?"

CJ thought about his conversation with Special Agent Coulter when they were transporting him to the FBI field office the day he'd arrived in St. Petersburg. "I'll tell you later. Trust me for right now. That's the pronunciation. She obviously changed her name when she came to the United States. It's not a stretch from Éibhleann O'Donoghue to Eveleen Danohough. The name she used on the birth certificate, by-the-way, was Éibhleann Ó Caiside. She used her actual first name but a false last name."

"You sure you don't want to fill us in on how you're so smart on this?"

"Let me bask in my brilliance for a while." He pointed to the scribbled return address. "So, who is this?"

> *Michael O.*
> *Lisburn*
> *Co. Down*

"Sure doesn't look like Eddie Hall, that's for sure," Parker said.

"Can't disagree there."

"And what about this?" Stella said, pointing to the addressee.

Éibhleann O'Donoghue
Droichead Nua
Co. Kildare

"And what is *Droichead Nua*?"

"No idea. Look it up on your *iPad*."

She pulled out the *iPad* and after a minute or so said, "It's the Irish name for Newbridge, a town in the county of *Kildare* in Ireland; not Northern Ireland." She looked down through the stacks of letters. "All of these are from Michael O of *Lisburn*." She entered *Lisburn* into the search box. "It's in Northern Ireland, southwest of Belfast. This stack spans about four years it appears."

"And that's where my stack picks up," Parker said. "Most say Michael O as well, though some are just Michael."

"Same here," CJ said. "He remains in *Lisburn* until May 25 of 1981. The return just says Michael. No town or county. That's the last one."

"What's the postmark say?"

CJ turned the envelope and then said, "I think it's *Ballycastle*. Where is that?"

Stella entered it in the search box. "Northern Ireland," she said after a time. "On the northern coast, if that's important. So, what does it all mean?"

"Two months after the *Battle of the Bogside*, during which Douglas was born and given the name Douglas O'Reilly, Danohough, then O'Donoghue, began correspondence with a man by the name of Michael O. Could he be Michael O'Reilly, Douglas' biological father?"

Stella held up her hands as though shaping a picture frame. "It's a sad love story about two people, in love but forced apart as a result of the political drama around them. A different kind of Romeo and Juliet. In the middle of a bloody battle, Douglas is born and then given up in hopes that he would land in a loving home. Michael heads off to Lisburn in Northern Ireland and she to Newbridge, or *Droichead Nua*, in Ireland. Sadly, she discovers that she can't live without him and begins a letter writing campaign to win him back, but it appears the life together that she has dreamt of, that she gave up her baby for, never comes to pass. She is left forever forlorn, not only for the loss of him, but also for the loss of her baby, regret at the decision she was forced to face. Maybe over the years they occasionally get together, but can never make it work."

"A made for TV movie," Parker said. "Very nice."

Stella tapped the last envelope with the *Ballycastle* postmark. "What I want to know is what happened in 1981 when all the letters stopped, and where is Michael O now?"

"We'll have to open the letters to find out," CJ said. "Are you guys okay with that?"

They both agreed.

"Where should we start? The end or the beginning?"

"Let's find out what happened in the end." Stella picked up the envelope and opened it.

Chapter 45

They all stared at the letter, a single sheet of notepaper with only a few brief words.

Róis,

For reasons I cannot say, I must leave me beloved Éire. It be best I not write again. Please do not try to find me.

Be well,

M

"He just left?" Stella sounded flabbergasted. "Why?"

CJ pointed to the *iPad*. "See if you can figure out if anything significant happened in May of 1981 in Northern Ireland, something that would send Michael fleeing from his country and cutting communications with his friends." He picked up the letter as though to closer examine it. "I wonder where he fled to. This last letter was postmarked in *Ballycastle*; on the coast, you say? Did he take a ship to somewhere?"

"An easy jump to Scotland from there," Parker said. "Then on to England and who knows where. Being over thirty years ago would make him a bit difficult to follow."

"There was the 1981 hunger strike," Stella said, poking her finger at her *iPad*.

CJ put down the letter. "Hunger strike? By who?"

"That would be whom," Stella said. "By whom."

"Whatever."

"Irish Republican prisoners had gone on a hunger strike in the Maze."

"Maze?"

"A prison." She continued to scroll. "On May 5th the first of ten died. His name was Bobby Sands."

"I don't see why Michael would be fleeing his country because of that. Was there anything else in May, closer to the 25th?"

They waited while she searched the web. "Here's something. On the 19th five British soldiers were killed by a roadside bomb planted by the Provisional Irish Republican Army."

"That could be interesting," CJ said. "Six days later he's left Northern Ireland, saying goodbye to a friend of at least twelve years, without so much as a forwarding address."

"They were just pen pals," Parker said.

"They were more than pen pals," Stella said. "For one he called her Róis, like the flower rose I'm sure. That's more personal. Also, she saved the letters. At least to her, their relationship meant something."

"Exactly," CJ said. "They could have met up every few years, or every few weeks for that matter; occasional lovers. We may learn more about that in the letters. In any case I think he had something to do with that bomb and was on the run."

"It's not a stretch, CJ," Parker said. "Still, who is this guy now?"

"His letters to her may not tell us who he was. We don't have her letters to him, but we do have her diary."

With that Stella pulled the diary to her and carefully opened to the first page.

On the name plate was the name, Éibhleann Róis O'Donoghue, born 2 December 1948 in *Droichead Nua*, Ireland, Co. Kildare.

"So he used her middle name," Stella said. "Róis."

"Maybe that's the name she went by," Parker said. "Might kill your theory that it was an endearment. It was just her name."

"Maybe," Stella said.

"Interesting, though, where she was born," CJ said.

"What's so interesting about that?" Stella said.

"First of all, remember that Ireland and Northern Ireland are two different countries. Northern Ireland is under the British flag while Ireland is an Irish Free State. At just barely twenty-years-old Éibhleann leaves her country to be with someone across the border. I'd be willing to bet her parents weren't happy with the decision. She gets pregnant by him, a player in the PIRA or whatever organization is dealing blows against the British military during that period. About the time she goes into labor things are getting hot and heavy around Derry. Violence erupts as Douglas is born and this young woman makes a hasty decision. She doesn't want to raise her baby in such violence so off Douglas goes, into another life. Chances are she later changes her mind but by then it is too late. He is gone.

"Devastated, she flees back to the comfort of her parents in *Droichead Nua*, however, she loves Michael, cannot just forget about him. She begins a letter writing campaign to win him back, which, may or may not have been successful."

"It's obvious that they never married," Stella said. "Otherwise there wouldn't be all these letters and her name would be something other than O'Donoghue or Danohough."

"True. It does appear that she never married at all." CJ pointed at the diary. "Turn the page. Let's see what she wrote."

Stella turned quite a number of pages. "I don't like prying into this young girl's life at the age of fourteen, so I'm going to skip all this early stuff." She continued to turn pages and then stopped. "Here! Summer of 1968. There's Michael's name."

At first it was just his first name, then in September she wrote,

I am so tired of milking cows. Michael says he has to
go back to Londonderry and asked that I should go
with him.

WOW!!!! YES!!!!
Mrs. Michael O'Raghallaigh
He hasn't asked me yet, but he will. I know he will.

There were hearts all around the name.

"There's your Michael O and I'll bet the last name sounds just like O'Reilly," Parker said. "The g-h is probably silent."

CJ straightened up and stretched a bit. "So, when she put his name on the birth certificate, she had enough wherewithal to change the spelling to O'Reilly. But she wouldn't give up the father's full name, even in an unofficial document that she created."

Stella said, "I think she knew before he was even born that it was what she was going to do. She planned it. It wasn't a spur of the moment decision."

CJ pointed to the book. "Keep going. What happens next?"

She flipped through more pages. "Bla... bla, here we go. September 18th she writes that she is in Londonderry and her parents are pissed. She won't tell them where she is." She turned a few more pages. "A little bit more about that on the first of October. She talks about her sister and... the next entry is in November where she goes on about her love for Michael, but again misses her sister. More about never milking a cow again. December 25th she is lonely for home, Christmas with her mum and sis." She read for a few seconds. "And here is where she realizes that she has missed her period; on Christmas day."

Stella paged several times again, quickly scanning the feminine penmanship. "January 29th entry." She held it up so that the men could see.

I'm pregnant. How do I tell Michael?

Stella continued browsing. "She tells him in the middle of February. He is not happy about it."

"That's all fine and good," CJ said. "Skip to August. What does she say around the time Douglas is born?"

She paged forward, looking at dates, and then said, "Here we go. Early August she is concerned that Michael doesn't want the baby. She wonders how to give him up for adoption." She keeps turning pages, reading fast. "Talks about that every few days. She's very tired, depressed. Tries to call her mum but gets her dad. He refuses the reversed charges. A couple of days later she tries again. Same thing."

"This girl is mixed up and hurting," Parker said.

"August 12th she writes that the world has gone crazy."

"That's when the violence started," CJ said.

"Yes, and she's feeling labor pains. Then there is nothing until August 16th. She writes, 'Tried calling Mum. Not at home. Haven't seen Michael since before. All the crazy has stopped, but. Is he dead? In hospital? Wally say he was injured, but okay, busy. Michael doesn't want the baby. It is hard. He cries. Always crying. I wish I had me mum. Today I will... leave him.'"

"Leave him? Leave who? Michael?"

"No, Douglas." She holds up the diary and points to the next line.

He deserve better home. They will find him a home.

And then Stella pointed to two more lines.

Michael don't want him
I'm bad mum

"The 16th of August was when Douglas was left on the doorstop of the hospital," CJ said. "What did she write after that?"

Stella turned the page and then a few more pages. "Nothing. That was the last entry."

"Nothing? How can that be?"

She pushed the diary away. "She was a confused young girl who had to make a terrible decision. She gave up her baby and forever after, regretted it. She likely fell into a deeper depression upon returning to her parents' home, and tried hard to put it all behind her, which meant not talking about it even in her diary. Her diary went the way of childish memorabilia. She may have never opened it again but kept it with her as a stark reminder of what she did; in a way, her punishment."

"Do you think she told her parents?"

Stella shook her head. "I doubt it. Her heavy secret to bear."

"She returned to milking cows," Parker said.

They all sat in silence for a time. Finally CJ said, "Okay. It's a sad story for sure, one for the likes of Nicholas Sparks to listen to *you* talk, but that's not what we're here for. What I want to know is where did Michael go and where is he now?"

"I think you need to contact your FBI son," Parker said. "Didn't you say something about being told the night you arrived here that Agent Coulter implied they were looking for Douglas' parents?"

"I can't really say he implied it," CJ said, "but he didn't deny my suggestion that it was what they were doing." He leaned back for a few moments. "I'm thinking that it is actually Douglas' father who they are after, the man who fled Northern Ireland after killing or being involved with the killing of five British soldiers. I don't think Douglas' mother was anything more than a means to that end."

"Allegedly killing five British soldiers," Parker corrected.

"Allegedly."

"But we're still not getting anywhere near understanding where Michael disappeared to," Parker said. "We're going to have to go through the letters."

CJ pulled his stack toward him. "Then let's do it."

Little more than thirty minutes later they all sat back.

"That was a bust," CJ said. "No talk about Douglas or the IRA."

"Except in the first letter," Parker said. "What was it he said? 'I'm so sorry about the baby. At least you are okay.' That tells me that she led him to believe that the baby died at birth. After that the letters gradually turned mushy, 'I can't wait to see you' stuff."

"That's not mushy," Stella said. "It was sweet. I don't know why it never went past the two or three times a year rendezvous, though."

"They didn't start that for what, five years?" Parker said. "It took them that long just to get back to an occasional roll in the hay."

Stella slapped Parker on the shoulder. "It was more than that to her, I'll bet. She was being patient. One step at a time."

"We still know nothing more about where he went," CJ said. "Not even a mention of a relative or friend outside of the island who he might have gone to. I think we're dead in the water."

"What I didn't do was Google his name," Stella said. She started to type and then said, "How was his last name spelled?"

CJ opened the diary, paged until he found the name. "O apostrophe r-a-g-h."

Stella looked over at him. When he didn't continue, she said, "What?"

He turned the diary toward her and pointed. "You didn't mention that."

"What? What are you pointing at?"

CJ tapped it. "His full name. You never mentioned the middle name."

Her eyes got wide. "That's a different entry. I never saw that. Must have skipped over it. Do you think...?"

"What are you two talking about?" Parker said.

CJ rotated the diary so that Parker could see the name where it was underlined three times, surrounded with dozens of little red hearts.

Mrs. Michael Edmond O'Raghallaigh

"O... kay," Parker said. "Edmond. It is a little suspicious, isn't it. Still could be a coincidence."

"Maybe, but when you look at the last name, O'Raghallaigh, remove the first four and the last four letters, what do you get?"

"Hall," Stella said. "Edmond Hall."

"I'll be damned," Parker said.

CJ put down the diary. "Hellooooo Eddie." He pulled out his phone. "Time to call my favorite FBI agent again."

Chapter 46

"Yeah, Dad?" Josh said just when CJ thought he'd be leaving a voice mail.

"I'm not in trouble again, Josh."

"Good to hear."

"Have you found the paintball shooters yet?"

"People are working on it. Why do you ask?"

"Just curious. I might have something else for you."

"What do you mean by something else?"

"My hunch is that you've been looking for someone, an individual who might have had something to do with the death of a few British soldiers about 31 years ago. That would be in 1981 if you don't have your calculator handy."

"Where do you come up with this stuff, Dad?"

"I guess you don't care to hear what I've got to say."

"Fine. What have you got?"

"Do you know the name, Michael O'Raghallaigh?" CJ spelled it for him.

"I do. What about him?"

"You've been looking at Eddie Hall."

"We have. So?"

"They're one in the same."

"And you know this because?"

"Let's just say, I know."

"What else do you have?"

"What do you mean what else do I have?"

"You just told me something we already know. Now can you tell me where Eddie Hall is at the moment?"

"You mean you lost him?"

"We never really had him. At the time that we were at his home..."

"You mean when I showed up to help you interview him?"

"Yeah, that time. We didn't have anything on him at that time. He was simply a person of interest in the Danohough killing, was soon dismissed."

"But that was before he was linked up with Michael O'Raghallaigh."

"Correct. I just figured that out a short time ago. So when did you figure it out?"

"Just a few minutes ago."

"Really."

"Really." When there came a long silence, CJ said, "I was kind of hoping you guys had him in custody. I'd sure like to talk to him again."

"Sorry to disappoint you, Dad. I'm sure we'll find him. When are you going home?"

"In a day or two. What about you?"

"Whenever Taffer is done with me. I go where I'm told. How did you figure it out?"

"It was just a matter of putting the clues together."

"Where did you get your clues? I had to do some deep digging."

"It appears that Eveleen Danohough was actually Éibhleann Róis O'Donoghue, and she kept a diary when she became pregnant with and gave birth to Douglas back in 1969."

"Her diary?"

"You should have thought of that, my fine FBI son. Douglas' father was Michael Edmond O'Raghallaigh. A cub scout could easily see Eddie Hall in that. Oh, and there are also some twelve years of letters that he wrote to her, which she kept, before a roadside bomb killed five British soldiers in 1981. That's when he disappeared, to the United States I'm assuming, and changed his name."

"You got lucky."

"Isn't that what half of this is, luck?"

Silence.

"Have you figured out yet how Eddie Hall figures into the paintball attack?"

"Haven't found a connection other than being the boyfriend of Danohough who was the biological mother of Douglas Rothbower who was our mole inside the UIRA."

"Compromised mole," CJ added.

"That's only a maybe. It hasn't been ruled out, though."

"What is it with you guys? You aren't willing to admit that you screwed up? They knew about him plain and simple and was using him to feed you false information. They practically came right out and admitted it to me. While you were running down false leads, they were planning their paintball attack.

"Also, Eddie Hall was Douglas Rothbower's biological father."

"You're certain of that?"

"I just told you, it's in Eveleen's diary. If you want to run their DNA to make it one-hundred percent certain, then go for it."

"We don't really care, Dad. It wouldn't make any difference in our investigation. No point in spending tax dollars on it."

"I see your point, Josh."

"I'm glad you do. I've got to go."

"What aren't you telling me?"

"What do you mean, what aren't I telling you?"

"You're an FBI agent. You're trained to withhold information, even if for no reason other than that you can. Don't tell anyone anything."

"No, Dad. That's not how it goes. It's don't reveal anything to the general public which may jeopardize, compromise or impede the investigation."

"Am I the general public, Josh?"

"As a matter-of-fact, Dad, yes you are."

"Even though without me you'd probably be nowhere on this thing."

"I wouldn't go so far as to say that."

"You've an entire slew of FBI special agents between here and the beltway working this thing twenty-four seven. I show up to find the father of a dead Arizona girl and stumble onto what you guys haven't been able to find with all your expertise and electronic gadgetry."

"Stumble is the correct word, Dad."

CJ ground his teeth for a few seconds. "I'm just trying to help, Josh. Why is it every time I attempt to feed you information, you give me crap?"

"Who's giving who crap here, Dad? You call up to give me information that we already have and then bad mouth us."

"We're on the same side here."

"Doesn't sound like it. I've got to go. Thanks for the info, Dad. I think we can manage the rest without you. Go sailing with Stella and then go home."

CJ opened his mouth to respond only to realize the connection was dead. He looked up at Stella and Parker.

"That didn't sound like it went very well," Parker said. "What do you think he's not telling you?"

"That was just my way of seeing if he'd spill something to me. Don't you use that technique in interrogations?"

"Suspects, but not an FBI agent."

"You *were* a little harsh with him," Stella said.

"Who's side are you on?" When CJ saw the set of Stella's jaw he added, "I'm sorry. It's just that..." *Just what?* he thought, looking at Stella. She just stared at him, waiting. "I don't know. I want us to be like father and son, not like FBI agent versus some stranger on the street who only gets in the way."

"Have you ever thought that maybe that's what he wants, too?"

"He sure doesn't show it."

"Do you show it to him or do you push yourself into his work life? What do you know about his personal life, Clint? Have you asked him about girlfriends, where he lives in Denver, what he does with his spare time, hobbies, anything that is not job related or Fed related? Serial killer or IRA related? Have you ever thought that maybe what he wants is not another cop sidekick, but a father?"

"He's the one who ran away; not so much as a *postcard* to tell us he was okay. Nearly seven years without a word and then he shows up out of the blue as an FBI agent. Does he expect that I'll just jump back into the father-son role?"

Stella reached over and placed her hand on CJ's. "Chances are he is just as confused by it all as you, Clint. I think you need to ease back a little. Give it time. Let your father, adult son relationship heal naturally."

"I think he's dammed scared," Parker said.

"Scared of what?"

"Of losing you. You've cheated death how many times since he showed back up in your life? four? five?"

"I've lost count."

"Parker is right," Stella said. "He wants you to go home because he's scared that he is going to lose the father he's just gotten back."

CJ sat back and seriously considered their words. But what about him? Could it be that he's scared of losing his son again?

Chapter 47

When CJ pulled up in front of the DuPont house, he and Stella declined Parker's invitation for dinner, saying that they'd had a late lunch, that they had other plans. They did promise to join the DuPont family for dinner the next evening as they weren't planning on flying out until Thursday.

The three of them remained seated in CJ's rental in front of Parker's house discussing Eddie Hall.

"So you're done with this case?" Parker asked. "You're thinking that any further effort to talk to Hall is useless?"

"If he was involved in the summit attack," CJ said, "he is certainly in the wind. Their plan was very well executed, despite the screw-ups involving me."

"What bothers me," Parker said, "is if he was an officer in the UIRA he'd have to have been involved in the decision to kill Danohough and Douglas. That doesn't jive with what we've discovered about his and Danohough's relationship. She was obviously still in love with him, asked him to marry her."

"Maybe he wasn't in love with *her*," CJ said. "Maybe he was just using her."

"For what?"

"Good question. It does seem that he really didn't know about Douglas until recently."

"Do you think maybe that it pissed him off that she gave Douglas away and then never told him about his son actually being alive. Remember that we did learn that she told him that the baby died at birth."

"Did we learn that or did we form a conclusion based on a few inconclusive entries in her diary?" Stella said.

"Good point," CJ said. "In any case, would he have been pissed off enough to have her killed?" CJ really couldn't imagine that.

"Maybe others wanted her out of the way when they discovered that her son was an informant," Parker said. "and he was pissed off enough that he didn't vote against it. You know, like a board of directors for UIRA voting to off Eveleen Danohough. All in favor indicate so by raising your right hand. Whatever the procedure, he may have abstained."

"You two watch too many cop movies," Stella said.

"This is real life, Sweetheart," Parker said in a hardboiled detective voice. "We whack 'em like we see 'em."

After Parker got out of the car, Stella said to CJ, "What other plans do we have?"

"I sort of just want to be alone with you."

"I like that." She appeared to consider his statement for a few seconds and then added, "What do you mean by sort of?"

"I'm thinking I want to go by Paddy's McGee's Irish Pub one more time."

"Why?"

"Don't know. Maybe just to bring Paddy and Rebecca up to date."

"Do you think they'll know more about Eddie Hall now that we have his real name, or do you think they've been withholding for some reason?"

"If they're not telling us something, it may not be because that's their intention," CJ said. "I think they've told us everything about him they think they know. If we throw out his real name, maybe we'll trigger memories about things they don't know they know."

"Kind of what I was thinking."

Twenty minutes later they stood just inside the pub entryway looking at the crowd of people waiting to be seated; not a surprise after seeing the parking lot.

"I don't think this is going to be easy," CJ said as Hannah rushed by, taking no more notice than a quick glance and a brief smile. "It looks like the entire crew is on duty and they're buzzin'."

"Something about Tuesday nights?"

A young lady who CJ hadn't seen before came up to a nearby podium, looked at a list and called, "Boyd, party of four?"

About a third of the waiting crowd followed after her.

"So, I guess we wait."

They stood to the side for about a minute, then the young lady returned and took their name, writing Washburn on her list. CJ saw that there were three names before his.

Again, CJ and Stella stepped aside, out of the way. From their vantage point CJ could see Maire and a middle-aged man working the bar. Hannah, Rebecca, and another woman were working tables. Both Paddy and the older cook were on the grill. There were two other young men beyond the grill working dishes. One of them came out and started bussing tables. From what he could tell, Paddy's McGee's Irish Pub could use a few more staff.

Then he noticed a crowd of people at the bar, centered around the best viewpoint of the widescreen TV. They weren't watching a football game or sports highlights. They were watching CNN and what looked to be the latest report from the *Orlando World Center*. He touched Stella's arm and pointed. "That's why this place is so busy."

"Maybe we ought to come back later," Stella said. She watched the changing images for a few seconds and then said, "Oh!"

"Oh what?" CJ's gaze had shifted to watching Rebecca, hoping to catch her eye.

"Do you know what today is?"

CJ thought for a minute and then said, "September 11th." When the significance of the date occurred to him, he looked back up at the monitor.

"Do you think there's a connection?" Stella asked.

"I certainly hope not. Would be very insensitive."

"Just a coincidence that the G8 mini-summit was held in the World Center on 9/11?"

"I would want to think so."

Stella turned away from the view of the monitor and the image of the first World Trade Center building collapsing. "I'm really not ready for dinner anyway, and there's no way anyone is going to be able to break away to talk to us. I'm also afraid someone's going to recognize us."

"No news cameras ever got us and hopefully, our names didn't get released. I'm sure Paddy doesn't even know we were involved."

"Yeah, still, why don't we come back in a couple of hours? This is just too much."

With that, CJ stepped up to where the list lay and crossed off his name. As he started to turn away, he spotted Rebecca looking at him from across a half dozen tables. He pointed to his watch and then held up his hands, displaying all ten fingers. She nodded her understanding and went on with her duties.

"We'll come back at 10:00," he said as he guided Stella back out the door. "Rebecca got the message. What should we do now?"

"I don't really want to go back to the hotel and just sit and do nothing. I feel antsy, like I want to keep moving."

"Let's go down to *The Pier*, then. It's a pleasant evening to walk the waterfront. How's your arm doing?"

"It's sore. Your ribs?"

"Could probably due with a whole new set. These feel worn out."

"I'm starting to wonder about this PI stuff." She stopped at the car and leaned against it. "I've got this gun that I carry and I'm afraid that if I should need it I'll be too scared to use it. And then I'm scared of what will happen if I do use it. I'm also scared that I'll pull it out and use it when I don't need to."

"The SIG Sauer scares you?" CJ said.

"No. That isn't what I mean. Guns have never scared me. My father taught Sara and I both how to shoot and instilled a respect. It just never occurred to me what it would be like to actually be in a position to have to pull it out to use it on a person that wasn't printed on a paper target."

"Most police officers go their entire careers without using their guns on anyone."

"Yeah, but when they do doesn't it screw with their heads a bit?"

CJ thought about the bullet he put through Tommy Clark's eye. As much as he tried to deny it, he was having to admit that it took something away from him. "Yes, it does."

"I don't want my head screwed up anymore than it already is."

"Your head isn't screwed up."

"I just wore a suicide vest that I thought was the real thing. If that doesn't screw with someone's head then they aren't human. I don't know if I'll ever get over that."

CJ leaned against the car next to Stella and put his arm around her. "We're soul mates, you and I, equally screwed up."

While they'd leaned against the car, CJ had noted a late model dark sedan parked on the street. Under the street lights it'd appeared that there were two people sitting in it. He didn't recall if it was there when he'd parked. When he pulled the rental out of the parking lot he'd kept an eye on the sedan for a while, but with traffic he couldn't be certain that it'd pulled out as well before he had to take a turn and lose sight. He'd thought its lights had come on, but he wasn't sure.

Why would someone be following him now?

By the time he'd turned onto 2nd Avenue to take them toward *The Pier*, he'd dismissed it or simply forgotten about it, more in tune with Stella sitting next to him, looking forward to a nice walk with her in the warm night air.

The Pier was not nearly as quiet as they expected it would be on a Tuesday night. He pulled the car into the last parking lot, choosing a spot near the ticket kiosk. While Stella waited, he ran his credit card to obtain a ticket, which he then placed on the dash. Then, hand-in-hand, they climbed the steps and headed out for the quarter of a mile walk along *The Pier,* on the end of which stood a structure that looked like an inverted pyramid.

Briefly, CJ thought about the two cars that had pulled into the parking lot after him, one light colored, one dark. He wondered if he should have paid more attention to them, at least the dark one. He glanced back. Several people where at the kiosk, but from the distance and the low light he wouldn't have even known his own mother. Would someone who was intent on doing them harm take the time to purchase a parking ticket? *You're being paranoid again,* he told himself.

"They're going to tear it down," Stella said.

CJ turned to see what she was talking about. They'd stopped at a sign that said that *The Pier* would close May 31st of 2013 in preparation for demolition so that the new "Lens" design pier could be built in its place.

"Wonder what a Lens design is?" Stella said.

"No idea."

They walked on a few paces until suddenly a pelican flew up and landed on a piling post less than ten feet in front of them.

"Ah... Clint. What does he want?"

"How should I know. Maybe he thinks we'll give him dinner." CJ held out his hands to the bird, demonstrating that they were empty. "I don't have any fish."

"He is huge!" Stella stepped a bit closer.

"Be careful," CJ said. "He might..."

"Might what? He's obviously used to people."

Suddenly the bird spread its wings and flapped himself a few feet into the air.

"Eek!" Stella jumped back. "What's he doing?"

"Showing off."

With that the pelican turned away to soar some fifty yards before landing on another piling post farther down *The Pier.*

"Wow. That was neat." Stella pointed past the bird to the odd-shaped structure on the end of *The Pier.* "Gracie said that there's an aquarium in there. Let's check it out."

"Probably closed at this hour, but you never know?"

CJ noted several other strolling couples farther on. "This must be the place to go for an evening stroll." Still hand-in-hand he pulled Stella to a stop to look out into the darkness of the bay and the lights reflecting across the water.

"I like this," Stella said, leaning on the railing.

"Me too."

"It's romantic."

"My thoughts exactly." CJ started to put his arm around her shoulders, remembered her gunshot wound and slipped his arm around her waist instead. "Wish we had something like this around Tucson."

"It *is* very pleasant, isn't it Mister Washburn?"

Stella stiffened against CJ's arm.

The unmistakable Irish brogue came from a man behind them. CJ turned his head to look into the face, surprised at who he found. "Eddie Hall, or should I say, Michael Edmond O'Raghallaigh."

Chapter 48

Next to Eddie stood the woman who CJ referred to as "The Boss" when he and Stella were shackled in the house only twenty-four hours before. CJ looked beyond them but saw only a family walking off *The Pier*, a mother and father, a middle school-aged girl holding her mother's hand. It appeared that Eddie and The Boss were alone, nonthreatening.

"It's good to see you out and about," Eddie said, "no worse for wear." He took a deep breath and slowly let it out, looking past CJ, out toward the dark water. "It surprises me though, and saddens me, that you know my real name."

"It wasn't hard." CJ looked from Eddie to the woman. "You two, together, were in charge of this entire thing? The fake vests and paintball guns?"

Eddie brightened up. "Quite an undertaking, wasn't it. In charge of it all? Well, I am not so sure. It was a well executed cooperation among many. I really tried to keep my distance, though I was somewhat involved in some of the ideas, especially the writing of the statement. The execution part under Isabel's guidance," he put his hand on the woman's hand where she rested it on his arm, "of Rory and his team was flawless, wouldn't you say?"

"It was quite convincing," CJ said, "and their exit very smooth. What's your endgame?"

"There is no endgame, Mister Washburn. That was it. We fulfilled our mission and are now disappearing, almost before your very eyes."

"Almost but not quite. Aren't you taking a risk by hanging around? Not only do I know who you really are, but now, so does the FBI."

Another deep breath. "Loose ends, Mister Washburn. Loose ends."

CJ thought about the Eddie he interviewed in Clearwater. This didn't seem like the same guy. That Eddie was distraught over Danohough's death, seemingly confused by it all. Was that a topnotch acting job? This Eddie was cool and in charge, confident. Did he bamboozle everyone, including the FBI?

CJ had been watching the man's eyes when he talked. Even in the low illumination of the pier lighting he could see that they were alert, clear when he spoke of the successful mission, clouded over when he spoke of loose ends. The man's confidence was weak. His thirty-year-old secret was out and he was again on the run for murder, but there was something else.

"What about Eveleen and Douglas?" CJ said. "Were they part of your plan that went smoothly?"

The woman started to roll her eyes and then checked it. The look on her face was unmistakable, though. There was no love lost over the two deaths.

Eddie, however, presented a very different look. Maybe regret; maybe a deeper sorrow. "Eveleen's death was..." He shook his head. "Sad." There came a long silence before he continued. "Douglas however.... Despite everything, the FBI was getting too close."

"Despite everything? You mean despite all the false information you fed Douglas to pass to the FBI."

Eddie looked a bit surprised. "Yes."

"Why are you here right now? Why aren't you hunkered down somewhere, in deep hiding or in route to some distant destination?"

"I have unfinished business."

"With us?" CJ said, indicating himself and Stella. "What business? And how did you find us? Are we carrying a tracking bug?"

Eddie held up his hand. "Not to worry, Mister Washburn. I was not tracking you by some electronic means, nor did I have someone following you and reporting to me. All those involved are gone, except for the two of us."

"Are you saying that you just happened to run into us by accident, that on your way out of town you decided to have a romantic walk on *The Pier*?"

"We are, as a matter-of-fact, on our way out of town. I'd considered stopping for dinner at McGee's pub, but found the parking lot full. We were parked on the street talking about the fact that it probably wouldn't be a good idea anyway. Isabel's face is not known, but mine certainly is and by now they, meaning the McGee's, may have me connected with what went on with the summit."

"And then we walked out."

"You could have knocked me over with a feather, as they say."

"And so you followed us. Why?"

"I want to know who killed Eveleen. You're the only one who seems to be coming up with answers."

With those words came a look of surprise on Isabel's face, and she didn't even try to hide it from CJ. She just glared at him as though daring him to say anything.

"You truly loved Eveleen."

Eddie didn't respond, thus did not deny it. The woman shifted her glare onto the back of his head.

"But even though you loved her you were using her," CJ continued. "Six years since you became business partners. This couldn't have been in the planning for six years. This mini-summit was scheduled no more than a few months ago. Did you use her in some other way for all that time, and for what purpose?"

"In a sense, yes, it has been in the planning. Just as one plans for the future by building a nest egg, we have been planning by building associations, real-estate and contacts. In the end, credibility. We had no idea in what ways it would develop."

"So by becoming a partner in an American business you gained credibility. It wasn't hard, seeing as you and Eveleen were lovers forty-three years ago, made a child together who you later had killed?"

Even in the low light CJ could swear he saw Eddie's face and neck turn red. Too much being revealed in Isabel's presence? he wondered. Who was Eddie's real lover right now?

Eddie stepped up close to the rail, looked out into darkness. "Evie lied to me those many years ago."

"Evie?"

"Eveleen. I called her Evie back then. She told me that the baby was still-born. And then I come to find out that he indeed survived his birth and then she dumped him on a doorstep like a bag of trash."

"You're still angry," CJ said. "I get that. Then why kill him?"

"Obviously, you haven't figured it all out yet."

"Figured what out?"

"Douglas, the Douglas who was an FBI informant, Douglas Rothbower, was not my son. Nor was he Evie's son though he certainly led her to believe such. Initially he came to St. Petersburg searching for his biological mother, but he quickly understood that he was on the wrong track despite the fact that a lot of the clues fit. It was because so many clues fit that the FBI stepped in and recruited him, asked him to play the part."

"Why?"

"Because they were after me."

"They were after you for the killing of five British soldiers in 1981, a roadside bomb."

Eddie turned his head to CJ, surprise on his face. "You're as good as they say." He returned his gaze to the night. "Yes. I will confess it here in the dark. That was certainly me. I was young and stupid."

"You had to have been in your thirties. You should have grown out of your stupid phase by then."

"Thirty-three. Some days I think I'm still in that stupid phase. That bomb wasn't supposed to kill anyone. It was meant to scare and make a point. I got a little too carried away with the charge. A heavy burden of regret that I've had to carry."

"So you jumped ship, so-to-say, ran away from your country, changed your name and became an American citizen."

"It wasn't quite that simple. I passed through a number of countries, gained a number of false identification documents, one of them being a British birth certificate giving me British citizenship. I then migrated to the United States, eventually obtaining a dual citizenship."

"So, you're one hundred percent certain Douglas was not your son."

"Yes."

"How can you be so sure? Did you talk to him about it?"

"No. I didn't even know that that was a possibility until last week. She introduced him as her son a few months back, but seeing as I was told forty-three years ago that my son had died, I didn't even consider that he might be mine, didn't make any kind of connection. Douglas could have easily been in his mid thirties."

"But you maintained communications with Evie for twelve years after the Battle of the Bogside. You had romantic reunions several times a year. If she had any other children or other relationships, you'd have known."

"We didn't get back together in that way for a number of years. And how do you know all of that?"

"Five years. I'm an investigator. It's what I do."

Eddie continue to stare out into Tamp Bay while Isabel continued to stare at the back of his head.

"You never thought about how old Douglas was because you didn't want to know, or you were too naive or stupid to not do the math. You assumed and then concluded, becoming convinced. You were never willing to put all the pieces together for fear, whether conscious or not, that you wouldn't like the result. It was also easier to believe that he was just an FBI plant who pretended to be her son.

"Here's the thing, Eddie," CJ added. "Douglas had a birth certificate." CJ had not seen it but his hunch was that it still existed and was in Douglas' personal effects somewhere. Or he had a copy and his adoptive parents had the original. Even if it no longer existed, with the surprised look on Eddie's face, CJ knew that his comment had hit the mark.

"It's not a hospital issued birth certificate," CJ continued, "because, as you know, Douglas was not born in a hospital. Evie drew up a birth certificate by hand which she left with Douglas when she dropped him off on the doorstep. That handmade certificate stayed with him all these years. Evie described it in her diary, even drew a miniature replica of it as one of her entries."

Eddie's mouth was hanging open. "She had a diary?" he managed to say.

"Yes she did and for many years, up until the day she gave Douglas up, she was very faithful with her entries. On that certificate, young, scared Evie tried to create all the information she thought a real birth certificate should contain, including the father's full name. Convenient for you and in some twisted logic in which she thought she was protecting you, I'd guess, she left that line blank on the one she left with the baby. She even gave a false name for the mother; Éibhleann Ó Caiside. However, in her diary she recorded the full, correct names of the mother and father. Her diary didn't lie."

Eddie's chin dropped to his chest.

"Éibhleann Róis O'Donoghue and Michael Edmond O'Raghallaigh." CJ spelled out the father's last name for him. "Aka Eveleen Danohough and Eddie Hall. For whatever reason Evie entered Douglas Edmond O'Reilly for the baby's name, the shortened version of the last name, on both birth certificates. When the Rothbower's brought Douglas across the big pond to Chicago, he became Douglas Edmond Rothbower. Yes, Eddie, Douglas was in fact your son. You had your son murdered."

With slow, almost painful effort, Eddie turned to CJ. "No," he said, his voice cracking. "I did not have him killed." He continued turning until he was facing his companion. "*You* killed him, Isabel. We talked about it and agreed that we'd just kidnap him and store him away until it was all over. We weren't going to kill anyone. That's what this was all about. We wanted to make our point peacefully, non-lethal. And then he turned up dead, so what did I do? I turned a blind eye.

"Shame on you, Isabel. And shame on me for letting you get away with it."

"I didn't kill him, Eddie."

"Of course you didn't. You hired someone else to do the dirty work. Who was it?"

"No Eddie!"

"Don't even bother denying it. You wanted him dead and then it happened. Who did you hire to kill Douglas?" He took a quick step toward her; she countered with a back step.

"Who!?"

"Alan!" As soon as she said it, Isabel seemed to regret the admission. She gave CJ a look that appeared to say, 'Keep your mouth shut.'

"I don't know who killed Eveleen," she added quickly. "That was probably a robbery or something. The police may even know by now."

Eddie seemed to be confused by it all, maybe wanting to believe her because it was just easier that way. The thing was, CJ wasn't the type to keep his mouth shut, especially when all the pieces were flying together, when the full truth was staring him in the face.

"Let me tell you what I know, Eddie," CJ said. "The morning that Douglas was killed, knifed and dumped into the bay, the killer bumped into me and lifted my wallet, which he then threw into the bay with Douglas. I got just enough of a look at the man to suspect that it was the same man who kidnapped me in the elevator yesterday afternoon, and I know for a fact that that was Alan. Same shoes. Same Khaki pants. The individual who tried to pass himself off as Eddie Hall when Stella and I discovered Eveleen murdered, was Alan. Do I need to put the pieces together for you Eddie?"

Eddie took a step toward Isabel. "You murdered both of them!"

Isabel shook her head at him. "I had to do what had to be done, Eddie."

"You had no right," he said softly. "I may have been angry with her, but I still loved her. And my son... my son." And then he yelled, "NO RIGHT!"

"Don't even look at me like that, Eddie, or talk to me like that. He was a threat. He had to be eliminated. Both he and your precious Evie. Of course I knew you loved her, your *partner*." She said *partner* like it was a bitter poison on her tongue. "And how was I to know Douglas was your son?"

"You're done! I've had it! You've been like an anchor around my neck for this entire thing and now I find you've been doing things behind my back. What else have you done?"

"No, Eddie."

"Whatever it is it can't be worse than killing off my family, you... bitch!"

Isabel took a step back and then suddenly had a gun in her hand. "Fine! I'm a bitch."

With barely a pause, Eddie rushed at her and grabbed the gun. They struggled, she grunting, he yelling. "Stop it, Isabel! Don't be stupid!"

She kneed him in the groin and he nearly dropped to one knee, his hold on her hands and the gun the only thing keeping him upright. Suddenly, with one last effort, he surged to his feet and smashed her in the face with his forehead. She fell back, his grip on her hands taking him with her. She hit the ground with a head-splitting crack, Eddie on top of her, and then the gun exploded.

It all happened so fast that at first CJ didn't have time to react. Now as he ran at them, Eddie rolled off of Isabel, blood bubbling from his chest. CJ skidded to a stop when he saw Isabel pointing the gun at him. She shook her head, her aim unsteady.

"Stop right there," Isabel growled, her words slow, barely audible. Her head dropped back to the pavement, tried to rise and then dropped again. She shook it. "Stop right there." Then she lifted her head, held it and started screaming, "Stop! Stop!" all the while appearing to try to get an aim on him. CJ wasn't moving but she was shifting the gun back and forth as if he was.

Suddenly, from the side, came Stella, so fast that CJ didn't know what was happening until she hit him, sending him stumbling one way while she bounced the other. It was in that split second that the gun went off again. In the next second Stella kicked Isabel's hand so hard that the gun went flying. Then she dropped on top of the woman, the pink SIG Sauer pressed to her head.

"Don't even move, Bitch!"

Chapter 49

When the first responder arrived, a St. Petersburg police cruiser, CJ was holding pressure on Eddie's wound, not able to tell whether it was life threatening or not. Eddie was breathing but otherwise motionless. Stella was sitting on Isabel's back, having nothing to secure her with. Once she had Isabel on her stomach, she'd slid the SIG Sauer back into the hidden compartment in her purse. She and CJ had exchanged a look.

God, CJ was suddenly proud of her.

Right after it had all gone down, CJ had yelled at a distant observer to call 911 and then with one bloody hand had pulled out his phone and called Parker DuPont.

And then they had waited.

Now the police cruiser was roaring toward them, the EMS van thirty seconds behind. The cruiser skidded to a stop and two uniformed officers came flying out.

"She shot him," Stella stated, pointing to Eddie. Then she pointed to where the gun lay, twenty feet away. "Her gun is over there. No one has touched it."

In a matter of minutes the officers had the scene secure, Stella sitting to the side, Isabel handcuffed and in the back of the cruiser. CJ had released his pressure hold on Eddie, passing him over to the EMS techs. They wasted no time preparing him for transport.

CJ sat down next to Stella. "How're you doing?"

"Good. Real good in fact."

He put his arm around her. "You were amazing, the Stella I know and love."

She snuggled up against him. "Maybe now I can get closure with this entire thing, being able to sit on the woman responsible for this morning."

"She's not the only one."

"Yeah, but she may be all I need. I had a burning desire to punch someone back for scaring the hell out of me. She'll certainly due."

"We only got the top dogs."

"I don't care about the rest of them," Stella said. "These two are good enough."

CJ extracted his arm and pulled out his phone. After wiping blood from it onto his shirt, he speed-dialed Josh. When Josh answered, CJ said, "Where are you?"

"Back at the hotel. Where are you?"

"Were relaxing down on *The Pier*. You might want to join us, though I doubt you can get here before they hall Michael O'Raghallaigh away."

"What? Who's they?"

"EMS. I think maybe you have about two minutes. The other head of the Irish side of the summit operation is also here, though I don't think she's going anywhere for a while, at least not before the detectives show up."

"I'm on my way."

CJ then called Parker.

By the time twenty minutes had passed, Josh, Agents Taffer and Coulter, as well as Detectives DuPont and Gorky had arrived along with three additional police cruisers and another EMS vehicle. They were working on the back of Isabel's head, where she'd hit the pavement. CJ was certain that she'd suffered a concussion. *The Pier* was secured. Those wanting to go on, couldn't. Those wanting to get off, had to wait for a police escort to walk them past the scene.

After Detective Gorky reminded Parker that he was on medical leave, Parker sat down next CJ and Stella.

"So, what the hell happened?" Parker asked.

"According to Eddie, they spotted us coming out of McGee's Irish

Pub. We came down here for an evening stroll, wanting to put this entire thing behind us for awhile, when he and Isabel–last name Carroll if I heard it correctly from the uniform–approached us. Eddie wanted to know if I had any idea who killed Eveleen Danohough."

Parker looked surprised. "I figured they'd have skipped the country by now, or at least the state."

"They should have, but as we learned a few hours ago, he and Eveleen had a long history together. He was angry with her and in love with her all at the same time. He couldn't leave without answers to his questions."

"So how did Ms. Carroll wind up shooting him?"

"In the process of our conversation, he figured out that the person who ordered the hit on Eveleen and Douglas was the woman standing next to him, his partner in this morning's event. My impression was that she wasn't happy with his and Eveleen's relationship and had Eveleen killed, using her relationship with Douglas as an excuse. Until I laid out the facts for him, the diary and all, Eddie didn't believe that Douglas was his or Eveleen's son. When he realized the truth, Eddie confronted Isabel. She pulled out a gun. They wrestled and the next thing I knew the gun went off and he had a bullet in his chest. I can't say if it was intentional or accidental. She did, though, make a serious attempt at killing me."

"Christ. How did you get the gun away from her?"

"I didn't." CJ pointed to Stella with his thumb. "Kung Fu Stella here took her down."

Parked leaned across in front of CJ and with his good arm presented Stella with a hi-five. She grinned and slapped his hand.

"I wish I could have seen that," Parker said.

"It was awesome," CJ said.

"Parker."

They all looked up at Detective Gorky walking toward them.

"Yeah," Parker said.

"Thought you'd like to know. Just got a call from the uniform at the hospital with the victim. They lost him."

Parker nodded. "Thanks Don." As the detective walked away, Parker said to CJ and Stella, "So, you found out who Douglas' biological father was, and now he's dead. That closes it for you guys, I guess."

"Pretty much. Unless you, being St. Petersburg Police, or the Feds need us around for any particular reason, we'll head out..." CJ looked over at Stella. "Thursday? Tomorrow?"

"We've already talked about this, Clint. Thursday. We're going sailing tomorrow followed by dinner with the Parkers."

"Just confirming is all, making sure you haven't changed your mind."

"Nope. Not changing my mind. Want top-of-the-line life jackets, though."

After a time, Detective Gorky broke them free, securing an agreement that they report into the department at 8:00 a.m. sharp to provide their statements. After Parker departed and as CJ and Stella walked back to the car, CJ called Gianna.

Without even a hello, Gianna answered with, "Okay, CJ, don't even tell me that the Irish Army fiasco in Orlando I saw on the news had anything to do with you. I really was expecting a call from you earlier today if it had."

"Unfortunately, Gianna, I cannot tell you otherwise. That's a story for a time when we can sit together with a glass of very expensive wine that you supply."

Gianna seemed to laugh and groan at the same time. "Fine. Tell me what I need to know right now. I've got a fight going on between my sister and Doug's parents as to where he shall be buried. I'd ask if the police there are ready to release his body except that I don't know where to ship him, Illinois or Indiana."

"You could leave him here with Rebecca, his second wife."

"I've got World War Three about to start here. Do you want to go for the holocaust?" Gianna took in and then let out an audible breath. "Seriously, what's happening?"

"Douglas' biological mother is Eveleen Danohough, and she is dead, but you already know that."

"That she's dead, I didn't know. When did that happen?"

CJ closed his eyes and tried to think. "I'm not sure. Maybe Sunday. Events are starting to stack on top of each other."

"Fine. It just creates another wrinkle, or maybe it'll smooth one out. Don't bother expanding on that story. I'll just add another bottle of wine when you get here. Go on."

"His biological father was Michael Edmond O'Raghallaigh. He is now, also dead."

"You were involved in that?"

"Yes."

"Do I need to get you out of jail?"

CJ laughed. "No Gianna. Sorry to disappoint you. He was killed by Isabel Carroll, his partner in the Irish Army fiasco, as you called it, just a few hours ago. Thanks to Stella I am not dead and Isabel is in custody."

"Keeping that story for the wine party?"

"Yes."

"Did Stella have to use her little SIG Sauer?"

"You knew about that?"

"Of course I knew about that. She came to me for advice in anticipation that she'd be traveling with you back when you flew to Indiana. Did it get fired?"

"No, but she did get to do a show and tell for Isabel Carroll."

"I definitely can't wait for the wine party."

"We'll bring the crackers. We're on our way to meet with Rebecca and her family one last time, just to bring them up to speed. Anything I need to tell her?"

"Other than that I'm sorry for her loss, not really. I really do feel bad that she's going to be left out in the cold. There's nothing I can do, except..."

"Except what?" CJ said.

"Don't you even tell my sister I told you about this, but what

Rebecca needs to do is get an attorney who can help her establish proof that Douglas is the father of her baby."

"You mean DNA testing?"

"Correct. And she needs to start that right now before Douglas' body is shipped away. Get his DNA on an official record. Shouldn't be hard, though it'll cost her a bit. Don't need to do any invasive DNA testing on the baby until after birth."

"I'll slip that info to her. Anything else?"

"Nothing that I can think of."

"I'll be back in Tucson Thursday. Will talk to you then."

CJ put the phone away and said to Stella, who was sitting in the driver's seat listening to the call. "Off to see Mister Magoo."

"Who?"

"Mister Magoo. You don't know who Mister Magoo was?"

"Never heard of him and what does he have to do with Rebecca?"

"Magoo was a cartoon character who was extremely nearsighted and continually denied it. He'd be talking to a bush or a fire hydrant, thinking it was a child. He'd always get into trouble that he was not even aware of and then get out of it."

Stella just stared at him. "And?"

"Never mind. We're off to see Mister McGee and Rebecca. It sounded funnier in my head than I guess it was."

She reached up and touched the scab on his head. "Maybe you *did* receive a concussion, a tad bit of brain damage."

CJ brushed her hand away. "Just drive."

Chapter 50

It was after 11:00 p.m. when CJ and Stella entered the pub. The entire family was still there, the hired help, except for one of the dishwashers, apparently gone. Less than twenty percent of the tables were occupied.

Rebecca saw them first and came right over.

"I thought you said 10:00."

"I did. But now I've got answers to all your questions." CJ looked over her head, saw three sets of McGee eyes on him. "We all need to sit down somewhere, together."

Rebecca turned around and scanned the tables. "We're still open so we can't all go back to the office." She pointed. "How about that table? That section has already been cleaned and closed off to customers and we can see when someone needs something or wants to pay their bill and leave."

"Sounds fine."

CJ and Stella pulled two tables together and then sat. Several minutes later Rebecca joined them.

"So, what's going on?" she asked.

"We'll wait until everyone is here," CJ said. "For just you, though, I advise that you find a lawyer."

"A lawyer? Why?"

CJ went on to tell Rebecca what Gianna had told him about securing Douglas' DNA. "Do it tomorrow," he concluded. "I don't know if anything will come of it, but it's worth a shot for your baby. Even if he didn't want it, it still carries his blood."

And then all the McGees were there. Rebecca, of course, was also a McGee. She'd revert back to her maiden name before long, CJ was sure. He cleared his throat.

"You all heard about the UIRA attack on the G8 mini-summit this morning, I assume."

"It's all that's been talked about all day," Paddy said.

"We haven't watched much of the news so we don't know how it's being reported. You do know that fake suicide vests were involved along with paintball guns?"

"Yes."

"This is not to become general knowledge. As a matter of fact if I don't get sworn secrecy here, I will not divulge anything more about that attack."

Paddy looked between his wife and daughter and then at Rebecca.

"Yes," the women all said.

Paddy held up his right hand. "I vouch for us all. Not only yes but an Irish, *hell yes!* Nothing passes McGee lips after tonight."

"I can accept that," CJ said. "Stella and I were wearing the suicide vests. We were forced at gunpoint."

"Oh my God!" Maire, Paddy's wife, said.

"The hell!" Paddy said.

Hannah and Rebecca just stared at CJ, their hands to their open mouths.

"We didn't know they were fake until almost the end. Nor did we know about the paintball guns. We thought it was all real and lots of people were going to die, including us."

"How... when?" Paddy seemed confused as to what to ask.

"We'll tell you everything that lead up to it in a minute, but there's something else." CJ turned to look at the woman still dressed in black. "Rebecca, the leader of the group that attacked the summit this morning was your biological father-in-law."

Rebecca looked surprised and confused. "My father-in-law? Who was my father-in-law? Doug never said he had a father, just his mother, Eveleen."

"Eddie Hall was Doug's biological father. He was here hiding from the authorities, wanted for the killing of five British soldiers in 1981. His real name was Michael Edmond O'Raghallaigh. Do any of you know Isabel Carroll?"

The family looked between each other. Hannah said, "There was an Isabel that Eddie came in with once. Stern looking woman. Very dark-red hair, straight to her shoulders."

"That's her," CJ said. "The two of them ran the UIRA organization out of Florida, planned and executed the attack this morning."

"Where are they now?" Paddy said, "Michael O'Raghallaigh and Isabel Carroll? On the run I imagine?"

"He's dead, shot by Isabel. She's in custody." And then CJ and Stella went on to outline the previous thirty-six hours, stopping once when a customer had to be dealt with and then a second time when Paddy shooed the few remaining customers out and closed early.

"So, what about Rory and his crew? Any idea where they are?" Paddy said.

"Heading for parts unknown, I imagine," CJ said. "They'll likely be on the terrorist lists. They'll be watched for in Ireland and Northern Ireland, so I doubt they'll head that way until things cool down, if they ever cool down. The Feds know exactly who two of them are, can probably figure out the others and are certainly working with MI5, Scotland Yard and Interpol. If I were them, I'd be making name changes, buying up new IDs. As a matter-of-fact, I'd be willing to bet that that was in the plan all along. They may have already had new identification ready which was probably the reason they didn't care if we knew their names."

"A big sacrifice for a cause," Paddy said.

"People give their lives for causes every day," CJ said. "It's a choice one makes. For a time they're going to be wanted for not only the fake bomb attack this morning, but also for the real bomb Saturday morning and the murders of Douglas and Eveleen. The Feds should, however, figure out that those were carried out by a professional hit man who Isabel Carroll hired. She confessed it to Eddie in front of

Stella and me so I'm sure we'll be called to testify about that. I'm sure the hit man has already turned to smoke."

They all sat in silence for a time, maybe thinking about choices, maybe thinking about something else. What CJ was thinking about was his stomach.

"You wouldn't happen to have a leftover steak hanging around that grill of yours, would you, Paddy?" he said. "I'm starving."

"Me too," Stella said.

Paddy sat back in his chair. "I'm sure I can butcher something. I think we can all use a little sustenance. Hannah, take orders. Let's get this dinner party a hoppin'."

By 9:30 the next morning, Stella and CJ were walking toward the rental, having spent the previous hour and a half writing and going over their statements for Detective Gorky.

"How're you feeling?" CJ said, taking Stella's hand as they turned into the parking lot.

"Good. Real good, actually."

"That's the high one gets when a case like this closes and they're still walking and breathing, having sustained only minor bruises."

"I was shot and your ribs were broken. I don't consider that minor."

"It is when you consider we could be returning to Arizona in a couple of fancy boxes."

"True."

"You ready to go sailing?"

"I want nothing more than to put my feet up and watch those sails catch the wind."

When they got to the car, she released his hand and then grabbed his arm and snuggled up close to him. "By-the-way, when are we going to New Zealand?"

Thank You...

...for reading *Sailing into Death*. If you enjoyed this book, please consider *Lost & Forgotten*. Imagine waking one day with a new face and no memory, an opportunity to pick a new name and start a new life; a clean slate. Orphaned as children, separated for 22 years, Melissa is intent on finding her identical twin, Marissa; however Marissa is now Mariah and not who she used to be. Melissa's search brings her to Los Angeles, crossing paths with Tyron, the only person aware of the truth, a person with immoral intent. As Melissa searches for her twin and Mariah searches for who she was, they are both faced with first time romances. Their brief crossing of paths and wisps of twin psychic connections provides one hope, and the other confusion. Tyron hatches a plan to bring them together, for a price that includes more than just their money. *Lost & Forgotten* is story of wealth and poverty for far from pretty identical twin sisters as one meets evil in her search for her other half, and the other struggles to start a new life and find out who she was.

And now, the first two chapters of *Lost & Forgotten*...

Chapter 1

May 15

"When I grow up I'm going to be beautiful."

"No you're not."

"Yes I am. We're both going to be beautiful."

"We're always going to be ugly."

"Don't say that! Momma says ugly is a bad word."

"Bad or not, it's still true."

The two girls began slowing their swings, still in perfect rhythm, forward and back, side-by-side. Without being consciously aware, they dropped their feet at the exact same time and brought the swings to a perfect stop as though part of a choreographed routine.

"But I know we're going to be beautiful some day."

"Maybe you will, but I won't. I'll always be ugly."

"No you won't. When I become beautiful, so will you. It always works like that because we're identicals."

"Identicals is not a word."

"I know, but it's what Momma always uses. We're her identicals."

"It's a silly word."

"Sometimes silly is fun."

The girls fell silent as Becky Farsi appeared out of the school doors and started toward them. Her head was down and she was walking fast. Thirty feet from the two girls she looked up. Her surprise was brief before she put on her 'I'm superior and beautiful and you're not' look, and cut a wide berth around the playground swings. The twins looked down at their identical shoes until Becky was out of sight.

"Becky made me sad and angry today."

"I know."

"Where were you?"

"In the library. Where were you?"

"In my classroom."

"We were far apart."

"It's getting stronger, isn't it?"

"Yeah. She made fun of our scarves, didn't she, Marissa."

Marissa looked at her sister. "I didn't tell you that. How did you know? Did you actually see it happen in your mind?"

"No. I just felt your sadness and then you got angry, and then I knew."

"Like we had become one."

"What does that mean?"

Marissa thought for a second. "It's like our minds merged into one big brain. It's been happening for a while. Haven't you felt it? When we were in the math bee, we helped each other."

"I didn't give you any answers."

"No. That's not what I mean. We were like one very powerful brain that we both could use."

"Weird."

"I know."

"Is that why nobody likes us?"

"That, and because we're ugly."

"No. That can't be it."

"Because we're different."

"We're special. That's what Momma says."

"I don't want to be special anymore."

"We're twins. Identicals. We'll always be special, Marissa."

"Sometimes I wish you'd go away."

Melissa looked at her sister in shock. "You don't mean that!"

Marissa sighed. "No, I guess I don't. But don't you sometimes wonder what it'd be like to be by yourself?"

"No. I've never thought of that. I can't imagine ever being without you."

"Doesn't it bother you that you can't be mad alone, that I always know what you're feeling?"

"I've never thought of it as being a bother. It's nice to share."

"Pretty soon we're going to be able to read each other's minds and then we won't have any privacy."

Melissa hopped off her swing and looked at Marissa. "You really don't want me around anymore, do you!"

"That's not what I said."

"Yes you did. You said you wished I would go away. Well, what if I did? Who'd brush your hair? Who'd you talk to just before you fall asleep? Who would you have when Becky Fart-face starts picking on you?"

Marissa giggled. "That's what we should do. Start calling her Fart-face. Becky Farsi Fart-face."

"Yeah! That would be funny."

Marissa stood up and together they picked up their identical backpacks and started walking in the direction of home. In the background of the warm May afternoon was the sound of a commercial airliner lifting off the runway two miles away. It was a sound heard often by those in the upwind path, a sound mostly ignored.

"How did you do on the math test?"

"Why do you ask me? I always get them all right, just like you."

"Just wondering. I figure one of us has to make a mistake eventually."

"What?" Melissa shouted. The two girls, in identical blouses and identical skirts, turned their identical misshapen faces toward the huge passenger jet. Melissa pulled Marissa to the ground and they covered their heads with their backpacks and cowered against the roar that shook their little bodies.

At barely two miles off the end of the runway, commercial airliners normally have more than sufficient altitude to avoid scaring the daylights out of a couple of ten-year-old girls on a school playground. Above the girls the airliner was at 200 feet and losing altitude, the pilot having already frantically reported to flight control that there was a hydraulic failure. One of the seven people who survived out of the 159 on board—they would become known as the miracle seven—would remember looking out the window and being surprised at seeing the girls lying on the ground, just before realizing that there was something deadly wrong.

Two blocks beyond the girls, the jet slipped below 100 feet. Instead of trying to regain hydraulics, the pilot was unsuccessfully attempting to steer the massive flying machine toward an open field. He felt a shudder on contact with the chimney of one house, thought of his wife and child, and saw a woman run out of the next house and look directly at him, and then draw her last surprised breath.

The girls jumped to their feet and watched the tail of the huge plane disappear beyond the oak trees and tops of houses, and then heard the explosions and saw the horrendous fireballs in the sky. They took off through the opening in the fence, across the street and down the avenue that ran directly to where they lived. People were coming out of their houses and running in the same direction, toward the flames and smoke shooting high in the air. The girls ran and ran and ran. More and more people were running with them; women were screaming and crying. Two men ran past them, shouting, and there were sirens.

And then they stopped.

They moved no farther than the corner sign marking the cross streets of Berry Lane and West Third Avenue. They were holding hands and staring. Their hearts raced and tears streamed down their misshapen cheeks. It was not the raging fire that stopped them. It was the fact that the house, which they called home since the day they were born, where Momma sang songs and called them her identicals, was gone. They also knew that so was Mamma. Today was her day off from work. What they had yet to know was how totally alone they were yet to become.

Chapter 2

August 28

Mrs. Frank Croons dried her hands, flipped the towel over her shoulder and picked up the portable phone. "Croons residence," she said with her usual upbeat, happy voice. She listened to the caller and then said, "Yes, this is Patricia Croons." She didn't recognize the caller's name, but her tone and the words, child welfare, were enough to dampen her cheerfulness. She eased down onto the sofa and listened to the reason for the woman's call. It was short and to the point and Patricia had no more to say than, "I see. I understand." She glanced at the mantel clock. "Sure. I'll have her ready. Why so little time?" The only explanation she was given was that adoptions at that age were hard to find, and sometimes, when a good placement pops up, quick action was warranted.

"What about family?" Patricia asked. "Hasn't there been anything?"

"Afraid not," the woman said. "As you already know, the father died in a hunting accident when they were two. There are no living relatives."

Patricia Croons returned the phone to its cradle and remained sitting. When she finally pushed herself up, the clock read 5:15. Frank would be home in fifteen minutes. The agency would be here at 7:30. She returned to the kitchen, dropped the towel into the sink and looked out at the girls in the backyard. A thunderstorm had rolled in an hour before. After the thunder and lightning were gone, leaving a steady rain, the girls put on their yellow rain slickers and went out and sat on the bench next to the flower garden. There they still sat like two canaries enjoying the rain. But there was no enjoyment in their lives and every day that Patricia watched them her heart ached for their sadness. She and Frank did everything foster parents can imagine to make their lives happy. But there was only so much they could do. It was time that would heal, and for Melissa and Marissa she had a terrible hunch that that time would be very long.

And now it was going to be even harder.

One of them—she had yet to be able to tell them apart—was being adopted. Not both of them. That would be too much to wish for, wouldn't it? They were going to be split. Who was it that decided what's best for these girls? Patricia slammed her hand down on the counter. "Why! Won't they be better off anywhere together, than anywhere else apart?"

But of course there was no answer to her question. She picked up the towel, uselessly wiped away her tears and then retrieved her own rain slicker and stepped out to talk to the girls. They were only days away from celebrating their eleventh birthday, as though the word celebrate had returned to their vocabulary. It was to be a backyard party. As Patricia hunched down in front of the emotionless faces, she understood that there would be no point in a big party, especially for just one. Such a party would only enhance the level of abandonment they already felt.

To mask her tears Patricia left the hood of her slicker back and let the rain beat upon her face. She knelt before Melissa and Marissa and forced a smile. They gave her a slight smile in return, maybe amused by the water running down their foster mother's face. Hell, she thought, I'd run naked and throw myself in the mud with everyone and anyone watching if it would make them laugh.

She gulped down a lump of something stuck in her throat and then hated herself for what she was about to say. She hated the aviation people. She hated the government bureaucracy. She hated the situation God had thrown these little girls into. She hated the fact that she had chosen to become a foster parent. She hated having to pretend as though it was a happy day for these two unfortunate little girls.

"I have good news!"

* * * * *

To purchase Lost & Forgotten in eBook or paperback visit:

Desert Bookshelf Publishing
www.desertbookshelf.com

About the author

A retired graphic designer, James Paddock lives in Florida with his wife, Penny, a retired teacher. Novel writing, which keeps his sanity, if there is such a thing, is his passion and gives Penny, an avid reader, something to look forward to every few years. Together they claim five children and many grandchildren, and they, of course, are all beautiful and highly intelligent.

James began his writing efforts in 1993 with the publication of his very first short story. He became hooked on the craft of storytelling and soon began longer works, completing his first novel, *Elkhorn Mountain Menace*, a story of terrorism in rural Montana, in August of 2001, only weeks before 9/11.

To order additional copies of this book contact:
Desert Bookshelf Publishing
orders@desertbookshelf.com
www.desertbookshelf.com

Made in the USA
Charleston, SC
09 March 2015